STILL LIFE

STILL LIFE

TWO SHORT NOVELS

Sanford Friedman

Saturday Review Press | E. P. Dutton & Co., Inc. New York

LIBRARY
University of Texas
At San Antonio

An excerpt from *Still Life* first appeared in *Works in Progress*, No. 2, and an excerpt from *Lifeblood* first appeared in *Works in Progress*, No. 8.

An excerpt from *Lifeblood* ("The Birth of Attis") first appeared in *Shenandoah*, Vol. 24, No. 3 (Spring 1973).

LIBRARY OF CONGRESS CATALOGING IN PUBLICATION DATA

Friedman, Sanford, 1928–
Still life.

CONTENTS: Still life.—Lifeblood.
I. Friedman, Sanford, 1928–   Lifeblood.   1975.
II. Title.
PZ4.F8989St   [PS3556.R564]   813'.5'4   74-28060

Published simultaneously in Canada by Clarke, Irwin & Company Limited, Toronto and Vancouver
ISBN: 0-8415-0368-0

To Bob and Abby

CONTENTS

STILL LIFE

Before entering the dining room, Anna Maria peeped on tiptoe through the little round window in the swinging door. The room was dark—the señora's way of telling Maria she could clear, to say nothing of conserving electricity . . . always the electricity. The switch that controlled the overhead light, a German fixture of chromium and frosted glass designed in the twenties, also turned on the picture lights over the four paintings in the room—the slice of beef liver, basket of plums, plate of oysters, and the landed pike, hooked by a fisherman out of the viewer's sight—but after twelve years with the Wahls, Maria no longer noticed the paintings. What she did notice instantly was that the double glass doors leading to the living room were closed. Usually these doors were left ajar by the señora, who expected Maria to close them while clearing as a sign of deference. But not tonight. Tonight there was no deference, only secrecy, distress. Yet now that Danny had come home, wouldn't you think the family would be rejoicing, saying prayers of thanks, instead of sitting in there like that: Señora Wahl at the piano, her hands not on the keyboard but covering the crown of her head as if she were being pelted; the señor, hidden by the newspaper from behind which his cigar smoke poured like smoke from a house on fire; Claude, the law student, picking his nose; Jerome pacing the floor and smoking too— And Danny? where was

Danny? In the chair blocked from view by the piano? . . . To catch a glimpse of this chair without seeming, at the same time, to be spying, Maria began to remove from the rectangular ebony table the napkin rings, silverware, and dirty dishes.

It had been this way all day, starting at breakfast with that fight between Jerome and his mother about who should bring Danny home from Connecticut—Maria had never really understood why the hospital was so far away, but gathered from certain remarks made by the señora that it had something to do with the special climate required to cure lung disease—mother and son accusing each other of being unfit to deal with Danny, calling each other terrible names: snake and selfish brat, ignoramus, good-for-nothing, mad woman, maniac; till Jerome shouted that if his mother went, Danny would be sure to have a relapse; and the señora screamed, "You—it's you who should be locked up"; whereupon, Señor Wahl, speaking for the first time, exclaimed, "Bite your tongue! you're *both* insane," and forbade either one to go, declaring that he would leave the gallery early and go himself; to which his wife responded with such bitterness that whatever she said drove both men out of the house. Left alone, the poor woman had gone to the piano but couldn't play, couldn't sit still, decided instead to set the table—at nine in the morning, even before the breakfast things were cleared, she had begun to set the table for dinner, and was still not finished at twelve forty-five when, lucky thing, she had to meet her sister for lunch; otherwise, she might never have finished, judging by the number of times she had changed the cloth, rearranged the candlesticks, fruit bowl, and shears, altered the children's seating arrangement—she had even interchanged two of the paintings, but the dust marks on the wall were too conspicuous, and she finally restored the paintings to their original positions. Remembering now her employer's behavior, Maria scratched her scalp and murmured in English, "Cuckoo," a word to which she was so partial it had become the children's nickname for her. Even more cuckoo, perhaps, was the frantic way in which the señora had struggled, later that afternoon, with the cardboard box from the bakery, pulling and clutching and tearing at the string until, in her exasperation, she broke not only the string and box but the cake inside, and burst into tears. Imagine! tears, when almost the first thing we learn in this life is not to cry over spilled milk, yet there the señora stood in the pantry, sobbing her heart out over a layer cake. And all this—this *tumulto*—on the day of Danny's homecoming. It made no sense. "Cuckoo," Maria said aloud.

2.

At the head of the table now Maria could see the other side of the living room. The chair behind the piano was empty. Had Danny gone to bed already, tired from the trip, or was he in the opposite corner in front of the windows? To satisfy her curiosity Maria edged to the glass doors and peered through one of the panes. Almost simultaneously the señora stood up, came to the door, and opened it, but only a crack, as if barring the way to a suspicious-looking stranger.

"What is it, Maria?"

For a moment Maria stared in silence at the señora's face, at her cold imperious features, expressionless and pale as tallow. "No—no anything," she stammered and quickly turned away, hearing the door click behind her.

"What was it?" Wahl inquired casually from behind the newspaper.

Hunching her shoulders Mme. Wahl shut her eyes, shook her head, and made a sour face. "No any-ting."

Jerome flew at his mother. "Why do you always mock her?"

"Je-rome," Wahl cautioned his son in a tired sing-song.

Jerome ignored the interruption. "Always so superior. What have you to be superior about? What, I ask? You think your English so much better? For your information—"

"Oh, be still!" the mother hissed.

"No—you!" Rushing across the room to the second set of doors, those that led to the foyer and rear of the apartment, Jerome quickly closed them.

"Open those doors!" commanded Mme. Wahl.

"Not until you change your tone!" From his own, it was obvious Jerome was struggling to suppress his fury. "For once we're going to act or try like—try to act like—"

"Ha-ha! 'Try like,'." Claude jeered at his older brother. "Speaking of g-g-good English," he stammered in a cracking voice over which he had not as yet, at twenty, gained complete control.

"Shut up, you! That's exactly what I mean," Jerome went on, "a perfect example. For once we've got to act like *other* families: cheerful and relaxed. We must, you hear? must! At least pretend—for *his* sake. His—his sanity depends on it!"

Less to silence her son than to obliterate from consciousness the abhorrent reference to Daniel's sanity, Mme. Wahl brought her fist down on the Bechstein. The strings resounded eerily. "*Imbécile!*" she cried, expressing in a word both her annoyance with herself for striking the piano, as well as her profound contempt for the idea that there could be anything like a causal relation between the family's behavior and Danny's illness. "You'll open those doors, I said."

"And I said, no!"

"This is still my house, and I'll—"

"*Your* house?" Jerome turned to his father for support, but Wahl was entrenched in the newspaper.

"Do you pay rent?" Mme. Wahl rejoined with self-satisfaction.

"So that's it! I'm to pay rent now. It's not bad enough—" Jerome checked himself.

"What? what's not bad enough?" His mother took up the challenge. "If you hate it so much, why do you live here? Why don't you get married—get out? You have no complaints coming. Eleven shirts a week! Do you know what it costs, your laundry alone? I wonder sometimes what you do in those shirts."

"Since when do you pay Cuckoo something extra—even a cent— for the laundry?"

Mme. Wahl darted a glance at the dining room. "Be quiet, she's listening."

"Slave labor, that's what—"

"Quiet, I said. Eleven shirts! lipstick on all— Open those doors, if you know what's good for you."

"C-c-come on, Jerry," Claude butted in, "open up."

"What do *you* know about it?" Jerome turned on his brother, adding with disdain, "Dimitri."

"Calling me D-D-Dimitri d-d-doesn't make you Ivan, not by a long shot. You're the oldest, remember."

"And you're Dimitri—or better yet" —he scrutinized his brother's thick shapeless lips and pitted skin— "Smerdyakov."

"You should know, F-F-Frankenstein."

"Is that the best you can do? For your information—"

"Marcus," Mme. Wahl appealed to her husband, "the doors, they must stay open. Suppose he wants something, calls out—"

" 'Who, if I cried out,' " Jerome recited scornfully, " 'would hear me among the angelic orders?' "

Confused by the quotation Mme. Wahl grimaced. "What?"

"I said, 'Who, if I cried out—' "

"Jerome!" Wahl lowered the newspaper irritably. "Enough now! Open the doors."

Stern though his father sounded, Jerome was quick to catch signs of dissimulation—a playful rolling of the eyeballs behind the massive horn-rimmed glasses, a rapid opening and closing of the palm to gesture helplessness—familiar signs that had the same meaning whether made at the gallery for the sake of a sale or here

4.

at home for peace-and-quiet's sake: "Humor her." Jerome relented. But no sooner had he opened the doors than he saw his mother advancing toward them. "Where are you going?"

"To see what he's doing," she answered without thinking.

"No!" Again the doors were closed. "You *know* what he's doing—I told you before—reading."

"Oh, yes," she remembered now, "reading. But why?" —her face expressed genuine bewilderment— "why isn't he here with us? Surely, that's not why he left the table. He reads too much, it isn't normal—*healthy*," she corrected herself, "he'll ruin his eyes—always the dimmest light he can find. And just *what* is he reading, tell me? Those poets again? Verlaine? Baudelaire?"

"Why should I tell you?"

"All right, don't! don't tell, I don't—"

"Emily Dickinson, for your information."

"Who is that?" Her enormous eyes narrowed with suspicion.

"A famous—"

"Oh, what's the difference, anyway? They're all alike: twisted, degenerate, all of them. If he must read, why not something decent, stimulating—intellectually, I mean, not filth—someone like Anatole France: worldly, wry—"

"Oh, no," Jerome moaned, "anything but France."

"Why? why anything? why do you scoff? Don't be so quick to show your ignorance. Was this—this Dickinson person a member of the Academy? . . . What now? what's so funny?"

"You tell her, Claude."

"She c-c-couldn't be, Maman, she was American."

"She? I thought you said Émile."

"Emily."

"*She* . . . . Ah, so that's it, of course, that teacher of his—or whatever she is, librarian—at school."

"Miss Kerns?"

"Oh, dear," Mme. Wahl struck her cheek, reminded suddenly of the message that Miss Kerns had called while she was out to lunch. Well, whose fault was it that she had forgotten? Only a cryptographer could read Maria's infantile scrawl.

"What about her?"

"It's all *her* fault."

"Miss Kerns?"

"Yes, yes, yes."

"What's her fault?"

"Everything! the whole—this whole—everything with Danny—it all goes back to her, his seeing her, visiting her apartment— Did

5.

he ever drink before? did he smoke? not till *she* got hold of him. If you want my real opinion, she's at the bottom of it all—everything—she's the one who did it to him."

"Did what? *what?*" Jerome demanded.

". . . Changed him," she murmured almost in despair, "like this."

"Oh, Maman," Claude tried to cheer her up, "if only you could see Miss Kerns—she's skinny as a rail, f-f-flat as a board—"

"I'm not discussing her figure— *Mon dieu!* if I thought *that*— No-no, her influence: those books she has him reading, plays she takes him to, that *danseuse*, Graham—harmful—definitely harmful. I don't want him seeing her, don't want her calling—that's all there is to it."

"What on earth are you talking about?" Jerome threw up his hands. "In the first place you have no say in the matter—"

"Oh, don't I!"

"No! It's *his* affair, entirely his. Can't you get that through your head? Just stay out of it for once—don't go near him, don't interfere!"

"Interfere?"

"Exactly."

"With my own child?"

"Child! He's seventeen, a man."

At a loss to deal with such presumptuousness, such ignorance, at a loss to explain to this callow, heartless son of hers what it means to be a mother, Mme. Wahl stared at Jerome in dismay, her lips puckering slightly, as if about to spit.

"And secondly," Jerome went on, "what I don't understand—you act as if he were home for good, instead of—"

"We'll see," Mme. Wahl remarked mysteriously.

"What do you mean, see? There's nothing to see. What do you think 'gradual'—what the doctor said, 'gradual readjustment'— It's only for the weekend, a sort of trial, to see how he does . . . *gradually*. Danny understands that, accepts it—why can't you?"

Again Mme. Wahl confronted her son in silence, her contracted brow and outraged eyes speaking for her. Why couldn't she accept seeing her baby, the person she loved most in the world, worth more than all the rest put together, of an entirely different order from the rest, someone altogether good, selfless, even saintly—on that, his saintliness, everyone agreed—accept his going back to that—that *place*, when so clearly he was sane, as sane as anyone . . . a little sickly, perhaps, sensitive, moody sometimes, but then, that was *Danny*, his nature, the very thing that made him different

6.

from the rest—only different, not *insane*. Even the doctors realized that—why else would they have sent him home? And if he was well enough to come home, he was well enough to stay. "Maybe someday, Jerry," she replied bitterly, "when you're a parent, you'll understand."

"Maybe so, but in the meantime, he's expected back—Sunday afternoon."

"We'll see."

"Why do you keep saying that? It's ridiculous! Papa, tell her—" Seeing the urgent appeal in his father's expression, Jerome broke off. Though by no means willing to abandon truth for the sake of his mother's foolish hopes, he nonetheless modified his tone. "It does no good to think that way, Maman, only makes it worse, harder for everyone."

"In a way, you know"—conscious of his wife's nervous state, Wahl's tone was gentle, even a trifle apologetic—"the boy is right, Germaine."

"Naturally! when wasn't he? Is that why you took him with you today? Or were you afraid you'd lose the way after seven months?" Till now she had had no opportunity to confront her husband about his latest betrayal: going back on his word and taking Jerome to Connecticut. Though she had seen Danny at the hospital just the week before, she had been too excited this afternoon when the doorbell rang, too unnerved by Maria's screeching, and that snoop of an elevator man, worse than any Paris concierge—oh, how she despised him!—ogling the boy as if he were deformed; too upset by Danny's whole appearance—so thin, pale, tentative—to comment on the fact that he was with not only his father but Jerome: the two of them flanking him, her angel, like gendarmes, as if he were a prisoner . . . protecting him like bodyguards, protecting him, moreover, not from the world but from her, his own mother, as if *she* were the prisoner, a prisoner in her own apartment. Well, wasn't that what they were doing now? restraining her, holding her against her will in this smoke-filled overheated room (the thought impelled her toward the windows), and what they had done at dinner when Danny left the table? What had made him excuse himself like that? The broken cake? Something someone said? So many things, all of a controversial nature—was there any neutral topic any more, even gastronomy?—had been discussed at dinner: family, friends, politics, the Vietminh, General MacArthur, the Korean War . . . .

Mme. Wahl raised the window. The November air was raw. Shading her eyes she looked out at the thermometer: 39° What was that in centigrade? 9°? 6°? No matter how she tried, she simply couldn't accustom herself to the American system, American sights—to seeing out there that ugly asphalt avenue, the pride of New York, instead of the Musée Galliéra with its little green park, that unassuming, unspectacular, merely *human* little park, the exact opposite of this monstrous Maginot line misnamed Park Avenue . . . . To do away with the offensive sight Mme. Wahl shifted her gaze from the tar-black street, fourteen floors below, to the pink and purple tints, reflected in the windowpane, of Monet's *Boulevard des Italiens* on the wall behind her back. Was that what had driven Danny from the dinner table? the discussion, as always, of art: the current retrospective of that lunatic Soutine at the Modern Museum, the Albi Toulouse-Lautrecs at Knoedler's. . . . Albi, their trip to Albi years ago, before the war. Could Danny possibly remember that? He couldn't have been more than three at the time. Though God knows the Albi cathedral was enough to frighten any child. Or had he left the table because of the other Monet, the little *nature morte* in the dining room? How many times in the course of the meal had she caught him staring, almost in a trance, at that slice of liver? What *was* it about that drab little picture that intrigued him so? After all, it wasn't downright depressing like the Vuillard, lurid like the Moreau. And yet, hadn't she herself had the impulse that morning to switch it with the Manet? Hadn't she remembered to seat him with his back to the Courbet? Was there no safe place anywhere for Danny?

"*Chérie,*" Wahl broke the silence, "come sit down."

Her back to the room, Mme. Wahl could not be certain whether her husband was addressing her or Jerome, saying Jerry or *chérie.* Not that it made much difference—between Marcus and herself, *chérie* had long since lost its authenticity as a term of endearment.

"Did you see the Philharmonic review?" Wahl went on as his wife turned away from the windows. "Apparently we missed nothing. The Dvořák he calls 'saccharine.' "

"Wasn't it 'g-g-gardenia-scented?' " Claude suggested.

"Maybe so, let's see . . . 'Dvořák's Cello Concerto . . . plaintive cry'. . . . Here it is. Oh, lord." Wahl chuckled. "It's even worse: 'gardenia-flavored pathos.' Some phrase, hum?"

"What do you expect from Mitropoulos?" Jerome scoffed. "*Dimitri,*" he goaded his brother, "Mitropoulos."

"He's as g-g-good as Walter any day."

"Don't be an ass!"

"And the Schumann?" Mme. Wahl inquired with concern.

" 'Schumann's Symphony No. 2 in C,' " Wahl obliged by reading the review aloud, " 'which came at the end, was the brightest spot in the program—' "

For the first time since dinner Mme. Wahl smiled. "Very good."

" '—the composer's illness and roman—' "

The smile vanished from her lips. "What was that?"

" '—the composer's illness and romantic nature notwithstanding.' "

"What does it mean: notwithstanding?"

"*Néanmoins*, Maman."

"*Néanmoins?* Uhh!" she grunted as if stabbed, "the idiot!" She could not bear to be reminded of the mad Schumann, the Schumann who had taken dictation from the ghost of Felix Mendelssohn, who had hurled himself off the Düsseldorf bridge—that was not *her* Schumann. "*Néanmoins*: Beethoven's deafness; *néanmoins*: Chopin's consumption; *néanmoins*—"

"B-B-Bravo, Maman." Claude applauded. "That's it! you show him, make him eat his *néanmoins*."

"How do you mean?"

"Play something."

"Good idea," Wahl agreed.

"Now?" She hesitated, glancing toward the foyer doors.

Misinterpreting this look as a request for his approval, Jerome assented. "Why not? Go ahead."

"All right." On her way to the Bechstein, which had belonged to her mother, Mme. Wahl removed her garnet bracelet, also an heirloom from her mother, and laid it with care on the glass-topped table beside a low upholstered cube of an armchair, one of four in the room. "What shall it be?"

"*Fantasie*," Claude called out.

"No," Jerome differed, "the *Third Étude*."

"Naturally! if I ask for *F-F-Fantasie*—"

"Dum dum dum deeee dum," Jerome vocalized the étude's bass line, while accompanying himself solemnly on an imaginary piano.

Taking advantage of the sudden relaxation of tension, Mme. Wahl, already seated and busy shuffling the scores on the rack, turned to Claude and remarked matter-of-factly, "*Chéri*, go ask Danny to come and join us."

"No!" As if it were a reflex action, Jerome dashed back to the doors and took up his post. "He'll come, if he wants, without being asked. Just start playing" —he raised both hands like a conductor signaling the orchestra he was ready to begin— "the étude, please."

"I'd rather die than play the étude."

"Why? Just because *I*—"

"*Fantasie*, Maman!"

"If not the étude, then *Carnaval:* da dum, da dum, da dum-da-dum—"

No, she would not play *Carnaval*, nor *Fantasie*, nor any of the études. She was not the least bit interested in displaying her virtuosity, considerable though it was, but simply in bringing Danny into the living room, luring him, if need be, from the rear of the apartment. For that there was only one effective ruse: *Kinderscenen*. Yes-yes-yes, that would do the trick, something from *Kinderscenen*, the composition Danny loved above all, the music Schumann had written for his beloved Clara. What was more, she knew just the morsel that would entice him . . . . Her stocky fingers poised now, Mme. Wahl touched the keys with as little effort or ostentation as it took to lower her eyelids.

"Oh, no," Jerome complained, "not *Träumerei*."

"Shhht!" Wahl silenced his son. The newspaper open to the entertainment section, Wahl's eye reverted to a photo in a movie ad he'd been studying before Jerome distracted him, a photo of an Italian starlet, an amazon of a girl standing cross-legged and calf-deep in what appeared to be a swamp or rice paddy. Posed fullface, her body turned just enough to reveal its prodigious contours, she was wearing a v-neck sweater and a pair of shorts, the briefest shorts Wahl had ever seen on a girl, as short as panties, except that they weren't silk or nylon, some coarser stuff like denim, maybe even lederhosen—what a charming idea . . . her lover's shorts—did they have a fly?—what a facilitation!—it was hard to tell, not only because the photo's scale had been greatly reduced for the ad, but also because the shorts themselves had ridden up her thighs almost to the fork, the folds of the material bunching so alluringly over the belly and mound. And that band across the thigh? was it merely a shadow or the top of a black mesh stocking? Stockings in a swamp? Again it was hard to tell, hard to tell whether or not she was wearing a brassiere. Indiscernible though the nipple was, from what you could see of the chest underneath the sweater, it certainly looked like she had nothing on. And yet, were that the case, were musculature alone responsible for the brazen stance of those colossal breasts—Wahl expelled his breath. But, of course! he realized suddenly, this was the very girl, the film star Boris Napotnik had been going on about the other day at the studio. What a pity to have missed his customary Friday visit to Boris' studio this afternoon, particularly since that new little Japanese model—Miko? Mika?—was scheduled to be there again. What an adorable creature—those eyes, those teeth, those haunches—so accommodating,

10.

eager to please. They were all like that, supposedly, the Japanese, submissive to the point of servitude. It might, of course, kill the sport, that kind of almost fanatical cooperation, so unlike Western women—this one in the ad, for instance, all defiance: tits like a twin-engine fighter; whereas, Miko's . . . plums, ripe greengages late in August when the skin turns tan. Such an extraordinary balance between modesty and shamelessness, the Japanese. They say their tongues are supple as snakes—no orifice inaccessible—and that all of them without exception are double-jointed, able to do anything, assume any position, perform any service, any act you ask—no need to ask, they volunteer, ask *you:* Shall I crouch now? Would it please you in my mouth? Oh, Miko! Miko . . . . Was there still a chance to set something up for the weekend? Tomorrow afternoon, perhaps? Would Boris be back from dinner yet? . . . Inching his wrist out from under the blue oxford cuff, Wahl gave his watch a furtive glance. Too early to call, give him another half hour or so `. . . .

The moment his mother's fingertips touched the keys, Jerome's attitude toward her changed completely, changed, he was aware, because she herself changed so completely whenever she played— even a trivial mawkish tune like *Träumerei.* No longer the *grande bourgeoise,* championing Anatole France, condemning Soutine, penny-pinching on the laundry, ridiculing the maid, violating her children's integrity, prying and nagging and neurasthenic—at the piano she became an artist: altogether serious, dedicated, self-possessed. Even from behind, seeing only a quarter view of her patrician profile, straight back softened by her cream-colored satin blouse, freckled arms, wavy auburn hair lustrous in the lamplight, Jerome could tell she was a different woman, no longer at odds with her environment, estranged from her husband, tormented by her children, by herself, driven from room to room, unable to find a resting place among all that modern furniture and nineteenth-century art—no, now she seemed quite relaxed, at home; Vuillard's *Salon*—the painting over the piano, of a cozy Third-Republic interior aglow with muted yellows and burnt umber—the perfect background for her recital.

As always when conscious of his mother's incongruities, Jerome was baffled by his own. Not five minutes ago he had wanted to murder the woman; now he found himself gravitating toward her, touched almost to tears by the masterful simplicity with which she was performing *Träumerei,* as if the little tune were issuing straight from Schumann's heart, unmediated by his mother's stubby

11.

fingers. God! why couldn't she be like this, the artist, all the time? How much easier, less confusing things would be . . . . Coming to a standstill just beyond the turned-back lid of the Bechstein, on which he rested his folded arms, Jerome could see not only his mother (how much like a De La Tour Virgin she looked just now with her features in repose) but also his father and brother across the room. How right, Jerome decided, that he should end up standing there, aligned with his mother; Claude on the sofa beside their father. At heart, he and his mother were so alike—what else explained their constant bickering?—alike in appearance (almost the image of his mother, Jerome felt that nature had even improved on the original: straightening the imposing nose, sharpening the too-full jaw—no wonder his high school class had voted him Best Looking Senior), alike in temperament and character—though not, of course, in intellect, where he naturally excelled. From whom but Maman had he inherited his talent for painting? he reflected, dreaming of the day when he would take his rightful place at Wahl Gallery—not on the "floor" with his father but on the walls with the masters. His father had no real feeling for art . . . other than the art of love—heh-heh! No-no, that wasn't fair. His father had an excellent eye, a good business head, abundant culture, skillful salesmanship—all that was lacking was imagination, creative imagination; that came from his mother. No doubt about it, she was the one he took after, just as Claude took after their father. Except that in Claude's case, instead of improving on the original, nature had debased it: coarsened the features, softened the physique, dulled the wits, reduced to cloddishness all the charm and suavity. In Claude you could really see their father stripped of his veneer—the hedonist unmasked. Had it never occurred to Marcus, in the course of all the banter about Ivan and Dimitri, Alyosha and Smerdyakov—had it never even crossed his mind that he himself, as head of the family, was, ipso facto, Fyodor Karamazov? . . .

At this point, Jerome's attention shifted from his father and brother to the painting by Boris Napotnik on the wall behind their backs. Titled *Jeune fille en chemise verte*, the large seven-by-five-foot canvas (the largest in the living room) was a portrait of a slightly buck-toothed though beautiful Slavic girl with almond eyes, a triangular face and raven hair, highlighted by streaks of lavender. To protect her modesty the girl, whose viridian blouse was unbuttoned from top to bottom, clasped the front of the garment in her strikingly ugly hands, her dreamy expression verging on vacuity. Tonight, as never before, *Jeune fille en chemise verte* offended Jerome. Not only was it a mediocre work of art, utterly derivative of Mo-

12.

digliani and vastly inferior to all the other paintings in the room, it was an absolute affront to Maman. How dared his father hang this portrait of a former mistress here in the apartment? (Jerome remembered the model, Theodora, with considerable ambivalence— remembered himself at the age of thirteen or fourteen going with his father and brothers to Uncle Boris' studio, not on a Sunday afternoon as usual, but on some holiday or other, and falling in love with Teddi at first sight; remembered it was Teddi's beauty that had stimulated him to paint his first oil. In reality, there was something so improvised and awkward about the blouse in *Jeune fille en chemise verte*, Jerome sometimes wondered whether it hadn't been donned because of him and his brothers, because they had taken Uncle Boris and Teddi by surprise that afternoon, turning what had started as a nude into a clothed portrait . . . . But speculation of this sort began only later, long after Teddi had vanished from the scene and Jerome grasped more fully the nature of her relation to his father. By then his love for them both was infused with hatred, the kind of hatred, part jealousy and part indignation, Jerome was experiencing now, staring at the portrait.) Did his father imagine Maman knew nothing about Teddi and the others? Of course she knew, had always known that Uncle Boris ran a private brothel for her husband. The monthly stipend the gallery paid Napotnik for his "art" fooled no one but Napotnik—poor self-deluded simpleton. No wonder Maman was miserable most of the time. No wonder she resented painting, resented her husband, resented New York, resented even the lipstick traces on his own eleven shirts—in that respect, but in that alone, was he his father's son. No wonder she clung so desperately to Danny—except for music, he was the only uncorrupted element in her life. Why, then, had this happened to *him*? Why was it always the Dannys, the Alyoshas—the really beautiful and pure in heart who had to pay the price? Why couldn't it have been Claude? . . .

Claude welcomed *Träumerei*, if only because it shut his brother's trap. The idea of Jerome as Danny's advocate infuriated Claude. He could tolerate Jerome's hot air, his arrogance, obstinacy, egomania, and pride, but not his hypocrisy. Having suffered at the hands of his older brother every form of violence and cruelty short of fratricide, Claude could not trust Jerome's altruism where Danny was concerned. He took it as the sign of a guilty conscience, an attempt on Jerome's part to cover up the past. In their boyhood Jerome had expressed no altruism, shown no mercy to Claude. On the contrary, he had treated Claude like a slave, worse than a slave—a slave who performs his duties is entitled, at least, to go about his business unmolested, but not Claude. In addition to being Jerome's slave, forced to do his bidding on pain of death, Claude had also been his brother's whipping boy, punished time after time for Jerome's own evil nature. If Jerome misbehaved, if he received bad grades at school, lost a game, or crossed a friend, he invariably took it out on Claude: locked him in the closet, kicked or punched him till he cried. On top of that, Jerome had a habit, developed at an early age, of belittling Claude, belitting his mind, appearance, speech, clothes, interests, actions, everything about him—as if by diminishing Claude, Jerome could somehow aggrandize himself. Yet the moment the situation was reversed and Claude treated Danny the way he, Claude, had been treated by Jerome, he was accused of being a barbarian, a bully. After all, Danny was only a child, delicate and defenseless—and no ordinary child, at that. In Jerome's eyes, as well as in everyone else's—there was no one Danny had not deceived—their little brother was a saint: altogether innocent, selfless, good—their own home-grown Alyosha. To the same extent that Jerome vilified, tormented, and depreciated Claude, he sanctified, protected, and idealized Danny. The inequity of this double standard made Claude's blood boil, made his soul cry out for justice. Yet he sometimes wondered whether Danny was any better off than he was, had any more reality for Jerome; or whether Jerome regarded them both as mere functions, components of himself—the bad and the good, the base and the noble, the flesh and the spirit—opposites in an endless dialectic of which Jerome himself was the synthesis. But that was quite another matter, more complex and puzzling than Jerome's hypocrisy—a good example of which could be seen this minute as he lounged like a lizard over the Bechstein, his expression one of loving appreciation for Maman whom he really despised.

As for Danny, Claude alone saw through his so-called illness, knew it for what it was: an *act*. What else could you call behavior so blatantly deceitful and premeditated, so calculated for effect? Maman liked to think he had changed overnight, that overnight her little angel had turned into a devil, become recalcitrant and vicious, foulmouthed and filthy minded, an entirely different person—but that was nonsense. He had always been that way: a sneak, a liar, a snake in the grass, so innocent in front of Maman, never to blame for anything and therefore never punished; but the minute she turned her back, out would come his tongue, up would go his thumb to his nose—infantile gestures of defiance—because it was always Danny who started the trouble: pulled your hair, scratched or kicked or bit just like a girl; and if you dared retaliate, why then, of course, he would turn on the tears and go whining to Maman. He had always been a crybaby, a weakling who hid behind his sickliness; he had always held his breath, postured, thrown tantrums, talked to himself or else refused to open his mouth, brooding and pouting instead. That was nothing new. There was nothing new about any of it—except, perhaps, the voices, those voices he claimed to hear nowadays. But that sort of thing was highly suspect. Juridically speaking, there was no way in the world of verifying "voices" —especially when heard solely and exclusively by a confirmed liar. That a handful of psychiatrists had been convinced by Danny's hallucinations, carried no weight with Claude. It wasn't just the courts that took a dim view of the testimony of psychiatrists—the whole world did—psychiatrists were known the world over as a bunch of quacks who bled their patients for all they were worth. No-no, Claude was not convinced. Far from it. He had, in fact, a strong suspicion his brother made the voices up, fabricated them for a definite purpose—the same purpose Danny had for doing everything he did—to attract attention. That was the crux of the matter, the key to all his behavior—Danny was a show-off, an exhibitionist for whom voices, breath-holding, tantrums, posturing, silences, suicide threats were nothing more than stratagems to gain attention. Even his poems were written to ingratiate himself with their parents or, at least, with Papa. Papa put altogether too much emphasis on literature. Painting was one thing—a business, after all—but poetry quite another. There was no excuse for it. Anyone could write a poem— "Cement, cement, I've spent my days in cement." —that didn't make you a genius. Nor did acting insane. . . . Of course, the minute he was put away it became a crime to say such things, a crime even to *think* them. Somehow madness made you sacred, inviolable, above justice. Surely Danny understood that, had understood it long before the fact; surely his desire for preferential treatment, special privileges, had prompted him to act insane. Why else would he have gone to such extremes, allowed himself to be locked up? More important, why if he were truly mad, certifiable, would he have been released? Didn't that prove he could turn it on and off at will? Once inside the madhouse, he had doubtless changed his mind, found the place not to his liking (though God knows why—it cost enough!), preferred to come back home. . . . Ahh! but that was his mistake, his fatal mistake. Even Maman had remarked on it: "If he's well enough to come back home, he's well enough to stay." Exactly! Either you were nuts or sane—you couldn't be *both*. By

15.

coming home, the little imp had tripped himself up, trapped himself—that much was clear; moreover, there had been some indications this evening, such as Danny's perfect conduct throughout dinner (even when he left the table, he had asked to be excused), that he himself realized the fact, realized there could be no two ways about it. If he wanted to stay, he would have to behave himself, cut the act; otherwise, back he would go! Fair enough. Poetic justice was better than no justice at all. It would be interesting, to say the least, to see what Danny would do now.

> For You have I prepared myself:
> set the wooden staves in place,
> stuck the funnel in my mouth,
> inserted the plastic tubes and hose.
> For You alone, your fluidity,
> I long. Spill into me, over me,
> anoint me like a gangland stiff,
> destined for the river bed,
> where, at last, self-fulfilled,
> impervious, it comes to rest,
> itself its tombstone and its tomb.
> But hurry, hurry, harden quickly,
> lest one false move crack the mold.

This poem, written by Danny two days ago in anticipation of his homecoming, had been painstakingly transcribed into a pocket-size spiral notebook, which lay open now in front of him on the desk. Beside it was a volume, also open, of Emily Dickinson's poems. Of the four poems on the two showing pages, one— "After great pain, a formal feeling comes" —was marked with a meticulous check. For a while, after leaving the dinner table, Danny had sat incanting this poem to himself, but the final stanza—

> This is the hour of lead,
> Remembered, if outlived,
> As freezing persons recollect the snow:
> First chill, then stupor, then the letting go.

—disturbed him so much, he had had to stop. Turning, then, to his own poem, he had tried to rework it. There was something equivocal about the tubes and hose—their ability to conduct both in and out, to drain as well as to supply—that troubled him. Troublesome, too, was the dangerous contrast between fluidity and rigidity. He wanted no mistakes about that, no misunderstandings.

16.

His intention in writing the poem had been purely Conservationist, orthodox, in no way deviatory, radical. And yet, for all his efforts, he had failed to eliminate these ambiguities. This failure, which Danny could only pray would pass unnoticed or, if not unnoticed, unpunished by the Committee, had brought on a bout of nail biting.

For Danny nail biting was no simple matter—an occasional bit of manicuring: a little nibbling here, trimming there—it was a highly complex and savage compulsion. Begun at a very early age in imitation of his brothers, both of whom had long since stopped, Danny's nail biting had gone through many stages. Dismissed, at first, by his mother and his beloved nurse, Fräulein Frummerman, as "naughty," it wasn't long before the naughtiness had turned into a "nasty habit," necessitating punishment. Thereafter, every time Danny bit his nails, he was called "bad," and his hand was slapped; when that failed to break the habit, the bitten nails were painted with a bitter-tasting liquid the color of iodine. But since the taste of this preventative was far less disagreeable than its stigmatizing appearance, Danny was driven to suck and bite his nails more than ever in an effort to erase the stain. And the more he did, the more he was criticized, told that only babies bit their fingernails, informed that boys with bitten fingernails were not allowed to go to school, cautioned that girls refused to marry boys who bit their fingernails, warned that swallowed fingernails were indigestible and could only be removed from the stomach or appendix, in which they lodged, by surgery. Apart from making nail biting the crucial issue in Danny's life, these remarks touched off an enduring inner conflict. On one side was his passionate determination to be a good boy, to please Papa, Maman, and Fräulein Frummerman by putting a stop to this vicious habit; on the other was his uncontrollable need—aggravated, if anything, by these remarks which filled him with anxiety and shame—to tear himself to pieces.

Instead of subsiding in time, the struggle became ever more intense, desperate, significant, a kind of test—a test not only of will and self-control but also of *character*. His repeated inability to pass the test, his tendency, rather, to fail it ever more miserably, convinced Danny of his fundamental wickedness, weakness, worthlessness, childishness and depravity. The fact that he was handsome, virtuous, good-natured, and obedient, he overlooked. Whatever goodness others saw in Danny was utterly belied for him by his bitten fingernails. They abrogated all external authenticity, became for him the outer sign of an inner ugliness and evil. He considered himself a devil—how often had Fräulein Frummerman called him *Teufel* or *Teufelkind*—a creature possessed by demons over which he had no control. To conceal this hideous fact from the world, he began to conceal his hands. At the dinner table he held his knife and fork in his fists, at school he held his pencil as if he had no other fingers but the thumb. When it came to games, he was forced to improvise ways of picking up cards, moving checkers, rolling marbles. Certain games such as patty-cake, cat's cradle, or pitching pennies, he simply refused to play. (To his mother's chagrin, he also refused to practice the piano.) If a coin dropped he was helpless to retrieve it. To open a penknife or knotted shoelace, he was obliged to use his teeth (more and more his teeth were made to substitute for the fingernails they themselves had devoured, and his dreams teemed with lions, tigers, wolves, and beavers); the tops of boxes, lids of cans, even candy wrappers resisted him.

In these and countless other everyday activities Danny found himself seriously handicapped. Increasingly, he looked on his bitten nails as both the cause and effect of all his misery: his feeling that everyone was staring at him, judging him, that he was unlike other boys, more delicate and moodier, physically and mentally inferior—inferior to his brothers, inferior to his friends—that not just his hands but all of him, he himself, was good for nothing, helpless, useless; increasingly his bitten nails attested to his badness: his tears and tantrums, kicking and biting, lying and tattling and being a sneak. Worst of all he blamed his nail biting for the loss of Fräulein Frummerman, who, as his mother later pointed out, had refused on the eve of the war to accompany the Wahls to America because she was "no longer willing to take care of a boy who bit his nails."

To atone for all the unhappiness and displeasure nail biting had caused his nurse and parents, Danny strove to make himself exemplary in every other way. Taking to heart the maxim "Children should be seen, not heard," he all but tiptoed through the world—obedient, polite, soft-spoken—excusing himself at every turn. On the subway he gave his seat to women, at street corners he helped the blind, in elevators he removed his cap, after meals he replaced his napkin in the napkin ring. He kept himself immaculate—body scrubbed, hair slicked down, shoes highly polished—never used a dirty word, never picked his nose, never, if he could help it, farted. Frugal to a fault, he seldom spent a penny on himself, saving up instead to buy expensive gifts for his family and Cuckoo. At all times he tried to be helpful, thoughtful, unselfish. If there were errands to run, dishes to wash, straightening up to do, Danny volunteered. All in all he behaved less like a growing boy than an apprentice, indentured not only to his family but also to the world at large in whose eyes, as a result, he seemed a model child.

In his own eyes, however, he saw himself quite differently. Since his good behavior, far from being an end in itself, was simply a means of combatting his nail biting—combatting, that is, the devil within—Danny paid little attention to the valor and tenacity with which he fought the battle. All that mattered was the outcome, a consequence about which he could think only in absolute terms: total victory or total defeat. When, therefore, instead of stopping, his nail biting grew worse and worse, rapacious to the point of self-cannibalism, Danny surrendered to his inner demon, losing thereby all sense not only of his good behavior but of his physical being, his body in the world. Like his bitten fingernails, on which he gazed eternally, he saw himself as ugly and altogether powerless—powerless to use his hands, powerless to persuade by speech (who but Cuckoo wanted to listen anyway?), powerless to oppose or even to resist by means of physical force. What power he did possess, as shown by his teeth, by his tantrums and nightmares, seemed utterly fiendish and destructive, under the sign of his inner demon, and Danny disavowed it—curbed his movements, curbed his tongue, isolated his outer self from his inner demon.

Once this breach had been effected, into it moved a force more powerful than either Danny's inner demon or his outer self, more powerful than both combined. Though it seemed to speak in the voice of conscience, it acted more like Momus, the god of censure who finds fault with the faultless and is perfectly implacable. Because Danny himself was so critical of his nail biting, he accepted as his due the much harsher criticism of Momus—he had it coming to him, he told himself. And yet Momus' criticism was by no means limited to nail biting. So high were his standards that nothing Danny did or said could measure up to them—even his best behavior wasn't good enough for Momus. Omnipotent, ubiquitous, Momus was quick to catch and comment on the merest peccadillo—a fingerprint or inkblot on the page, a sloppily crossed "t," a single hair out of place, the briefest lapse of memory. In more important matters such as homework, tests, reading, writing, spelling, sports, Momus was unremitting in his disapproval. Even in areas where there was no right or wrong, no accepted standard, Momus berated Danny for eating too fast, reading too slowly, being too thin, taking too long on the toilet. Even when his behavior was irreproachable, when, for instance, he got 96 in English, hit a triple, or wrote a sonnet, Momus needled him for not getting 100, hitting a homer, being as good as Milton. On those rare occasions when Momus seemed to approve of something Danny did, it was only to take away with one hand what had been given with the other—to expose his good behavior as nothing but deceitful, a vain attempt to camouflage his inherent evil. Most distressing of all, perhaps, were the countless times Danny initiated an action positive beyond a doubt of his veracity or innocence, yet completed it all but convinced by Momus that he had been lying or guilty. Eventually Danny found it difficult to do almost anything—read or write or study, hit a ball or memorize a lesson—so intimidated was he by Momus. His outer self thus enfeebled, his inner demon seized on every opportunity to mutilate his fingernails—and then it was that Momus, forever lying in wait, stepped in to show them both who was boss. This show of strength was never verbal: no matter how excoriating, words were not enough to express Momus' scorn on these occasions—it took the form of a third degree. Using techniques learned from G-men and the S.S., Momus completely violated the integrity of Danny's outer self, reduced his inner demon to absolute subservience. Just how it was done, Danny was made to forget, but he emerged from these closed-door sessions a confessed sinner, broken and hopeless, only too eager to recant his selfhood.

By the time he came to adolescence Danny had endowed his nail biting with all sorts of overtones: sexual, psychological, astrological, religious. The fact that his zodiacal sign happened to be Gemini, the twins, more than confirmed the breach between his outer self and inner demon, it made the split predestined, irreparable. Furthermore, his sign provided his duality with a distinct and tangible form: the Dioscuri, brothers who by the slightest mutation could be made to stand not only for Danny's double nature, but also for Jerome and Claude, himself and Claude, Jerome and himself, Cain and Abel. At Sunday school the voice of Momus, which heretofore had vaguely resembled certain familiar human voices, took on at first the awesome authority of Abraham, Moses, Jeremiah, and then the absolute authority of Yahweh Himself; so that what had been more or less a private struggle to overcome a nasty habit gradually assumed the cosmological significance of a sin against Almighty God.

From a classmate in junior high Danny learned that nail biting was a dead giveaway for another "nasty habit"—only masturbators, he was told, bit their fingernails. Since he himself was guilty of both these unspeakable practices, the statement seemed indisputable, and he believed it without question. What he had sought to keep a dark secret, turned out, to his horror, to be common knowledge. Everyone who crossed his path—his family, friends, teachers, classmates, every stranger on the street knew him for a masturbator. Henceforth, his already frenzied struggle to overcome his nail biting became even more desperate, imperative. How else could he conceal his sinfulness, his onanism? He had to quit biting his nails, simply *had* to . . . but couldn't. To stop biting his nails, he had to quit masturbating, simply *had* to . . . but couldn't. In his mind the two became inextricably implicated, inextricably associated with his inner demon, all but interchangeable. To resist or suppress the one caused an outbreak of the other—an outbreak which, in turn, provoked an onslaught from Momus who, in the name of Yahweh now, tormented him as if Danny were already among the damned in perdition.

Finally, even his madness—his posturing and hallucinations, cowering in corners and keeping his hands as far from his teeth as possible, even Robespierre's proclamations—all of it seemed in one way or another related to his nail biting.

At the desk now Danny sat perfectly still (except for the movement of his eyes), as if in obedience to his own warning that one false move would crack the mold. His right forefinger, wrapped in a bloodstained handkerchief, rested on the page of his spiral notebook. Though he could no longer concentrate on either the notebook or the volume of Emily Dickinson's poems, he had left them open on the desk as a precaution—a precaution not against the members of the Committee who were, after all, undeceivable, but against the spies in his own household by whom he was determined not to be caught idle.

As for the C.P.S., Danny couldn't quite believe, despite the Committee's current absence, that it was gone for good, out of his life forever, couldn't believe it wasn't somewhere within striking distance, wouldn't turn up sometime in the course of the weekend. Until this afternoon he had gone along with Dr. Nordhoff's careful explanation of the weekend as "a kind of field trip," an opportunity for Danny not only to put into practice what he had already learned about himself at the hospital, but also to make new discoveries, gather fresh impressions for future use. But the moment he set foot in the car, Danny had been seized with doubts. That was the reason he had insisted on putting his small overnight bag in the trunk. Not because there wasn't room on the back seat, but because of his dreadful suspicion that one or two Committee members—not Mortlock, of course, or Monk or Zinc, who were above having to stow away, but Lashmit or Fowler—were hiding in the trunk. That the trunk was empty proved nothing, except perhaps their unwillingness, with so many other means of transportation available to members of the Committee of Public Sanity, to travel like cattle.

As the afternoon wore on and Danny watched himself forfeit—first to Papa and Jerome, then to the doorman, elevator man, Maman, Cuckoo, Claude—whatever selfhood he had managed to attain after seven months of treatment; as he watched himself relapse so readily into all his former attitudes, as if he didn't understand that his very survival depended on his asserting new ones, Danny began to discount what Dr. Nordhoff had said. All that about a field trip was just a lot of bull. Quite obviously the real reason for his being sent back home was to see whether or not—on his own, away from Dr. Nordhoff's care and the impregnable defenses of the hospital—the C.P.S. would continue to keep hands off; or whether Robespierre would have him taken into custody again. That was the crucial question, and whatever the answer, merely asking it was in itself, Danny realized, a terrible setback, certain to have serious consequences.

Some of the consequences were already apparent. Though he knew better than to let on he had noticed, Danny was only too aware of whoever it was who kept opening and closing the living room valve, letting the mounting pressure escape; whoever kept plucking the French-blue coordinates of the plaid wallpaper, causing the walls to vibrate; whoever kept darting about the bedroom, spinning first one, then another of the countless white helms, the nautical motif printed on the blue cotton cushions, curtains, bedspreads.

To counteract these distractions, Danny had fixed his gaze on Jerome's full-scale copy of Watteau's *Gilles*, which hung on the wall beside his bed, diagonally opposite the desk. By studying the central figure—who in Jerome's version possessed the features not of Watteau's model Corneille van Clève but of Danny himself, who had sat for his brother—he hoped to absorb some of Gilles' evident composure. At the moment, however, he felt unsettled, dislocated, staring at this portrait of himself, his own head stuck onto the shoulders of an early eighteenth-century Frenchman, dressed up as Pierrot and posed on a knoll in the woods where he stood towering (taller than the background trees) over four other figures, three of whom, two men and a woman, could be seen from the waist up, standing in a gully behind the knoll and pulling a donkey on which another man was mounted. Dressed though Gilles was in the traditional white clown jacket and pantaloons (the sleeves inches too long; the trouser legs inches too short), there was nothing comical about him. On the contrary, the ill-fitting costume only increased the pathos of his appearance. There he stood—full face, arms at his sides, feet slightly spread, body erect yet perfectly relaxed, shoulders sloping—singled out, isolated from his fellows for no apparent reason, like one of Aaron's goats—but whether sacrificial victim or scapegoat, God alone knew. Whatever his fate, it was obvious from his mute submissive attitude that Gilles was resigned to it: expecting nothing, demanding nothing, self-contained. The opportunity to take a different stance—to rebel, protest, supplicate—had clearly passed, if indeed it had ever existed for this modest gentle soul. For Gilles the vast range of man's potential responses had been reduced to one, the definitive one: acceptance. Hence the knowing look of sorrow in his eyes as he stared down from above—sorrow not for himself but for what he faced, what he saw before him: the Eternal Waste.

Of the others, the group in the background, only Laurent, the youth in the gold sombrero with the upturned brim serrated to suggest a sunflower, saw something too, something which left him dumbfounded, eyes and mouth agape. But unlike Gilles, who was staring straight ahead, Laurent's eyes were fixed on a point to the southwest; and whereas Gilles was altogether pensive, Laurent looked astonished, almost awestruck, as if he were seeing now for the first time something Gilles had long ago perceived and turned from in despair.

There was, however, the possibility that Gilles was only feigning, pretending detachment on orders from his master, Hector, by whom he had been posted on the knoll to divert attention from Vittorio and Emilia. In contrast to Laurent, these two ignored what was happening in the southwest; their one concern was to get Lobo, Hector's mount, into the forest. Judging by the strenuous way Vittorio and Emilia were tugging at Lobo's rope, pitting against him their combined weight and strength, and by the look of savage fury in the animal's eye, the donkey was resisting them. And with good reason, too. For though he could not now see the leering man astride his back, earlier, when Hector mounted him, Lobo had seen his black skullcap and black robes, had seen Vittorio's scarlet vestments and Emilia's cleavage under her taffeta shawl; above all, Lobo had seen, just ahead, at the edge of the forest toward which he was being tugged, the forest's guardian spirit in the form of a limestone bust mounted like a herma on a pillar eight feet high—a bust of Pan, the god in whose name the impending rites would shortly be performed.

Despite his impassive countenance, Gilles was doubtless aware of what was going on behind his back—aware of the goateed god with the Oriental eyes and pointed ears, of Lobo's rage and Hector's leering, Laurent's astonishment and the impatience of Vittorio and Emilia to get into the forest. Surely Gilles knew, far better than the rest, what was about to happen; moreover, he knew something the others, the Enragés, didn't know, something which perhaps explained his immobility and muteness—Gilles knew why Pan had turned to stone.

Danny cocked his head. Somewhere, far away, someone was playing *Träumerei*. Was it being played ironically to mock him for musing over Gilles? To mock the painting? Where was it coming from? The apartment upstairs? The living room? Maman? Was Maman playing, serenading him as she used to when they lived on Avenue Pierre I de Serbie? . . . The tranquil little tune seemed to simplify the world, make it a safer place, much as it once had been when he helped Grand-maman Nathan scoop the marrow from the marrow bones; when Fräulein held his hand to assure his balance on the parapets in the Trocadéro gardens; when Maman herself invited him to sit beside her on the piano bench—a privilege never vouchsafed Jerome or Claude—and played for him alone, in the bay of the huge salon with its many windows and bowls of lilacs, a command performance of *Kinderscenen*.

With the bloodstained handkerchief wrapped around his forefinger, Danny wiped away a tear. At the same time, as if the tear signaled a thaw, he felt at last the impulse to get up and trace the music to its source, hoping thereby to regain the lost security evoked by *Träumerei*. But first, to forestall the family's questions, he unbandaged his finger. The bleeding had stopped. Near the fingertip, which still retained the crescent impressed on it by the missing nail, the newly exposed skin was colorless; farther up, however, toward the moon, where not just the nail but pieces of flesh had been torn away, were little crimson potholes, magenta ridges, and jagged snow-white peaks; while in the open side-wounds and along the mutilated cuticle lay deposits of gore.

In addition to depressing him, the sight of his finger offended Danny's sense of order and he quickly set out to improve its appearance. First he sucked the blood away. Then he took from the top drawer of the desk a rusty pair of tweezers with which he pried up and plucked out tiny slivers of fingernail and hangnail inaccessible to his teeth. Of these, only the nail fragments were preserved: laid out one by one like archeological specimens on the open notebook. The rest, the flesh, he popped into his mouth and devoured. Resisting the temptation to eat the parings too, he turned back to

24.

the drawer and removed with great care a white envelope, dated 1950, which he placed face down on the desk. For a moment, as he stared at the bulging envelope, he began to gnaw his pinky, but caught himself and stopped. Aware, now, that he was being watched by Hector, Danny screened the envelope with his left hand, opened the flap and peered inside. Amassed therein, like the bones and skulls once piled high in the charnel houses surrounding the churchyard of the Innocents at Paris, was a mound of bitten fingernails. In all there were several hundred fragments, some ingrained with dirt, some the color of ivory, some no thicker than a hair, delicate and curling, others, thumbnails, broad and crude, still others bearing bits of wizened flesh—the aggregate, a brittle, spiky, desiccated horde that at the slightest tilting of the envelope murmured of its hellish thirst. And yet, from Danny's point of view, this little bone-yard was no *memento mori*. Rather, it signified the possibility of salvation. Profligate though he was, he hoped, by garnering the evidence against himself, to atone for his sins and gain redemption. And so, he picked up the notebook, dumped the new bits of fingernail into the envelope, closed the flap, and returned it to the drawer where he reposited it in front of several others, identical to the one in his hand but dated 1949, 1948, 1947.

Under the spell of the music now, he tucked the bloodstained handkerchief into his pocket and stole out of the bedroom. But in the hall he hesitated. Through the closed glass doors at the other end, he could see Maman and Jerry in the living room. Involuntarily, Danny rubbed his thumb over the tip of his forefinger, feeling the nail's absence. Maman had begun to play *Träumerei* again, and Jerry was protesting. Danny drew back within the doorjamb. As he stood there, out of sight but listening intently, he suddenly realized that *Träumerei* contained the seeds not only of Schumann's madness but of his own, that somewhere intermingled in that reverie of marrow paste and lilacs, Grand-maman and Fräulein Frummerman, everlasting love and fusion, was the cause of his undoing. If he answered its call, all would be lost. . . . And yet, to turn a deaf ear, withhold himself, go back to his desk and sit in solitude awaiting "the hour of lead"—that was no solution either. That was not the reason he had agreed to come home for the weekend. He was there because he was well enough now—at least in Dr. Nordhoff's opinion—to rejoin his family, take his place beside them without having, at the same time, to put aside himself. Though Danny doubted the truth of this statement, he knew it could be tested only in the living room, knew it was there, and not at his desk, that he would have to face the music.

Inhaling deeply, he crept from his hiding place and started slowly down the hall.

Even before her son entered the room, Mme. Wahl knew he was at the door. Her heartbeat quickened, lungs drew deeper breaths, body tensed, teeth began to gnaw the walls of her mouth. In contrast to the ease with which she had played these notes the first time, they sounded deliberate now, willed and stiff. All at once her mind, which had been inert, empty of all thought, was in turmoil. Should she stop playing and turn around? Pretend to make a mistake? Go on as if he weren't there? Was he *really* there? . . . Instead of turning, Mme. Wahl glanced at Jerome, hoping his expression would confirm her premonition. Yes-yes, his eyes were fixed not on the keyboard but on the doors behind her back where Danny must be standing. "Enough," she said with a sigh.

"Don't stop now," Jerome objected.

"First you complain about my going on, then you—"

"P-P-P"—Claude stammered—"Pay no attention, Maman."

"Really, Jerry," Mme. Wahl continued, "there's just no pleasing you." Much as she wanted to turn around, Jerome inhibited her, and she hated herself for allowing him to influence her actions. "What are you staring at, anyway?" she inquired testily, using curiosity as an excuse to follow the line of his gaze.

"Maman!" he grumbled, too late to stop her.

Standing with his back pressed against the wall, Danny was so slight as to be almost indiscernible in the dark hall. Even his profile, framed in one of the panes, was obscured partly by a lock of black hair, partly by the hand whose fingernails he was gnawing. But the instant his mother turned her head, Danny dropped the hand to his side, and Mme. Wahl could see that he was scowling, disfiguring his beautiful features. . . . Don't do that, she said to herself, echoing an old saw she had reiterated since he was a child: What if your face froze that way? Remaining seated, she pivoted on the stool and held out her arms as if to an infant learning to walk. "*Viens, donc, chéri, viens.*"

"Let him be," Jerome said half under his breath.

"Oh, be still!" she rejoined out of the side of her mouth. "I've had enough of you for one day."

"What now?" Wahl put aside the newspaper and stood up.

"P-P-Pay no attention," Claude repeated, not indicating whether he was addressing his father or mother, referring to Danny or Jerome.

Still seated, arms still extended, Mme. Wahl beckoned Danny with her fingers. "Come on, pussycat."

Wahl, having reached the double doors, transferred what remained of his cigar to his left hand in order to free his right for the knob.

"Look out!" his wife exclaimed as the second door swung open with the first, and she saw her baby about to be pinned behind it. "You'll crush him."

"Crush him?" Wahl snorted and rolled his eyes heavenward, beseeching God for patience. "It's nowhere near him. Is it" —he turned to Danny for corroboration—"*mon petit?*"

Nauseated though Danny was, as always, by cigar fumes, he forced a little smile and shook his head in token agreement.

"But why do you stand out here," Wahl went on, "like an orphan? Why—"

"Marcus!" Mme. Wahl disapproved of his using the word orphan in front of Danny who, after all, had just been released from an institution where—judging by his hollow cheeks, the circles under his eyes, and his heartbreaking expression—he had not slept or eaten in months, and had been altogether miserable, mistreated.

Wahl ignored the interruption. "Come and join the fun. Maman was just playing for us, a little Schumann recital."

"Hardly a recital," she dissented modestly.

" 'The c-c-composer's illness and roman—' "

"Tssst!" Mme. Wahl silenced Claude.

"*Néanmoins,*" Jerome chimed in.

"G-G-Gardenia-scented—"

"Flavored," Jerome corrected his brother not in his usual critical manner but helpfully, playfully. Then, raising his hands once more like a conductor, he signaled Claude and, at the silent count of three, the brothers uttered in unison, "Gardenia-flavored pathos."

"Oh, be still!" their mother snapped, "*both* of you."

"Your brothers are joking about a review in the *Times.*" As Wahl explained the reference, he laid his hand gently but firmly on Danny's shoulder in an effort to draw him out of the corner.

To escape his father's touch, Danny freed himself with a shrug and slipped into the living room.

Cheered by his entrance, Mme. Wahl spun around light-heartedly to face the keyboard again and began to play, by way of a salute, the first piece that came to mind: the "Bridal Chorus" from *Lohengrin.*

Claude was quick to sing the accompaniment:

> "Here comes the groom,
> All dressed in white. . . ."

The incongruity of both the selection and the non-rhyme brought on a fit of loud, high-pitched laughter which, when combined with his stammer, made Claude's next remarks all but unintelligible. ". . . ide . . . b-b-b—"

Jerome acted as interpreter. "He wants to know where the bride is."

"No, no" —Claude shook his head and waved his hands— "who . . . whoooo?"

"Who but Cuckoo?" Jerome suggested. The idea convulsed Claude. His laughter was contagious; Jerome began laughing too. For the moment there was a feeling of real camaraderie between the two.

To top his brother, Claude made what seemed to him an even funnier suggestion. "Wait! I've got it. M-M-Miss Kerns."

"Myra—ha ha! Myra Kerns. Of course! ha ha ha! Of course!"

At mention of Miss Kerns, Mme. Wahl stopped playing.

From her lowering expression Jerome clearly understood she was in no mood for more, but he was enjoying himself too much to stop. "How about it, Maman? Would you have her for your daughter-in-law?"

> "Here comes the groom,
> All dressed in white . . . ."

"Idiots!" Pivoting on the stool again, Mme. Wahl turned away from Jerome and Claude in disgust, and beamed at Danny. "Don't listen to them, darling. They don't know what they're saying. Imbeciles, both of them—sometimes I wonder where they came from, whose they really are." This remark, as old and familiar as the sound of her voice, was greeted with giggles by Jerome and Claude. To sum up their misbehavior, Mme. Wahl resorted to another pet expression, the name given during the Revolution to the ultraradicals who opposed Robespierre. Anxious that there be no mistake for whom her barb was intended, she glanced over her shoulder at Jerome: "Enragés!" Doing so, however, Mme. Wahl missed Danny's reaction to the word. She did not see him whirl around to face the double doors with such rapidity that inertia made the flesh pull away from his skull; did not see him clap his clenched fists to his chest as if to protect himself from assault; did not see her husband also turn to detect the cause of Danny's agitation. All she saw was the look of perplexed concern that suddenly came over Jerome's face.

By the time she turned back, Danny had turned back too—his

hair disheveled, thumb in his mouth. "Don't bite your nails! Come here, my pigeon." Once again Mme. Wahl held out her arms. "Let me have a look at you. You know how long it's been since I've seen you—*really* seen you: to feast my eyes on you? *Ça remonte plus loin que j'ose penser*. . . . What's the matter? Don't you like Maman any more? You want to break her heart?" Slowly, perfunctorily, Danny walked into her open arms, which closed with the speed of a triggered snare. "Mmm-mmmuh!" She hugged the breath out of him. His back and shoulders stiffened. Relaxing her hold, she turned her attention to his hair: smoothing it down, combing it out of his eyes.

With an almost violent jerk of his head Danny pulled away, out of his mother's reach.

"Don't be so—" She started to speak in anger, but stopped herself. Instead, she took hold of her wrist and began to massage it zealously like an animal licking a wound.

Wahl, meantime, had crossed the room and sat down in one of the three cube-shaped chairs grouped around the glass-topped coffee table on which was displayed a sculpture by Rodin. "So, *mon petit*, tell us: how goes it? How does it feel to be home again?" The answer was barely audible. "What? Only 'all right'?"

To avert his father's questioning gaze, Danny riveted his eyes on the Rodin. Cast in bronze, the piece was a study of a hand and truncated forearm. Its overall height, including the rugged little base designed to keep the forearm vertical, was about eighteen inches. The unnatural position of the hand, bent back at right angles to the wrist, suggested the hand of an athlete, holding a shot—except that the fingertips were flexed too far to accommodate a shot and looked, instead, as if they had recoiled in pain (the palm was deeply gouged), like the arms of a starfish lanced through its center. It was evident that *rigor mortis* had set in. (With his forefinger Danny touched the spot where the chisel, wielded by the sculptor against the hand, wielded by himself against the starfish, had entered his own chest.) Even so, the hand was still alive, still struggling against its destiny, still strong enough, despite its mutilation, to pulverize a stone, yet powerless to lift its little finger, robbed forever of its life by the very bronze that gave it immortality.

After waiting in vain for Danny to speak, Wahl went on. "Well, what have you been up to? What were you reading?"

"Danny!" Jerome exclaimed. "Listen to this. This'll kill you. Guess what Maman thinks the poet's name is? . . . Émile!"

"Emil und die Detektive," Claude was quick to add. This reference

gave Claude the opportunity to embark on one of his most familiar routines: a merciless impersonation of their former German instructor. "In casez uf sobriety—eh, *pardon*—dubiety ve must rezort ourselfs to ze pluperfect—"

"My bracelet!" Mme. Wahl cried out. While massaging her wrist she had grown increasingly aware of something missing, something lost—something very precious, very dear to her—but only now did she realize what it was. "Mother's bracelet!" Leaping to her feet, she looked in all directions, her hand groping along the ledge of the music rack. "I had it—here! here!—a minute ago. Where could it have gone?"

Though Jerome and Claude knew exactly where the bracelet was, they found their mother's hysteria too entertaining to bring to an end. She was forever mislaying her belongings and then imagining them stolen by some member of the servant class: handyman, superintendent, delivery boys, part-time maid or, worst of all, the back-elevator man, a wily Albanian with whom Cuckoo was altogether too familiar to suit Mme. Wahl. The moment something disappeared she invariably turned to Danny for help, convinced her "*petit*" was endowed with a sixth sense for finding things. More often than not he was successful. When he failed, however, she would not rest until her husband filed an insurance claim, usually the day before the missing item miraculously reappeared in one of her own bureau drawers—a materialization that made her suspect her family of playing tricks on her.

"Danny darling, help me. It's Grand-maman's garnets. I know I had it on this noon. I distinctly remember Françoise saying— Oh, my God!" She clapped her palms to her temples. "You think it could have fallen down . . . into the strings?" Seizing the lamp from the music rack, Mme. Wahl held it over the hammerheads.

"M-M-Maman, you look like Diogenes."

"Instead of making stupid remarks, maybe one of you so-called gentlemen would be good enough to help me."

"Gladly, Maman." Jerome came to her assistance. "What would you like?"

"To cut my throat! that's what I'd like. Raise the top, please."

Jerome did as he was told. "Supposing it *is* down there, Maman," he said with a straight face, "how will we ever get it out?"

"How should I know? Oh, I could kill myself—I'll kill myself if it's gone."

"Now, now, *chérie*," Wahl tried to comfort her.

As soon as the support was in place, Mme. Wahl thrust the

music lamp into Jerome's hand, ducked her head under the piano lid and peered into the instrument. *"Mon dieu!* the filth, the filth! Oh, that Maria—it's a wonder it has any tone at all. I must get hold of the tuner first thing Monday."

The moment his mother's head was out of sight, Jerome signaled his father frantically. When, at length, he caught Wahl's eye, he pointed at the side table and then pecked his finger in the direction of the garnets. Wahl didn't understand. To clarify, Jerome waggled his wrist like a woman showing off a new bracelet. Still at a loss, Wahl expressed his non-comprehension by protruding his lower lip, hunching his shoulders, and showing his palms. Observing these gestures, Danny turned with apprehension from his father to Jerome. For his brother's benefit Jerome repeated the pecking pantomime, adding this time the unvoiced hint, "The bracelet . . . BRACE-let." He desperately wanted Danny to be the one to find it.

Meantime, Claude, not realizing that Jerome had something more in mind than to let Wahl in on the secret, went over and whispered it into his father's ear. In the next second Wahl, too, began to signal Danny, peck his finger in the air, and mouth soundless words. "On the table . . . TA-ble!" At last Danny turned all the way around and spotted the bracelet. Whereupon Wahl, who was now enjoying the conspiracy as much as Jerome, said aloud, "Danny, be a good boy, and help Maman find her bracelet. It must be here somewhere. It can't have walked away."

"Oh, yes, my love!" Mme. Wahl's plaintive plea issued from under the piano top. "Please help. There's a reward, you know."

In the center of the room now, Danny hesitated, torn between the desire to please his family and the need to oppose them or, at least, not to betray himself. Tempted as he was to be a "good boy," do what was expected of him: pick up the bracelet and pronounce the simple words, "Here it is, Maman, I've found it," endearing himself, thereby, to everyone, to say nothing of collecting his mother's unnamed but only too familiar reward: a thousand kisses, a dozen of which would be meted out instantly and lavished on his brow—tempting as this prospect was, it also troubled him because, as Danny fully realized, the entire ritual depended on his willingness to be manipulated. In one stroke he could undo all he had achieved in months and months of therapy. And yet if he resisted, his refusal to participate in their game would surely give them just the excuse they were waiting for to pack him off, back to the asylum. . . . No, that wasn't true! He would have to go back no matter what, regardless of his actions. It was only Maman who

31.

kept insinuating— But if he couldn't stay, why had he bothered to come at all? The answer was only too obvious: he was *living* the answer right now. He had come to see what he would do in this very situation—whether or not he would pick up the bracelet. But even as he struggled to keep in mind the still unassimilated reasons why it would be damaging to his integrity to pick it up, every member of his family, every moment of his history, every muscle in his body compelled him toward the bracelet.

Seeing Danny move, Claude moved too, to intercept him. Now that he understood what was happening, Claude refused to be a party to this hoax, refused to perpetuate the myth of Danny's psychic powers. No, indeed. "Maman! Maman! L-L-Look! Here it is!"

"The bracelet? Where?" In straightening up, Mme. Wahl bumped her head on the piano top and cursed. But in the next breath she thanked God for her good fortune. "Where was it? Who found it? Danny?"

"N-N-No, Maman, *I* did. It was—"

"Liar!" Jerome, who was outraged by his brother's treachery, had all he could do to keep from hurling the music lamp at Claude.

"D-D-D-D—"

"D-D-D-D!" Jerome mimicked Claude mercilessly. "Driveling idiot!"

"Jerome!" Wahl smacked the arm of his chair for silence. "*Ferme ça!*"

"No one found it," Jerome explained to his mother. "It's been there all the time."

"What!" Mme. Wahl looked incredulous. "Where? *Where* all the time?"

"On the table, just where you left it when—"

"D-D-Did I say it wasn't?" Claude demanded in self-defense.

"Thank you, *mon cher.*" Mme. Wahl took the bracelet from Claude and patted his cheek. "Really, Jerry, you don't expect me to believe? . . . I realize, of course, how much it would please you. . . ." Despite her nonchalant tone she clearly had her doubts. In addition she was having difficulty closing the bracelet and was beginning to show signs of impatience. "Danny darling, tell me— you're the only one I can trust—was it on the table the whole time?"

"How should *he* know?" Jerome objected. "He wasn't in the room before. Ask Papa."

Taking her eyes off the bracelet, which she secured from falling by pressing it against her hip, Mme. Wahl gave her husband a timid questioning look. In response Wahl smiled sweetly, sadly, and made an apologetic face at having to confirm Jerome's statement. "Naturally! naturally! When wasn't he right? Always! Go ahead—*all* of you—*flûte!*" she cursed the still unfastened bracelet. "Nothing in this world would please you more—don't you think I know it?—than to please me—convince me—" she corrected herself. "There! you see? I don't even know what I'm saying any more, you've got me so insane." Scarcely had the word passed her lips, than she let out a pitiful little yelp and punished herself for making such a remark in Danny's presence by plunging her teeth into the heel of her hand. The bracelet fell to the floor.

Without a moment's hesitation Danny bent down and picked it up.

"My angel," his mother murmured, too ashamed to meet his eyes.

Danny put the bracelet into her open hand. The ring of still fresh tooth marks on the mount of Venus aroused his sympathy. Though he had seen her bite the hand herself, it now seemed as if the marks had been inflicted on her by someone else—himself, conceivably—and he felt called upon to heal the wound. But even as he reached out to touch the spot, he saw his bitten fingernails and instantly withdrew his hand.

The piano lid came down with a thud, startling everyone. "Why do you pick it up for her?" Jerome disapproved of Danny's action. "She should be made—"

Wahl snapped his fingers loudly in a vain attempt to check Jerome's fury.

"Both of them! *that* one too"—Jerome jutted his jaw at Claude—"that miserable—"

"M-M-Miserable what?"

"What? Made to *what?*" Mme. Wahl said defiantly, as she sat down next to the side table to deal with the bracelet. "What should I be made to do? I'd be interested to hear."

"Pick it up like-like *Sisyphe*— Oh, never mind. Whatever it was, would be too good for you."

"You're speaking to your mother now," she reminded him. "Remember?"

"How could I forget?"

"Well then, show some respect."

"For what? When you deserve it," he muttered, "I'll show respect."

"What did you say?"

"You heard me."

"Brat!"

"And *you*?"

"Keep still!"

"What are *you*?"

"Keep still, I said."

"I will not!"

"Spoiled brat!"

"Gorgon!"

"Marcus!" she called for her husband's support.

"Jerome!"

"No! She can't order me—order my respect like—like she orders Cuckoo—"

"Lower your voice!" his mother commanded.

"What should I respect her for? For not knowing what she's saying half the time? For being—"

Wahl leaped to his feet. "Enough!"

"Why? She said so herself. You heard her. I'm just repeating what she—"

"She! she!" Mme. Wahl exclaimed in exasperation. "Who is *she*?"

Whirling on his mother, Jerome reached out as if to strangle her. "*You*, you—"

Before Jerome could say another word, his father grabbed his arm. "Enough, I said." Even more restaining than the strength of his grip or the tone of voice, was the intense threatening look in Wahl's eyes, which kept shifting back and forth from Jerome to Danny, who was standing now diagonally behind his father, and for whose sake, quite obviously, the eyes were demanding silence. Once he had made his point, Wahl released Jerome's arm, turned to his wife and smiled warmly. "Speaking of bracelets, *chérie*, guess who was in the gallery this morning? . . . Mrs. Wickersham. You should have seen the one she had on: square-cut diamonds . . . a triple band . . . that wide"—with his thumb and forefinger he measured off two inches— "really, without exaggeration. Jerry, you saw it, tell your mother, am I exaggerating?" Jerome remained silent. "It must have cost—oh, God—a quarter of a million— easily! Pharmaceuticals must be doing well these days."

Mme. Wahl wasn't listening. Instead, she was watching Jerome with feelings of both triumph and outrage. As far as she was concerned the battle had not ended, was still in full swing, so that when she saw him move now toward the foyer doors, she simply took up where they had left off. "And just where do you think you're going?"

"What business is it of yours?"

34.

"I asked a question."

"Since when do I have to account to you?"

"Since always! You're still my child—whether you like it or not. As long as you live in this house—"

"Danny" —Jerome purposely turned his back on his mother— "I'm going for a walk. Want to come along?"

"A walk!" Mme. Wahl exclaimed. "What's the matter with you? Have you taken leave— Of course he doesn't—"

"I wasn't talking to you."

"Well, *I'm* talking to *you*."

"Danny?" Jerome repeated.

"Did you hear me? I said I don't want him—"

"You know, *chérie*," Wahl interceded, "it just might do them good—"

"Good?"

"—to get a breath of air."

"On a night like this? Do you know what the temperature is? He'll catch pneumonia. He isn't used to—"

"For your information" —Jerome had rushed to the windows to check the thermometer— "it's thirty-nine degrees."

"So?"

"So what are you talking about—pneumonia?"

"I'd rather not discuss it."

"Who brought it up? Did *I*?"

"I said I'm not discussing it. He isn't going out, and that's the end of it." For emphasis, Mme. Wahl rapped her knuckles against the arm of the chair.

"Papa!" Jerome appealed to his father.

"You know your mother," Wahl said dryly. "When she makes up her mind. . . ." So customary was this remark, there was no need to finish it; everyone in the room automatically supplied the missing words: God Himself could not dissuade her.

"But you said yourself. . . ." Jerome persisted.

"Apparently, what *I* say doesn't count."

Stung by her husband's irony, Mme. Wahl retaliated. "And what would *you* like?"

"I've *said* what I'd like."

"For him to catch pneumonia?"

"Don't twist—" Wahl broke out, but quickly controlled his temper. "I don't like your tone."

"Pneumonia! is that what you'd like?"

"I'd like you to change your tone, I said." Wahl's own tone was so bridled and ominous that the danger sign was unmistakable. In the silence that followed, a series of hostile, challenging looks were exchanged between Wahl and his wife, his wife and Jerome, Jerome and Claude—all with more or less the same purport: Lucky for you Danny's here or I'd finish you off.

At last Claude broke the silence. "Oh, Maman, l-l-let the hot-head go."

"Shut up, you!" Jerome snapped.

"Who's stopping him?" Mme. Wahl replied to Claude.

"G-G-Good riddance, I say."

"Shut up, I said!"

"*I'm* not stopping him. Go on! Go! go" —she exiled Jerome from the room with a sweeping gesture— "my *boulevardier*, go walk the streets, do what you want, destroy yourself—but Danny stays here!"

"You know what I think?" Wahl suggested with a sly expression. "I think the men should go together—*all* of us, out on the town—and leave the women to do as they please."

"Exactly!" Jerome was exultant.

Mme. Wahl sneered. "Very funny."

Wahl walked over to Danny. "How about it, *chéri*?"

"Marcus!"

"Let's take a little walk, just the four of us."

"*Three*, Papa," Jerome put in. "Let's leave *that* one here, with *her*, where he belongs."

"L-L-Like hell, you will!"

"No, no" —Wahl was relishing his wife's discomfort— "none of that. We must keep a united front, whatever the cost."

Determined now to put a stop to this subversion, Mme. Wahl stood up and interposed herself between her husband and son. "You know, my sweet," she said to Danny, using all her charm to win him over, "you never even touched your cake . . . your favorite too. I bought it specially for you . . . and then, not—not even to taste it . . . that wasn't very nice. Was it because she dropped it? You know how clumsy Maria is, you mustn't hold that against the girl . . . she tries, poor thing. She's saving it for you—I told her to. Why not have some now? Hmm? With a nice big glass of milk? You have to eat, you know."

"Maybe he isn't hungry!" Jerome objected. "Did you ever think of that?"

"A lot you know!" Mme. Wahl retorted shrilly. "Look! look at his pants, they're falling off his body." Then, turning back to Danny, she resumed her seductive manner. "Don't listen to them, darling. Listen to your mother. Maman knows best, *n'est-ce pas?*

Come along—Ooo, your hand's like ice" —she rubbed Danny's hand between her own— "And they, *messieurs les professeurs*, think you should go for a walk! Well, let *them* go, let them take their precious walk, we don't need them, do we? We'll have our own little party."

"That's what *you* think!" Jerome declared. "Papa—"

Now, in an abrupt reversal of his earlier position, Wahl motioned Jerome to be still.

"Come. There's ice cream, too, vanilla," Mme. Wahl continued, as she opened the double doors and led Danny into the unlighted dining room. "Careful of the chair," she cautioned, even though the light spill from the living room provided ample illumination. "Hold on . . . I wouldn't want to lose you." She squeezed his hand, no longer cold now but perspiring. "We're like *Orphée* and *Eurydice*, aren't we, my pigeon? Except that *you* should be leading *me*. No-no" —she promptly changed her mind— "it's better this way . . . otherwise you could never look back, never see me again . . . ever . . . . How would you like that?"

Danny didn't answer. He was, in fact, looking back, over his shoulder at his father, who was standing on the other side of the glass doors which Wahl had just closed to prevent Jerome's voice from carrying.

". . . lunatic! She'll ruin—"

"*Tout de suite.*" Mme. Wahl gave Danny's hand a slight tug. She was eager to release the swinging door which she was holding open for him with her elbow, eager to get him out of earshot of Jerome.

"Then take *her* out!" Danny heard his brother shout as the door swung closed, muffling his father's response.

Maria, still in uniform, was standing over the sink, her back to the door, doing the dishes. The sink was at the far end of the oblong room in front of a curtainless window which looked out on a courtyard across whose dark expanse other cooks could be seen at other lighted windows. On the white enamel kitchen table against the right-hand wall was a dinner plate containing a small slice of sauerbraten in its congealed gravy, a spoonful of red cabbage, and a dumpling—Maria's as yet untouched meal. Mme. Wahl prided herself on the fact that she, unlike most women of her position, permitted Maria to eat exactly what the family ate. The only difference she insisted on was that Maria use the "kitchen silver" rather than the flatware used by the family—otherwise there was absolute *égalité*.

"*Mon dieu!* it's hot in here. I don't know how you stand it, Maria. Why don't you open the window?"

The running water gave Maria an excuse not to answer.

"Maman," Danny frowned. "She's right in front of it. You said yourself how cold—"

"Ah! *poquito*." The sight of Danny dispelled Maria's usual morose expression. Her small eyes brightened, and she smiled broadly, showing her terrible teeth. "I think to myself: he go to sleep."

"No, Cuckoo, still awake."

"And starving," Mme. Wahl put in. "What have you done with the cake, Maria?"

"In the pantry."

The pantry, which extended off the kitchen at right angles, was nothing more than a narrow vestibule equipped with another sink, additional cupboards and counters, and two doors, one to Maria's bedroom, the other to the foyer. As Mme. Wahl went in search of the cake, Maria turned off the water and began to dry her hands.

"Don't stop, Cuckoo," Danny said. "She'll find it. What about *you*? Don't you want to eat?"

"First the dishes, then the dinner."

"Doesn't it get cold?"

"*Sí*. I like."

"Your food cold?" Glancing at the plate, Danny made a face. "Cold dumpling?"

"*Sí*." Again Maria smiled broadly. "Cuckoo, hah?" she parodied herself.

"*Sí*." Danny grinned. "Cuckoo."

"Maria!" Mme. Wahl called from the pantry. "How many times have I told you to put a damp cloth over the cake?"

To mitigate his mother's criticism, Danny shook his finger playfully at Maria who, in turn, puffed out her sallow cheeks and rolled her eyes sheepishly.

Coming back into the kitchen with a large slice of devil's-food cake, Mme. Wahl held the plate at arm's length as if she were exhibiting legal evidence. "Bone dry."

"I like it dry," Danny said in Maria's defense.

"Nonsense! Don't always be such a good Samaritan. You'll get no thanks for that—not in *this* life, you won't. They'll walk all over you." Mme. Wahl set the plate down hard on the enamel table. "*I* should know," she added bitterly on her way to the refrigerator.

While her employer was attending to the ice cream, Maria opened the drawer containing the kitchen silver, took out a fork, and set a place for Danny opposite her own. "Sit, *poquito*."

Ready as he was to accept the invitation, Danny had to wait till his mother closed the refrigerator before there was room enough to pull out the chair.

"No-no, *chéri, pas ici, la salle*—" Seeing Maria place a paper napkin on the table, Mme. Wahl interrupted herself and said with impatience, "What are you doing, Maria? He'll have it in the dining room."

"No, Maman, *here*."

"It's much too hot in here."

"No it's not."

"Not? It's suffocating."

"I'd rather—"

"Maria" —Mme. Wahl set down the container of ice cream on the counter— "do as I say."

In defiance of his mother, Danny sat down at the kitchen table. Though she said nothing, Mme. Wahl gave her son a spiteful look; in response he picked up the paper napkin and spread it on his lap. For an instant, as his mother started toward him, Danny expected some reprisal, but in fact her only purpose in coming over to the table was to get a serving spoon for the ice cream.

"I thought this was to be *our* party," she reproached him softly.

Danny steeled himself against his mother's hurt expression. "Cuckoo, come and sit down."

Maria hesitated.

Returning to the counter Mme. Wahl drove the spoon deep into the ice cream. "Maria" —her arm shot out— "the plate, please." In the brief moment it took for the cake to be transferred from the table to her outstretched hand, Mme. Wahl did nothing to conceal her resentment. Working her lips like a tropical fish, she trained her rancorous eyes on Danny till she stared him down.

As he looked away Danny's attention was caught by a message pad hanging from a piece of string tied to the extension phone on the wall just above his head. On the pad was a name he didn't recognize, a Mrs. or Mme. or maybe even Mina—it was difficult to decipher Cuckoo's curiously linear left-slanting script—the surname looked like Arms. But before he succeeded in figuring out the name, the cake à la mode was set down in front of him.

Too rich, too dense, too pure to seep into the cake, the mound of already melting ice cream rested on the hillside like a snow drift, spreading its smooth white softness over the surface of the black porous earth. Much as the snow craved the soil, longed to enter its secret silent passageways, ooze into its arteries, tunnels, and defiles, it dared not take the risk: to be befouled by the devil's-food, run to earth, to the bitter end . . . bittersweet . . . chocolate . . .

Katzenzunge Fräulein sent from Hamburg bombed and burning shipyards shattered buildings razed bodies babies tabby cats ablaze in the roaring inferno extinguishable only by snow . . . creamy thick bittersweet snow sprayed like fertilizer over the shame of the earth . . . scorched unfruitful arid earth, as much in need of the sacrament as the sacrament needs to be received—both in need, yet neither one—neither snow nor soil, moist nor dry, soft nor firm, white nor black—capable of communion. Deadlock . . . . Prompted now to mash the ice cream into the cake, Danny seized his fork, but stopped himself in the nick of time from disrupting the cosmic order.

As if she had read his mind, Mme. Wahl snatched the fork away from her son. "Wait."

Danny was startled, affronted. "What?"

"I'll get you one of ours," his mother explained as she headed for the dining room, confiscated fork in hand. The swinging door moaned shut behind her, creating a draft.

Jumping up, Danny opened the table drawer and grabbed another kitchen fork. Determined now to mash the cake and ice cream, he stood over the plate—his shoulders hunched, teeth clenched, face flushed—and raised the fork again, but once again he wavered, hand trembling, unable to strike for fear of the consequences.

"What the matter, *chico*?" Maria reached out to him across the table. "What you want?"

A stream of breath poured from Danny's lungs. To his great relief his arm began to lower, slowly, slowly, like a drawbridge, and his body subsided back into the chair. Conscious, then, of Cuckoo's small chapped hands, still outstretched, still wanting to help and waiting for an answer, Danny murmured, "Nothing," and looked up at her with a reassuring little smile. Despite Cuckoo's obvious concern and sympathy, her expression was more cross than kind. What made it seem so cross was the set of her eyebrows which inclined permanently toward the center of her forehead like the outline of a gambrel roof. The only other person Danny knew whose brows were set that way was Myra Kerns, except that in Myra's case they gave her face a suffering expression, whereas Cuckoo— Myra! Danny turned back to the message pad. M-i-r-a A-r? A-e? "Cuckoo."

"*Sí*."

Danny pulled the page off the pad and handed it to Maria. "Read me this." After examining it closely, bringing the paper to

40.

within an inch of her eyes and holding it at various angles, Maria shrugged. "Then spell it for me, can you?"

"*Sí*. No difficult to spell, difficult to say. M-i-r-a A-e-r-n-s."

"When did she call?"

"Lunch time."

"Why didn't you tell me?"

"I tell the señora."

"Tell me what?" Mme. Wahl said, coming back into the kitchen. In her hand now she held two forks.

"That Miss Kerns called," Danny said.

"Oh?" Mme. Wahl scratched her scalp. "Didn't I?"

"*No*, you didn't." In contrast to Danny's firm aggressive tone was a feeling of weakness in his stomach, peril in his heart.

"Well, I just happened to have a few other things on my mind today. You think the sauerbraten prepared itself? The table, the cake, the flowers— Sit down, Maria! Why don't you eat?" Maria did as she was told. "And you?" Mme. Wahl turned back to her son. "What are you waiting for? For the ice cream to—" Breaking off, she narrowed her eyes and made a wry face. "Just where did you get that fork?" Delighted to have foiled his mother, Danny could not help but giggle. "What's so funny?"

"You are."

"Give me that fork."

"Don't change the subject."

"The fork, I said."

"Why didn't you tell me Myra—"

"Oh, so it's Myra now!"

"I've always—"

"I don't know what kind of school—"

"You had no right—"

"—what kind of teachers—"

"She's *not* a teacher."

"First names, filthy books—"

"They aren't filthy."

"What do *you* call them—literature, I suppose?"

"Yes, exactly!"

"You and your father," she muttered dismissively. "And those plays she takes you to—also literature?"

"Yes!"

"Stop shouting, no one's deaf. Are we, Maria?" she added with incredible *sang-froid*. Unnoticed by Maria, who had bowed her head in embarrassment and was toying with her food, Mme. Wahl

41.

darted a sharp glance at Danny to remind him of the servant's presence.

For his own sake, rather than for Cuckoo's, Danny tried to catch his breath, calm his thumping heart, control his voice. "*Néanmoins*, you should have told me."

"*Néanmoins!* So, they've told you *that* already—"

"No one told me!"

"Behind my back—they couldn't wait, your brothers—"

"I discovered it" —Danny indicated the telephone message—"myself."

"—To ridicule their mother. The minute I turn my back, they have to tell—"

"They didn't, I said. It's *you*—you should have told me."

"About *néanmoins*?"

"About Miss Kerns!"

"What about her?"

"That she called!"

"Oh, but I did."

"What!"

"*Bien sûr*."

"When?"

"This afternoon, when you first arrived."

"But just now you said—"

"You weren't listening."

"I was!"

"If you had been listening—"

"I heard exactly—"

"Well then, if you *heard* . . . ."

"Just now, I mean, when you said—"

"No-no, you never listen, never hear, not a word—in one ear, out the other. Take now, for example: ten times, I've asked you ten times to give me that fork."

"You never told me, Maman."

"To give me that fork? I—"

"Not the fork! Myra! You never—"

"I most certainly did."

Unable to release his fury, Danny throttled it by clenching his teeth, clenching his fists, filling the room with a terrible screech, more macawlike than human. "*Liar!*"

Mme. Wahl lunged forward. "Don't you dare—" she lashed out, but quickly checked herself, rechanneled her rage. "Give me that fork!"

As a result of his outburst Danny felt too guilty to put up much

42.

resistance. By calling his mother a liar, he had somehow undone her lie, made himself the liar; by crying out against her injustice, he himself had become the wrongdoer, as culpable as if he had struck her. He released the fork.

Once the fork was hers, Mme. Wahl flung it, together with its mate, confiscated earlier, back into the table drawer, and substituted the sterling dessert-fork she had detched from the dining room. "Now eat your cake!" she said impatiently. At the same time she knew better than to wait and see whether Danny would obey her. Instead, she walked to the window, fussed with her hair, wiped the perspiration from her brow.

So pronounced was the silence in the kitchen that Mme. Wahl could hear the soap suds crackling as she bridged the sink to raise the window. The cold air darted in, attacked her wrists, her arms, pierced her almost to the heart, it seemed, for she suddenly felt like crying. But the cook in the kitchen opposite was watching her. Had the woman witnessed the whole scene? . . . The thought prompted Mme. Wahl to pull herself together. Turning back to the room she remarked, "Imagine showing off like that in front of—I'm sure you never spoke that way to *your* mother, Maria . . . . I should think not. No one in this world would dream . . . only *my* children. Sometimes I wonder—" She broke off, as Danny took from his hip pocket a small address book. "What are you doing?"

"Calling Myra."

"But you haven't touched your cake."

"I'm not hungry."

"Oh, so that's it! Now that I've taken the trouble—" Seeing him open the address book and run his finger down the thumb index, Mme. Wahl changed her tack. "Can't Miss Kerns wait until tomorrow?"

"I want to go and see her tomorrow."

"But I thought we had a lunch date. Have you forgotten?"

"No."

"Well then?"

"I'll see her after lunch."

"As you wish." Mme. Wahl cast a cold eye over her fingernails. "And when will we go shopping?"

Reminded of his own bitten nails Danny put down the address book and withdrew his hands from sight. "Shopping? For what?"

"Clothes, what do you think? Look at you: you have nothing to wear, nothing fits."

"They're good enough . . . for the hospital."

"The hospital! You're not going to spend the rest of your life in
43.

the hospital, you know. You'll be out of there by Thanksgiving—sooner, if only—" she broke off.

"Only what?"

"You'd behave yourself, not use such-such language. . . . Really, there's no reason why you shouldn't stay here now. All Papa has to do is pick up the telephone. No one can *make* you go back, you know, not if you don't want to. You don't have to do anything you don't want, *chéri*, not as long as *I'm* alive, you don't. . . . Once Maman is gone . . . ." Mme. Wahl toyed with the garnet bracelet, turned it around her wrist; tears came to her eyes. "Don't you want to stay?" she asked in a broken voice.

Resting his elbows on the table, Danny took hold of his head: the cranium cupped in his hands, the heels inserted in his eye sockets.

"What is it, darling? What's the matter? Tell Maman. Wouldn't you like to stay?"

Danny raised his shoulders as if to shrug, but didn't complete the movement.

"Please, darling, look at me. You want to go back to that place . . . break Maman's heart? Don't you want to stay . . . here with Maman?"

Danny's shoulders began to quiver, his body to shake, and a stifled sob broke from his throat.

With a quick, dismissive gesture Mme. Wahl sent Maria out of the kitchen. "Don't, don't, sweetheart"—she caressed his head—"there's nothing to cry about, nothing. Maman's right here."

"Oh, Maman!"

"Don't, don't . . . ."

". . . send me back . . . please—"

"*Back?*"

"Don't! don't! please!"

"No-no, *chéri*—"

"Don't send me back!"

"Never."

"Please!"

"Never," she reassured him, "never."

"I'll conserve—"

"Conserve?"

"Behave."

"Of course. Of course you will. Shh, shh. That's enough now, no more tears. All's forgiven . . . forgotten. Where's that angel face of mine? Let me have a look at it." Slowly Danny raised his head, wiped his eyes with his hand. "There it is."

"Oh, Maman!"

"No-no, no more tears, I said. . . . Don't you have a handkerchief? That's it—blow your nose—here, let me—that's my angel. Now then, let's see a smile, please. . . . Oh, you can do better than that."

"Where's Cuckoo?"

"She went to her room for a moment . . . embarrassed, I think. I can't say I blame her. Imagine fighting with Maman like that—like—like an *enragé*. And for what? A fork!"

At the word *enragé*, the hand that held the handkerchief stopped in midair. "*Enragé?*"

"Well what would *you* call it? Screaming like that, calling Maman names . . . ." She shook her head, not in disapproval but to rid herself of the memory. "*N'importe*. It's over now. Put away your handkerchief. I'll go and speak to Papa. You'll stay, my love, I promise you, you'll stay."

"No, wait!" he said with sudden urgency.

"What is it?"

Despite his mother's obvious concern, Danny did not answer. He was lost in thought now, his eyes expressionless, body motionless.

"What?" she repeated. "What are you thinking? How can I know— Please! I'm talking to you, darling, please don't go away like that, into yourself—it-it" —to allay her fear Mme. Wahl brought her hand to her heart for support— "it isn't healthy. Please, I don't understand, explain to me. Why shouldn't I talk to Papa?" Again she waited in vain for an answer. "Why?"

When at last Danny spoke, it was as if he were talking to himself, reminding himself of something about which there was no longer any choice, any hope. "I can't stay here," he stated flatly.

"Can't?"

"Mustn't."

"Why not? What do you mean? You just—didn't you just get finished telling me—"

". . . mistake . . . ."

"What? I can't hear you, darling. Please, take—put that—how can I hear you with that handkerchief in front of your mouth? . . . That's better. Now, what did you say?"

"I must not stay."

"Yes-yes, that I heard. But *why?* Why: must not? Wh-What do you mean: must not? Where did you ever get such a notion? Who's to stop you?"

"They'll find a way," he said softly but with absolute certainty.

45.

"Don't be silly! No one— *They?* Who is they? Dr. Nordhoff? Dr. Mizener? Who do you mean? . . . Answer me! Look at me, darling. Stop biting your nails. Please! Who is they?"

"No one, Maman."

"That's no answer! You think you're fooling me? You think I don't see how fright—how upset— If there's someone you're afraid of, darling—someone at that hospital—I've got to know! How else can I help you? . . . Tell me now, please *chéri*, tell Maman. Is it someone on the staff? One of the patients? . . . Please! don't keep making me ask you questions."

"I can't explain."

"But you must, must! One minute you say you want to stay, and the next— What changed your mind? . . . Are you trying to protect someone? Is that it? Has someone threatened you?"

Danny looked down at the discolored cake, the puddle of ice cream flooding his plate.

"That's it, isn't it? Someone at the hospital, that's what you're afraid of, so afraid you can't even tell Maman—"

"Not the hospital."

"Well, what then?"

Danny remained silent, staring down at the cake.

"Oh, please, sweetheart, please, I beg of you, for Maman's sake, tell me, tell me what it is."

"Here, Maman," he said almost inaudibly.

"What?"

"It's *here*," he whispered.

"What? *what's* here?" she asked, adopting his hushed tone.

"I must go back."

"Must, again?"

"To save myself! . . . the only way."

"Save? Please! You haven't answered my question. What's here? The thing you're afraid of? . . . No, surely not. This is your home, *chéri*, your home, where you belong. Have you forgotten? There's no one—nothing here to be afraid of. You're with Maman now—Maman who loves you more than all the world—and Papa, and your brothers. No one's going to hurt you *here*. I wouldn't let them. You know that, don't you, darling? You know Maman loves you more than all the world. So why must you go back?"

"Tonight, Maman."

"Ohhh." She breathed a sigh of relief. "So that's it—the night—that's what you're afraid of. Well now, we'll soon attend to that. Don't you worry, darling, Maman will stay with you tonight— Claude can sleep in Jerry's room."

"No, Maman, I can't!"

"Can't?"

"*Stay.*"

"All right, all right." She tossed her head, waved her hands. "We'll talk about it in the morning, after you've had a good night's—"

"No, now! I must go now."

"*Now?*" she said incredulously.

"Right away!"

"Have you any idea what time it is?"

"It doesn't matter."

"But it's after nine, *chéri.*"

"Please, Maman."

"Nine twenty-five."

"I mustn't spend the night!"

The finality with which these words were spoken—when all before had been so tremulous, entreating—frightened Mme. Wahl. Even more alarming was the edge of cruelty in Danny's voice, the sinister look in his eyes which made the words seem less a statement than a warning, almost a threat. "All right, that settles it. I'll go and speak to Papa—"

"Now, Maman!"

"Yes-yes, this minute."

"Tell him, please, to call the garage."

Since Mme. Wahl had but one thought in mind—to convince her husband that Danny must not under any circumstances be allowed to return to the hospital—she was caught off guard, confused by her son's request. "Garage?"

"To deliver the car."

"The car . . . . Oh yes, of course," she humored him. "You just make your call now, while I—"

"What call?"

"Miss Kerns."

"Oh." He shrugged. "Her."

"*Her?* What do you mean, her?"

"I have nothing to say to her."

"Nothing to say?"

As if to prove the point Danny closed the small address book and tucked it back into his pocket.

"I don't know." Mme. Wahl threw up her hands, shook her head wearily. "I just don't know—*ça me dépasse!* Ten minutes ago you would have thought the world depended on it; now . . . ." Dropping her hands she suddenly became defenseless, her tone tender

47.

and conciliatory. "Is it me, *chéri*—because of me? You think I object to your calling her . . . seeing her? Not at all. I don't object. *Au contraire*, I want you to call, want you to go out—you don't go out enough, as far as I'm concerned. Go, by all means go, but go with someone—go with girls—someone your own age—that Danzig girl you saw last spring—now there's someone: intelligent, pretty, her grandfather—you know her grandfather sat on the high court, don't you? Well, that's the sort of girl I mean, the sort you should be going with, not some old shoe like Maman."

"I am not *going with* Miss Kerns, Maman."

"Seeing, then, seeing her! Is that better? Why do you jump down my throat at every word? I'm only trying . . . . Please, *chéri*, call her now . . . for Maman's sake. It's not polite, you know, not the way you were brought up: to be a gentleman. . . . Shall I dial for you?"

"Maman!"

"You're only spiting yourself, you know. Miss Kerns doesn't know—I mean, what will she think when you don't return— Oh!" she interrupted herself, struck by an idea. "Is it because I'm standing here? If I leave you alone—"

Danny shook his head.

"Curious, isn't it?" she reflected. "How you expect Maman to do everything you ask—every little thing—speak to Papa, call the garage—"

"Yes, Maman. Please! You must!"

"*Must?* How so? Must *you* call Miss Kerns? . . . You see?" She smiled with self-satisfaction.

"All right, Maman, I'll call."

"*Bon!* that's my angel child." Mme. Wahl kissed the crown of his head. "Now, I'll go talk to Papa. Oh, and please," she added, on her way through the swinging door, "give Miss Kerns my warm regards."

Once in the dining room Mme. Wahl took a few steps and then, correlating her movements with those of the swinging door, slackened her pace, softened her tread, came to a standstill. With no one in the living room now to observe her—even earlier, when she went to fetch the fork, the living room had been empty—Mme. Wahl turned around and tiptoed back to the door. Though she appeared to be eavesdropping, her purpose was not to overhear her son's conversation, but only to assure herself that he was busy and safely out of earshot while she went inside to discuss with her husband this whole alarming business about the hospital.

48.

In the kitchen, meanwhile, Danny had dutifully taken out the address book again, rehearsed what, if anything, he had to say to Miss Kerns—after some deliberation he finally decided to inquire about Colette, her tortoiseshell cat—and picked up the receiver.

"—*à y reflechir, Boris, peut-être à l'heure du déjeuner*—"

Relieved though Danny was to find the phone in use, he felt like a transgressor, guilty and fearful, certain that his father had heard him pick up the receiver, would know exactly who it was and assume his son was eavesdropping. Holding his breath, Danny quickly deflected the hook, then noiselessly replaced the receiver.

His heart pounding now, he listened intently. . . . Mumbling . . . somewhere someone was mumbling . . . . Mumbo-Jumbo, God of the Congo . . . . Cuckoo's room? Cuckoo praying? Or was it? . . . Out of the corner of his eye he saw the shreds of cabbage on Cuckoo's plate wriggling, but pretended not to notice; saw the foam rise like lye to the surface of the devil's-food, but tried not to think about the mounting mass of caustic within; heard the door behind his back being opened stealthily, but dared not look; sat instead with bated breath, shoulders braced, teeth clenched, stomach muscles taut, awaiting his fate in dread.

"So!" his mother said, making known her presence, which caused Danny to jump with fright, "this is how you keep your word. I thought we had reached an accord: you to telephone, I to speak to Papa. But no—there you sit, exactly as I left you. Can't I trust you even for a moment? . . . What's the matter? Why do you close your eyes? What is it, *chéri*? Don't cover your face like that."

Even after an audible release of breath, Danny's voice, when he replied, seemed to lack support, as if he had forgotten to draw the next breath and were in need of air; nor was there a trace of disputation in his tone—he sounded just the way he looked: debilitated, beaten, almost in despair. "I tried, Maman."

"Tried?"

"To phone. It was busy."

"*Et c'est tout, chéri? Ma foi*, don't give up, try her again."

"Not Miss Kerns, Maman, Papa."

"Papa?" The smile disappearing from her face, Mme. Wahl eyed the wall phone with suspicion. "Papa is using the telephone?" When, after a moment's pause, Danny did not answer, she continued calmly, "Isn't that interesting." This remark, addressed to no one in particular, was meant to fill the silence, divert attention from herself while she walked around behind the chair in which her son was sitting and reached for the telephone. More or less reversing Danny's earlier procedure, Mme. Wahl placed her finger on the hook, brought the receiver to her ear, covered the mouthpiece, and then released the hook.

"—Miko, *il faut polir ton japonais, Marcus*. Uh-uh-uh-uh!"

The only thing that irritated Germaine Wahl more than Boris Napotnik's throaty, jovial Russian bass, punctuated repeatedly by those soft staccato belches, struggling to be laughter, was the man himself. She considered him—this *maquereau* who lived not only off her husband but also *through* him, taking a certain vicarious satisfaction from her husband's lechery—the bane of her existence, a creature fashioned by the devil, if not the devil himself masquerading as a *basso buffo*, a sort of Leporello to her husband's Giovanni, albeit a Russian Leporello, created not with Mozart's magic touch but with the heavy-handedness and morbidity of a Moussorgsky. Her loathing for the man appeared on her face the instant she heard Napotnik's voice. But loathing wasn't all. There were signs as well of frustration, jealousy, anger—all of which she did her best to conceal the moment she realized that Danny was observing her.

Like his mother's, Danny's expression reflected a mixture of feelings: accusation, disgust, resentment and even, in some subtle way that showed in his eyes and around the corners of his mouth, collaboration, as if he were in fact not his mother's judge but her accomplice.

Mme. Wahl replaced the receiver and produced a smile. "So he is," she remarked, answering the question she herself had asked earlier. "I'll just go in and tell him you're waiting to call Miss Kerns."

"No, Maman."

"Just eat your cake, *chéri*," she said over his apathetic objection, and swept out of the kitchen, heading at once for the master bedroom.

Danny placed both palms flat on the kitchen table and raised himself with great exertion. Once on his feet he stood staring at the room, studying and surveying it, not with the trained businesslike eye of a contractor, but rather like a housefly, whizzing about this way and that, alighting here and there, feeding at length on certain substances, scarcely touching others, always moving on to satisfy some persistent inner need. At present Danny's need seemed to be for surfaces—hard, gleaming, impervious surfaces: the white enameled table, waxed linoleum floor, white enameled sink, china and glassware, aluminum pots and pans, chromium-finished toaster, steel mixer-blades, stainless-steel blades of knives. As closely as he scrutinized these, Danny seemed to overlook, almost programmatically, all the softer, less durable things surrounding him—spices, sponges, towels, mops; the dumpling on Maria's plate, the still untouched layer cake. The exception was the little leather address book on which his eye came finally to rest, and which he slowly reclaimed and pocketed (as if to cover his tracks), before leaving the kitchen.

Coming through the swinging door, Danny hesitated. Of the six tubular steel chairs in the dining room, the two on the near side of the table (his own chair and Claude's) were not aligned—one was slightly askew, the other pushed in with so much force, Danny could feel its pain. And yet if he pulled it out, thereby using up his one allotted move, it would still not correspond to its mate. And if he pushed the other in, *both* would be in pain. And if he touched the metal? If he used his thigh? . . . By now such questions were in any case purely academic—his time was up, he had forfeited his turn.

Though he wanted to leave the dining room and was standing but two or three steps from the double doors which his mother had made certain to close behind her, Danny reversed his course, brought himself about slowly as a steamer, and proceeded in the opposite direction: clear around the table. Along the way he passed without a glance Monet's slice of beef liver, Manet's basket of plums, and the same artist's plate of oysters. When, however, he approached head-on Courbet's landed fish, *Le brochet,* he slackened his already torpid pace and came to a full stop in front of the canvas. The painting hung just to the left of the glass doors which transmitted enough light from the living room to illuminate the somber work adequately, if not properly. The effect of this indirect lighting was to accentuate Courbet's originally pronounced contrast between highlights and shadows—between, that is, the burnt umber and lampblack of the rocks on which the fish lay dying beneath a dark and brooding sky, and the whites of the flashing water, bright markings on the pike's contorted body, gleam in its at once pitiful and ferocious-looking eye, row of sharp shiny teeth that crenelated its gaping jaw, and the delicate silvery line held taut by the fisherman, standing out of sight, who had brought the creature to its doom.

In childhood Danny had hated the unseen fisherman with all his heart—hated him for letting the pike take the lure so deep into its guts that evisceration was unavoidable; hated him for breaking the fish's spirit, for bringing it, as it were, to its knees—which was, in fact, the way it looked, resting on its ventral fins, head raised, jaws agape; it looked (despite the final fury in its eye) exactly like a suppliant, beseeching some unseen tyrant to spare its life. And so, as a boy, Danny had come to hate the fisherman, who in certain respects so closely resembled Claude. In time, however, he began to think about him differently, as no mere mortal, but someone more like Momus, more like Yahweh (the up-sloping fishline, a kite string ascending to the heavens, to the very throne of God), and Danny's hatred developed into fear and awe. Still later, when in high school Danny had his first taste of philosophy, mythology, the unseen fisherman took on the less personal, more abstract significance of Fate, of Moira herself, tempering his hatred, fear and awe with doleful resignation. But then, quite suddenly last spring, he put his finger on it, figured out once and for all who the fisherman really was. Not, of course, Moira or Momus or even Yahweh, but the Supreme Being's hatchetman—Danny glanced out of the corner of his eye to see if anyone had overheard him think that thought—His minister plenipotentiary, he had meant to say, none other than the Incorruptible, keeper of the Sacred Reservoir, guardian of the Vital Force, his supreme eminence, Robespierre.

Now, as his eye reverted to the picture, Danny experienced a strong discomfort in his bowels—no sharp pain or hemorrhaging, nothing symptomatic of the grapnel; what he felt was simply tension, tension from the swallowed line, as if the fisherman, not content with having hooked him mortally, had tied him up as well, enmeshed his poor intestines, bound them fast, till he was helplessly constricted and at the mercy of his captor's whim—whatever that might be: to rip out his guts or merely toy with them by putting constant pressure on the line. In response Danny had the impulse to break the line, tear it in two with his hands or, that failing, sever it with his teeth or go and get the scissors or, better yet, the carving knife, and *hack*— In retaliation for these treasonous notions the fisherman tightened the line. He was preparing now, Danny realized, for the *coup de grâce*, wrapping the line deliberately around his hand to get a better grip on it before giving it the final yank, when liver, guts, pancreas and all would be hauled up through Danny's windpipe, clogging it, choking him—his own blood and slime and entrails glutting him, but not enough to kill him off; being still alive, still conscious, he had as yet to *taste* them, *see* them, his own insides, torn from his mouth and dangled temptingly before his eyes like the very bait that had brought him to his ruin. Understanding this, the futility of his position, Danny made no sudden moves, showed no signs of protest, lest he harm himself, hasten his demise. He stood, instead, stark still, gazing into the eye of the pike whose fury had abated now, as life ebbed out of him, reducing the baleful gleam to a flicker of pathos, one fully formed tear, trickling down Danny's cheek.

"Menteur!"

So loud was this outcry of his mother's that the sound carried the whole length of the apartment—from the master bedroom to the dining room—jolting Danny out of his trance. It was not the echo of Danny's earlier accusation, "Liar!" but the sound itself, signifying an open fight between his parents, which mobilized Danny now, drawing him out of the dining room, across the living room, toward the hall, as if his mother's cry, like a wave breaking on the shore, had a powerful reflux, pulling him after it. And so he went, compelled as he had always been since childhood toward the scene of battle—not as a mere observer, nor yet as a full-fledged combatant, but as a sort of self-appointed aide-de-camp to his mother. He went, moreover, with stealth, rather like a spy: tiptoeing through the living room, turning off the lights along the way, concealing his movements as best he could—for it was a convention among the entire household that the battle now in progress would never under any circumstances be acknowledged by anyone as having taken place.

Just as Danny reached the foyer doors, he drew back into the shadows at the sight of Jerome coming out of his own bedroom, hurrying down the hall and stopping for a moment to listen at the closed door of the master bedroom, before stepping furtively into the bedroom opposite—the bedroom Danny shared with Claude. At the same time, Danny became aware again of the monotonous mumbling he had heard earlier in the kitchen and had attributed to Cuckoo. This time, however, the mumbling seemed much closer at hand, as if Cuckoo were standing just the other side of the living room wall, in the pantry, listening to the fight as Jerome had done, and talking to herself about it or praying for her employer's survival.

Once Jerome was out of sight, Danny left the living room, took three giant steps across the no-man's-land of the foyer, and entered the hall. The overhead light was off, the hallway dimly illuminated by the light spill from the boys' rooms. Even so, Danny realized he would be seen by anyone unexpectedly leaving one of the bedrooms, and he decided to take cover. Rejecting as both too risky and remote the bathroom between the boys' rooms, he slipped into the linen closet. On the same side of the hall as his parents' room, the linen closet was situated back to back with the large walk-in closet in the master bedroom, thus providing an ideal listening post for Danny. Leaving the door ajar he could also overhear, though less distinctly, less consistently than the fight between his parents, the comments of his brothers from the other end of the hall.

"Never mind," Papa growled, "you were listening!"

"Not *me*," Maman defended herself, "Danny—"

"Always listening!"

"I tell you Danny—"

"*Non! Le menteur—c'est toi!*"

"*Moi? . . . Et le monstre?* . . . Arranging with Napotnik—with your *maquereau*—"

"It's the last time—I swear to God—the last time you'll ever—I'll-I'll have it disconnected—ripped out! Tomorrow—wait—you'll see— I'll rip it out!—no more phone! no more listening, invading of privacy— *C'est fini! Fini! Compris?*"

"And your *maquereau*?" challenged Maman.

"Stop using that word—"

"How will you keep in touch—"

"—it's unbecoming!"

"—with your *maquereau*?"

"Stop it, I said!"

"What? . . . Referring to your *maquereau*?"

"One more time, Germaine, just once more" —Papa's voice grew softer, yet harsher, hoarser, more threatening and savage, with every syllable— "I'll murder you!"

Ruthlessly Danny ripped the nail off his pinky. His bloodthirst satisfied for the moment, he ground and crunched the fragment between his molars. He was standing now sideways in the closet, ribs pressed up against the shelves, his right arm resting on a shelf just below shoulder height, a shelf on which bath towels had been neatly stacked until Danny elbowed them out of his way. And yet it was not to support his weight that he intruded upon the shelf; it was simply to get closer to his parents' room, bring his ear as close as possible to the closet wall, infiltrate the battle line, be on hand—if not to prevent, at least to postpone, the murder of his mother.

"You *would* too, wouldn't you?" Maman remarked, her voice turning tearful suddenly. ". . . Stop at nothing . . . to defend your pride . . . your *maquereau*."

"All right! Go ahead! Fine! That's it!"

"What do I care—"

"I warned you—"

"—what you do? Go ahead! murder me—"

"I'm getting out."

"—murder us all—"

"This minute!"

"—you all but have already."

"*What?*"

"Oh, my baby!" Maman's tears came now, flowing freely, released in a flood that threatened to sweep Danny off his feet; but he clung to the shelf, sank his teeth into a towel. "My poor, poor baby . . . terror! . . . a state of terror . . . while you sit in here . . . comfortably . . . telephoning to your *maquereau*."

"God damn you!"

"Yes . . . yes . . . *damned*—"

"No," Papa brought himself up short, "not tonight—"

"—damned—"

"—I will not fight with you tonight."

"—all of us . . . damned . . . cursed . . . ."

This lament of Maman's was followed by silence, a long suspenseful silence which left Danny holding his breath and wondering what was happening.

"Th-Th-That's it folks—round one. The ch-ch-challenger has retired to her corner now to nurse a bloody lip—"

"Ha ha ha!" Jerome was enjoying his brother's imitation of a sports announcer.

"Ch-Ch-Champ Wahl in t-t-top-notch—"

The closet door in the master bedroom was yanked open. Danny heard the rattle of a coat hanger from which a garment had been removed in haste.

"I'm going now," Papa announced, his voice much closer, more distinct—he was still standing inside or just outside the bedroom closet.

"Naturally," Maman rejoined, "naturally . . . . *Autruche!* For sure, the ostrich is going now. Why not? What else *can* he do, but go? . . . go and stick his head into *le sexe.*"

"*Merde!*" The closet door slammed shut.

The impact made Danny flinch, and his heart began to thump.

"Go . . . go, *autruche!* . . . sport yourself, show yourself . . . stick out that long neck of yours, your *grande tête* . . . . Go on! . . . I'll stay here . . . mind the house . . . it's my business . . . responsibility . . . the woman's . . . always the woman's . . . the woman's alone! . . . *You* go on; *I'll* attend to everything— Oh, God!" Maman cried out frantically, "God! . . . my baby . . . baby . . . help my baby!"

Again there was silence. In the distance Claude continued his mock-broadcast (informing his listening audience that the challenger had rallied, p-p-picked herself up off the mat), though by now Jerome, having ceased to be amused, had grown altogether irritable, impatient with both his brother and his parents. "If they don't stop, I'll—I'll— You're sure he's in the kitchen?"

"Ac-c-cording to Maman."

Danny, meanwhile, had set to work in earnest on what remained of his pinky nail: gnawing ever closer to the moon, burrowing in pain right down to the cutis, causing the blood to flow, tearing at the flesh, sucking the blood, chewing the flesh, torturing and devouring himself till the sound of creaking bedsprings stopped him short.

"Don't . . . don't pull away, *chérie*," Papa said softly, tenderly. "What is it? What makes you say such things? . . . Don't you see how much improved the boy is?"

"Improved?"

"Yes-yes. Haven't you noticed—"

"*Autruche*," Maman repeated, her tone no longer virulent, but pathetic and hopeless.

"No-no . . . *tranquille* . . . really! . . . Except, of course, for that—that moment at the dinner table—one or two moments—to me he seems altogether—"

"*Tranquille?*"

"*Oui!* Really, so much better—"

"*Tranquille?*"

"Don't you think—"

"I tell you" —there was a catch in Maman's voice— "he's in terror!"

"Why do you keep saying—"

"*Terror*," Maman screamed, and once again her tears broke loose, only this time in a torrent of anguish and hysterics. "Oh, God! . . . terror . . . terror . . . and no one . . . no one— I don't know . . . what . . . how— Save him! . . . save him—" At this point Maman emitted such a horrible sound—a harsh, prolonged, frenzied gasp—Danny could not help but remember Claude holding him underwater till he thought he would drown, holding him under the pillow till he thought he would suffocate, coming up for air, tears and mucus streaming now, he knew, down Maman's face, lungs collapsing, body brutalized, life itself *in extremis,* as she cried out in desperation, "Oh, *ma mère! ma mère! ma mère chérie* . . . help me! . . . help me! . . . kill myself!"

A tortured little wail leaked from Danny's throat.

As if in answer, Maman produced an even more pathetic and forlorn little vowel sound like the call of a mourning dove. "Ooo . . . ."

His face buried now in the crook of his arm, his arm resting on the shelf, hand clutching a towel, Danny tried in vain to restrain his tears.

"Come, come, *chérie*," Papa tried to console Maman, but Danny would have none of it, pulled away in revulsion. "You mustn't take it to heart so . . . eat your heart out so."

"He *is* my heart."

"How well I know it," Papa replied both bitterly and sadly, as if to himself. "He'll be all right though—you'll see—everything will be all right."

"*Tranquille, n'est-ce pas*, Marcus?" Maman stopped and blew her nose with vigor. Danny took the opportunity to blow his own nose, but quietly. That done, he wrapped the already bloodstained handkerchief around his bloody pinky—as much to prevent further onslaughts as to bandage it. When Maman spoke again she had all but recovered her normal tone, and sounded much calmer, almost philosophical. "Oh, *mon cher*, if this were Judgment Day, if the whole world were about to come crashing down on our heads, you would say, '*Tranquille, tranquille*'—providing, of course, you had *le sexe*."

"Germaine!"

"*Oui, oui, oui!* . . . you would go out and get yourself *le sexe* . . . and then—*voilà*—even Judgment Day would be transfigured, made *tranquille* for you. . . . Blind fool!" Again the bedsprings creaked. "I tell you he's in terror," Maman asserted forcefully, "frightened out of his wits."

"Yes-yes, but you don't say why, what—about what?"

"I don't know. He won't confide." Maman was on her feet now; Danny could hear her restless pacing. ". . . Someone at that hospital . . . he's too frightened to confide . . . even to me."

"Perhaps *I* could get to the bottom of it."

"*You*," Maman sneered. "You think he'll tell you what he won't confide to me?"

"Jerry, then."

"No! no one—he's too frightened, I tell you. . . . It's that hospital—someone at that hospital—of that I'm absolutely certain . . . ."

Stiffening, Danny turned very slowly, inconspicuously, and peeped out into the hall. He was sure he had heard a footstep, someone coming, but there was no one. As a precaution he pulled the closet door to, leaving it open scarcely a crack.

"*Donc*," Maman continued, her voice growing not in volume but intensity, "of one thing more I am also certain."

"Namely?"

"That he must never go back to that place, Marcus—never again—no matter what you say, I'll never let him go—never . . . never—over my dead body! . . . . He'll stay *here* now, here with us . . . where he belongs . . . ."

"Stay?" Danny repeated in a horrified whisper.

"And you," Maman went on with increasing power, "*you'll* stay too—for *his* sake, if not for mine . . . . *Le sexe*, Marcus, *est fini!* From now on the family comes first. The family must be sacred!"

" 'After great pain,' " someone murmured in Danny's ear, " 'a family feeling comes.' "

As if he were in church, participating in responsive reading, Danny murmured back:

> This is the hour of lead,
> Remembered, if outlived,
> As freezing persons recollect the snow:
> First chill, then stupor, then the letting go.

At some point, of which Danny was totally unconscious, he had removed the bloodstained handkerchief and begun to attack his pinky again with the predacity of a cannibal. The fear and agitation into which Danny had been plunged not only by his parents' fight, but also by the news that he would have to stay there now—no matter what!—not just the night or weekend, but forever, to face again the hour of lead, set off a melee of reactions: extreme anxiety, muscle contractions, stomach spasms, intestinal panic, retention of breath; feelings of acute helplessness, hopelessness, desolation—a melee for which there was only one possible remedy: his medication. Was there still time to get to the bathroom and take two tranquilizers before the onset of the hour of lead, the coming of the Committee?

"Let's go back now" —Maman set down something, a bottle of perfume or a comb and brush, on the glass top of the vanity table— "to the living room, and behave like *la famille Dupont* . . . like the Joneses," she added with a chuckle. "*D'accord*, Marcus?"

"*D'accord*."

". . . No more strife—"

"Germaine!" Papa exploded. "What are you doing? . . . Put that down! I thought we had agreed—no more listening—*none*, I said. Under no circum—"

"Listening; who's listening? *Rien de la sorte!* I have to know if he's off the phone, don't I?"

"Then go and see! Don't—"

"I *have* seen: he is! . . . Probably with the boys. . . . Are you coming?"

"In a moment. . . . Don't look at me that way— I have to use the bathroom. . . . And I'll use the telephone as much as I damn please," Papa declared, *"whenever* I please! This is still my house—I still pay the bills—and no one—no one's going to stop me—not you or anyone else! *Compris?"*

Maman did not answer.

Danny pushed open the closet door an inch or two and peeked down the hall. The coast was clear, the bathroom door wide open; he could easily slip inside unnoticed. The pills were in his toilet kit, the toilet kit on top of the hamper. There would be no need to turn on the light; he could find the bottle blindfolded. With luck the door leading from the bathroom to his and Claude's room would be shut—unless, of course, Jerry had gone back to his own room by way of the bathroom, leaving the inner doors ajar. In that case Danny could pretend to brush his teeth or something, and take the pills on the sly, without Maman's ever finding out. That was the main thing: to keep Maman from worrying, becoming even more upset than she already was.

His left hand now on the rim of the door, Danny glimpsed his pinky in the light. The sight of the mutilated nail filled him with fury, self-abhorrence, remorse. Bringing the finger to his mouth to succor it, salvage it, doctor it up before crossing the hall, he promptly ravaged it again. . . . Oh, God! there was no hope, no help for him—he was hateful, worthless, damned! He would remain a nail-biter the rest of his life, never be able to stop—never, never, never . . . a no-good, a nothing . . . always . . . nothing . . . his soul as hideous and evil as his bitten nails . . . his body, like his bitten nails, hideous and useless . . . a flyweight . . . flimsy . . . the body of an insect—cricket limbs, limbs like bitten fingernails: brittle, puny, freakish—clapped into a cage . . . caged like the insane— Insane! Oh, God! he'd be insane forever: sent back to the asylum for nail biting, strapped into a restraining jacket, given insulin shock, Enragés Control Therapy—for nail biting; and still not stop, still go on biting his nails the rest of his life, spend the rest of his life locked up, outcast and alone, a congenital . . . congenital-congenital (Danny's other hand had moved to his groin) nail-biter . . . congenital liar . . . congenital idiot—locked up like a genital to keep the world uncontaminated, safe from his disease . . . .

Conscious, suddenly, of applying rhythmic pressure to his penis, rubbing and caressing it, inducing its engorgement, Danny pulled

59.

away his hand in horror. As if he had made a hairsbreadth escape, his heart was beating frantically, and he heaved a sigh of relief. "Thank God . . . thank God," he said to himself, grateful not to have gone any further, not to have touched himself overtly, made direct contact with the flesh. Again he heaved a sigh, a sigh of real thanksgiving for the mercy he'd been shown: the precious, priceless gift of being spared perdition, the Eternal Waste, permitted instead to conserve the Vital Force. He must, he knew, get out of there at once—out of confinement, temptation's reach.

After making certain that the coast was still clear, Danny crept out of the closet, closed the door noiselessly, and tiptoed across the hall into the bathroom. (Despite the fact that the doors to both Jerome's and Danny's rooms were open, they were only partly open; furthermore, both doors were at the far end of the bathroom and both opened outward into the bedrooms, so that unless someone chose to come right into the bathroom or crane his neck around the door, Danny was safe from view—his only concern was not to make a sound.) No sooner had he reached the bathroom than he heard the door to his parents' room open and someone come out. Instinctively, Danny ducked behind the door by which he had entered, and stood perfectly still, listening.

"Psst! Maman!" Though Jerry spoke in a whisper, his voice was charged with belligerence.

"*Oui.*"

"Did you have to go and do that tonight?"

"Mind your own business!" Maman was quick to adopt Jerry's hushed though outraged tone.

"It *is* my business! Couldn't you have waited till Monday, till he—"

"There'll be no Monday." Maman's tone was self-complacent.

"*What?*"

"You heard me."

"What do you mean?"

"Ask your father."

"I'm asking *you*!"

"I have no time now."

"Where are you going?"

"To the kitchen."

"Wait!"

"What *is* it?"

"This has got to stop!"

"What are you talking about?"

60.

"This—this . . . *discord*." Still whispering, Jerry managed, nonetheless, to give the word explosive emphasis.

"Here's your father," Maman rejoined, "discuss it with him."

"Discuss what?" Papa inquired. "What are you all doing out here?"

"They're holding a c-c-council of State."

"Shut up, idiot!" Jerry snapped. "Papa, what's all this about Monday?"

"It's none of your business, I said," Maman repeated.

"You said I should discuss—"

"What's all the whispering about?" Papa asked. "Where—where's Danny?"

"In the kitchen," Maman replied. "I was on my way there, till I was stopped by this—this roughneck."

"Wait!" Jerry enjoined her.

"For what?" Maman countered. She had moved now down the hall, closer to the bathroom. Danny flattened his back against the tiled wall—tried not to budge, not to breathe. "What am I to wait *for*?"

"I want to know what you're going to say to him."

"What do you mean, say?"

"When you get to the kitchen."

"How should I know?"

"You've got to know!"

"Before I get there?"

"Exactly!"

"*Absurde!* . . . I'll know when I get there!"

"No! It's no good! There's got to be a plan."

"A plan?"

"Yes! We can't just sit around—"

"I suggest," Papa put in, "we all go now to the living room—"

"And then what?" Jerry interrupted. "Suppose he wants to read?"

"He's read enough!" Maman objected. "He's too excited, too upset. It must be something pacifying . . . diverting—a game of cards! that's what we'll do."

"And suppose he doesn't feel like cards?"

"Why wouldn't he? He loves cards!"

"No! You've got to let him do what he wants."

"Who's stopping him?" Maman had difficulty stifling her exasperation.

"*You* are!"

"Oh, leave me alone!" Maman flounced past the bathroom door.

"Wait! Come back!" Jerry rushed after her.

"What now?"

"*I'll* go!" Jerry declared. "I'll go get him. The rest of you go into the living room and wait." The sound of his footsteps receded down the hall.

"Big shot!" Maman complained. "Thinks he knows everything . . . always! . . . better than anyone else."

"All right, all right," Papa tried to smooth things over. "Let him go. What's the difference?"

"The difference is, *he* isn't running this household—not yet, he isn't."

"Claude" —Papa snapped his fingers— "*viens!*"

"P-P-Personally, I don't see what all the c-c-commotion's about . . . ."

Now that they were gone, Danny released his breath. He didn't move, however, didn't come out from behind the door. He was staring at his toilet kit, but didn't know why. He knew he had come into the bathroom for a reason, but couldn't remember now what it was, what had brought him there.

"Papa!" Jerome called out suddenly, "Papa! He isn't there!"

"What!" Maman exclaimed.

"Not in the kitchen!"

"Did you ask Maria?"

"Yes, yes—he isn't there, I tell you!"

"Where then?"

"How should *I* know?"

"He couldn't have gone out, could he?"

"*Out!* Oh, my God, my God! . . . No, he couldn't—wouldn't . . . without— Marcus, call downstairs—the house phone —ask them—Jerry, what are you doing? Where are you going?"

"Out."

"Out?"

"To look for him."

"Wh-Wh-What makes you think he went out?"

"Where is he then?"

"Who knows . . . he m-m-might be anywhere."

"Anywhere! . . . Marcus, what do they say?"

"No answer yet!"

"Naturally! never! never when you need them!"

"Hello? . . . hello! . . . . I don't know what we're paying rent for."

"Jerry! ring for the elevator—*vite! vite!* Ask him—"

"Hello! . . . hello!"

"If you ask m-m-me, he's h-h-hiding somewhere."

"*Bête!* . . . Here! make yourself useful—hold the door, while I go see what's happening with your father."

"Hello? . . . Damn it! . . . Hello!"

"Maman! Maman!"

"The elevator?"

"*Oui.*"

"Marcus! never mind! it's here, the elevator . . . . Jerry, what does he say? . . . Oh, thank God, thank God!"

"What? What, Germaine?"

"He didn't go down. . . . *Assez, assez, Jerry! Qu'il parte! Et toi, rentres ici!*" The front door slammed. "There's no need for the whole world to know our business."

"*Alors* . . . where is he?"

"D-D-Didn't I tell you?"

"What?"

"He's h-h-hiding!"

"Hiding?"

"Smerdyakov! . . . Suppose he used the stairs?"

"The stairs! Oh, my God! the stairs—I never thought—"

"Jerry, be a good boy—*descends voir*—"

"*Oui-oui, Papa, j'y vais!*"

Again the front door slammed. In the ensuing silence, Danny realized he still had the opportunity to reveal himself: stroll into the foyer and feign complete surprise at his family's distress . . . . "What's the matter?" "Matter! Where have you been?" "In the bathroom." "Didn't you hear us looking for you?" "No." . . . There would follow a great sigh of relief, laughter, embraces, a game of gin rummy . . . the whole episode quickly forgotten—if only he could go forth now and show himself . . . . But Danny couldn't. Something held him, made him hug the wall, pull the bathroom door to his rigid chest like a shield.

"The police, Marcus—hadn't we better call the police?"

"Let's wait and see—"

"But suppose— Oh, I don't know—don't know what to think."

"Let's see what Jerry—"

"Claude! What exactly are you doing?"

"L-L-Looking for my brother."

"Uch! *Imbécile!* . . . Come out of that closet."

"W-W-Want to bet I find him?"

"*Bête* . . . *bête* is right. . . . Marcus, you don't suppose— He-he

63.

couldn't have gone—not at this hour—to visit Miss Kerns, could he? At ten at night? No, surely not . . . . Ohh! what's keeping Jerry?"

"It's fourteen flights, *chérie.*"

Still listening intently, Danny heard a rush of air, as Claude yanked open the linen closet door. A moment later the light clicked on. "Maman! Maman!"

"What now?"

"L-L-Look at this."

"At what? what?"

"Look! He's b-b-been in here, obviously."

"Don't be ridiculous! It's that *cochonne*, Maria. You tell them a thousand times— Get out of my way and let me straighten up!—a thousand times you show them, demonstrate with your own two hands, and still they don't comprehend—never, no matter what— Where are you going now?"

"N-N-Never mind."

For a second Danny was fearful his brother was heading for the bathroom, but Claude went instead into Jerry's room. Danny could hear the parquet creaking as Claude advanced, evidently on tiptoe, toward Jerry's closet. There was no longer any choice for Danny. He would *have* to get out of the bathroom now (logically Claude would look there next), go into his own room, and pretend to have been there all the time. He would wait till he heard the closet open, and then, while Claude's back was turned, make a dash for it—the desk, Emily Dickinson . . . the hour of lead. . . . For You have I prepared myself: set the wooden staves in place—

Claude yanked open Jerry's closet.

"Go!" Danny coached himself. Sprinting the length of the bathroom, he dodged the sink, rounded the door, rushed into the bedroom, stopped dead in his tracks, and stifled a cry.

Seated in the easy chair diagonally opposite the bathroom door was a middle-aged man in a single-breasted gray flannel suit, white shirt, and foulard tie. Altogether relaxed, if not a trifle weary, his tall lean body was slouched far down in the chair, his long legs crossed at the knees, his complexion as pallid as the cigarette he was holding.

"Monk!" Danny exclaimed almost voicelessly.

Smiling agreeably Monk brought a patrician finger to his lips. "I came ahead," he explained in his usual mild monotone. "The only one, of course, respectable enough to use the front elevator. The rest will be along presently. . . . No sense biting your nails about it—things are bad enough." Monk cleared his throat. "But then,

64.

who am *I* to talk? sitting here smoking my fool head off. . . . I'd appreciate your not mentioning it to Mortlock . . . in which case I'll overlook the nail biting, as well as that little bit of hanky-panky in the linen closet. Is it a deal?"

Danny nodded.

"Good. Now then, if I were you, I'd sit down at the desk and start reading. Inspector Javert" —Monk smiled ironically and gestured in Claude's direction— "is hot on your trail."

Danny did as he was told. The spiral notebook and the volume of Emily Dickinson's poems were still lying open on the desk. Surreptitiously Danny placed his forearm on top of his own poem to conceal it from sight, and focused his attention on the Dickinson.

Monk chuckled. "Don't think you've put one over on us. It's already been microfilmed—your poem—copies distributed to every Committee member . . . though Lord knows what Fowler or Lashmit will make of it . . . . Personally, I like that line: 'anoint me like a gangland stiff,' but I doubt if it'll go down too well with the Incorruptible. Probably there'll be hell to pay—" Monk broke off. "Better start reading—here he comes."

"Robespierre?"

"Heavens, no! You're not all *that* important . . . yet. Your brother."

Keeping one eye on the bathroom door, Danny turned the page of the Emily Dickinson volume and began to read aloud:

> It felt a cleaving in my mind,
> As if my brain had split—

"No-no," Monk interrupted, "not aloud; he'll never fall for that. Just act natural."

So gradually, yet deliberately, did the bathroom door drift open (obviously only the slightest pressure was being applied), that for a moment Danny anticipated the arrival of one of the other Committee members—Fowler more than likely—until he spotted Claude out of the corner of his eye.

"Studying?"

It was a curious phenomenon, one of the most curious and puzzling in the world from Danny's point of view, that whenever he and his brother were alone (Monk, of course, having by now made himself invisible), Claude seldom stammered. Danny looked up from the book. Claude was sneering.

"Where were you hiding?"

"I've-I've been here all the time."

"All *what* time?" Claude shot back like a prosecuting attorney. "The time we've been looking for you—is that what you mean? In which case you must have heard us, *knew* we were looking for you! Well?" Danny was silent. "You phony. Couldn't even go through the first night without pulling a stunt like this. . . . *N'importe*, it's *your* neck." Claude paused. "Well . . . are *you* going to tell them or am I?"

"Tell them what?" Monk prompted.

"Tell them what?" Danny said.

Claude shook his head in disgust. "You phony," he repeated. Then, turning on his heels, he left the room by the hall door, calling out in a singsong as he went, "C-C-Come in, c-c-come in wherever you are. I've found him!"

Just as he was about to turn to Monk for reassurance, Danny caught sight of Fowler on the bed. Stark naked, the young man was stretched out shamelessly, lying with his hairy legs propped not against the wall but against Jerry's copy of the Watteau, his feet planted squarely on the middle of Gilles' groin (Gilles remained indifferent), one of his hands pillowing his huge curly head, the other fondling his uncommonly small penis. That was Fowler's paradox: built like a wrestler—however short and stocky, his physique was highly developed: compact, solid, powerful—he had a penis the size of a two-year-old's. "Come on, baby," he coaxed Gilles, wriggling his toes and digging them into the canvas, "don't be shy—get it up! . . . Oh" —Fowler pretended to see Danny for the first time— "hi, kiddo. How's tricks?"

"All right," Danny murmured. Much as he enjoyed some of Fowler's qualities—his energy, unorthodox charm, lack of inhibition, outrageous tongue, and puckishness—Danny mistrusted him, knew how utterly unscrupulous and selfish Fowler was, what a liar, what a psychopath. Yet his mistrust of Fowler was nothing compared to his mistrust of Lashmit, who at that very moment opened the closet door and stepped into the room.

At a glance Lashmit seemed as neat and well turned-out as Monk. He too was wearing a flannel suit (though his was charcoal gray), a white shirt and tie, and black oxfords. On closer inspection, however, one realized that the shirt was filthy, its cuffs and collar frayed, the suit was grease-stained, trousers unpressed, shoes badly in need of repair and polish. His personal hygiene was, if possible, even worse. Like Danny, Lashmit also bit his nails, but his were etched with dirt; his ears were filled with dollops of wax; he picked his nose with a passion; and his long black hair, treated for years with pomade or tonic in preference to shampoo, hung down like rockweed, matted and stringy. As if to distract from these glaring imperfections, Lashmit bedecked himself with jewelry. On his gnawed fingers he sported two rings: one a cat's-eye set in gold, the other a massive gold initial ring embossed with the capital letters UL (since Danny had observed this abbreviation on every electric wire and extension cord he'd ever seen in the United States, he was not deceived into thinking the letters stood for Ulysses, Uranus, or Uriah Lashmit, but was quick to deduce some reference to the Committee's indisputable jurisdiction over every form of energy: electric, solar, sexual—in short, the Vital Force); his sizable cuff links were Egyptian scarabs cut from turquoise; around his left wrist he wore a heavy silver identification bracelet, quite ordinary in every respect except that instead of bearing Lashmit's name, the plate was engraved with the one word, SURVEILLANCE. In contrast to all this uncleanliness and ostentation—these intimations of the underworld—were Lashmit's skin and eyes. Unusually large and black, his eyes were not, as might have been expected, the least bit intense or sinister, but dreamy, romantic, even gentle; and his swarthy skin was so soft and close-shaved as to seem (despite his thirty years) beardless, dotted here and there with beauty marks. In fact, had it not been for the scar which originated at the center of his right nostril and terminated toward the corner of his upper lip, scoring it and creating the impression of a harelip, though in no way affecting his speech—without this scar one might easily have been deceived by Lashmit's dark good looks into forgetting he was a killer. "All right, let's get it over with—taxi the thing."

"Keep your pants on." Fowler guffawed at his own joke, and began to play with himself to call attention to his nudity.

Ignoring Fowler, Lashmit addressed his next remark to Monk. "What are we waiting for?"

"The Incorruptible, obviously," Zinc replied, adding sourly, "and Mortlock."

Till now Danny had failed to notice Zinc, even though the man was anything but slight and sitting directly opposite him on the other side of the desk.

A black Irishman, Zinc too was a handsome fellow, despite the pockmarks on his face and the stoutness he unwittingly emphasized by wearing tight double-breasted suits with wide lapels and padded shoulders. (The one he had on tonight, for instance, was some nondescript blend of black and gray which looked at first like worsted, but was actually a synthetic fabric made of ashes.) At the outset of any social occasion Zinc was always personable, charming, hearty—he had a pleasing baritone—but as the evening wore on he inevitably became disagreeable, contentious, often bullying and cruel. His drinking was the problem. He was almost never without a glass of beer or bourbon in hand (long ago Danny realized that Zinc had a natural preference for beer, resorted to bourbon only when he was feeling insecure about his lineage and wanting to impress the others)—tonight he was drinking bourbon.

"What's keeping Mortlock?" Lashmit was picking his nose.

"Traffic, no doubt," Monk remarked. "I never thought I'd make it across town."

"Or that new broad of his," Fowler suggested. "If you ask me she's got teeth in her cunt."

"No one, to my knowledge," Monk said drily with his usual ironic grin, "asked you anything."

"Tough titty!"

"Not teeth, nails in her cunt," Lashmit put in, "*Its* fingernails." He motioned his head in Danny's direction.

Zinc removed the glass of bourbon from his lips just long enough to inquire, "Has the taxidermist been notified?"

"Yup."

"The carpenter?"

"Yup."

"Embalmer?"

"Yup."

"The priests?"

"Of course!" Lashmit showed his irritation by flicking a pellet of snot across the room. "What do you think I am? Everything's ready—everything! We've got enough nails now to stuff the thing twice over."

Fowler swung his legs down from the painting and sat up on the edge of the bed. "You mean we aren't going to use the ones It's been saving, the ones in the desk?"

Along with the others, Danny stood back and scrutinized himself sitting at the desk, eyeing the top drawer, but not daring to make the slightest move to protect his life's savings.

"Look at It," Lashmit jeered, "sneaking a gander—"

"A goose!"

"Get your hand out of there!"

"Naughty!"

"Bad!"

"Harder—"

"Bad!"

"—Slap it harder!"

"Idiot!" Lashmit went on, "they've all been confiscated, the nails—"

"Consecrated," Zinc suggested.

"—every last one of 'em, while *It* was in the living room, wallowing in Schumann."

"Léon Blum, you mean."

"I mean Schumann—don't tell *me*—when I say Schumann—"

"Poor Enragé," Monk remarked at the mention of Schumann, "flung Itself off the Düsseldorf bridge—"

"For jerking off?"

"No-no, for composing."

"Same thing!"

"—smack into the waters of the Rhine."

"The Rhone, you mean," Zinc corrected his colleague politely.

"The Elbe."

"The Hudson."

"Nile!"

"Yalu!"

"Loire!"

"Mississippi!"

"Spell Mississippi!" Fowler commanded. "No thinking."

Danny did as he was told. "M-i-s—"

"In Egyptian, idiot!"

"What's the capital of Michigan?"

Danny hesitated. He knew it was Lansing, but dared not say the word for fear they'd turn the instrument against him.

"Come on! Quit stalling!" Fowler had lost patience. "Let's fillet It!"

"E.C.T. It!"

"Why, when we can lionize It?"

"Lobotomize It, *I* say!"

"Nnah, let's taxi It first—"

"Where's the kit?"

"The syringe!"

"Really, gentlemen," Monk objected, "I don't quite see the need to discuss these matters till the others arrive. Besides," he turned to Danny, "Inspector Javert's coming now—bringing the keepers—better bury your nose in that book. . . . Yes-yes, just imagine," he mused, "into the icy waters of the Düsseldorf . . . . *Ventôse* 27th, if I'm not mistaken, the year 62 . . . ."

"Oh, my angel—thank God, thank God, oh, thank God!" Mme.

Wahl, who entered the room first, ahead of her husband and Claude, hurried toward Danny with outstretched arms. Her blouse had come out of her skirt on one side, and her hair was disheveled as if she had been tearing at it or scratching her scalp uncontrollably. "Where have you been? Didn't you hear?"

"You didn't hear us?" Wahl said simultaneously.

"How is it p-p-possible?" Claude cross-examined.

Having reached the desk, Mme. Wahl began to pet and hug Danny's head. "Oh, *mon chou, mon chou* . . . what a fright!" Like so much yard goods on a counter, Danny remained perfectly impassive to his mother's touch. "We were calling and calling, running like chickens . . . you had us half crazy . . . ."

"How c-c-come you didn't hear us, *mon frère*?"

"We thought—we didn't know what—what to think! Where *were* you, sweetheart?"

As his family pressed closer, crowded round the desk, Danny sat in silence, staring at his book. The closer they came, the more distant they sounded, hazy they seemed, as if he were inside an isolation booth, separated from the rest of them by walls of frosted glass. At the same time he too stood outside, with his family, looking in, observing his own aggressive silence, woebegone expression, repelling posture, but was helpless as they to affect the boy within.

"You haven't answered M-M-Maman's question."

"This book, *chéri*" —leaning over Danny's shoulder, her bosom pressing against his back, Mme. Wahl angled the volume of poetry to get a better look at it— "is it so—so fascinating, you didn't even hear us? Your poor brother is running— Oh, *mon dieu*" —she reminded herself with a slap on the cheek— "Jerry!"

Wahl turned to his son. "Claude, be a good boy: go find—" In the course of gesturing toward the foyer, Wahl was stopped short by the sight of Maria's scowling face framed within the doorway. The instant their eyes met, however, Maria withdrew from sight. Rather than upset his wife by confronting Maria across the room, Wahl went out into the hall to speak to the woman. Curious to know where he was going, Mme. Wahl left Danny's side and started after her husband. Seeing his parents move in succession toward the door, Danny, who was still anticipating Mortlock's arrival, looked after them in terror.

"Phony," Claude murmured under his breath.

Ignoring his brother, Danny craned his neck to see what was happening, but his mother was blocking his view. He could only see her fussing with her hair—smoothing it back from her temples and holding it down as if against a gust—could only hear his father whispering heatedly but indistinctly in the hall. Unable to understand what was being said or to whom, unable to see what was going on, unable to leave the chair or articulate his fury, fear, frustration, Danny began to pound the desk.

"Easy," Monk cautioned, and Danny instantly desisted.

"Phony," Claude repeated in a whisper, as Mme. Wahl turned on her heel and rushed back to her baby.

"What? what? what is it, *mon chou*? What happened? . . . Why are you making such a face?" With his fist still clenched, teeth bared, frightful eyes riveted on the door, Danny looked ready for animal combat. "Maria—it's only Maria—what did you think?—up to her old tricks again: spying, always spying—ignorant fool! . . . No-no," Mme. Wahl relented, "poor thing was worried too, I suppose. You had us all so worried, darling, disappearing in that fashion—not knowing what had happened, where you were—we were about to telephone the police."

"Which b-b-brings us back to the salient question."

"What question's that?" Wahl asked in a chatty manner as he reentered the room.

"Where D-D-Danny was."

"We searched everywhere, *chéri*," Mme. Wahl pursued the point, "everywhere—high and low—"

"You know" —Wahl chuckled— "it's really difficult to comprehend—"

"Y-Y-Yes, indeed."

"—how four people could search a house—"

"T-T-Tell us, *mon frère*, where were you hiding?"

Mme. Wahl made a face. "Hiding! Don't be ridiculous! He wasn't hiding, were you, darling?"

Danny didn't answer; again his eyes were fixed on the book.

"W-W-Were you, darling?"

"Oh, be still!" Mme. Wahl snapped at Claude. "Go find your brother."

"In a m-m-minute, as s-s-soon—"

"No, now!" Wahl commanded, but before Claude had a chance to obey, the front door slammed.

"I've looked everywhere," Jerome shouted from the foyer, "there's not a sign—"

"*Là! Là*, Jerry!" Wahl shouted back. "It's all right! We're all in here."

Out of breath and sweating noticeably, Jerome dashed into the bedroom. "Where *was* he?"

71.

Wahl shrugged and threw up his hands.

Jerome went over to the desk to put the question to his brother. "Where were you, Danny?"

Still staring at the book, Danny remained mute.

"Look at you!" Mme. Wahl criticized Jerome as she took out her handkerchief to wipe his brow. "Come here."

Jerome paid no attention to his mother. Instead, he bent over till his head was on a level with Danny's. "Where did you go, *mon frère*?"

A drop of perspiration fell from Jerome's brow onto the open page of Emily Dickinson's poems. Danny watched the teardrop, a perfect circle, spread over the small print till it circumscribed the words:

> never met this
> ended, or alone
> ithout a tighter
> Zero at the bone

Too late for tears, for irrigation of any kind—rivers, fountains, dew; sweat or sperm or sputum—he would have to spend eternity condemned to Lower Egypt, condemned in perpetuity to squeeze a single nonexistent drop of Vital Force from all the dust-dry bones and stones and fingernails of the Eternal Waste. "Embalm me," Danny murmured.

"Who?" Jerome responded gently. "Who's balmy?"

"B-B-Balmy! Is *that* where you went?"

Straightening up, Jerome glowered at Claude; then, turning to his father, he said without voicing the words, "I'll kill him!"

At the same time, Mme. Wahl took hold of her hair and, tearing at it, turned on Claude and whispered frantically, "Stop it!"

Bending down again to face his brother, Jerome resumed his gentle inquiry. "Sorry, Danny, I didn't hear." He shot a quick accusatory look at Claude. "Where did you say you went?"

"Yes, t-t-tell us, Dan."

"Oh, what's the difference?" Wahl tried to make light of the matter.

"Difference!" Jerome exploded. "Suppose—suppose he had had an attack—"

"Bite your tongue!" Mme. Wahl exclaimed.

"And lower your voice!" Wahl added. "What do you think this is? He *didn't* have an attack—"

"Thank God!" Mme. Wahl knocked on the desk with her knuckles.

"No difference!" Jerome muttered sarcastically.

"Of course there's a difference!" Mme. Wahl took Jerome's side. "It's not as if— We have to know—every minute! He can't just wander off like that. You can't just wander off, *chéri*."

"D-D-Did you wander off, *chéri?*"

Danny maintained his stony silence.

"Maybe if all of you got out of here," Jerome proposed impatiently, "and let me talk to my brother alone—"

"Of course!" Mme. Wahl scoffed. "To *you*, he'll talk! . . . Darling" —she interposed herself between Jerome and Danny— "tell Maman—just whisper in my ear—where did you go?"

"To the bathroom," Monk said.

"The bathroom," Danny murmured.

"Bathroom?"

"Which bathroom?"

"And you d-d-didn't hear us?"

"I must have dozed off," Monk said.

"Must have dozed off," Danny repeated.

"D-D-Dozed off?"

"Oh, my poor baby" —Mme. Wahl clapped her cheeks and rocked her head between her hands— "poor poor baby! You're *that* exhausted, you fell asleep sitting— Of course you're exhausted, worn to the bone. How could it be otherwise, after a day like this: your first night home . . . on the go since the crack of dawn . . . that interminable drive . . . all that reading . . . that lunatic in the kitchen—of course you dozed off, it's too much for anyone, too much excitement! . . . What's needed now," Mme. Wahl announced as she crossed the room and began to open Danny's bed, removing the cushions and turning down the cotton spread, "is a good night's sleep. One good night's sleep in your *own* little bed— *toute douillette* . . . nice clean sheets— I'm sure you haven't seen clean sheets in a month—God knows what we were paying for—"

"Maman!" Jerome censured her.

"Keep out of it!" she retorted sharply. "I was saying, sweetheart, one night at home in your own little bed—"

" '. . . In your own l-l-little bed again,' " Claude broke into song, and Jerome joined in on the chorus, " 'There'll be blue-birds over—' "

"Idiots! They're idiots, your brothers. Pay no attention, darling. Listen to Maman. One good night's sleep—I promise you: you'll wake up feeling like a different person. You'll see. . . . The idiots can sleep together. Claude, you hear? You'll sleep in there with Jerry tonight; I'll sleep—"

"Like hell he will!" Jerome objected.

73.

"*Ferme ça!*" Mme. Wahl growled. "I've had enough! You'll do as you're told, for once—both of you!" Then, turning back to Danny, she added sweetly, "Maman will sleep in here, *chéri*, with you."

"Tell her," Monk put in, "you're not used to having anyone in the room at the hospital—you have to sleep alone."

"Maman," Danny said faintly.

"*Oui, chéri.*"

". . . Alone . . . I have to sleep alone."

"*Pourquoi?*"

"I'm not used to anyone."

"Anyone! Since when is Maman just anyone?" Coquettishly transforming her offended expression into a smile, Mme. Wahl turned away and headed for the closet to fetch Danny's pillow.

"Maman!" Leaping up, Danny raced across the room and intercepted her before she reached Lashmit's hiding place.

Mistaking his outburst for remonstrance, Mme. Wahl stopped dead in her tracks and raised both hands as if in response to a stick-up. "All right, all right—if that's the way you want it. I wasn't thinking of myself, you know? Maman has a bed of her own, a perfectly good bed—"

"*I'll* get the pillow," Danny said, breathing heavily.

Troubled and perplexed by her son's behavior, Mme. Wahl grimaced and shook her head, shrugged and exchanged bewildered looks with her husband while Danny's back was turned.

Cautiously opening the door, Danny ventured into the closet without turning on the light. Though the pillow was on a shelf overhead, he focused his attention on the clothes poles, which flanked the side walls, casting his eye over the jackets on hangers, jeans on hooks, pajamas, robes, athletic gear, searching for some sign of Lashmit. Sure enough, once his eyes had adjusted to the dark, he spotted the Committee member, back turned, bending over something on the floor in the corner. Just what the man was struggling with—whether a foot locker containing the embalming equipment or the mummy case itself—Danny couldn't make out, since the object in question was being extracted from a kind of tunnel or vault whose existence had, until this moment, been kept secret from Danny. Nor was Lashmit ready to divulge the secret; the instant Danny discovered him, he straightened up and turned around—his scar more pronounced than usual—gave Danny a nasty look, and grumbled, "Scram!"

Frightened, Danny grabbed the pillow and held it in front of his face, using it as a buffer between himself and Lashmit. As he emerged from the closet he was careful to leave the door ajar so

74.

that Lashmit would have no cause, later on, to accuse Danny of attempting to suffocate him.

Seeing her son standing inert, his eyes closed, head couched on the pillow he was embracing, Mme. Wahl exclaimed, "Look at you, *chéri!* you're falling asleep on your feet."

"D-D-Dozing off again?"

"All right now" —she took command of both Danny and the situation— "out—all of you—out of here, and let me get the child to bed."

"Child again!" Jerome jeered.

Mme. Wahl guided Danny, who was still hugging the pillow, across the room and set him down on the bed. Thereupon, she too got down—on her hands and knees—and began to unlace his shoes. "*Regarde-moi ça*—not fit for a peasant. That a son of mine. . . ." The thought was dissipated in a sigh. "They're a scandal, *chéri*, really a scandal, your shoes. We'll have to buy another pair tomorrow— a whole new *ensemble*."

"Perhaps," Wahl put in, "the boy would like to visit his uncle tomorrow?"

Mme. Wahl sat back on her heels. "Which uncle?"

"Boris."

"What! Are you out of your mind? We have a million things to do—people— He wants to see Miss Kerns tomorrow— Oh, by the way, *chéri*, did you reach her?"

Danny didn't answer. He was peeping over the top of the pillow at his father and Jerome, who were whispering together and gesticulating animatedly.

"*N'importe*—it can wait . . . everything. We'll discuss it in the morning, after a good night's sleep. . . . Here: raise your foot . . . that's it. *Voilà!*" She put the pair of shoes aside. "I do wish you wouldn't wear white socks, *chéri*, they're so—so *voyou*. You have no others? We must remember to buy socks too—so many things— we'll make a list in the morning." As soon as Danny's feet were bare, Mme. Wahl began to wiggle one of his toes after the next, reciting a counting jingle:

> *Celui-ci a vu le lièvre*
> *Celui-ci l'a couru—*

Jerome turned away from his father. "Maman!"

Put on her guard by his belligerent tone, Mme. Wahl gave Jerome an icy stare. "What, still here? I thought I told you to get out."

"Danny's perfectly capable of undressing himself."

"Is that so!"

"Yes, that's so! He's *not* a child, in no way incapacitated—"

"For your information, he hasn't the strength—"

"Danny," Jerome appealed to his brother, "do you want her to undress—"

"*Her* again!"

"I think," Danny replied in a feeble voice, "it would be best—"

"There!" Mme. Wahl threw back her head in triumph. "You see? Now get out!" she barked, "*all* of you!"

"Maniac! He hasn't—"

"Don't you—"

"Danny, what were you saying, *what* would be best?"

Even as he tried to answer Jerome, Danny's eyelids lowered and his head drooped to the pillow.

"Danny—"

Mme. Wahl struggled to her feet to protect her baby. "Will you be still, and leave him alone!"

"Danny—" Jerome placed his hand lightly on his brother's shoulder— "what would be best?"

"Leave the child alone, I said!" Struggling to keep her voice down, Mme. Wahl not only tensed her vocal cords till she sounded almost bestial, but also forced her words through clenched teeth, grinding them to pulp—a mannerism anathema to Wahl.

"Don't be so emphatic!"

"Can't you see—" she continued in the same tone.

To settle the matter, Wahl resorted to a tone even more intense and savage than his wife's. "I said, don't be so emphatic!" In the next breath, however, he turned to his sons and remarked matter-of-factly, "Come, we'll all go out, and let the boy undress himself—you too, Germaine!"

"Will you look at him!" By now the tension and exasperation so evident in her voice had spread to Mme. Wahl's body—her knees were bent, back hunched, elbows pinned to her sides, fists shaking ineffectually. "He's sound asleep."

"*Tant mieux,*" Wahl retorted, "let him sleep."

"Sitting up? . . . He hasn't undressed . . . brushed his teeth . . . his pajamas. . . ."

Like the door of Hell harrowed by Christ, the pillow Danny was holding fell aside. "*I'll* get the pajamas."

"Oh, s-s-so you are awake after all, only f-f-faking."

Claude's assertion did not seem altogether unjust to Danny and might have passed unchallenged if it hadn't been for Fowler, who

76.

suddenly piped up with, "Of course It's faking" —an accusation which drove Danny to beat his own thighs and groan.

Hearing this, Jerome hurled off and walloped Claude savagely. "Damn you!"

In retaliation Claude shoved his brother half across the room into the desk. "F-F-Fucking dupe!" he sputtered as their father rushed between them and their mother shrieked at the top of her lungs, "Stop it!"

Danny's posture had changed noticeably since his fit of anger. He was sitting now, staring into space, stiff-backed as an Egyptian statue, palms pressed flat against his thighs.

"Now see!" Mme. Wahl declared half in distress, half accusingly, as if her husband and sons were solely responsible for her baby's present condition. In dread of one of Danny's attacks, during which his muscles would become rigid, she strayed into the center of the room and began tapping her temple rapidly like a telegraph operator, trying to get a message to her brain. When at last the message came through, she cried out, "The pills!" and bolted for the bathroom.

Her alarm thus transmitted to the others, they stood for a moment, suspended in fear, staring helplessly at each other, hearing the running water, the rattle of the pills, till Jerome made a move toward the bed. "Danny" —he tried to sound calm— "Danny?"

"*Oui.*"

Jerome heaved a sigh of relief. "You're all right?"

"Of course he's all right," Wahl replied cheerfully, eager to reassure not only his son but himself.

"He's all right?" Mme. Wahl echoed her husband breathlessly as she came from the bathroom holding two pills and a glass in her trembling hands. "You're all right, *chéri?*"

After waiting in vain for Danny to answer, Wahl spoke for him. "*Oui-oui-oui.*" He motioned to his wife to control herself. "He said so himself, didn't he, Jerry?"

Jerome nodded. "*Oui.*"

Unconvinced, Mme. Wahl advanced toward Danny with obvious trepidation, her voice subdued to a shaky undertone. "*Chéri* . . . *are* you all right? . . . Please: some sign . . . your arm . . . can you? For Maman—please, oh please! move it for Maman."

Exacerbated by his mother's behavior, Jerome turned to his father and, wielding his arm like a scythe, slashed the air to indicate that she should be taken out of the room.

"Here" —Mme. Wahl had hit on the idea of using the tranquilizers to induce Danny to move— "take this; it will do you good, *chéri.* Maman will hold the water, you just take the pills. . . . Here, be my good boy. . . . Please, please! my love."

Again Jerome gesticulated violently at his father, driving him to act this time. Coming up behind his wife, Wahl pressed his thumb into her back and whispered her name.

Startled, Mme. Wahl recoiled, spilling some of the water onto Danny who, despite the accident, remained immobile, staring into space. "Something! something! do something!" she implored Wahl under her breath.

"Come out now," Wahl replied firmly.

"The doctor—call the doctor—something!"

"The boys will help him undress."

By now even Claude had grown concerned. "*Oui,* M-M-Maman, we'll—we'll get him to bed."

"How?" she entreated frantically. "He can't move!"

"Danny" —Jerome took out his handkerchief to blot the water on his brother's trousers— "do you want to go to sleep?"

"Come, Germaine." Wahl tried to pull her away.

"Leave me be!" she snarled.

"Come out, I said."

"Can you undress yourself?" Jerome inquired softly.

Wahl gripped his wife's arm. "*Out.*"

"Out. Get them out!" came an order from above. "All of them, this instant!"

Though the speaker was invisible, his German accent was only too familiar to Danny. Mortlock had arrived. Rising briskly, Danny answered Jerome in the most natural, if impatient, tone of voice. "Of course I can undress myself. I'm not a baby any more." To demonstrate the point, he began to unbutton his shirt in the most businesslike manner.

"You see!" Jerome turned on his mother.

"Enough!" Wahl silenced his son. "Come: we'll go out now and let the boy get some sleep."

Mme. Wahl shut her eyes. Her chin began to quiver, face to crumble as she moved her head from side to side, trying hard to hold back her tears. ". . . Can't . . . I can't—"

"Control yourself!" Wahl demanded under his breath. "Boys," he said aloud.

"—can't take any more."

"Jerry!" Removing the glass from his wife's hand, Wahl freed his own by passing the glass to Jerome. "Sleep well, *mon petit,*" he said over his shoulder as he led the sobbing woman out of the room.

". . . haven't kissed him good night," she whined.

"Claude!" Jerome said sharply. "Come!"

"Shut the door please," Danny called after his brothers.

Before leaving the room Claude turned back, smiled knowingly and took a parting shot. "You even had *me* fooled that time."

As the door closed Danny heard Jerome threaten in an undertone to murder Claude, heard his mother burst into sobs, saw the Committee, including Mortlock, reassemble before his eyes.

In deference to his superior, Monk vacated the easy chair, strolled across the room and took Danny's former place, opposite Zinc at the desk. Fowler, still naked, was no longer lounging on Danny's bed but sitting on the edge of Claude's, his legs widespread, showing off his puny penis; while Lashmit stood guard, however lackadaisically, at the bedroom door, polishing his gold initial ring.

Mortlock ignored Monk's good manners, shunned the empty chair. Deep in thought, he kept on the move, expending his animal energy by endlessly circling the center of the room. He could seldom sit still, preferring as now to remain on the prowl, head lowered, hands behind his back, a cigarette hanging from his downturned mouth. A chain smoker, Mortlock was never without a cigarette, forever soiling his custom-made suits, besmirching the furniture and rugs, leaving in his path a trail of ashes like animal droppings. For someone his height (he stood a mere sixty-two or -three inches in shoes) he had a disproportionately large head, a head whose baldness exaggerated its size to such a degree it looked almost hydrocephalic, though neither cranium nor features were in any way disfigured. On the contrary, except for the mouth, compressed into a single lipless line, his face was rather handsome, graced with a proud straight nose, strong chin, prominent cheekbones, and large challenging eyes. Moreover, like many of his countrymen (despite his claim to being Viennese, he was clearly a Berliner), he could turn on the charm—especially for women—making himself so attractive he had his way with everyone.

After completing a countless number of circuits, which left Danny all but mesmerized, Mortlock cocked his thumb like a hitchhiker and motioned, to no one in particular, in the direction of the bathroom.

Lashmit was quick to pick up the signal. "Shut the other door!"

Danny did as he was told.

"*And* the blinds!"

Once the blinds were closed—the desk lamp remaining the only source of light in the room—Mortlock came to a standstill. "So, gentlemen, word's come down— Please, please," he interrupted himself to speak to Danny, "don't mind us. Go about your business. Get ready."

A shiver coursed through Danny's body. He was uncertain what Mortlock meant by ready—whether for bed or something worse—but dared not ask for fear of giving the Committee ideas.

Zinc read his mind. "It's being naïve, doesn't know what you mean—whether for bed—"

"Or bifurcation," Monk put in mischievously.

Raising his glass, Zinc toasted Monk across the desk. "It's *on* Its bifurcation."

"Touché."

"Sure, for bed," Mortlock returned to the subject. "You think the mad one can restrain herself, keep out of here the rest of the night? Not on your life! It wouldn't look right, you understand, arouse her suspicions, if she found you still up. Better put on the pajamas. . . . So, as I was saying, gentlemen, word's just come down: the opposition's trying to get through."

"Which faction?" The innocence with which Zinc put this question did little to conceal some deeper intent.

"Do I sense a note of ambiguity—"

"Ambigooity?" Zinc mimicked Mortlock's accent.

"So, you're at it again, I see."

"At what? The booze or the Incorruptible?"

"Where *is* the Incorruptible?" Lashmit was curious to know.

Mortlock took advantage of the interruption to get away from Zinc. "In the Green Room, naturally."

"What are they rehearsing?" Fowler asked.

In response Monk smiled pointedly. "The trial and death of Marie Antoinette."

Wild with excitement Fowler clapped his thighs together repeatedly. "For incest with her son?"

"You're forgetting yourself!" Mortlock reprimanded him. "We're Conservationists—*all* good Conservationists—whatever our petty differences." (Though Danny could see that this statement was aimed at Zinc, he somehow missed the point of it, as so often when it came to the Committee's infighting.) "We'll review the charges presently. Meanwhile, the faction I had reference to—let me make myself crystal clear—is the enemy, gentlemen, the *Enragés*."

"Holy cripes!" Lashmit exclaimed.

"Dear, dear," Monk sighed. "Not again."

"Sure again! Again and again and again!" Mortlock flushed as he grew more impassioned. "It is *they*, the enemy, not ourselves, that demand the constant vigil!" Obviously these remarks were also meant for Zinc. "However, there's no cause for alarm, gentlemen. We've thrown a boomerang around the house—the whole damn block—they'll not get through." Complacently, Mortlock flicked the ash off his cigarette.

Fearful of calling attention to himself, Danny suppressed an impulse to rub the fallen ashes into the carpet, as he had seen his mother do ever since he was a child.

"Of course," Mortlock went on, "they'll get a warm reception, plenty warm, let me assure you—we've got an arsenal on the roof."

"Ray guns?"

"Restraining jackets?"

"Sure, sure, everything, the works—electrodes, embalming fluid, anaesthetics, intravenous—"

"Ssst!" Lashmit drew Mortlock's attention to Danny. "It's listening."

"Sure It's listening." Leaving his colleagues, Mortlock walked over to where Danny was standing at the head of the bed. "I thought I told you to get undressed. . . . Heavens, don't look so put upon. Who do you think got you into this mess in the first place—*us*?" He waited in vain for Danny to answer.

"It's thinking," Lashmit reported.

"Sure It's thinking, saying to Itself, 'The Enragés rescued me the last time, got me out of here, maybe they can pull it off again.' Well, let me assure you, they can't! There's too much at stake this time—the power balance of the universe! *Gott!* what a feather it would be, what a *coup*, to abduct you again. *Abduct*," he repeated angrily, "you understand? Not rescue, *dummkopf!* What you call rescue, we call *doom*." So forceful was the impact of the final word, it left Danny blinking. "Now, get undressed."

Recovering himself, Danny obediently continued to unbutton his shirt.

"And don't forget to say your prayers," Fowler added with evident glee.

"*Aquinapay medinore*," Danny began to pray, "*aquinapay medinore . . . aquinapay medinore . . . .*"

At last Mortlock availed himself of the easy chair. "All right, gentlemen, let's get down to business now. Read the charges."

Zinc set down his glass with a thud. "Without the Incorruptible?"

"Sure without. Look here, Zinc" —Mortlock was back on his feet— "is it *my* fault if Robespierre stays away from an emergency session he himself called? prefers to remain in the Green Room all night, poring over police reports?"

"*Aquinapay medinore* . . . ."

"Perhaps" —Zinc took a long quaff of bourbon— "he's got wind of something . . . some internal plot."

"Plot! What plot?"

"To overthrow him."

"Sure, sure." Mortlock dismissed the idea with a flap of the wrist. "That's what they're designed for, those reports, to fill the Incorruptible's head with doubts, suspicions—"

"About whom?"

"A lot of phony charges—"

"About whom? I said," Zinc repeated.

"*Me*, of course!" Mortlock shouted. "And Lashmit, the E.C.T. men, *anyone* who takes the hard line, who understands that to govern is to make war!"

"Attaboy! Give it to him, baby!" Fowler and Lashmit egged Mortlock on.

"A plot to overthrow the Incorruptible, seize power for myself," he sneered. "Baloney! What am I, an Enragé, consumed with personal ambition? What do you take me for—Lucifer? Listen here, I'll let you in on a little secret: I ain't no Lucifer . . . any more than Robespierre's the Lord!" Along with the stream of cigarette smoke which poured from Mortlock's mouth came a decidedly cynical chuckle. In the next breath, however, he turned dead serious. "My only purpose in this life—think what you like, Zinc, who gives a fuck!—is to secure the Sacred Reservoir from the enemy—the enemy out *there*," he added fanatically, lashing his arm toward the windows, "not here! That's what concerns me, that's the cause—the only cause to which I'm pledged—not to you or Robespierre or any *verdammt* mortal, but to the One who will finally judge us *all*. And in His eyes, you can rest assured, there ain't no doubts, no imputations of disloyalty. The Supreme One knows what's what. So what do I care for your lousy accusations? I spit on them! My heart is pure, my destiny assured. Long after you're a speck of dust, I'll be bathing in the Blessed Waters, at one with the Sea of Bliss. So, go ahead! persecute me! persecute me while you can."

"Come-come," Monk tried to mollify him, "no one wants to persecute you."

"If not, then let's proceed." Enfolding himself in his jacket, Mortlock sat down ceremoniously. "After all," he muttered at Zinc, "you're not the judge—not yet, you're not—merely an attorney, a provincial lawyer like your precious Robespierre—and don't forget it! That Danzig girl, her grandfather is still Chief Justice."

"If so, where is he?" Zinc demanded.

"At dancing class," Fowler replied, putting on a pair of white cotton gloves, working each finger as if the gloves were kid.

Lashmit produced a small leather book, which Danny instantly recognized as his own, and looked up an address. "1185 Park Avenue."

"1189," Fowler disagreed.

"The Third Crusade."

"Give the dates of the First Crusade!"

"Richard Coeur de Lion."

"Lionize It!"

"Lobotomize It!"

"Lapidify—"

Mortlock rapped the arm of the chair. "Silence in the court."

"*Le coeur!*"

"The court!"

"Silence! I said." The clamor ceased. Ready to begin, Mortlock gave his lapels a final touch. "Commence the trial weekend. Read—" he interrupted himself, his eye on Danny. "Not yet in Its pajamas, I see. What are you waiting for, slowpoke, someone to assist you?"

"Me!" Lashmit volunteered.

In a flash Danny, who was standing now in his underwear, seized his shirt and trousers, and fled to the closet. Like an actor making a quick change in the wings, he could hear the drama on stage continue as he stripped.

"Don't you see what Mortlock's up to?" Zinc appealed to the others, "this conniver—"

"*Genug!*"

"He's using this case to provoke civil disorder—"

"*Lügner!*"

"—impose martial law—"

"*Schweinhund!*"

"—create an absolute dictatorship—"

"*Verräter!*"

"No, *you*," Zinc shot back, "you're the traitor! Gentlemen, I accuse this man of treason!"

At this, pandemonium broke loose. Everyone began to shout at once, "Mutiny!" "Slander!" "*Sans-culottes!*" "*Sieg heil!*" "Jew!" "Pig!" "Poet!" "*Über alles!*" "Kill!" "Kill!" "Kill!"—till Mortlock, spotting Danny at the closet door, raised his voice above the rest and bellowed at Lashmit, "Soundproof It!"

Instantly Danny's wires went dead. As he emerged in his pajamas from the closet and sidled to the bed, he could see but no longer hear the Committee. Mute himself, he stood in wonderment and watched the dumb-show whose outcome would, he knew, settle his fate once and for all.

Without the general clamor which, judging by everyone's vigorous jaw action, continued unabated; without the verbal content of the battle to distract him, it was perfectly clear to Danny that Zinc, though twice the size of his opponent, was no match for Mortlock. Using a completely defensive strategy, Mortlock stood his ground like a little citadel in the center of the room, forcing Zinc to storm him again and again. And each time Zinc did—each time the giant Irishman, flushed and grimacing, charged the small Berliner—Mortlock repulsed him with incredible ease, either by simply straight-arming Zinc or by raising his leg and shoving him back, staggering.

Throughout all this, Fowler, using the bed like a trampoline, kept jumping up and down wildly and hurling anything within reach—pairs of socks and tennis shoes—at the combatants. At one point, when Zinc sallied out brandishing a sheaf of documents which Mortlock promptly slapped from his hand, sending the papers flying in all directions, Fowler rushed around collecting them and crumpling them into balls for extra ammunition. Lashmit, also wild with excitement despite his glazed expression, was biting his fingernails—but only those on the right hand; with his left, plunged deep into his trouser pocket, he was playing with himself. Of all the Committee members Monk alone seemed insouciant. He was rocking back and forth on the rear legs of the desk chair, back and forth, back and forth, obviously bored—so bored, in fact, that during one of the final bouts. he somehow, without his colleagues' knowledge, managed to get an audible message through to Danny. "Don't despair. They can't keep at it forever. The Enragés will soon be here."

Shortly after this something either occurred or was said—Danny had no way of knowing—which terminated the battle abruptly. All of a sudden Fowler flew at the windows, raised one slat of the blind and peeked up at the sky, but apparently saw nothing, for then everyone turned his attention to Lashmit, who carefully covered his eyes with the flat of his hand—a customary gesture, familiar to Danny, called "fluoroscoping," a technique whereby the Committee was able to bring into view the activities of anyone anywhere on the face of the earth—and stood stark still for a moment before speaking. Whatever it was that Lashmit saw and then reported caused the Committee members not only to resume their former places—Mortlock in the easy chair, Fowler on Claude's bed, Monk and Zinc at the desk, Lashmit at the door—but also to turn the sound back on.

"Commence the arraignment," Mortlock said in a perfectly flat businesslike tone which showed no evidence of strain. "Read the charges—misdemeanors first."

As one, Zinc and Monk produced two enormous scarlet briefs from which they began to read antiphonally.

"The defendant stands accused of:"

"Thinking."

"Dreaming."

"Speaking."

"Spitting."

"Spitting?" Monk lowered his glasses the length of his nose. "Obviously a typo. It never spits. Its father spits."

"Strike spitting," Mortlock said. "Continue."

"Breathing."

"Eating."

"Drinking."

"Shitting."

"So what was the typo?" Lashmit interrupted.

"Let spitting stand," Mortlock ruled.

"Spitting."

"Shitting."

"Farting."

"Objection!" Monk rose slowly. "Here, I should like to remind the court of the defendant's vigilant effort to restrain Its flatulence, at least in public."

"Overruled!"

"Hard-ons."

"Headaches."

"Wet dreams."

"Pissing—"

"It tries to do it quietly—"

"No excuses!"

"—against the side of the bowl."

"Overruled!"

"Sweating."

"Shouting."

"Shedding tears."

"Bed-wetting—"

"But that was years ago."

"Need we remind the defense that time is not of the essence here? Continue!"

"Kicking."

"Cursing."

"Biting."

"Pinching."

"Puking—"

Mortlock rapped the arm of his chair. "In reference to the charge of pinching—is the court to understand penny-pinching or just plain pinching?"

"Both!"

"Come now," Monk objected, "has the defendant that many merits that we can afford to condemn his paramount virtue, frugality, as a vice?"

"Objection sustained!" Mortlock ruled. "Come to the felonies."

"Hot dog!" Fowler exclaimed.

"Silence in the court!"

Danny watched the two attorneys flip through the briefs till Zinc found the place. "Two hundred seventy-eight," he prompted his colleague. "The defendant stands accused of nail biting in the first degree."

"Now here" —Monk got to his feet again— "I should like to bring to the court's attention the nails themselves, so neatly packeted and preserved, which indicate—well, if not exactly Conservationism in the strictest sense, at least the defendant's good intentions; albeit," he added ironically, "the Eternal Waste is paved with good intentions."

"Come to the point!"

"May it please the court, I move to place in evidence the envelopes of fingernails."

"Motion granted. Produce the envelopes."

Though Mortlock had addressed no one in particular, Danny quickly realized the order was meant for him. Taking pains not to disturb the proceedings or call attention to himself, he hurried over to the desk, tiptoed around Monk, opened the top drawer noiselessly and removed the four bulging envelopes.

"Furthermore," Monk continued, "I should like, at this time, to request that a count be taken of the nails themselves in hopes that their prodigious number may in some small way influence the ultimate mercy of the court."

"Request granted. The clerk will proceed with the count."

Confused by the term clerk, Danny hesitated.

"Well, what are you waiting for?"

Mortlock's harshness sent Danny scurrying back to the bed where he sat down at once and carefully emptied the contents of the first envelope, the one marked 1947, onto the night table.

"And don't try to pull a fast one," Lashmit cautioned, "we know the total before you begin."

Amassed before his eyes, the mound of nails looked strangely solid, monumental, almost immemorial, like a pyramid. And yet, the moment Danny reached out to touch them, count them, they seemed to come alive, possessed of a will of their own—the will to elude him like worms or cling together like filings caught in a magnetic field. The only aid that could possibly have simplified the task for him was his missing fingernails, the very nails he now found himself compelled to count. Starting at the perimeter, where certain tiny fragments lay strewn about like bonus points in Pick-Up Stix, Danny moved them one by one across the table with his index finger. ". . . three, four, five, six—" But even as he did, these isolated bits stuck to his fingertip, and he was obliged to detach them with his thumb before continuing: "—six, seven— six . . . five, six—" Unsure, he started over. "One, two, three, four . . . ." The task seemed like a preview of what was in store for him, a foreglimpse of the Eternal Waste; and Danny wondered whether he would be made to load his celestial bark not with practical provisions but solely with his bitten nails. ". . . fifteen, six— fif— fourteen? . . . fifteen? . . . One, two, three, four . . . ."

As he went on he began to sweat, his fingertips growing stickier, causing the nails to adhere in bunches—often two or three at a time would cling to his forefinger, then to his thumb—the perspiration making them more difficult to detach, more difficult to count. ". . . thirteen, fourteen, fifteen . . . eighteen, nineteen—"

"It's cheating!"

"One . . . two . . . three . . . four . . . ."

". . . jerking off in the first degree!"

"—seven-seven-seven!" Danny tried with all his might to concentrate on what he was doing, tried to keep track of the count, not to eavesdrop on the proceedings . . . .

"In the month of *Germinal* alone, It committed the atrocity ninety-seven times; in *Floréal*, eighty-six—"

"Eight-six . . . eighty-six—no! seven—seven-eighty— One, two, three, four . . . ."

The more often he started over, the more distraught and agonized Danny became, till finally, maddened with frustration, he began to bite the still-growing nails on his free left hand—even as he attempted with his right to tally up the dead ones on the night table—tearing at himself, ripping away what remained of his middle fingernail, devouring the flesh, drawing the blood, committing before the C.P.S.'s very eyes a first-degree felony.

That the Committee took no notice of him was little short of a miracle. Having come to the charge of "Writing poetry in the first degree," each of the members had been furnished and was studying a copy of Danny's latest effort, when suddenly there was a terrific crackling noise like electric static, amplified to a deafening volume, which caused everyone but Danny to drop what he was doing, leap to his feet, and rush about in confusion. The din went on for a full minute before subsiding, whereupon the Committee broke into an uproar.

"Interference!" "It's *them!*" "Enragés!" "Air raid!" *"Luftwaffe!"* "Sound the signal!" "Jamb the wave lengths!" "Get their coordinates!" "Take a reading!" *"Mach schnell!"* "North-northwest!" "Check the sonar!" "Radar!" "Searchlights!" "Fluoroscope!"

Once again Lashmit placed the flat of his hand over his eyes, as everyone fell silent. "They're swarming in like bats, thousands of 'em . . . the sky's thick with 'em—not just guys, broads too, all in the nude—tits and cocks swinging like clappers . . . wings beating . . . fangs bared . . . lipstick . . . nail polish . . . hair streaming—heading straight this way, coming in from the north, over the park."

Mortlock glanced at his watch. "How much time have we got?"

"A couple minutes."

"Enough to finish up. Resume the trial. *Mach schnell!* Come to the summation. The defendant will rise."

Unable to move, Danny was torn between a desire to obey the court's order and a determination not to lose track of the count: thirty-seven.

"What's the matter? Still soundproofed?"

"It's using delaying tactics."

"Let's finish It off!"

"Rise, I said!"

. . . Thirty-seven, thirty-seven, thirty-seven, Danny repeated over and over to himself as he got to his feet, and Zinc came forward to deliver the summation.

"Gentlemen, you see before you not just a hardened criminal, a raving maniac, a disrupter of the cosmic order, a writer of revolutionary tracts, an incurable nail-biting onanist, a mama's boy, crybaby, sneak, snake in the grass—someone, in short, who can't even *count*—"

"Speed it up!"

"—You see an atheist, an enemy of God—virtually a deicide, gentlemen, a desecrator of the Vital Source, dissipator of the Vital Force—"

There was a soft knock at the bedroom door.

Taken by surprise, Mortlock flinched. "What's that?"

"Enragés?"

"Impossible!"

"Too soon."

"It must be *her*."

"Holy Moses!"

"The light" —Fowler gestured frantically— "the light!"

"Douse the light!" Lashmit ordered in a whisper.

Danny dashed to the desk and switched off the lamp.

"Quick: to bed!"

"Quick! quick!"

Inching his way through the dark, Danny reached the bed and scrambled under the covers.

The knock came again, followed this time by a soft but anxious, "*Chéri?*"

"Don't answer!"

"Pretend you're asleep."

"And no funny business!"

"We're watching."

Slowly, silently the door opened, admitting a shaft of light, partially eclipsed by Mme. Wahl's stationary figure.

Danny shut his eyes.

"*Endormi?*" The floor creaked under her cautiously advancing feet. "*Bon.* . . . Sleep, sleep, my angel." The mattress wobbled as she sank down on the edge of the bed. "Oh but please, please be well tomorrow . . . no more sickness, please . . . I've had enough, more than I can take—my God!—more than any soul should be made to suffer in one life: first Maman— Oooh, Maman! Maman! *Ma mère adorée!* . . . why did you leave me? . . . why always—why is it those we love the most? . . ." Her shaking body shook the bed.

. . . Thirty-seven, thirty-seven, thirty—

"You know that, don't you, darling? know I love you more than life itself? You're all I have, all I want, everything, my heart's desire . . . so don't be sick—for Maman's sake, don't be sick— don't do it to me, please!"

. . . Thirty-seven. . . .

"You don't want to make Maman sick as well, do you? . . .

89.

That's the way it will end, of course—you'll see—they'll come and take Maman— Oh, God! Me! me! *chéri*, not you! It's me—I'm the one—I've always known—I'll go insane!"

"Maman!" Jerome uttered in a loud rasping whisper.

"Shhh! he's sleeping."

"Exactly. Come out."

"Un moment."

"Non, maintenant!"

Mme. Wahl heaved a sigh. *"J'arrive."*

"My God! it's hot in here," Jerome remarked.

"What are you doing?" Again the bed wobbled as Mme. Wahl rose abruptly. "Close that window!"

"He'll suffocate!"

"Close it, I said!"

"Shhh! you'll wake—"

"I want that window—"

"Shhh! Come out of here."

"Let go of me!"

"Out, I said!"

"Lower the blind at least."

"Leave it!"

The door clicked shut. Danny opened his eyes. Now that the Venetian blind had been raised, there were a few faint pools of light on the ceiling, but otherwise the room remained in shadow, perfectly still, silent . . . except for someone's heavy breathing in the corner.

"Quick now! come to the verdict," Mortlock declared. "How do you find the defend—"

"Wait!" Lashmit broke in. "Don't anybody move! There's someone in this room with us."

"What!"

"Who?"

"Robespierre?"

"Not one of *us*, schmuck, one of *them*."

"They're here?"

"Where?"

"Turn on the light."

"The light!"

"No! leave it off! You'll give our positions away!"

"Where's It hiding?"

"Who's It near?"

"If you'd shut your traps you'd hear!"

When everyone was silent Danny heard again the heavy breathing coming from the corner just beyond the head of his bed.

"If you ask me, there's more than one."

"How many?"

"Hard to say . . . half a dozen, maybe more."

"More!"

"How'd they get in—"

"Infiltrated!"

"Sure infiltrated! but how?"

"Slipped in with the mad one—"

"Through the window."

"Of course!"

"Christ! there's one right here!"

"Where?"

"Right beside me—breathing down my neck!"

"Shhh: listen. . . ."

"I don't hear a thing."

"Can't you *smell* It?"

Despite the open window, there was, in fact, a distinct, almost overpowering aroma in the room of musk and manure which made Danny salivate.

"The fur. . . ."

"The hooves. . . ."

"The fornication. . . ."

At this, the Committee's voices were all but drowned out by a resumption of the crackling noise.

"Quick!"

"Take cover!"

"They're coming in—"

"Call for reinforcements!"

"Make yourselves scarce!"

When at last the noise died down, the Committee seemed to have dispersed. There wasn't a sound. Even the breathing in the corner had ceased. All that remained was the musk and manure, acting on Danny like a stimulant: arousing his senses, causing his head to spin. Then suddenly he caught a whiff or thought he did—no, there was no mistaking it—a whiff of something intermingled with but altogether different from the excremental smell, something spicy, fragrant, delicate . . . perfume . . . sandalwood perfume. So intoxicating was the composite aroma, Danny sat up in bed and swallowed hard to clear his head. Though there was nothing he could see or hear, he nonetheless looked around, mistrustful of the silence, the dark, the Committee's disappearance. As he rested on his elbows, trying to trace the perfume to its source, and listening expectantly—for what? he didn't know—all at once he heard a rustle of taffeta, the click of amber beads and bracelets, a slight metallic tinkling, followed by someone politely clearing her throat.

"Good evening, Danny, I'm Emilia."

Though he couldn't see the woman in the dark, Danny felt certain she was a stranger. Not only had he never met anyone called Emilia, he had never heard her voice. Its principal quality was a deep rich huskiness, in no way hard or coarse or strident, but feminine and mellow, open and direct—a huskiness that conveyed at once great warmth and vitality as well as something sorrowful, mysterious. This combination of the vigorous and the poignant, the straightforward and the arcane made it difficult to guess Emilia's age. She sounded neither young nor old nor middle-aged; she sounded ageless. To complicate matters, she had a slight but very charming accent which Danny couldn't place. It might have been Albanian or Austrian, Greek or even South American. And then, besides the accent, were all those other signs suggestive of the Middle East: the tinkling earrings, beads and bracelets, sandalwood perfume. There was, moreover, that other *smell*, so hard to reconcile with the friendly, kind, compassionate voice—with any *human* quality—which put Danny on his guard. However sympathetic she sounded, however benign, he mustn't be misled, mustn't forget that Emilia was an Enragé, armed with fangs and claws.

"Don't stiffen," she said, "we aren't going to hurt you."

"We?"

"Yes . . . this is Vittorio."

"How do you do," Vittorio slurred, not in a sullen or hostile way, but merely with indifference.

"And this is Laurent," Emilia added.

"Hello." Laurent sounded more boyish than Vittorio, warmer, more responsive.

"And I'm Hector," a third man said with such hauteur that Danny wondered whether the speaker, who was doubtless older than the rest, was vexed by the indignity of having to introduce himself or was simply supercilious.

"We've come to take you out of here," Emilia went on, "away with us . . . where you belong."

"Back to the hospital?"

"Not necessarily," Hector replied in much the same grand manner he had used to introduce himself.

"Where then?"

"We must take a trip," Emilia explained.

Danny shrunk back on the bed, his shoulders pressed against Jerome's copy of *Gilles*. "Where?"

"Wherever you like," Laurent answered with ease. "There's no set place. . . . We could go to the vineyards of Burgundy, the olive groves of Greece; to Smyrna for ripe figs or Florida for tangerines—the kind that practically peel themselves. I know some orchards—purple plums and cherries, kumquats and bananas just waiting to be picked; and apricots whose nectar—if you stop to savor it—fuse you in a flash with all creation. . . . Or else we could go to a garden I know, shaded by persimmon trees, where banks of peonies astound the hummingbirds to a standstill in midair; and bushes of azaleas bloom in colors without name, colors so bright they make you blink in disbelief you ever used your eyes before."

"We could go to the Aegean," Emilia proposed, "to the sponges' spawning ground, sponges so submissive . . . soft, once you squeeze them, your hands revert to infancy—to a time before you had the need or teeth to bite your nails, a time when you were busy reaching out, instead: finding, feeling, grasping . . . the sponge. . . . We'll dive for them, and dig for clams—the little ones, no larger than a seedless grape. Swallow the liquor; you'll find yourself immersed at once in the waters of the seven seas. . . . It's there we'll swim and splash and play until we're too exhausted to do anything but let ourselves be washed away . . . ashore . . . onto the sands of some forgotten cove where we can stretch out naked in the sun and fall asleep . . . fast asleep, only to reawaken, refreshed and ready to be borne again on the rising tide."

"Let's not forget the caverns," Hector said, "the underworld where the dead decay, the seed takes root, and the oracle speaks through his medium, the serpent: body coiled, throat outstretched, head upheld—speaks of neither past nor future but of himself, the serpent, coiling and uncoiling, gliding to and fro among the decomposing corpses and germinating seeds. . . . If you hold on to my robes, my sleeve, we'll descend together, down into the caves, caves with single chambers large enough to house Versailles. You can't imagine the sights you'll see down there—parakeets and hippogriffs, mosques and minarets, pagodas with eleven tiers, Hindu temples, Shinto shrines, carved Moroccan screens—and all of it, everything you see: composed of dripstone. . . . I'll show you whole cities of stalactites and stalagmites, moon-colored cities aglow in the dark; blue and green and gold; I'll show you Bagdad

93.

and Persepolis, Isfahan and Angkor Wat in the bowels of the earth.
. . . You know how long it takes to form an inch of limestone—a single inch? Seven hundred years. Seven centuries of water flowing—rivers, streams—rushing, gushing, trickling, seeping, dripping drop by drop, building inch by inch, eroding and creating the cave itself two hundred million years. . . . That's time! that's process: the true meaning of stone: continuance, not cessation."

"Let's get into the forest—"

"That's enough," Emilia interrupted Vittorio, "we're wasting time. We can't hold off the Committee forever. . . . Listen to me, Danny, you must get up, get dressed—"

"Dressed?"

"So that we can leave—the minute the family's asleep."

"I just undressed."

"You can, of course, stay the night," Hector needled Danny, "stay with the Committee, if you prefer."

"No need for threats," Emilia rejoined. "He understands, knows he's better off with us—don't you, Danny? . . . Of course. . . . Please trust us then and do as I say—will you? . . . Good! . . . First, I want you to come away from the wall . . . just relax your shoulders . . . let your shoulder blades release the wall. . . . That's it."

Danny hesitated. "I'll need to take some things along."

"Only yourself."

"Clothes, I mean."

"Whatever you wear will be enough. . . . Now, lean forward . . . that's right: move toward me."

"I'll have to pack."

"Just slide yourself across the mattress . . . that's the way."

"Handkerchiefs: six or seven . . . underwear, seven sets: a change for every day . . . and socks: three pairs of white, three brown—unless I wear my black shoes—"

"Don't stop moving, Danny, keep coming toward me."

"Six or seven shirts: four white, two blue, the black-and-red plaid—"

"A little more—"

"And ties—how many ties? . . . the black knit, blue-and-white stripe—"

"That's good, Danny. . . . Now lower your legs over the sides."

"And slacks: the gabardine, a pair of jeans—"

"Don't hold back—"

"And sweaters: the sleeveless and the turtleneck . . . the shetland—should I take the cardigan?"

"Now bend your knees—we have to hurry!"

"Money!"

"We have enough. . . . Let your left foot touch the floor."

"Tickets!"

"*We'll* attend to that."

"Toilet things!"

"Now the right foot."

"Medication!"

"You won't need it any more. . . . Just feel the floor under your feet."

"My books!"

"Take hold of the edge of the bed . . . that's right."

"The Dickinson!"

"Let your hands support your weight."

"Rilke!"

"Lean forward, Danny."

"Yeats!"

"And now—"

"My notebooks!"

"—I want you to stand up."

"Stand up?" Danny recoiled.

"Yes-yes, we must get out of here! Quickly! Don't be afraid. Trust me, please, it's our only chance!"

"To escape the Committee?"

"Not just the Committee—the Eternal Waste."

"Let's hurry then!"

"Yes-yes! . . . That's it . . . that's right: raise your body . . . more . . . a little more . . . there! Good boy! . . . Now, let's go over to the closet— No-no, not the desk."

"I have to leave a note."

"After you've dressed."

"There won't be time."

"There will, if you hurry."

"Maman—"

"Shh! they'll hear you in the living room. . . . Come along."

"I must be quiet."

"Yes. . . . Here we are, here's the closet. You get dressed; I'll wait over there with the others. Just call me when you're— What is it, Danny? What's stopping you?"

"That smell."

"You find it so unpleasant?"

"Not your perfume."

"I know which smell you mean."

95.

"Emilia?"

"Yes."

"Why didn't you let Vittorio speak?"

"Trust us, please."

"What did Vittorio—"

"You must—"

"—start to say?"

"—trust us!"

"Where are you *really* taking me?" Danny asked in dread.

"Into the forest" —the moment Vittorio opened his mouth, there was an intensification of the musk-and-manure smell, as if it were on his breath— "the primeval forest where herds of red deer roam among the giant oaks. We'll form a herd ourselves, the five of us, and dance barefoot around the sacred trees, worshiping their permanence and power. . . . At first we'll will our movements: toss our heads forward and back, jerk them this way and that, swing our arms, fling them wide, rear our thighs, stamp our feet, spin ourselves around in circles—round and round without restraint: spinning, whirling, wildly, wantonly, endlessly whirling till the willing stops and we, still whirling, no longer whirl ourselves but, being whirled, begin to lose ourselves among the sacred oaks, animated by their immobility, empowered by their permanence—to *uproot* them!"

"Enough!" Emilia tried to silence him.

"Carried then," Vittorio ignored the interruption, "crashing through the forest, crushing underfoot the ferns, rushing headlong toward the far-off bellows of the rutting bucks, bellowing so loud we put the birds to flight—in flight ourselves, flying faster than the finch, swifter than the faun, sweeping down the rocky slopes, bounding over brooks and gullies, leaping ridges, racing through the underbrush—yai! yai! yai!—in hot pursuit of the fleeing faun, our prey, brought down at last—yah-heee!—down in terror by the five of us, falling on it tooth and nail, tearing it limb from limb, ripping out its organs, guts: eaten raw—blood dripping from our hands, dribbling from our jaws, partaking of the sacrament, sharing it, the six of us . . . at one with the flesh . . . at one with the blood . . . at one with the Divine. . . ."

"Stop! not another move! I, Robespierre, command it!"

Danny felt his muscles lock, trapping him in the closet doorway.

"So," Robespierre continued, "caught in the act again, I see— red-handed—trying to make a getaway. Sneak! Turn my back, and what do you do? Quick! into the forest . . . at one with the Divine— The Divine!" he sneered, "with *them?* And you, you fool, listen, swallow it whole, hook, line, and sinker. Imbecile! You haven't the brains you were born with. Encounter the Divine with them, this pack of Enragés? Encounter the Divine by running wild—trampling ferns, uprooting trees, tearing apart the hart and drinking its blood, eating it raw? Fah! Haven't you had enough of that? Haven't you learned your lesson yet? . . . Apparently not; apparently you need to be taught it again—once and for all!"

"Don't listen to him, Danny," Emilia entreated, "there's still time."

"Wrong!" Robespierre contradicted her. "Time's run out, there's no more time."

"We still can go—"

"No more space!"

"Release your arms," she pleaded with Danny.

"For what?" Robespierre's question was rhetorical. "To uproot trees?"

"Unclench your fists!"

"To tear apart the hart?"

"Unlock your jaw!"

"To drink its blood—eat it raw?"

"Yai! yai! yai!"

"Silence! I've heard enough!"

"Raw!"

"Enough! Commence the ceremony!" Robespierre's command resounded through the vast granite hall. "Summon the priests."

From the distance came the sound of many feet moving in unison a step at a time, shuffling slowly but persistently over the granite slabs—first the bare soles of the right feet brushing the stone with a swish, being brought down with a thud, pausing in silence; then the left feet: swish . . . thud . . . pause—the procession of priests in perfect step, swaying as one from side to side, advancing as one down the huge unlit colonnaded hall: swish . . . thud . . . pause . . . swish . . . thud . . . pause—then, suddenly, the cadence of their footsteps drowned out by their voices, their voices taking on the tempo of their feet, the priests still coming on but chanting now, chanting in chorus. "Only in silence, the silence of the tomb; only in stillness, the stillness of stone; only in stiffness, the stiffness of board; only in the mummy case, encased within the coffin, can there be deliverance—deliverance from struggle, deliverance from strife, deliverance from suffering the Eternal Waste." . . . Swish . . . thud . . . pause . . . swish . . . thud . . . pause. . . .

"Every flicker of the eyelash brings tears to another's eyes; every breath you draw makes another gasp for air; the lifting of the little finger stabs the mother to the heart! O, deliver It! deliver It from moving, deliver It from feeling, deliver It from loving the Eternal Waste." . . . Swish . . . thud . . . pause . . . swish . . . thud . . . pause. . . .

"Holy, holy, holy, the Vital Force conserved; holy, holy, holy, the worshiped Vital Force: given in trust, in sacred trust, to man on earth to be conserved. Holy, holy, holy, the unspent Vital Force, conserved in life, restored in death, returned intact to the Vital Source, the Sacred Reservoir; holy of holies, the All-holy Himself."

The instant the prayer ended, Robespierre resumed command. "Technicians, are you ready?"

"We are."

"Carpenters, have you Its measurements?"

"We have."

"Then get to work! Cut the planks, carve the wood, save the sawdust for the packing."

The order given, saws began at once to drone, mallets to tap, chisels to gouge, planes to whish, files to rasp, sawdust to settle audibly like grains of sand.

"Artists, mix your paints. Don't waste the gold— It isn't worth it! Stick to sepia and black—a touch of blue, if you like, for the eyes."

A large tin can rattled hollowly as the turpentine was poured with splashes into several mixing bowls.

"Tailors, have you spread the sheets?"

"We have."

"Are the pads made up, bandages unrolled?"

"They are."

"Then cut the cloth—keep it uniform, smear the undersides well."

Instead of using scissors, the tailors rent the cloth by hand, producing a sharp ripping sound, strip after strip.

"Surgeons, once you've removed the vital organs, eviscerate It totally, you understand?"

"We do."

"Lay out the instruments."

One by one the scalpel, forceps, trocar, needle holder, needles, nippers, clips clinked against a slab of stone—an improvised, unsanitary instrument table.

"Watch out there, morticians! don't spill the tannic acid. Set it down carefully."

A great wooden vat came to rest with a thump.

"Are the Canopic jars in order?"

"They are."

"Air-tight? leak-proof?"

"Absolutely."

"Prepare the sodium carbonate."

Judging by the prolonged pouring sound, the Na_2CO_3 was being mixed not in beakers but in tubs to create several gallons.

"Faster there!" Robespierre supervised. "Step it up!"

Now that everyone had received his orders, there was a terrible racket as the various technicians pursued their tasks simultaneously—hammering, sawing, chiseling, planing, ripping cloth, mixing soda, mixing paint, laying out the surgical instruments, taking up and putting down all sorts of vessels and containers. To add to the din was the chorus of priests, chanting over and over at regular intervals, "Deliver It from moving, deliver It from feeling, deliver It from loving the Eternal Waste."

"Don't listen to them!" Emilia suddenly whispered in Danny's ear.

"Don't listen!" echoed Vittorio, Laurent, and Hector.

"Don't you see what they're up to?" Emilia went on, still in a whisper. "Listen to *us*—quickly now, before it's too late—try to feel—anything!—feel your heartbeat, feel your breathing—"

"Deliver It from breathing . . . ."

"Feel the flow of your blood—"

"Deliver It from feeling—"

"Feel your flesh—"

"Deliver It from loving—"

"Hug yourself! Feel yourself! Feel your strength!"

"—the Eternal Waste."

"Feel your rage!" the Enragés exhorted him.

"It's felt enough!" Robespierre silenced them, "enough sorrow, enough suffering for one life—all that's left is terror, pain—"

"Untrue!" Emilia exclaimed.

"The fangs and claws—"

"Listen, Danny, listen: you've got to feel, got to move—"

"Stay where you are!" Robespierre commanded.

"It's the only way!" Emilia said.

"She's lying!"

"The only way to get out alive!"

"*Dead*, she means—they're trying to trick you."

"Ignore him, Danny!"

"Trying to steal your Vital Force!"

"Just listen to me," Emilia whispered. "Concentrate on what I'm saying, what I'm *doing* . . . . Don't you hear it? . . . Listen carefully . . . listen," she murmured. Once again there was a rustle of taffeta, click of beads, clink of bracelets, a delicate metallic tinkling. "I'm dancing, Danny, moving my shoulders, moving my hips—all of us are—swaying our bodies, swinging our arms—"

"Stamping their hooves!" Robespierre jeered. "Priests!" he called out with a snap of the fingers.

"—So much pleasure, play . . . . Try it, Danny, try to move. Release your arms, unclench your fists—"

"Only in stillness," the priests resumed chanting, "the stillness of stone . . . ."

"Don't resist—no one's going to hurt you, Danny—let yourself go: start with your fingers, start with your toes—"

"Only in stiffness, the stiffness of board . . . ."

"Come on, Danny, don't hold back—"

"Only in the mummy case, encased within the coffin . . . ."

"Come to me, Danny, come from your keep—"

"Interred within the pyramid . . . ."

"Unlock yourself, unlock your heart—"

"Can there be deliverance . . . ."

"Come out of there now—"

"Deliverance from loving—"

"Out of yourself, into the open—"

"—the Eternal Waste."

"Into my arms!"

"Whore!" Robespierre bellowed. "There you have it! you see for yourself what she's after—the filthy whore!—trying to sap your Vital Force. They'll stop at nothing—suck you dry!"

"Come to the orchards, come to the ocean."

"Go if you dare!"

"Come to the caverns—"

"The risk is yours!"

"Come to the forest—"

"Remember their fangs!"

"Come, move your pelvis."

"Remember their claws!"

"Come, move your buttocks."

"Don't move a muscle!"

"Come, move your thighs."

"Stay as you are!"

"Raise your arms!"

"Stand perfectly still!"

"Open your eyes!"

"On pain of death!"

"To save your *life!*"

"Only the Supreme One can save It now!"

"Only we, the Enragés, can!"

"The Conservationists!"

"Come, stamp your feet!"

"Conserve yourself!"

"Beat your fists!"

"Conserve your Vital Force!"

"*Use it*, Danny!"

"Use it, and you're lost!"

"You're lost unless you use it!"

"Lost to the Eternal Waste!"

"O deliver It!" the priests, as one, cried out. "Deliver It from moving, deliver It from feeling, deliver It from loving the Eternal Waste."

"Quick now!" Robespierre declared. "No more talk. Let's get going! Skip the incision—there isn't time! Leave the guts, organs—everything! Just use the syringe—inject the fluid into Its anus—two three quarts—then plug it up!"

"Holy, holy, holy, the Vital Force conserved." . . .Swish. . . thud. . . pause. . . swish. . . thud. . . pause . . . .

"*Aquinapay medinore*," the high priest prayed, "*aquinapay medinore.*"

"Forget the headdress!" Robespierre rushed on. "Forget the mask! Just bring the sawdust—hurry—bring the sheets, the strips of cloth!"

"Holy, holy, holy, the Vital Force conserved." . . .Swish. . . thud. . . pause. . . swish. . . thud. . . pause . . . .

"They're coming now, Danny," Emilia warned, "coming with their instruments, their ice-cold tongs, to wrap you up, bind you hand and foot forever, bind you inch by inch with bands of linen tougher than rawhide, tougher than any restraining jacket—a whole restraining *suit* from which you'll never escape, never break loose—"

"*Aquinapay medinore.*" . . .Swish. . . thud. . . pause. . . swish. . . thud. . . pause . . . .

"They're coming, Danny, coming with their sacks of sawdust, their moldy sheets, to lay you out, wind you up forever: encased within the mummy case, entombed within the coffin, interred

101.

within the pyramid—those giant granite slabs: airless, motionless, mute forever: a living corpse, confined forever: untouchable, unchangeable, invincible forever: immortal in your death."

"*Aquinapay medinore.*" . . .Swish. . . thud. . . pause. . . swish. . . thud. . . pause . . . .

"Don't you understand?" Emilia cried out. "They're coming to embalm you!"

"And *they*?" Robespierre shouted back. "They'll have you drinking blood!"

"Embalm you alive!"

"The blood of your brothers!"

"Move, Danny, move!"

"The blood of your parents!"

"Touch the doorknob!"

"Your father's blood!"

"Touch the wall!"

"Do you *dare*?"

"Turn on the light!"

"The blood of Maman!"

"Run, Danny, run!"

"Remember the forest!"

"Run for your life!"

"Death!"

"Run!"

"Run, and they'll make you jump!"

"Yes, Danny, yes—"

"You hear that, fool?"

"—Run and jump and leap—"

"—Hear what they're saying?"

"You've *got* to, Danny!"

"They're going to make you jump!"

"You have no choice!"

"Jump to your *death*."

"For your life!"

"The *dying* life!"

"The living death!"

"*Aquinapay medinore.*" . . .Swish. . . thud. . . pause. . . swish. . . thud. . . pause . . . .

They're here, all around you
holy, holy, holy
closing in
the Vital Force conserved
get away

holy, holy, holy
away
the worshiped Vital Force
for the sake of your life
morticians
the sake of yourself
take up the corpse
get away
seize It, I say
fight, fight, fight them off
give up
fight
be still
for life
death
kick flail
still
bite hit
perfectly still
rip claw
locked
punch pound
hidden
hammer gouge
safe
screw scream
be still
murder
still
murder
still
bloody
blood
murder
Maman
kill
Papa
kill
Claude
kill
still
kill
still

life
death
rage
no
wrench
no
uproot
no
stampede
no
yes
no
yai
no
yai
wait
yai
stay
yah-heee
stop
run
after It
run
stop It
run
block It
run
catch It
run
cut It down
run run
there It goes
run
that way
run
stop It
faster run
stop
faster than the finch
stop
swifter than the faun
stop
sweeping down the slopes

head It off
bounding brooks
hunt It
leaping ridges
snare It
run
bag It
run
bring It down
run run
not that door
run
that door parents
run run
not that door
run
that door brothers
run run
cornered
forest run
trapped
trees
trapped
leap
trapped
jump
death
life
stop
carried
no
crashing
no
crushing
no
rushing
no
head on
no
window
no
flight
no

sill
no
stand
no
jump
no
jump
no
jump jump jump
"Yah-heee!" Danny cried out, doing as he was told.

LIFEBLOOD

I

At Apollo's command a council of the gods had been convened to deal with the problem of the hermaphrodite Agdistis. Zeus stayed away—not only because the subject had already been discussed too much, but also to avoid quarreling with Hera—and many of the other gods followed suit. The crippled master-craftsman Hephaestus preferred his work to the permanent indifference of his wife Aphrodite. Demeter and Persephone were detained in the underworld. Hermes was up to his usual tricks. A foul mood kept Poseidon at sea; and the ever-distant Artemis remained predictably aloof. Only Hera, Aphrodite, Athena, and Dionysus answered Apollo's summons.

From his opening remarks it was evident that Apollo had lost patience with Agdistis and was determined to deal with the monster once and for all. Yet nothing about the god's demeanor gave the slightest hint of anger. His breathing was regular, his voice controlled. He made no impatient gestures—never reached for his quiver or bow—showed no signs of flushing or perspiring. And though he stood, as was his custom throughout a council, striding back and forth past the other seated gods, every golden hair and ringlet on Apollo's head remained in place. Even his white linen mantle never slipped or billowed as he strode; its folds, as if starched, scarcely stirred. Moving, the god seemed motionless; near at hand, far away.

"It's gone too far," Apollo summed up. "The creature holds nothing on earth or in heaven mightier than Itself . . . knows no limits, no constraint. It must be stopped—this sacrilege!"

"Sacrilege?" Dionysus echoed with irony, his breath wafting the saffron veil that covered his face and beard. Unlike Apollo, Dionysus was clothed from head to foot—his body sheathed in an ankle-length Eastern robe over which was cast a heavy plum-colored stole, his head enveloped in a colorful kerchief, so stuffed with hair that it sagged at the nape like an udder. Only his lively chestnut eyes and long black lashes, white hands and bare feet, visible under all the trappings, attested to the presence of the god.

"Yes, sacrilege," Apollo reasserted, whereupon he started to enumerate the hermaphrodite's transgressions.

"That's the least of it!" Hera interrupted. She was seated at the head of the council on one of two identical gold thrones, her large sandaled feet resting on a gold footstool. Indeed, everything about the goddess was gold: her diadem, beads, bracelets, rings, fibulae—even her full breasts, under the honey-colored overfold of her peplos, resembled two gold orbs. At her slightest movement, Hera's body glittered in the morning sunshine, her great cow eyes gleamed with golden lights. Her voice alone was not golden, not at least in council when, as now, she often sounded harsh and strident. "Come to the point, Apollo—lechery, rape! . . . leaving Its loathsome progeny all over the countryside."

"And which of us is guiltless of that?" Aphrodite remarked, "except, of course, Athena." Ironic though her tone was at first, it became straightforward in reference to the virgin goddess about whom she was simply stating a fact. Like the absent Artemis, Athena was invulnerable to the goddess of love; but whereas Aphrodite feuded constantly with Artemis, she managed to tolerate Athena. Seated now next to each other on neighboring thrones the two goddesses created a striking contrast.

Unhampered by the rigid confines of the marble throne, Aphrodite looked like a lounging cat: her right elbow resting on the back of the throne, right leg forward, left curled under her rump, body angled in opposite directions—the upper half toward Hera at the head of the council, the lower toward Dionysus at its foot—a position that accentuated her exceptional beauty. So too did her diaphanous chiton which was open down the right side and girdled at the waist, leaving exposed her prominent hip, voluptuous buttock, thigh, and calf. Yet, what made her so alluring was not her body, not her nudity, not the fragrance of the oil with which she was anointed, nor the wreath of fresh roses crowning her head—what made Aphrodite irresistible was her eyes. Intensely alive, provocative yet soothing, intimate and warm, her eyes were like the flames of a fire in a hearth—once you looked into them you couldn't look away. Like flames, they took possession of you, held you fast, did away with reason, distance—the distance that objectifies and separates—did away with everything but reverie and desire, inducing you to participate again in some forgotten mystery whose rites, though long since lost to consciousness, your senses still acknowledged. Her eyes transmitted instantly both the need for and promise of perfect union, total fusion, absolute oblivion. They seemed to challenge you, in turn, to go up in flames, made you yearn to be ignited, consumed, delivered from yourself, from all restraints. Enthralled by her gaze, you were ready—whatever the consequences—to betray your family and friends, principles and honor, as well as all the other gods. Whether you ended up a dancing flame or heap of ashes was immaterial—all that mattered was the present moment, the living contact between your eyes and Aphrodite's.

In contrast to Aphrodite, Athena was leaning forward, poised on the edge of her throne, as if she were about to spring up and sprint off into battle. Though not in complete battle array, she was holding a spear and wearing a Corinthian helmet. The helmet, however, was not in place—pulled down over her head—but pushed far back, well above the hairline, so that its bronze profile converged with the part in Athena's hair just at the center of her frontal bone toward which the tip of the nosepiece pointed as if to call attention to her brain. The eyeholes had much the same effect. Situated over the crown of the skull, they gave the impression that her cerebrum had eyes of its own. As a result, the rest of her body, from the neck down, seemed merely secondary, more like a base than a torso for the helmeted head.

Though always serious and thoughtful, she appeared just now to be a trifle restless too, if not downright bored, impatient as ever with these councils—with talk in general—and eager to be on her way. The fact was that Athena much preferred the company of mortals to that of her fellow gods. Still, she felt obliged, since Aphrodite had brought her into the discussion, to state her opinion. "Unlike you, Apollo, I find myself impressed."

"By what?"

"The creature's courage."

"Courage, Athena?" Keeping his distance, Apollo came to a standstill. "Can there be courage where there is no fear?"

"What troubles me," Athena ignored the question, "is Its mindlessness."

"Oooooo. . . ." This prolonged singsong note of dissent came from Dionysus, causing his veil to flutter again. "It uses Its wits."

"Like courage without fear," Apollo retorted, "wits without reason amount to nothing—nothing but brute force . . . the nonhuman: a paradox, to say the least, in man."

"But since It's not a man. . . ." Dionysus reminded Apollo.

Athena thumped the floor with the shaft of her spear. "Precisely! that's precisely why Agdistis is of no *real* interest."

Swift as swallows, Dionysus' eyes darted over the assemblage in search of a supporter. "Surely you, Aphrodite, don't agree?"

Before answering, the goddess began to move slowly, smoothly like a serpent, coiling and uncoiling, expanding and contracting, slithering forward on the seat of the throne, sliding her left foot up and down the length of her right calf, gliding her hands over her breasts, over her belly and haunches, licking her lips avidly as her expression grew ever more intense, malevolent, until she came to rest hunched on the base of her spine, her pelvis arched, thighs spread, held wide by her hands, concentrating all her power in her loins from which the very sound of her voice seemed suddenly to issue. "Of no real interest? On the contrary, I'm fascinated," she hissed, "enough to kill—kill It! I say, for Its slight to me, Its utter indifference, utter contempt for intimacy."

"Intimacy!" Hera scoffed. "What about matrimony?"

Dionysus chortled. "With whom would you suggest It enter into matrimony—Itself?"

There was a blaze of gold as Hera's arms slashed the air. "Then do away with It! Let's rid the earth forever of this pestilence."

Apollo, seeing his chance to settle the matter, strode into the center of the council. "Are we agreed?"

"Yes! yes! yes!" the goddesses concurred.

Only Dionysus took exception. "Just a minute, please. Aren't you forgetting something—all of you?"

Hera narrowed her eyes. "Kinship?" she guessed, "your kinship with Agdistis—is that what you have in mind? That you were both brought into the world by Cybele? That you are, in fact, blood brothers?"

"Or *sisters*, as the case may be." Dionysus enjoyed his own joke.

Apollo cut through the laughter: "What difference does that make?"

As abruptly as the laughter had started, it stopped. Dionysus became motionless, grave. "Why, all the difference in the world. It would be like trying to get rid of *me*, Apollo. Just how would you go about it? Even if you and Artemis were to shoot your deadly arrows simultaneously—you, Apollo, aiming at the male; your sister at the female—you could not do away with It. Agdistis is immortal."

Apollo stood his ground. "Agdistis is a menace," he stated irrefutably. "There are many ways of dealing with a menace . . . other than by destroying it."

"Such as?"

The question released a flood of proposals— Let's get Hephaestus to fashion a set of unbreakable chains. Hurl It into the sea! Exile It to the wolf-country. Pack It off to the Lestrigonians. Cast It down to Hecate.—a flood that might have gone on indefinitely, had not Hera brought it to a stop. "Wait! I know!" she exclaimed, grasping the arms of her throne. "Emasculate the monster."

The suggestion met with varying responses. Apollo was quick to approve. Athena, after a moment's thought, pronounced the plan sensible. Aphrodite, on the other hand, hesitated, torn between a vindictive desire to punish Agdistis and grave misgivings about the means. To agree to unsex the creature would, in effect, be like committing self-mutilation, turning the blade of the knife against herself. Only Hera could have hit upon the idea; it expressed so perfectly Hera's point of view—everything she stood for, stood against—would come as such a victory not only over Agdistis, but also over Aphrodite herself. After all, it was one thing to rid the earth of the creature's offspring, and quite another to eliminate Its desire. No! the idea was untenable, threatened Aphrodite's whole domain. "Cut off Its hands, Its feet," she declared, "put out Its eyes—anything but *that*."

"But you yourself," Hera reminded her, "said kill the creature."

"Kill, not castrate!"

Apollo intervened. "Try not to dwell on the *idea*, the abstraction, Aphrodite. Consider, instead, Its offense to you. When, if ever, has Agdistis shown you the least respect—not to mention reverence? It behaves as if you didn't exist . . . uses Its member brutally, destructively, to flaunt Its strength—never to celebrate Aphrodite. What does It know about your wonders? Has It ever heard of yearning: the tug of the heart more powerful than gravity, the sea's attachment to the moon? Ever experienced ardor: the melting of the bones, the merging of the marrow? Ever dreamed of yielding, yielding to another, following another to the ends of the earth? How could It, being double-natured?"

"That's the crucial point" —Athena turned to Aphrodite— "Its double-nature. Just now the creature's self-sufficient, self-contained. It has no need for anything—not only you, but all of us—anything other than Itself."

"Its all-important, overriding self," Apollo added. "That's why I favor Hera's plan. Perhaps with gelding, that will change."

Aphrodite sighed, looked sad, regretful for a moment, before she said with vengeance, "Do it then!"

From the general stir in the chamber it was evident that a major hurdle had been overcome. Hera beamed. Athena relaxed her grip on the spear. Apollo turned on his heels and strode toward the foot of the council. When he came abreast of Dionysus, he didn't stop or slow his pace, but went right by without so much as glancing in the god's direction. Not until he was forty feet away did he turn back and speak. "That leaves only one of us opposed."

As everyone's attention shifted now to Dionysus, the gods were amazed to discover him napping: eyelids closed, body motionless, blanketed like a babe under the heavy stole. Just as Hera was preparing to rouse him harshly, she noticed something odd about the saffron veil. The others saw it too: a grayish circular stain over the mouth as if Dionysus were drooling in his sleep. In the next second, however, it became apparent that he was not asleep. Suddenly the ashen blot turned rose-red before their eyes. Fascinated, they watched as Dionysus stuck his tongue out bit by bit till the rosy tip, visible through the moistened silk, projected the veil six or seven inches from the face; whereupon, the covered tongue wavered back and forth like a feeler exploring the surrounding space, before it gradually withdrew, taking with it through the parted lips the surplus cloth, creating as it disappeared into the mouth an austere slit which proceeded to open and close regularly, monotonously as if Dionysus were munching the veil or chanting a spell— a wordless silent spell. Then out it came again, the rosy tip protruding slowly, wavering, withdrawing; the lipless slit reciting the inaudible spell.

When the sequence had been repeated several times, Apollo lost patience. "Stop playing games, Dionysus. We aren't here to watch you perform. Open your eyes! Come out of yourself, your *feelings*—your feelings are of no interest to anyone but you. Say what's on your mind, what you think, what you *know*. If you have a better plan than Hera's, state it! If you're opposed, let's hear your argument."

Though he ignored Apollo's request to open his eyes, Dionysus responded audibly, coherently. "My argument? *Me*, Apollo, argue? No, surely not. You're mixing us up, aren't you? speaking of yourself, not me—not *mine* the precepts, prohibitions, the certain knowledge of anything. . . . Say what I 'know'? I know nothing. I deal in fluids: phlegm and sap and blood, not solids . . . forms . . . eternal forms—except to sink my teeth into. Hee-hee! My tongue comes forth of its own accord, tempted toward sensations: tastes and textures: slimy tidbits, meaty morsels. My tongue is free, flexible like me, flowing with saliva, not ideas—immutable ideas—like yours. Opposed to alteration? Why would I be . . . opposed to anything so primary, so promising, so fraught with possibilities? No, indeed. I'm in accord. Let's do it! By all means, sever them! cut them off! The sooner the better. Let's devour them like figs, scatter them like marbles, juggle them like balls."

"At last!" Hera exclaimed with satisfaction, and the others joined in, expressing their contentment too. Apollo alone remained silent.

Sensing this, Dionysus raised his eyelids. Judging by the crow's-feet and the twinkle in his eyes, it was evident that he was smiling broadly behind the saffron veil. "What makes you hesitate, Apollo?"

"Your accord . . . it comes too easily."

"Oooo," Dionysus cooed, "you make me sound so difficult. Whatever for? After all, this isn't the first time we've been in accord . . . profound accord. Don't tell me you've forgotten?"

"Apparently."

"Forgotten the night you trusted me—"

"Let's not pretend, Dionysus. I've never trusted you—never could—it's not in my nature."

"Oh, but you're mistaken. You trusted me once, long, long ago when you were just a tot—perhaps that's why you've forgotten."

Apollo eyed him coolly, keeping his distance. "Forgotten what?"

"When you slew the Python."

Though Apollo didn't move, the distance between him and Dionysus seemed suddenly to increase, as if Apollo's eyes, like the legs of mortals, were empowered to take a few steps back in order to gain a desired perspective. "How could I forget," he said dispassionately, "forget an act for which I had to atone nine years? . . . And how could you remember—remember something which occurred before your birth?"

In contrast to Apollo's eyes which had become an overall field of flawless azure, undemarcated by pupils, irises, or whites, Dionysus' pupils darkened, dilated radically till the whites were all but eclipsed with rage. "Before my birth! I tell you I was *there*, Apollo, beside you . . . with you . . . *in* you. You couldn't have done it without me."

"Nonsense, Dionysus. I did it with this bow" —Apollo signified the weapon, suspended from his shoulder— "my father Zeus' gift to me. It was my destiny—to deliver the world from the Python— the reason I was born."

"Why, then, did you atone for it?"

"Because I was polluted."

"Polluted by your destiny?"

"Only afterward, years later, in the light of day, did I understand it to have been my destiny."

After a calculated pause, Dionysus raised an eyebrow. "Frankly, Apollo, I don't see how your tale disproves my statement: that I was there beside you."

"Perhaps it doesn't; perhaps you were . . . with me, *in* me, as you say, on that night, much as I was in the Python—inside the serpent itself, I mean, in its belly, not just its cave. But once outside, out of that miasma, once I understood the lesson of the bow— what it means to get the proper distance, take the proper stance, aim the arrow accurately, judge the wind, know the cast . . . and also," Apollo added in a more exalted tone, "how, eventually, the bow can be transformed at will into a lyre, an instrument not of death but song, the selfsame wood and string producing lyrics of enlightenment when handled understandingly, with skill—once I had recovered, cleansed and purified myself, removed the scales from my eyes; once I saw with clarity the natural world: the mountain peaks, pines, olive groves, eagles wheeling down below; once, in short, I recognized my relation to the sun, you and I parted ways, Dionysus."

"Yet here we are, still together."

"No," Apollo stated flatly. "I stand here now bathed in light— pellucid light unmarred by motes—stand here gazing down this double row of fluted columns, blazing white against a deep blue sky. At the other end I see a vista—also blue, gentian blue— endless, unobstructed space: the universe, of which I know myself to be a part, an intrinsic part, protracting me beyond myself: forward, outward into everlasting light." Breaking his gaze, Apollo turned back to the assemblage. "Even at this distance I can see distinctly the sixteen beads of Hera's necklace, the indignation in her eyes; in Aphrodite's cheek I see a dimple of disdain for all this talk of distance; and from Athena's posture I discern her waning patience. Only *you*, Dionysus"—Apollo strode forward now to confront his antagonist, though still at a distance— "I cannot see."

"Maybe you're suffering from sunblindness, Apollo."

"No, indeed, Dionysus. I see you seated over there in the shade—your formless bulk all bundled up behind that veil. I see enough, quite enough, to see precisely what it is I cannot see—and never have—your *face*."

"You can always gaze into my eyes," Dionysus suggested coyly.

"When, that is, they're open. But even then, they're much too shifty, changeable . . . like the moon on a cloudy night—one catches only glimpses."

"Perhaps that's all there ever is or can be—glimpses." As if to conceal himself further, Dionysus drew the stole closer to his body. "After all, it wasn't I who started this, questioned our accord."

"That's correct!" Athena sprung to her feet. "What counts is the accord. Look here, Apollo, this is the seventh council you've convened to deal with Agdistis. I myself have attended five—all of them failures, an utter waste of time . . . until today. Today, at last, we've accomplished something. We're in agreement, all of us, not only to punish Agdistis, but on the nature of the punishment. In the name of Zeus let's settle it now, once and for all!"

"Thank you, my dear," Dionysus expressed his appreciation to Athena, before turning back to Apollo. "And just who, if I may ask, have you in mind?"

"For what?" Apollo said with suspicion.

"To perform the delicate operation—Hera herself?"

"Don't be disgusting, Testiculous!" Hera rejoined.

"Who then?" Dionysus pursued the point. "You, Apollo, slayer of the Python?"

Ignoring the remark Apollo walked away and addressed himself to the goddesses. "Hermes, of course. We'll summon Hermes at once."

"No-no," Dionysus called after him. "No need for Hermes." The crow's-feet reappeared as his eyes brightened and enlarged in a leer. "*I'll* do the job myself."

Apollo stopped in his tracks, his back to Dionysus. "*You?*"

"Don't sound so incredulous, Apollo. What could be more natural than for me to do the job? . . . with a slight assist, of course," Dionysus added matter-of-factly, "from my guardian Silenus."

Deep in thought Apollo paced the marble floor in silence, his brows knit, eyes keen, lips slightly parted as if he were about to speak.

After what seemed an interminable pause, Hera finally broke the silence. "What is it, Apollo? What are you waiting for?"

"He's up to something," Apollo murmured, "some trick, some trap."

" 'Some trick, some trap,' " Dionysus mimicked. "First, when I

115.

sanctioned Hera's plan—'some trick, some trap.' And now again, when I volunteer my services—'some trick, some trap.' Tricks and traps" —there was an abrupt transition now from mimicry to acrimony— "are not my stock in trade. Hermes is the trickster, not I."

"Still engrossed in his own thoughts," Apollo said to himself, though loud enough to be heard by all. "He's being too cooperative. I must be overlooking something, some consequence I can't foresee."

"*You*, Apollo," Dionysus jeered, "you, the all-knowing, all-seeing, overlook some consequence? Impossible! . . . I will admit," he conceded pseudophilosophically in an obvious attempt to nettle Apollo, "castration isn't death—something neat and final, altogether reliable like death. But then, what is? Short of death, there's always the possibility of some happenstance. That's the risk you run."

"With *you*."

"With anyone!" Dionysus declared, his anger mounting. "That's what really troubles you, isn't it? what you mistrust—not me, but *anything* short of death. It's not for nothing you're called 'the death-dealer.' "

"And you," Apollo retorted coldly, keeping his back to Dionysus, " 'the annuller.' "

"Listen, death-dealer, it wasn't I who convened this council. If it were up to me, I'd leave Agdistis alone, let It stay the way It is. You're the one who insists on punishing the creature."

"It *must* be punished!"

"Then what difference does it make," Hera interceded, "who does the dirty work?"

"Exactly!" Athena agreed.

Now, for the first time since Apollo had walked away, he turned and trained his ice-blue unapproachable eyes on Dionysus. "I don't want *his* participation."

"Want it or not," Dionysus thundered, "I'll be there, I'll participate. I participate in all mutations. Wherever blood or sap or semen flows, expect to find me too."

Once again Athena thumped the floor with the shaft of her spear in an effort to settle the dispute. "Fair enough. If Dionysus wants to do the job, let him, I say." She turned to her fellow goddesses. "Are you agreed?"

"Agreed," Hera and Aphrodite said in unison.

"And you, Apollo?" Athena went on.

"I have a premonition," he replied softly, "a premonition of disorder far worse than anything that now prevails."

"Do you or don't you agree?" Athena pressed him.

Despite his evident misgivings, Apollo heaved a sigh of resignation and said, "I do."

Leaping up, Dionysus let out a jubilant cry, so shrill it made both Hera and Aphrodite cover their ears. When the sound died down Dionysus stepped forward toward the center of the floor till he was more or less on a line with Apollo who was standing some fifty feet away, his eyes still fixed on Dionysus. Even at that distance Dionysus found himself affected, held at bay, by the force of Apollo's gaze. "So you want to see my face!" he shouted. "That's easily arranged. All you have to do is come a little closer—close enough to lift the veil."

Apollo didn't blink, didn't stir. "I'll keep my distance, thank you," he responded drily, "and you keep yours."

"As you like. Perhaps you'll see it anyway—at least a glimpse, 'catch a glimpse'—if you're quick."

Hera slapped the arm of her throne with impatience. "I thought you had a job to do, Testiculous!"

"I do, I do," he reassured her. "I'm on my way." Offhand as this remark sounded, what followed was anything but casual. Like a hierophant Dionysus crossed his arms over his chest, lowered his head and bowed in succession, first to Hera, then to Aphrodite and Athena, and finally to Apollo. His head still bowed, he closed his eyes and proclaimed, "Hidden the holy, hidden from sight—the heart alone bears witness." Having finished this brief incantation, he straightened up, walked to the center of the floor, facing Hera, stretched out his arms as far as they would reach, turned the palms upward toward the heavens and closed his eyes again. Standing now perfectly erect and motionless, the purple stole draped over his outstretched arms, the loose-fitting full-length robe hanging from his frame, the saffron veil covering his face, Dionysus looked like a gigantic lifeless effigy of himself. It wasn't long, however, before he commenced to move in place, rotating rather slowly at first, though not without considerable grace, taking small but demonstrative steps, dipping his right leg, then the left, seesawing his outstretched arms, swinging his hips, swaying his head, making distinct quarter-turns until he came full circle and started again, quickening his pace as he repeated the circuit over and over; the purple stole stirring now, fluttering, floating on the wind; the saffron veil clinging to his face; the blood-red skirt ballooning out as Dionysus gained more and more momentum; whereupon, he began to jerk his head back and forth with such abandon his kerchief came undone, releasing a stream of long black hair which, like the

117.

stole, was borne on the air, flying straight out with the force of his whirling body, whirling ever-faster now, faster than the eye could see, so that the many colors of his finery blended into a neutral gray; and the various appendages—hair and skirt and stole— blurred into a solid cone, spinning faster than a top across the floor, spinning so fast he seemed at last to be standing still like a tornado seen from afar, at which point Dionysus shouted out in ecstasy, "Ooo-eee! ooo-eee!" and vanished from sight, leaving behind, like a little memento lying in the center of the marble floor, the saffron veil.

II

Awakened early by a bluejay perched in the willow overhanging Its lair, Agdistis reached surreptitiously for a good-sized stone (one of several kept on hand for ammunition) and hurled it at the squawker, silencing it forever. Pleased with Its marksmanship, the hermaphrodite stretched Its limbs the length of the seven-foot lair, yawned mightily, and then wriggled and rubbed Its back against the bed of earth to rid Itself of a bothersome flea. The hour was still too early, the sky too gray, to predict what sort of day it would be, except chilly, not yet spring, despite the festival preparations It had recently observed in the vicinity of Pessinus. . . . No, today was not the day It had been waiting for: the day It could cast off Its sheepskin cloak.

For a moment the hermaphrodite lay back, looking up into the leafless tree and listening with pleasure to the distant roar coming from the mist-covered pond, the source of the Sangarius River. Soon, however, the sound reminded Agdistis of Its bladder, and It got up to relieve Itself.

At Its full height Agdistis looked both formidable and comical— comical because of Its cloak, stolen from a shepherd a head shorter than Itself. The garment hung down only to Its hips, covering Its back and monumental breasts, while leaving exposed the lower portion of Its buttocks, powerful thighs and legs, as well as Its penis which, at this moment, stood erect. Taking the member firmly in hand, Agdistis restrained Itself just long enough to locate Its prey (the jay lay dead, legs in the air, on the far side of the tree), before It began to urinate. The spray fell wide of the mark. Observing this, Agdistis took two or three steps back, to compensate for the trajectory, till It scored a bull's-eye.

When Its bladder was empty Agdistis hurried over to the sodden bird and got down on all fours to sniff it. The urine made the otherwise bland, musty-smelling breast feathers altogether savory. Agdistis licked them clean. That done, It broke off the bluejay's head and legs, tore out the tail feathers, and popped what remained into Its mouth. Satisfied for the moment, the hermaphrodite returned to the lair. There, It picked up a wooden wind instrument, an aulos—Its only worldly possession other than the cloak—and headed for the pond.

The great gushing splashing roar of the spring drew Agdistis swiftly through the woods and underbrush to the water's edge. The mist had not yet lifted. At close range, however, the mist lost much of its opacity, becoming almost transparent. From where Agdistis stood It could just make out the mass of seething water in the middle of the pond. To get a better view It went around the u-shaped bend in the bank till It reached a little spit on the opposite side—the spot on land closest to the source itself. Now It could distinctly see the bubbles being belched up by the spring, bubbles the size of muskmelons, blistering the surface, bursting into foam, flecking the green with froth, turning into backwash or drifting aimlessly into little eddies, little random rivulets, until the tow became too great, whereupon the water wheeled all at once downstream toward the current—the fresh spring water feeding slowly, smoothly into the current, becoming the on-going current, gathering momentum rapidly, rushing ahead, flowing in streaks, streaming faster than the eye could see out of the pond and into the river, as ever-new bubbles erupted with a roar.

After a moment, Agdistis raised the aulos to Its lips, placed Its fingers on the holes and began to play with passion not a tune— what came out was utterly devoid of melody or rhythm—but a series of ascending minor notes (many of which were held in vibrato for a full half minute), so high-pitched that they could be heard over the roar of the spring. In its effect the piping sounded less like music than a plaintive call, the call of a giant water fowl, expressing at daybreak the mounting strain of some imperative need. And presently, as Agdistis played on, the call was answered—not vocally but visually—by a pair of lovely though albinic hands emerging like a shot from the very heart of the spring. The hands were followed in rapid succession by a sleek pair of arms (also albinic), prominent elbows, a head of pure-white dripping-wet hair molded like a mask to the features it concealed, deep hairless armpit hollows, and upturned breasts whose rose-tinted nipples were the only touch of color in an otherwise alabaster bust.

As quickly as the nymph appeared, she disappeared, leaving Agdistis holding Its saliva-flooded instrument. It knew from past experience better than to pursue the creature who was far too fast, slippery, and clever to catch. Long ago, when Agdistis first took Nana by surprise, disporting herself in the pond, It had charged right in after her, plowing through the shallows, plunging to the bottom, searching the bed, the banks, the bushes, but all in vain. It could find no trace of the nymph. Where had she gone? Downstream? Into the mud? Under a rock? Her disappearance left Agdistis mystified and cross.

In the course of the following months the chase was repeated three or four times, but always with the same result—Agdistis was given the slip—until one summer day It discovered, quite by accident, her means of escape. Agdistis happened to be standing then on the very spot It stood on now, when suddenly It spied Nana swimming right below the surface. Taking a flying dive at her, Agdistis entered the water and opened Its eyes just in time to see the nymph vanish through a barrage of bubbles into the mouth of the spring. So that was where she went! For days thereafter Agdistis tried in countless ways to crash the spring: charging at it head-on or with Its back turned, relying on sheer brawn to overpower it, straight-arming it, worming Its way into it underwater, taking running jumps from the spit and coming down on it feet first, but every effort failed, and It finally gave up in disgust.

After that, several months went by without a sign of Nana. Then, one dusk when Agdistis was feeling especially restless, roaming around the pond and piping to amuse Itself, the nymph suddenly reappeared, only to disappear the moment Agdistis noticed her and stopped piping. This time, however, Agdistis made no attempt to catch the creature. On the contrary, to show Its indifference It raised the aulos to Its lips and went on playing, whereupon Nana appeared and disappeared again. By the time Agdistis began to discern some connection between Its piping and Nana's epiphanies, the light had faded, leaving Agdistis alone in the dark to find Its way back to the lair, where It pondered the magical power of Its aulos till It fell asleep.

The following dawn It could scarcely wait to race down to the pond and resume piping. Sure enough, after a moment Nana appeared and disappeared, just as she had the night before. Fascinated by this new-found power Agdistis summoned her again. Again she appeared and disappeared. The cycle might have been repeated indefinitely had not Nana finally waved her white hands like a flag of truce and made some other signs to assure safe-conduct, after which she emerged from the spring and swam into the shallows where she settled in a prone position a few yards from

Agdistis—close enough to be heard over the roar of the spring, yet far enough away to escape if necessary. Now, for the first and only time, Agdistis got a close look at Nana's face—at the pink pupils of the lidless bulging eyes, the bridgeless nose that was really little more than a pair of nostrils situated above a jutting mouth whose lower jaw receded right into the neck without the slightest suggestion of a chin. Reposing on her folded arms, only the nymph's head and shoulders—skin as white as chalk, hair as fine and straight and colorless as corn silk—showed above the surface. The rest was submerged—a pale amorphous mass swaying to and fro and undulating in the moss-green silty water which the nymph kept stirring up, so that Agdistis couldn't see the outline of her body, couldn't tell whether she was kicking her feet or flicking a caudal fin.

"Stop doing that!" she complained irritably, adding in the same breath, "and don't try to pounce on me either—you won't succeed." Agdistis remained silent, motionless, obviously intrigued but undecided. "I'm Nana, the daughter of Sangarius. My father's very strict with me—you've no idea. Goodness! if he knew I was talking to you now" —Nana broke off and sealed her lips with three knobby nailless fingers, as if the consequence of speaking to Agdistis were either too dreadful to divulge or had only just occurred to her— "The gods be thanked he's still away. Why, if I so much as show myself to a landsman, he immures me for a month and beats me every day— Don't misunderstand, it's not the beatings I object to, it's the confinement—depriving me of circulation— I'm nothing, you see, unless I'm swimming." The prospect made Nana shudder. "Imprisoned for a month simply for showing myself—just once, mind you, not four or five times like last night and six this morning—and to *you*" —she sounded scandalized— "you of all landsmen: the polluter of the waters. Don't think your sacrilege has gone unnoticed. Father's registered more than one complaint against you with the gods. So you can see for yourself why it's so imperative to stop doing that."

"Doing what?"

"Piping."

Agdistis studied the aulos for a moment, ran a finger over the open holes, glanced at Nana who looked now like a suppliant abased before a tyrant in whose hands she saw her fate. A mischievous gleam came into Its eye. Agdistis brought the instrument to Its lips and tilted back Its head, about to play again.

"Don't!" she pleaded.

"Why? What has my piping to do with you? Go away if you don't like it."

Nana shook her head as if in a daze. Her expression was troubled, a trifle pathetic. "I can't," she confessed ruefully. "I hear that sound and find myself moving toward it helplessly, unable to resist. Your piping has some power over me—I don't know what it is, don't begin to understand. You pipe and I appear, despite my better judgment, despite my father's wishes, despite the certain punishment I know to be the consequence, I appear . . . well up like the waters of the spring . . . as if I *were* the waters, rather than their mistress. . . . What you don't seem to understand," she went on, her tone changing suddenly, becoming sharp, "is that I have a job to do down there: to supervise the waters, keep them flowing uncongested, channel them, chase them if need be, out of the earth into this basin. Once here, of course, I'm through with them, Father takes charge—it's his responsibility, as ruler of the river, to conduct the waters safely into Poseidon's hands. . . . Well now, you can see for yourself how little time I have to waste. There's much too much to do down there—arduous, everlasting work. . . . Oh yes," Nana conceded, "once in a great while I'll come up for a breath of air, to stretch my limbs, relax a moment—much as I was doing that morning you molested me—but let's not speak of that. What concerns me now is your piping. It's got to stop!" she scolded shrilly. "You understand? Leave me alone! Stop calling me!"

Agdistis was watching Nana closely, Its eyes intense with concentration. But whether It was listening to what she said or lost in Its own thoughts, hatching some sinister plot, she had no way of knowing, because the hermaphrodite didn't speak.

"Please! Try to understand. Don't you see? You're disrupting my life. Look at me: half out of the water already—next thing you know I'll be on land." Nana paused a moment to consider the possibility, peered past Agdistis at the alien bushes, alien trees, but the prospect made her so uneasy, she averted her gaze. "I don't know what's come over me—to show myself, talk to you like this. My whole life I've been content to be down there, where I belong, in the virgin spring. I've never felt dissatisfied before. Now, suddenly, it doesn't seem enough . . . I have a need for something more—I don't know what—something ter-ter—" she stammered. "There! You see? I can't even speak the word."

Under the guise of being helpful, Agdistis inched forward to the tip of the spit. "Terrible?"

Nana shook her head and heaved a sigh. "Terrestrial," she confided. "Could that be it—the element I'm yearning for? All at once I feel so incomplete, as if I needed to unite with something new—other than water, I mean—something altogether foreign, unfamiliar. I'm not even sure it's earth. Could it be— Oh, what's the use? How can I say, how can I know what I haven't yet experienced? . . . But if it's unexperienced, why is my body so quick to respond? Could it be that what I'm yearning for is something I'm already part of, that's already part of me? It's so perplexing. Could it be—" she broke off again, her brows contracted in uncertainty. "Your aulos! That's the only thing I'm sure of. It's your piping that makes me feel this way: incomplete. But why? Tell me. I don't understand. Who are you, anyway, Polluter of the Waters?"

As if to answer the question, Agdistis bent over in a half-crouching position: legs apart, hands on knees, holding now, in addition to the aulos in Its right hand, some other kind of pipe or flute between Its thighs.

Nana shielded her eyes.

"What's the matter?" Agdistis said solicitously.

"The light," she explained, "I'm not used to it. I better go back now, before it gets too bright."

"Wait!"

"No," she objected, her hand still protecting her eyes. "My father will punish me."

Before she had a chance to move, Agdistis was on top of her, straddling the slippery nymph front to back, encircling her waist with Its powerful legs till It had her in a scissor hold. The impact of Its weight plus the constricting strength of Its legs left Nana winded, unable to scream, unable to squeal, unable almost to breathe. In desperation she squirmed and wriggled pitifully, kicked her legs, reached up behind her back, grabbed Agdistis by the hair and yanked with all her might. In retaliation Agdistis seized her ankles (saw at last her webbed feet) and lifted her bodily out of the water, struggling to Its own feet even as It raised Nana's writhing torso on high, holding her still front to back, but outstretched now and hanging upside-down, her head alone remaining in the vicelike grip of Its thighs. A moment later Nana felt herself being lowered, manipulated clumsily, her buttocks bouncing over Agdistis' breasts, her head being shifted to the insides of Its knees bending gradually to underprop her descending hips, till both of them were virtually squatting: Agdistis in the water, Nana in her captor's lap, but upside-down and being prodded now by a stake—prodded first in the base of the spine, then between the buttocks—Agdistis breathing rapidly, heavily, heaving and grunting with excitement as It drove the painful stake deep into her bowels.

Crying out, Nana arched her back with such a sudden violent jerk, she freed both her buttocks and her head, but Agdistis still had hold of her ankles. She was floundering in the water now, stroking, splashing frantically, trying to kick, to swim away, but getting nowhere, restrained by Agdistis, who was roaring with laughter at her plight. Making one last heroic effort, Nana did a semi-somersault, doubling back under herself and coming up between Its legs, below some sort of pendent pouch into which she promptly sank her pointed teeth; whereupon, Agdistis let out a bellow loud enough to be heard underwater and relaxed Its grip just long enough for Nana to break away and swim back into the source. And from that day to this, Agdistis had revenged Itself by playing the aulos every dawn.

When It finished piping, Agdistis lay down on Its belly and, without a word of thanks to the gods, lapped a quart of water from the pond. Refreshed, It slipped the leather thong, to which the aulos was attached, around Its neck, and set out to find some food.

Beyond the woods was a vast mountain-rimmed plateau, thousands of feet above sea level. In the distance, to the north and south, were snow-capped peaks; while straight ahead, as far as the eye could see, to the east (where the sky was already light, though the sun was not yet visible), stretched a perfectly flat, semiarid waste—the Phrygian steppe. Except for some patches of umber soil, the steppe was covered with scrubby grass, dotted here and there with delicate white and yellow flowers. The immensity of the open space, the silence and the solitude coming, as they did, after the roar of the spring and the closeness of the trees, stimulated Agdistis to break into a jog. Unhampered by the ankle-deep grass, It moved along freely, swiftly, effortlessly, looking mighty and proud, if not altogether proprietary, rather like a monarch surveying his domain.

After eating a litter of newborn rabbits, Agdistis set forth in earnest, heading roughly east, toward the rising sun, though by no means in a straight line. Sometimes It veered to the north, sometimes to the south, depending on whim; then, too, It changed Its pace every so often, whenever the spirit moved It—jogging at times, sprinting at others or taking a series of giant strides, bounding like an antelope, Its breasts bobbing, aulos and hair whipping from side to side or floating on the wind, Its tough feet raising puffs of dust as It gamboled across the steppe, over which It seemed, more than ever now, to be incontestably sovereign.

By mid-morning, It had almost reached the great highroad which links the Aegean port of Ephesus with the Assyrian Empire, cutting obliquely across the kingdoms of Lydia and Phrygia, Galatia and Cappadocia. Agdistis was heading for the stonework bridge, two thirds of the way between Ipsus and Pessinus, where the highroad, running north and south, spans the Sangarius. (From its source the Sangarius flows due north for approximately thirty miles, thence east southeast for another ninety, before veering sharply north again; so that once Agdistis left the spring, It also left behind the river, until now, when their paths were about to cross again.) But long before It came to the highroad, It had caught sight of something on the horizon: a small dark mass, trailing dust, which, when Agdistis stopped to study it, continued moving, and which, on closer observation, appeared to be a caravan, making its way toward Pessinus. Judging by the distance between them, Agdistis concluded that It would reach the river and, more important, cover of the bridge, well ahead of the caravan. Agdistis had, in fact, ample time not only to quench Its thirst, but also to revenge Itself on Nana again by giving back to the river the water It had taken earlier from the source.

Minutes went by without a sound, except for the ceaseless sound of the Sangarius, flowing against the masonry piers. After a while Agdistis lost patience. Keeping Its head down, It clambered up the rocky bank past the right abutment to a spot, several feet below the level of the bridge, where, squatting, It could watch the road without being seen. The caravan was still quite far away, yet near enough now for the hermaphrodite to discern that what It had taken for a caravan was nothing more than a single wagon, covered by a cotton awning and drawn by a team of mules. It was clearly not a royal wagon—neither the sideboards nor the wheels were painted, the awning was undyed, and there was no military escort—all of which suggested that the wagon was being driven by two men at most, and was probably transporting goods. What sort of goods would be entrusted to only two men? Surely nothing more valuable than produce—a shipment of cheese from Ipsus perhaps. But Ipsus was too near-by to warrant using a team of four mules. No, the wagon must have come much farther, from Lydia most likely, in which case it might be loaded with olive oil, figs, pottery, tiles. Yet no wagon would come alone all the way from Lydia. Others must be following. . . . Agdistis scanned the road. There was nothing in sight for miles. Perplexed, It scratched Its scalp. What could it be carting then, and to whom? Ought It to attack or let the wagon pass? It could hear the wheels and sideboards now, rattling too loosely for a really heavy load; could see the bearded driver dressed in a tunic and hat—not the conical Phrygian kind with flaps, but a wide-brimmed Lydian hat for traveling— could also see, though only barely, the hat of another man, standing on the far side of the wagon, his back to both the driver and Agdistis. Behind the men, in the middle of the wagon, stood something else, something so tall it seemed to touch the awning overhead, but what it was, Agdistis couldn't make out.

Scarcely had the hermaphrodite decided to let the wagon start across the bridge and then attack it from the rear, when the driver suddenly drew in the reins and stopped, a good five yards short of the bridge on the opposite side of the road. Agdistis ducked Its head. Though It could no longer see the men, It could distinctly hear their voices.

"Listen to me, will you? If we stay here, we can have our lunch, water the mules—"

"Water the mules! What's wrong with you? Don't you see how steep that bank is? You'll never get them down alive."

"Want to wager?"

"Well, even if you get them down, you'll never get them up again—that, I promise you. What's the rush anyway? They'll last till Pessinus. It's only another hour or so."

"That's just the point! If we go on now, we'll get there in daylight."

"So?"

"Our orders were to deliver the thing to the woods *after dark.*"

"Before dark, after dark—what's the difference?"

"To get there, we have to go around the citadel, don't we? The woods are north of the citadel, aren't they?"

"So?"

"So, as we come along the highroad in broad daylight, we'll be spotted by the sentinels, taken into custody, charged with sacrilege, and put to death—that's all."

"Death! For what? It's not as if we *made* the thing, we're only carting it."

"Smuggling it, you mean. We're not in the pay of the authorities, you know—the *people* ordered this thing. Don't you understand? These people aren't enlightened like us, they're barbarians. Not the king, of course; naturally King Midas and the priests—the whole royal household—worship the Olympians like us. But the rest of them—the populace, everyone outside the citadel—they're ignorant, superstitious, still believe in the ancient gods—Agdistis and the like. Sure, by day they pay lip service to the Goddess and the Maiden, but at night they light torches, take to the woods, drug themselves on hemp fumes. And there's nothing Midas can do to stop them. So, he turns his back. So do the priests—they have no choice. But when it comes to us—that's a different matter. We don't live in Pessinus. We're foreigners, not Phrygians. With us, he wouldn't hesitate to set an example, show the populace what happens to those who disobey the law, offend the Olympians, worship forbidden gods."

"But *we* don't worship forbidden gods."

"Who's going to listen to that, once they've caught us with the goods?"

"I guess you're right."

"You guess! . . . Come on, let's take a look at the riverbank."

Agdistis waited while the men got down from the wagon, said something to the mules, and then resumed their argument about the steepness of the bank. As their voices trailed off, the hermaphrodite crept from Its hiding place and, crouching, sneaked along the roadside. When It was opposite the wagon, It stood up cautiously, so as not to startle the mules, and slowly crossed the road. Peering around the end of the wagon, It could see the men, still at road level, though at some distance now and continuing to move farther away in search of a descent for the mules.

Agdistis turned back and looked into the wagon. To Its surprise the interior was empty, except for two quivers and bows and some provisions in the far right corner, and, in the center, the massive object of which It had caught a glimpse earlier, but had not been able to identify, and still could not, because it was shrouded in cloth, bound with twine. From ground level the object appeared to be about eight feet high (it did, in fact, touch the awning overhead) and three feet wide. Agdistis checked again on the whereabouts of the men, who by now were quite far away, before It climbed into the wagon. The mules snorted, but luckily didn't bray. Squatting, Agdistis broke the cord at the base of the object and peeked under the cloth. Planted squarely in the middle of a rectangular pedestal, secured to the floor by a wooden frame, was a life-size pair of reddish-brown feet. Agdistis realized almost at once that the feet weren't real, weren't flesh, that the divisions between the toes were simply incised lines. Yet It had seldom seen a life-size statue before, and wanted to reassure Itself. The terra cotta felt cool, smooth, hard; it was odorless and, when licked, its color deepened. Working rapidly, Agdistis undid the rest of the cord and began to tug at the dusty cloth, trying to pull it off. But even as Its eyes met another pair of eyes—mere pellets of clay, painted black and stuck onto a rugged face with a great jutting nose—the cloth snagged and had to be released from a large upright phallus. When, at last, the statue was unveiled, Agdistis stepped back in amazement.

The majestic figure, standing in a frontal pose, bare arms

akimbo, not angular but elbowless and semicircular like the handles of a huge amphora—the figure seemed to return the hermaphrodite's gaze, expressing simultaneously aggression, benevolence, generosity, and absolute indifference. The highly pronounced curves of its shoulders, breasts, and hips were covered by a heavy full-length mantle, painted green and incised with a series of V's, arranged in a more or less regular pattern of overlapping rows, suggestive of scales. The lower front half of the mantle was raised (as a result, the back half, which remained at ankle length, created the impression of tail feathers), pulled up almost to the waist, where a powerful pair of mittenlike hands held the rolled cloth in such a way as to make the rigid phallus they revealed seem a kind of offering. Crowning the figure was a large basket, piled high with pomegranates, out of either side of which emerged the pale blue body (neither the head nor tail was visible anywhere) of a serpent, so ubiquitous and long it appeared to be moving in opposite directions at once, as if it were a pair of serpents, coiled around the figure's neck and arms, breasts and torso. Because the basket seemed at one and the same time to be the serpent's origin and goal, it was difficult to tell whether the creature was the donor or recipient of the pomegranates; whether, that is, it was responsible for providing the fruit in the first place or busily making off with it, back to the Underworld whence both the serpent and the fruit had come.

Still eyeing the statue in amazement, Agdistis took hold in rapid succession of Its nose, breasts, penis (matching Its own flaccidity with the idol's tumescence); fingered the leather thong around Its neck (finding the thong sadly lacking in comparison with the serpent's circumference); and finally brought a hand to Its head, half expecting to discover Itself crowned with a basket of pomegranates. Then all at once It raised Its fists and feigned a punch, as if to provoke a fight with the figure. The statue didn't stir. Agdistis faked another punch. Again it didn't stir. After a third try, Agdistis lost patience and began to move about lightly on the balls of Its feet, sparring (albeit unilaterally) with the statue, taunting it now not only physically but verbally. "Come on, erect-one! Come on, coward!" Still the statue didn't stir. As a last resort, Agdistis pulled back Its leg and aimed a kick at the statue's groin. This time, however, It misjudged the distance and actually connected with the clay; whereupon the phallus flew into the air, hit the awning overhead, rebounded, and plummeted to the floor where it landed with a bounce, unbroken. When It realized what had happened, Agdistis bent over, picked up the phallus, and burst into laughter. The more It related the object in Its hand to the gaping hole left in the unmanned statue, the funnier it seemed, causing Agdistis to laugh louder and louder, more and more uncontrollably, convulsively, till It rocked the wagon, and tears rolled down Its cheeks.

The mules began to bray.

Stifling Its laughter, Agdistis rushed to the back of the wagon and looked out. The men were returning on the run. Agdistis glanced over Its shoulder to assure Itself that their weapons were still in the corner.

"You see—I said it was the mules."

"I'm telling you, that was no mule."

"What was it then?"

"You heard it yourself—sounded like laughter."

"Yeah-yeah, so you keep saying, but whose?"

"How should I know? I never heard anything like it. Might have been Sangarius for all we know. Or—Curse those mules! Stop your braying, will you! I can't hear myself think."

"Could have been Sangarius, you were saying, or? . . ."

". . . Oh . . . yeah . . . well, you know, it's awfully close to festival time."

"You mean . . . the *shades*?"

"I-don't-know, I-don't-know! Whatever it was, we better make our offering to Sangarius right now! Come on, let's get the stuff."

Agdistis dismissed the idea, which flashed through Its mind, of bagging the men by throwing the cloth from the statue over their heads. Counting, instead, on Its superior strength and position, as well as the element of surprise, and the fact that the men were unarmed, Agdistis centered Itself in the open end of the wagon, gripped the edge of the platform with Its toes, crouched—the phallus still in hand, but held now like a cudgel—and waited, ready to pounce.

As the men, who had fallen silent, rounded the end of the wagon, Agdistis let out a terrifying war cry and, brandishing the phallus, swooped down on the two, landing less than a yard from their feet.

Taken unawares, the men let out a shriek, but once they actually saw their assailant, they lost their voices altogether; their eyes bulged, jaws fell, blood drained from their cheeks, and their teeth began to chatter. When, at last, one of them regained the power of speech, his voice was scarcely audible. "Alive! It's come alive!" he stammered. Thereupon the two started backing away, holding up their trembling hands in a feeble attempt both to protect themselves and pacify Agdistis, until the distance between them seemed safe enough for the men to turn and take to their heels—the first tripping over his own feet as he fled back up the road to Ipsus; the second running pell-mell out onto the steppe, eastward toward Cappadocia.

The minute they were gone, the hermaphrodite began to laugh again, even more uproariously than It had at first, laughing now in retrospect about the whole incident—statue, phallus, mules, men: the look of panic on their faces, their quaking limbs, pleading hands, rabbitlike retreat. When It was limp from laughing, Agdistis turned, gave the statue one last quizzical look, laughed again, and then set off—with no apparent lessening of energy—in the direction from which It had come, no longer empty-handed now, but proudly bearing the phallus overhead like a standard.

III

Two men, one muleback, the other leading the way on foot, were approaching a woods at the end of a glen. The rider boasted a full black beard, half a foot long but neatly trimmed almost to a point, a splendid head of thick black hair, garlanded with ivy, and a delicate neck adorned with a string of dried figs. He was wrapped to the waist in a plum-colored mantle, draped rather rakishly over a long red gown. But in order to straddle the mule, he had had to hike up the gown well above the knees, revealing a pair of legs and thighs which, for a man, were uncommonly fair (almost as if they had never been exposed to daylight), flabby, and hairless.

Compared to his companion, the fellow on foot seemed youthful and athletic. His carriage was erect, physique trim, gait energetic. Yet, judging by his naked body he was obviously ancient, old enough to be the rider's great-great-grandfather. In certain areas, especially about the face and neck, his weathered skin was so deeply wrinkled it resembled the bark of an oak; while elsewhere, around his chest and abdomen, it sagged like melting wax. Every bit of hair—the fuzz that fringed his bald crown, his bushy eyebrows, patriarchal beard, bristles obtruding from his snub nose, abundant chest and pubic hair—all of it, including his flowing equine tail, was white as snow. The ears, too, were long and pointed like those of a horse.

As for the mule, it was carrying not only the rider, but also a bulging triple-necked wineskin, which hung down on one side and was counterbalanced on the other by a kettledrum. In spite of its burden, the animal stepped along at a lively pace, almost prancing, its head held high, as if it clearly understood the importance of the personage it was carrying.

"You're sure we're heading right, Silenus?" said the rider. "Your cataracts aren't leading you astray?"

The old satyr looked back over his shoulder and frowned. "Quite sure, Dionysus. How could I forget—the source of the Sangarius, the place where Midas' men took me prisoner?"

Dionysus chuckled, remembering the incident years ago when he had ransomed the drunken satyr from King Midas for a wish. Silenus frowned again, as if to rebuke Dionysus for laughing. "Still a sore spot, old friend?"

The satyr ignored the question. "Watch your head now," he cautioned as they reached the woods.

"I wish you could have seen his face, Silenus."

"Midas'?"

"Apollo's—when I volunteered to do this—his cheeks turned red, red as my gown . . . with rage, I suppose, though he, of course, would never admit it, never admit any emotion."

"He will soon," Silenus remarked mysteriously but with unquestionable authority.

Aware of his guardian's exceptional gifts—Silenus was both a sage and a seer—Dionysus said, "Would you care to elucidate?" Once again the satyr looked back disapprovingly, but said nothing. "What's the matter, Silenus? Why do you keep giving me dirty looks? Have I offended you in some way?" The satyr flicked his tail in silence. "Tell me, please."

"I'm getting too old for this sort of thing," he muttered crabbily, as if to emphasize his age. "I'm not immortal like you, you know."

"For goodness' sake! why didn't you say so straight away? Come, we'll change places: you ride, I'll walk."

"No-no." Silenus turned around and raised his gnarled hands to dissuade the god from dismounting. Dionysus reined in the mule, which came to a halt. "Don't misunderstand. I'm not the least bit tired—physically."

Leaning forward, Dionysus looked down at his guardian with concern. "What then?"

Silenus came closer, close enough to wrap his arm around the mule's neck and finger its mane, while he looked up at Dionysus searchingly, his right eye keen, his left half shut, opaque and blind, staring vacantly into the trees. "Tell me, Dionysus, why did you involve yourself in this escapade?"

131.

"Because it's said that Agdistis is my sibling, the offspring of Cybele."

"Do you believe that?"

"What difference does it make? *Others* do—even the gods. I mean to put a stop to it."

"By gelding Agdistis?"

"How else? There can't be two of us, two sons, in relation to the mother," Dionysus stated forcefully. "Only one . . . one to one . . . no room for trinities. Let Agdistis be a daughter, if It likes, or let It be a mother, and worship the son, as all women must."

"And the son?"

"Will worship the mother, as all men must: love her everlastingly, selflessly, surrender unconditionally, till she loses her wits for love of him and, for fear of losing him, takes him back into herself."

"And when the mother dies?"

"The mother is immortal," Dionysus rejoined matter-of-factly.

"*Yours* was not."

"Mine was murdered, murdered by my father, Zeus, struck down by lightning."

"So the story goes," Silenus scoffed.

"Wait! Come back! You can't say something like that and then just walk away. Explain yourself!"

Silenus turned back. For a moment he stood in thoughtful silence, studying his hand, as if he were reading his palm or finding in the knobby joints evidence of his mortality. "Perhaps I should— since no one else knows the facts—perhaps the time has come."

"What facts? Tell me, Silenus. If my mother wasn't murdered, how did she die?"

"A natural death, in childbirth . . . or, to be exact, just after parturition." Silenus walked slowly toward the mule and placed his hand on Dionysus' bare knee, as if to lessen the impact of what he was about to say. "In the beginning, Dionysus, you and your mother were one: twofold, yet combined, complete unto yourself . . . exactly like Agdistis." Unable for the moment to assimilate this statement, Dionysus seemed to age a generation as he knit his brows and grimaced in silence. "All your father did with his celebrated thunderbolt was sunder you—"

"So he *did* kill her after all."

"No. Your mother died not from the blast, but from being bisected, from having done to her what you're about to do to Agdistis." Silenus removed his hand from his protégé's knee and challenged him sharply, "Now then, do you still intend to go through with it?"

"Of course," Dionysus replied without hesitation. "What choice have I?"

"You could make an exception."

"Nonsense! Not to go through with it would be a denial of everything I am, everything I was created for, everything you yourself ever taught me."

"Yes, of course," Silenus murmured. "You're right. Forgive me," he said, half sarcastically, half in earnest. "I was being senile, silly." The satyr turned away. When he had gone a few paces, he suddenly knelt on the ground, his back to Dionysus, covered his head with his hands, and cried out to the heavens, "O god! dear god! grant my wish: let me not be here to see the outcome."

His curiosity aroused, Dionysus dismounted from the mule and walked over to Silenus. "Why? What do you mean by that?"

"I mean" —the satyr looked up, his right eye fierce—"that with a little luck I'll be dead."

Dionysus knelt beside his guardian. "Dead? No. Don't talk like that, even in jest. Please," he said with feeling. "What would I do without you, old friend?"

Silenus shrugged. "Just what you've always done: live and die and be reborn."

"And if I spare Agdistis" —Dionysus took his guardian by the shoulders— "will you stay with me? Will you go on living then?"

After exchanging a long heartfelt look, the satyr slowly shook his head. "No, dear boy."

"Why not?"

"Because I've had enough of it," he said, his expression turning scornful, his tone bilious, "I'm sick to death of it!"

Dionysus looked incredulous. "Of life?" The satyr nodded. "But it was *you*," he protested sadly, "who taught me to love it— everything about it—even the butchery, even the blood." A tear rolled down the young god's cheek.

"Now-now, none of that. I'm still very much alive. Come!" In an abrupt change of mood Silenus slapped his thigh and sprang to his feet. "Let's get on with it!" Dionysus picked himself up with effort. "Goodness! don't look so downcast. The fact that this may be the last such prank I have a hand in, can only make it that much more delectable. Besides," he confided with relish, as he bent over and interlocked his fingers, creating a stirrup for Dionysus to remount the mule, "it will be a sweet revenge on Midas."

133.

"What has he to do with it?"

"Have you forgotten what I said to Midas when he asked me what Man should prize most?"

"You never told me."

"Take a guess."

"Gold, I assume."

"No, indeed." Silenus grinned slyly. "That was *his* idea, not mine. What I said—to which, of course, he paid no attention at the time, but may be forced to yet—I said, 'O miserable, ephemeral creature, child of chance and suffering, why do you ask me something you'd be better off never hearing, never knowing, since the thing in question is utterly unachievable anyhow?' 'What? What is it?' he pressed me. 'All right,' I said, 'if you insist: what Man should prize most' " —a look of malicious glee came into the satyr's eye, as he bared his yellow-brown teeth and snarled— " 'is not to be born . . . not to *be* . . . to be *nothing*. . . . Short of that,' I added lightly, 'the next best thing is to die young.' "

Dionysus laughed gaily. "Ever the optimist, dear heart."

"I do my best."

"Gee up!" Dionysus said, at which command both the satyr and the mule moved on. "Still, I don't understand what Midas has to do with Agdistis."

"You will," Silenus sang out over his shoulder, "you will."

"That's the second time today—no, the third—you've said something like that. Explain yourself."

"Patience . . . patience . . . all in good time."

"No!" Dionysus halted the mule again. "*Now.*"

Silenus stopped too and turned around. "What can I tell you?" he said, showing his ancient palms.

"Plenty! Stop acting so innocent."

"Well" —Silenus screwed his little finger into his ear and scooped out a dollop of wax which he promptly ate— "perhaps a . . . premonition."

"Of what?" Dionysus demanded in a tone that brooked no further evasion. "Tell me!"

"Very well," Silenus said solemnly, whereupon he started turning his head every which way, looking all around, peering into the underbrush and up into the treetops in search of something. By and by he walked over to a lofty ash which stood about seventy-five feet high and was three feet in diameter. At the base of the tree he paused a moment and then began to walk around it from right to left, making three complete revolutions, at the end of which he stood facing the trunk, his back to Dionysus. Raising his arms high overhead, he touched the tree tenderly and kissed its furrowed bark. Except for intermittent birdcalls, the woods were perfectly still. When the spirit moved him, Silenus turned around, pressed his spine against the trunk, dug his toes into the ground, tilted back his head as if to get the sun, and, reaching round behind him, embraced the tree with fervor.

Whether it was the flood of sunlight or the power of suggestion or the satyr's protective coloration that made all distinctions disappear, Dionysus couldn't tell, but as he watched and waited, he saw his guardian gradually blend into the tree, becoming part of it, indistinguishable from it—his long white beard and tail no more than strands of Spanish moss—so that when, at last, Silenus opened his mouth to speak, it was very much as if the tree itself had begun to speak, and even the birds fell silent.

"O sacred tree, whose topmost limbs attain the heavens, whose roots reach down to Hades, whose sturdy trunk mediates between the two—speak through me. . . . O sacred tree, abider in three realms at once, realms of which I, too, am part—abide with me. . . ." As his voice died away, Silenus was suddenly seized by a paroxysm: his head jerked from side to side and his body shook convulsively, compelling him now to hold onto the tree not for the sake of communion but for dear life.

When the fit had passed, Silenus, though still on his feet, looked decrepit, limp, and lifeless, almost disembodied. But presently he resumed speaking, chanting actually, in a voice by no means feeble, but powerful and sonorous, as if it were issuing from a cave. "Once again the mother, once again the son, the lover, slaughtered, slaughtered by the father, slaughtered by the mother, slaughtered by the son, the blood-drenched earth bringing forth another crop, begetting yet another corpse. . . . So it ever was, so it ever will be, over and over, world without end: first the fusion, then the fission—the fusion and the fission from which there's no recovery, only a continuing. . . ."

After a brief silence, the birds began to sing again. Silenus straightened up, opened his eyes, blinked a few times, smiled, flicked his tail, and bounded away from the tree.

Dionysus did nothing to conceal his irritation. "Riddles! always riddles, Silenus. I know less now than when you started."

"Sorry, dear boy. But, as you know, I have little control over these matters. Come!" he declared, looking up to gauge the position of the sun. "It's well past noon. We'd better get along. There's a lot to do before Agdistis returns."

Moving on, Silenus led the way, as he had from the start, but at a faster pace now, going at a trot. Before long, he pricked up his pointed ears. "Hear it?" he called back to Dionysus.

"Hear what?"

"Listen." From the distance came the sound of gushing water. "The source," Silenus explained, adding playfully, "cataracts indeed!"

When they reached the pond, the satyr stopped and pointed to the barren spit. "That's where It drinks. Its lair" —the pointing finger moved eastward ninety degrees— "is over there. Best leave the mule in the woods, I think, behind the spit."

"Whatever you say," Dionysus agreed, and they proceeded to the place indicated.

Once there, Silenus helped his protégé dismount, and then hitched the mule to a sapling. From what followed, it was clear which of the two was the worker, which the idler. Not that Dionysus was incurably indolent; he simply had no mind for practical matters, found it easier to step aside and keep out of the way of someone who did, someone like his guardian who, in fact, was already busy unloading the mule, staggering under the weight of the wineskin.

"Give me a hand!" Silenus called out.

Dionysus was perfectly willing. "Where shall we put it?"

"Down!" came the terse reply.

Lowered clumsily, the wineskin landed with a bump that would easily have burst a less well-made bag, but only left this one quivering like an enormous pudding on the ground. Dionysus watched it settle with fascination, while Silenus went around to the other side of the mule, unstrapped the kettledrum and stick, and lugged them down toward the pond where he concealed the instrument behind a clump of bushes to the right of the spit.

By the time he rejoined Dionysus, the satyr was wiping the sweat from his brow. "I've put the drum behind those bushes down there. See where I mean?" Dionysus nodded. "Good. That's where you'll be stationed. Now, then, where's the noose?"

"Noose?"

"The one Hephaestus made."

"Oh!" Dionysus tapped himself on the forehead.

"Don't tell me you've forgotten it!"

"No-no. I remember now. Hephaestus recommended horse-hair—said it would be our best bet by far."

"Well" —Silenus extended his hand— "where is it?"

"It isn't . . . yet. We have to make it."

"Make it! Confound it, boy! Why didn't you say so earlier? All that time we were in the woods—" Muttering to himself, Silenus marched over to the hind end of the mule and grabbed its tail.

"Wait!" Dionysus stopped him. "It can't be from just *any* old horse."

"Why not?"

"Because there are certain specific requirements—ductility, durability, pliancy, color—"

"Come-come, Dionysus," the satyr grumbled, "we're wasting time. Where do we get it?"

Dionysus tried in vain to keep a straight face, as he looked his guardian in the eye, but broke into a broad grin.

"Oh, no!" Silenus stamped his foot. "Nothing doing!"

"My goodness," Dionysus said, feigning surprise, "I thought you'd be pleased. You can't imagine how flattering Hephaestus was about your tail."

"Oh, yes I can. And that's the way it's going to stay."

"O, the vanity of age."

"Never mind! You haven't volunteered your beard."

Dionysus brought his hand to his chin defensively, as if to protect his manhood. "Certainly not! Why should I, when Hephaestus clearly specified your tail? Come on, dear heart," Dionysus coaxed, as he inched closer to his guardian, "be a sport. All we need is two fine hairs. It will only sting for a second."

After due consideration and a great deal of grimacing, Silenus finally consented to suffer the indignity like a man, but even as he bent over to accommodate Dionysus, his surprisingly cooperative attitude was belied by a wicked leer. No sooner had the god squatted to select the hairs, than the satyr raised his tail and let drop half a dozen perfectly formed oat-flecked turds. In retaliation Dionysus seized not two hairs but a fistful which he yanked out by the roots, whereat Silenus placed all his weight on his outspread palms, kicked his legs backward into the air, and delivered a blow to the jaw that sent the young god reeling.

Once they had regained their equilibrium, the satyr and the god began to exchange a series of sulky, spiteful, accusatory looks, but not a word was spoken—not even when Silenus snatched his tail hairs away from Dionysus and proceeded to tie two of them together in a square knot. After rigorously testing the strength of both the knot and the almost invisible filament, and finding them satisfactory, he went on to make a noose at either end of the horse-hair thread. That done, he walked over to a nearby willow, shinnied up its tall black trunk with the sureness and dexterity of a honey bear, and climbed into the upper branches where, facing east and shielding his eyes from the sun, he scanned the horizon. "There!" he suddenly exclaimed, "there It is, just entering the woods. Quickly now!" Almost before these last words reached Dionysus' ear, the satyr was back on the ground and issuing his next directive. "The wineskin!"

No matter how helpful Dionysus tried to be, he managed somehow to frustrate every attempt the satyr made to move the unwieldy bag. Either he wound up heading in the opposite direction from Silenus or lost his grip on the slippery skin, tripped over a root or dropped his garland, but after several minutes of strenuous exertion they were just about where they had started. Aware that time was running short, Silenus offered to carry the bag himself, provided Dionysus could load it onto his back, but even that proved to be too taxing for the god. Finally, Silenus got down on all fours, wedged his clavicle under the bag, pried it up, heaved it over his right shoulder, struggled to his feet and, in a determined effort to get the ordeal over with, sprinted the five hundred yards or so from the woods to the end of the spit. Dionysus tried to keep abreast of the old satyr, but even empty-handed he lagged behind, and soon gave up and walked the last furlong, panting all the way.

By the time the god reached the end of the spit, Silenus had already unplugged the bag. The deep-red wine was gushing with gurgles out of the triple spout into the spring, coloring and clouding the clear green water. Judging by their pained expressions, both men were sorry indeed to see the wine go, almost as if they were losing their blood. When the last drops had been squeezed from the deflated bag, Silenus kneeled down, cupped his palms, and scooped up a handful of water.

"Wait!" Dionysus objected. "What are you doing?"

"Just testing the strength, to see that it's not too diluted," the satyr explained, quickly quaffing the whole draft before Dionysus could stop him.

"Well," the god said begrudgingly, "how is it?"

Silenus sat back on his heels, shut his eyes, smiled blissfully and murmured, "Divine." In the next second, however, he pricked up his ears, sprang to his feet, and exclaimed in a whisper, "Quick! It's coming. Into the bushes! And don't come out till I tell you." The satyr waited to make sure that Dionysus was completely out of sight before he himself retreated from the spit and scampered up a tree in time to see the hermaphrodite emerge from the underbrush.

Agdistis looked both exhausted and exhilarated, as if It had just participated in a decathlon. It was panting and perspiring; Its di-

138.

sheveled hair had become entangled in the thong to which the aulos was attached, and Its long rosy tongue was literally hanging out. And though It was still carrying the phallus, the hand that held it was no longer raised on high, but hanging limply at Its side, the phallus pointing down like a baton in the hand of the losing runner.

Agdistis headed for the spit. Once there, It practically dropped to the ground from exhaustion and stretched out prone to quench Its thirst. As It lowered Its head toward the water, It noticed the curious discoloration, smelled the unfamiliar scent, and wondered for a moment if Nana had revenged herself by excreting some pollutant into the spring, but Agdistis was much too parched to give the matter a second thought. To Its surprise, the water, though unexpectedly piquant, seemed particularly tasty, and the hermaphrodite couldn't get enough of it.

All of a sudden, as It went on drinking, Nana issued like a shot from the source, flew into the air, did a stylish somersault, and landed on her back in the water. Uncertain whether or not the nymph had noticed It, Agdistis stopped drinking and held perfectly still. At the same time, Silenus, astonished by this unexpected turn of events, motioned to Dionysus from the treetop to take a look at what was happening. The young god crept with caution out of the bushes and, seeing the nymph, clapped both hands over his mouth to keep from laughing out loud.

Nana was indeed behaving most peculiarly. Still floating on her back, she would, every so often, fling an arm overhead or kick a leg with such abandon, it was a wonder her limbs remained attached to her body. Even more antic than her movements was her vocalism. She seemed, at first, to be producing merely a series of unrelated, high-pitched, endlessly protracted vowel sounds, but as Agdistis, Dionysus, and Silenus went on listening, they realized she was singing—singing, moreover, at the top of her lungs some eccentric ditty of her own composition whose lyrics (if, indeed, there were any) could not be heard over the roar of the spring.

Unable to lie still another second, Agdistis, inspired no doubt by both the wine and Nana's example, suddenly stood up, stretched Its arms overhead and, beating time with the phallus, began to sing in much the same fashion as Nana, only basso, and to execute on land and in an upright position, the same kind of erratic, impassioned, slow-motion movements that Nana was making in the water—swinging Its arms and swaying Its hips, flexing Its legs and doing all sorts of capers and kicks. Far from scaring the nymph away, the hermaphrodite's sudden appearance encouraged Nana to give herself up completely to the moment; and though they seemed to be paying no attention whatever to each other, they were in fact engaged in a duet, albeit a drunken one, which despite its absurdity and dissonance suggested a love duet.

As their singing grew louder and their movements more frenzied, Nana, in a sudden burst of energy, broke water like a fish, flipped into the air and, catching sight of Dionysus before she fell back into the pond, began pointing toward the shore and shouting with religious fervor, "Iacchus! Iacchus!" acclaiming the god by his most solemn appellation, whereupon Dionysus felt honorbound to come forward and reveal himself; and Silenus, convinced the game was up, covered his eyes, but Agdistis, not seeing the god, and mistaking the appellation for Its own, got carried away and, twirling the phallus high overhead, cast it as a kind of keepsake across the pond at Nana, who came so close to being hit she darted in fear back into the source, just as Agdistis let out a jubilant cry and, keeling over backward, landed flat on the ground near the end of the spit.

Silenus signaled Dionysus not to move until they were certain Agdistis was unconscious. After waiting a minute or so, during which time Agdistis showed no signs of life, the satyr climbed down out of the tree, and he and Dionysus converged cautiously on the dormant body. The hermaphrodite was lying with Its right heel resting on Its left shin, Its legs forming a scalene triangle. Working rapidly, Silenus readied the horsehair filament, slipped one noose around Agdistis' right foot and the other around Its scrotum, tightening both as much as possible without disturbing the creature's sleep, after which he and Dionysus withdrew into the bushes. There, the satyr took hold of the kettledrum, hugged it to his chest, and, squatting, straddled the instrument, supporting its bulk between his haunches; while Dionysus picked up the drumstick, waited for Silenus to give him the go-ahead, and then began to pound the parchment with all his might, creating an earth-shaking din.

Agdistis woke with a start and bolted upright, triggering the lethal snare which closed in a trice, stretched taut, and tore off the fated testicles. As the blood spouted from Its groin, Agdistis, who was, as yet, too drunk to understand what had happened, screamed in agony and took hold of Itself to ease the pain. Instead of abating, the pain grew worse, causing the hermaphrodite to gnash Its teeth, flail the air with Its bloodstained fists, and jump up and down till It could bear no more and, thinking Itself on fire, plunged into the pond. Still unable to find relief, It soon charged out again and, racing inland, plowed through the underbrush as if It were being pursued by the Furies, and disappeared howling into the woods.

When the sound died away, Dionysus and Silenus came out of the bushes and went to the spit to retrieve the testes, which the young god wished to take back to Olympus as both a trophy and proof of the bloody deed. To their amazement the remains were nowhere to be found. After searching the area thoroughly, they finally gave up, collected their gear, reloaded the mule, and set off in the direction from which they had come, leaving the blood-and-wine-polluted spring to purify itself, the blood-drenched ground to dry in the midday sun.

No sooner had they gone, than the winter-hardened soil near the end of the spit, where the testes had disappeared, began to thaw and crack and then to bulge until the blood-steeped earth broke open and fell aside in lumps, allowing a pale green shoot to sprout up leisurely but steadily toward the sun, at the same time that its stem enlarged in circumference and turned into wood, protected by a smooth gray bark from which a score of twigs spread out gradually, becoming budded branchlets, even as the burgeoning shrub continued to grow higher, fuller, putting forth a thousand shiny lance-shaped leaves, followed in short order by a sudden burst of scarlet blossoms whose crinkled petals unfolded to the sun, flourished momentarily, and then began to fall, leaving behind a host of purple calyxes, which presently commenced to swell into irregular spheres, big as oranges but brilliant red with a leathery rind, resplendent in the sunshine and weighing down the sturdy branches of a full-grown pomegranate tree.

IV

A pale white hand, made paler by the light of a full moon, emerged from the pond at the tip of the spit and reached out toward the pomegranate tree, then stopped in midair, its four stubby fingers trembling, too timorous to touch the ground. After a moment the hand began to stir again, hovering just above the shore, until it found the courage to alight, not assertively but tentatively, the fingertips alone touching down. In contact with the ground the already shaking hand shook uncontrollably, as if with palsy or plain excitement. When the tremor passed, the fingers, moving either singly or collectively, began to feel around, wavering antennalike, inching forward by contractions in the manner of a caterpillar, advancing cautiously into the unknown. The farther the hand progressed, the more evident it became that it wasn't just exploring the terrain but seeking something in particular, something out of reach yet so acutely coveted it tempted Nana for the fist time in her life to leave the water and come up onto land.

How strange—worse than strange, utterly disagreeable—to be supported by this solid, unyielding, stationary element. No wonder her father had forbidden her, on penalty of death, to venture onto land. But why so harsh a punishment for something so unsatisfying? What were the advantages of land? You couldn't swim, couldn't submerge, couldn't be carried forward or back, couldn't float, couldn't do almost anything. Worst of all, perhaps, was the feeling you experienced on land of being without a body, of incorporeality. On land there was nothing but air to oppose and contain you, nothing you could feel yourself inside of and inseparable from, no element to claim as *yours* and, in return, be claimed by. On land you lost your place in the order of things, were left alone in space, altogether on your own, a solitary outcast, cut off and expelled from the whole physical universe. Was that what her father had meant by penalty of death? Not that he would personally kill her, but that the punishment administered itself, that you began to die the minute you left the water? . . . The possibility frightened Nana. But even so, she was determined to get what she had come for: a pomegranate, the only one that had as yet fallen from the tree. Just why she wanted it, she didn't know—any more than she knew what drove her to respond to Agdistis' piping—all she knew was that she had to have it. . . . She could see it now, lying on the ground, glowing in the moonlight, an irresistibly voluptuous sphere, compelling her to pick it up, touch and fondle it, even perhaps to taste it.

As Nana crawled away from the water toward the fruit, she was stopped in her tracks by someone sobbing, sobbing so loud the sound could be heard over the roar of the spring. A shiver of sympathy coursed through her body, and she suddenly remembered, though only dimly, the waters of the spring turning red and tasting sour; remembered feeling something she had never felt before: a lovely kind of levity and titillation; remembered singing at the top of her lungs and leaping out of the water, astounded to behold Dionysus on the shore. Had it really happened or was it all a dream? Had she really been possessed and ravished by the god? If not, then what explained the miraculous emergence of this tree (surely it was real and she awake) in whose shelter she was crouch-

142.

ing now? Who was sobbing in the woods? What was she doing on land, risking her life for a piece of fruit? . . . As if to answer all these questions, Nana reached out and clasped the pomegranate.

O! how satisfying it was to hold something in your hands that stayed, instead of running through your fingers instantly like water. O! how wonderful to be resisted yet affirmed by something solid, something altogether other than yourself, yet close enough to call your own. O! how incredible the intimacy engendered between a pair of hands and a piece of fruit. Perhaps she had made a mistake after all, perhaps there *were* advantages to be found on land.

Once again Nana was distracted by the plangent sobs coming from the woods. Keeping a firm hold on the pomegranate, she turned her head to listen, torn between her passion for the fruit and pity for the sufferer. For some inexplicable reason she sensed that the two were interrelated, that somehow her gain was the other's loss, but now that the fruit was hers, she wouldn't consider giving it up. Moving swiftly like a fiddler crab, she sidled off the spit and eased her body back into the water.

As soon as the distance between herself and the shore seemed safe, the nymph relaxed, turned over onto her back, and floated in the moonlight, the pomegranate secure in the cup of her navel. But as she fondled the fruit she found that its serrated sepals scratched her, and she bit them off. When the pomegranate was smooth as a ball, she began to roll it around her abdomen, over her belly and up and down her rib cage, tickling herself till she squirmed with pleasure and had to stop for fear of dropping the fruit into the water; she rolled it next between her breasts, making herself triple-breasted, a condition which delighted her so much that even three seemed insufficient, and Nana longed to be covered with clusters of breasts; she rolled it round and round her own small breasts, stimulating the nipples to stand erect; rolled it then the length of her torso, as far as her arm could reach, down the inside of her right thigh and up again, and over the hairless groin, and down the left, and back to the groin where with mounting passion she rolled it up and down the cleft countless times until the fruit induced the lips to part, and Nana, in a transport of excitement that made her squeal and thrash her head from side to side and drive her soles against the water, took the pomegranate, rind and all, deep into herself, flipped over twice involuntarily and, diving down, disappeared back into the source, as the sobbing from the woods gradually subsided.

Even at so great a distance: several hundred miles from the river's source, at its confluence in the north with the Black Sea, Sangarius was quick to detect signs of pollution. Discounting the urine, which, as he well knew by now, came from Agdistis, first there was the wine, then the blood in such profusion that Sangarius could only attribute it to some profane sacrifice or homicide, and finally another type of blood, unmistakably Nana's, though, oddly enough, not menstrual. Obviously something was amiss, so much so that the river god decided there and then to investigate the matter.

Sculling with his powerful tail, Sangarius wheeled about in the narrow estuary, churning up the salty water till it turned as white as his scaleless skin, and headed upstream. Under the best of circumstances it was a trying feat to swim seven hundred miles against the current, a feat that demanded the most strenuous and unrelenting exertion of both the tail and arm muscles, but under the present pressured circumstances in which Sangarius felt anxious and suspicious from the start, it was not the least surprising that he was in a particularly truculent mood by the time he reached the source.

Since Nana was not immediately visible in the pond, Sangarius wasted no time looking for her, but plunged right into the spring and swam the length of an unsloping duct which led, in turn, into the underground portion of the river. Except for one thin beam of daylight flooding through a small sinkhole overhead, the limestone cave was completely dark. Sangarius stopped and listened for Nana. Hearing nothing, he assumed she must be hard at work in the rimstone pool just beyond the present chamber, driving the pent-up waters over the pool's stalagmite dam.

"Daughter!" Sangarius called out in a thundering voice that echoed and re-echoed through the cavern.

"Father?" came the faint intimidated reply.

"Come here at once!"

Nana did as she was told, surfacing a moment later at a respectful distance from Sangarius. "Are you well, Father?"

"Never mind that! What's been happening here?"

"Here?"

"Did you have an accident?"

"No, Father."

"How, then, do you explain the blood?"

"Blood? What blood, Father?"

"Yours!" he exclaimed, adding as an afterthought, "We'll deal with the other matters later."

"Mine?" Nana fell silent, too puzzled to speak.

"I can't hear you!"

"I-I don't know what explains it, Father—unless" —she hit on a happy idea— "it was my time of month."

"Don't lie to me!" Sangarius exclaimed. "Your time came ten days ago." The waters shifted noticeably. Nana pulled back, fearful that her father was coming at her in the dark, but Sangarius moved instead into the beam of light which was strong enough to illuminate his ferocious eyes and bared sharp teeth. "Come over here where I can see you." Nana obeyed. But Sangarius, not yet satisfied, grabbed her by the hair and pulled her head back until her terror-stricken face was directly in the light. "The truth now!"

"I-I don't know. Please! please believe me, Father."

"What about the wine?"

"Is *that* what it was?"

"Answer my question! Where did it come from?"

"I don't know."

"Again you don't know!" Infuriated, Sangarius lifted Nana by the hair a foot or so out of the water and shouted, "What *do* you know?" Nana yelped and stiffened her body against the pain, but put up no resistance. As the words do-you-know resounded through the cavern, she awaited stoically the moment when her scalp would part from her skull, and she would be delivered forever from this tyranny and pain. "Answer me!" he resumed with vehemence. "Whence came the wine? Whence the blood?" Rather than risk her father's further wrath by repeating "I don't know," Nana remained silent. "Don't try my patience, child, I'm warning you! I asked: whence came the blood?" To make his daughter speak, Sangarius gave her hair a savage tug, but to no avail. "What? Still no answer? Still 'I don't know'? Stubborn hagfish! Very well" —he lowered his voice menacingly— "there are other ways of finding out."

Nana felt an abrupt and terrible increase of pain as her father yanked her by the hair almost completely out of the water, holding her high with one hand, while with the other he grabbed her groin, parted the lips and probed her insides, causing the nymph to cry out incoherently not only against the pain and humiliation, but against this brutal violation of her selfhood.

Finding his fingers unobstructed, Sangarius began to bellow, "Whore! whore! whore!" and, taking hold of his daughter's hair with both hands now, swept her half-submerged body back and forth in the riverbed until the agitated waters splashed the cavern walls, and Nana lost consciousness, and Sangarius, still bellowing

145.

"Whore!" dragged her by the hair out of the river onto the rocks where, working by the light from the sinkhole overhead, he bound her inert body upright to a limestone pillar. When she was secure, he set about reviving her, drenching her still-dripping flesh from head to toe.

Nana recovered gradually. Her lidless eyes, which had rolled back in their sockets, began to focus on her father, who was completely underwater now except for his head and massive shoulders, showing white above the surface at the river's edge where he was waiting with obvious impatience for Nana's full attention. Eager, as always, to mollify and please him, she tried to draw closer, but couldn't move, and realized instantly what her situation was—the only question being how long the confinement would last. However long, the prospect filled her with despair, and Nana bit her lip to stay the tears.

"Your hands are free to cover your face," Sangarius remarked in a voice no longer unrestrained but stony, cruel, sardonic, "free to hide your shame."

Too broken in spirit to raise her hands, Nana simply hung her head as the tears streamed down her cheeks, and she tried to stifle a little, plaintive, high-pitched whine.

"If you're crying now, what will you do when you hear your fate?"

"How—how long this time, Father? How long do you intend to keep me here?"

"Until you starve to death."

"Death?"

"Did you think you were immortal, whore?"

Nana shook her head forlornly. "But if you let me die, Father, who will tend the spring?"

"The spring will tend itself."

"*Itself?* How can it, Father?"

"Do you really think the spring needs *you*, a whore, to help it flow?"

"If I am what you say, then, no" —her voice broke with emotion— "it has no further need of me—but someone else, someone new, a virgin must be trained to take my place."

"Fool! Do you honestly believe the spring needs *anyone*?"

"Yes, of course."

"You had better be enlightened then. Listen to me. When you were pure I permitted you to play in the spring—"

"Play!" Nana protested feebly. "Is *that* your word for hard labor?"

"Be still! and let me finish. Even when pure, you were nothing more than an ornament, a kind of dainty decoration—someone who for lack of any other skill could, at least, freshen the waters, sweeten the spring, grace the pond—but nothing more! You understand? You *never* had a purpose. Never never were you *needed*—not by me, and surely not by Poseidon. The waters of life need no one to assist them; they flow of their own accord—ceaselessly, irreversibly—the less interference the better! What you call hard labor was something I contrived to keep you out of trouble. So long as it worked—well and good. You made no contribution," Sangarius summed up, "but neither did you contaminate!"

"You-you—" Nana faltered. "You mean that all—all those years you forced me to drive the waters, oversaw my drudgery, acted as my taskmaster, my scourge—was all that tyranny, that toil for nothing, a waste of effort?"

"Absolutely meaningless," he stated flatly.

"My whole life—*meaningless*?"

"More meaningless by far than your death will be—at least your death will serve a purpose."

After a brief silence, during which a pathetic sound, half moan, half whimper, escaped from Nana's throat, she recovered herself and said dispassionately, "Then let me die this minute."

"No, indeed! Filth doesn't disappear like that, it putrefies—and that takes time."

Instead of pressing her appeal, Nana repeated to herself, as if she were trying at once to assimilate the fact and ponder its significance, "The waters flow of their own accord . . . . I think I understand now *why* I must be put to death—"

"To purify the spring, of course."

"—why the penalty for going onto land is death—"

The water rippled audibly as Sangarius' tail recoiled. "Land?"

"What tempted me to leave the water—"

"You left the water?"

"—was *need*, some need to be united with the earth; and once there's need, there must be death."

"Answer me! You went onto the land?"

"Yes, Father," she replied without a moment's hesitation or trace of fear, her voice growing more and more exultant as she continued. "Not only that! I drank the wine. I sang my song. I saw Dionysus on the shore. I felt the god come into me. I followed him on penalty of death. I found myself on land, I gratified my craving for the fruit of the tree."

Wild with rage Sangarius began to bellow again, "Death! death!

147.

death!" and to beat his daughter not with his fists but with his mighty tail, inflicting terrible contusions and welts, lacerating her delicate flesh with his razor-sharp fin, causing the child to scream and howl which, far from making the father relent, goaded him on to thrash her harder until she swooned, and the river god released an earthshaking roar and dived out of sight, leaving his daughter to starve to death.

The following dawn Agdistis awoke unrested from a bad night's sleep, disturbed by dreams of terrific violence and strife. Not yet resigned to the absence of Its testicles, the hermaphrodite examined Itself on the chance that It had only dreamed the mutilation, but Its sore blood-encrusted groin dispelled such hopes. Rising despondently, It left the lair and squatted in shame behind a nearby bush to urinate. When It was through, It removed the sheepskin cloak from Its shoulders, as It had done the last two mornings, and wrapped it like a skirt around Its waist. Finally, by force of habit rather than enthusiasm, It took up the aulos and wandered down to the pond.

The ground at the end of the spit was strewn with pomegranates. Two days ago, when Agdistis had first laid eyes on the fruit, It felt too miserable to try one, but yesterday It had done so, and found the tartness to Its liking. Now It picked up another, peeled the rind, pulled apart the pulp, and devoured the crimson seeds. Ready, then, to greet Nana and the new day, Agdistis leaned against the tree trunk and raised the aulos to Its lips. The piping sounded more unearthly, the reedy high-pitched notes more protracted and doleful, the calling out more needful and imperative today than ever before. Yet, despite this fact, Nana did not appear. Agdistis stopped playing, utterly perplexed by her unprecedented absence. After a brief pause It piped again, this time sounding a single treble note, an unequivocal summons, sustained for a full minute. But still the nymph did not appear. Just as Agdistis was about to pipe a third time, It heard a distant cry coming, if It judged correctly, from the northwest. To confirm this impression It piped and heard the cry once more, whereupon the hermaphrodite set out in the direction of the sound, stopping every so often, as It hurried through the underbrush, to get Its bearings by piping again and waiting for the response to guide the way.

Emerging from the woods, Agdistis reached the bottom of a natural amphitheater of stratified rock, and began to climb the receding terraces, undeterred by the jagged stones and crabgrass underfoot, but going on, scaling the rises with ease and mounting ever higher till It reached the summit on which sparse clumps of ailanthus, scrub oak, and pitch pine grew, and from whose lookout It could view not only the source far below, but also what seemed the whole of creation: the vast Phrygian steppe, flanked by snowcapped mountain chains, stretching as far as the eye could see into the inferno of the rising sun.

Agdistis looked in vain for the creature who had summoned It, certain now that it could not have been Nana calling from this wilderness too barren even for a bird. Mystified, Agdistis piped again. From somewhere very far away behind Its back came the eerie answer, "Here!" Agdistis turned around, but saw no one. It piped again. Again It heard the distant cry, issuing, or so it seemed, from the bowels of the earth. Getting down on all fours, It began to crawl over the arid ground in search of It knew not what. Then, suddenly, though It had not piped, It heard the cry again and stopped in Its tracks. "Where are you?"

"Here!"

"Where?" It shouted out impatiently.

"Under you!"

Backing up, Agdistis discovered a fissure in the ground, into which It promptly peered, but could see nothing. "Who is it?"

"Nana," came the faint reply. "Help me, please."

"How?" The hermaphrodite pressed Its ear to the ground, while Nana related her grim tale. As she spoke, Agdistis began to experience an emotion It had never felt before. The feeling arose from Its own recent suffering, which seemed to match Nana's so closely it enabled Agdistis not only to understand her plight, but share in it by shedding tears. "How can I save you," It asked when she had finished, "set you free?"

"You can't," she said without self-pity. "There's only one thing you can do."

"What's that?"

"Bring food."

"Gladly. But how," It added rather hopelessly, "how will I get it to you?"

"Through the sinkhole."

"Through this? There's no food small enough. And how would you get it, if you're bound?"

"My hands are free."

"What food could it be?" Agdistis wondered aloud.

"The only food I know—scuds and mites and algae—all of it comes from the water," the nymph explained almost apologetically, before lapsing into silence.

"Wait!" Agdistis suddenly exclaimed. "I know!"

"Where are you going?"

"I'll be back," It assured her.

Fleet as a chamois It descended the hill, bounded down the levels of the amphitheater, sprinted into the woods and out again onto the spit where It snatched up the first pomegranate It could lay hands on and started back without even stopping to catch Its breath, completing the circuit in a matter of minutes. Breathing heavily, Agdistis kneeled beside the fissure. "Nana."

"You're back?"

"Yes. Tell me," It said, as It pared the rind, "where are you in relation to the sinkhole?"

"About two feet away."

"And when you stretch your hands out?"

"The light beam hits my knuckles."

"Good! Do it now," Agdistis instructed her, "stretch out your hands and cup the palms."

"What have you brought?"

Holding a single seed between Its thumb and forefinger, Agdistis dropped it carefully, like a pebble into a well, through the fissure and waited in suspense for a response from below. In a matter of seconds It heard a little exclamation of surprise. "Did you catch it?"

"Yes. What is it?"

"Taste it."

After a moment Nana reacted with enthusiasm. "Are there more?"

"Many," Agdistis informed her with delight, and proceeded to feed her the entire batch seed by seed.

"Thank you," she said when she was done, "for my life."

Every day thereafter, first thing in the morning the hermaphrodite went to the spit, collected two pieces of fruit, and climbed up to the sinkhole where It sat down on the ground, peeled both pomegranates, fed one to Nana, and ate the other Itself.

In the succeeding months Sangarius came to the cavern several times to observe Nana, but despite his surprise at finding her still alive, he was not at all disappointed by what he considered the prolongation of her suffering.

In time, however, as her womb began to swell, Nana feared that her father would notice her condition—which she herself was at a loss to understand—grow suspicious and kill her on the spot. To

150.

forestall such an event, every time she heard him approaching, the nymph would feign unconsciousness, letting her body go limp and hanging her head so that her long corn-silk hair completely veiled her enlarging breasts and womb. But when she was alone, which was almost all the time, her thoughts would turn invariably to her changing body. Day and night she wondered, pondered, puzzled over the altogether mystifying paradoxes of her condition. Left to starve to death, she found herself feeling more and more alive. Reduced to a diet of pomegranate seeds, she felt singularly healthy and strong. Condemned to solitude, she seldom, if ever, felt alone. Wrenched out of her element, it seemed at times as if that element had been internalized. Held captive, her body had been freed at last from toil, her imagination liberated. Told her life was meaningless, she was more convinced than ever of its real significance. But just why she felt the way she did, Nana hadn't an inkling. As often as she asked herself the question, she simply had no answer, no understanding of what was happening.

Finally, one summer's night, even as she slept, the answer came: she felt a body—another body inside her own—stir, and she awoke. A ray of moonlight was shining through the sinkhole. She placed both hands on her distended belly and felt the living thing inside stir again. Looking up, she saw the sinkhole open slowly to reveal the moon and stars and Milky Way, numinous in the infinitely unfolding firmament. She heard the everflowing river at her feet. She felt the fetus kick and knew, at last, the answer. Just as she was enveloped by this cave, and the cave by the earth, and the earth by the heavens, and the heavens by the gods, so she, too, enveloped *them*: the gods, the sun, the moon and stars, the earth, the waters of the earth, the Underworld, and every holy living thing— all that ever was or would be in the universe was there in her hands this minute, alive inside her womb, palpably alive, everlastingly alive like herself inside the timeless, deathless All.

After that there were no further doubts or questions, no more anxious thoughts of any kind, none whatever. She prevailed in joy over her father's sentence, flourished in her limestone prison, gloried in her pregnancy, felt increasingly fulfilled, increasingly robust and hungry—so much so, that Agdistis was finally obliged to supplement her daily diet with a second pomegranate which, instead of eating outright, Nana hoarded, sucked and savored for hours on end, knowing as she did that each and every seed contained the elixir of life.

Her labor started sometime after dark, but whether at midnight or much earlier she had no way of knowing, because the whole

151.

day had been dark, overcast, one long enduring dusk climaxed by a tremendous downpour, unusual for November, more like a summer storm complete with deafening thunderclaps and terrifying bolts of lightning aimed directly at the cavern roof, as if Zeus himself were displeased with her and determined to blast her to bits. Nana was terribly frightened. But her fear of the storm was as nothing compared with the fear induced by labor. Having vaguely envisioned a gradual painless transmutation of herself, more or less alike in process to the larva becoming a butterfly, the pistil a piece of fruit, Nana was altogether unprepared for childbirth, unprepared for labor pains, unprepared to find her body at the mercy of a force more radical than the raging storm.

It came in waves, this inner force, huge mounting, cresting, crushing waves of pain, which convulsed her body and made her groan. Try as she did to withstand each new onslaught by bracing her back against the limestone pillar, the next successive wave was always more powerful than its predecessor, and broke with overwhelming impact, causing Nana to cry and scream and strain against her bonds. In its reflux the wave took away all her recent insights, all her answers. It took away the moon and stars, the earth, the Underworld, and gods, from all of which she had imagined herself eternally inseparable, and demolished them. It took the whole extensive universe and reduced it in a trice to nothing—nothing but this fear and pain. O! how had she deluded herself into thinking she was generating life, when so obviously this force was not a force of life but death, an all-destroying force against which she was utterly alone, utterly defenseless. "You're going to die," she told herself, "you're going to die." She knew that now to be her fate, knew it as indisputably as she had known the night before that she would live forever. O! Her groans and cries echoed through the cavern, but instead of subsiding the pain increased, coming now in tidal waves till something inside her body burst, and Nana lost consciousness.

By the time she recovered, the storm had passed, the pain had ceased. She was dripping wet, especially about the thighs, drenched by what she assumed to be sweat; limp with exhaustion and chilled to the bone, yet grateful to be alive and out of pain. But presently the pain resumed, assaulting her with a vigor so intense it made what she had suffered earlier seem mild by comparison. In a matter of seconds her head swelled up till it felt as big as her womb, and she was sure it would burst. What started as a scream became an agonized groan, as she clenched her teeth against the pain. Reaching up, she grabbed the pillar with both hands, holding on for dear life, even as the force amassed within launched a full-scale attack, a fight to the death, bearing down with such unremitting might she felt her insides coming out.

When, at last, the attack abated, Nana gradually relaxed her grip, released the pillar, and lowered her hands to her pelvis. Just as she had feared, her insides *had* come out! She could feel them now, covered with slime, protruding from her body. Bringing her befouled fingers to her nose, she identified a saline smell, as well as the smell of blood, and was reminded she was dying. In the next second the spasms began anew, recurring now in quicker cycles, but with a difference: the fear and pain were gone—or, if not exactly gone, at least no longer dominant, the center of concern—and with them went her tensions, her physical resistance. It was as if her body had suddenly acquired a mind of its own and knew precisely what to do despite her brain—knew just when to muster all its strength and when to let it go, when to take a breath and when to release it, when to be active and when serene—knew not only how not to oppose, but also how to assist the body inside her own by contracting and relaxing her muscles in time with its tidal rhythm; knew at last that she was not in the throes of death but birth, that she herself was not the subject but the agent, not the river but the riverbed, the medium through which this living force, this sacred cosmic energy was coursing, and that her only earthly purpose now was to facilitate its passage. And so she labored selflessly, assiduously through the night into the small hours when suddenly the body inside her own plummeted with such terrific gravity Nana had to grab the pillar once again to keep from being pulled down with it; and, holding tight, she threw back her head, fixed her eyes on the sinkhole, clenched her jaw, and let the inner body go, ejected the vital force out of her womb into the world, relinquishing it in an ecstasy of jubilant laughter and joyful tears, which all at once was answered from below with a resounding robust bawl; and, reaching down, Nana found a cord coming from her insides, severed it instinctively and tied it off; but even as her fingers made the knot, she realized that her work was done, her destiny fulfilled, that she had just exchanged her own specific life for life itself, and Nana died in peace.

At dawn, when Agdistis came to the sinkhole to feed the nymph, It was amazed to be greeted not by Nana but a bawling infant. As often as It called her name, Nana didn't answer; instead, the infant bawled more lustily. Perplexed, Agdistis pared one of the pomegranates and dropped a seed down the sinkhole, but not

153.

only didn't Nana answer, the infant continued to bawl. At a loss what to do, Agdistis sat down on the cold damp ground and waited, cupping in Its palms Its greatly enlarged and aching breasts.

By mid-afternoon Sangarius, attracted by the fresh blood and afterbirth, came to the cavern and, finding Nana dead, laughed triumphantly; but wanting to get rid of the whoreson too, he seized the still-bawling baby, dove with it down the duct, and left it under the pomegranate tree to perish.

Through the fissure Agdistis heard the river god's gloating laughter, heard the baby's bawling cease, called to Nana one more time before It realized she was dead. Too bereaved to move, It spent the rest of the afternoon sitting in silence, still holding Its breasts from which, toward dusk, there suddenly spurted two small jets of milk.

In the waning twilight, which corresponded closely to the hermaphrodite's mood, Agdistis left the sinkhole, plodded down the levels of the amphitheater, and headed toward Its lair. Soon after It entered the woods, It heard a baby screaming and was reminded of the baby in the cave that dawn. Hurrying in the direction of the sound, It found the helpless infant on its back, beating the ground with its fists and kicking like a frog, as it cried and screamed itself hoarse. Not having eaten all day, the hermaphrodite's first impulse was to devour the child. Accordingly, It picked the foundling up by the wrist—provoking it to bawl all the louder—and began to examine its dangling body: prodding and squeezing the tender flesh (which Sangarius, doing the work of a midwife, had unwittingly bathed clean) in search of the choicest parts. Unable to decide between the belly and the buttocks, Agdistis shifted the baby from Its right hand to the bend of Its left arm, pressing the convulsed and shivering body close to Its own in order to examine it more easily, when all of a sudden the child took the hermaphrodite's teat into its mouth and started sucking greedily. This turn of events was so unexpected, so agreeable and soothing that Agdistis completely forgot Its own hunger in favor of the foundling's, whose crying had by now subsided.

Taking care not to disturb the infant as it went on feeding, the hermaphrodite sat down under the pomegranate tree and gazed at the pond. Huge glandular bubbles, milky in the moonlight, were erupting from the spring, bursting into froth and fanning out over the slowly moving water whose surface glinted and twinkled as if it too, like the heavens above, were studded with numberless stars. The baby had begun to gurgle, but to Agdistis, who was feeling very drowsy now, everything seemed interfused. It could no longer differentiate between the baby's gurgles and the sound of the source, between the source and Itself, Itself and the infant at Its breast, the flow of milk and the river's flow, the flood of moon and stars gushing out of the ground and out of Its nipple, nurturing the infant in Its arms and all the Orient . . . . Nodding, Agdistis pulled the sheepskin out from under Its rump, wrapped it snugly around Itself and the still-feeding infant, and, utterly content, fell sound asleep.

V

High above the workers' district and the outlying deposits of salt and clay, safely inside the citadel of Pessinus whose cyclopean walls surrounded the palace, temple, cemetery, cistern, and granary; behind the less massive but no less impregnable palace walls topped with iron spikes; past the royal orchards of pomegranate, pear, olive, fig, and citrus trees; beyond the royal stables, storehouses, arsenal, fountain, and sacrificial altar; at the far end of the vast flagstone courtyard; under the gilded guardian lions on the pediment over the portico of the Hall of Honor; ensconced on a throne of highly-polished basalt placed in front of the hall's gold-plated and ivory-inlaid portal, sat King Midas, listening inattentively to his chancellor. A swallow had built its nest on the inner side of the entablature, and the king was watching the bird feed its young.

"It's spreading like an epidemic," the chancellor was saying. "Every other day someone else claims to have seen the creature— not just woodcutters, herdsmen, farmers, but people in the city: women, children, potters, smiths—not only do they claim to have seen It, they swear they've heard It *speak*. Apparently, It comes right into their back yards in broad daylight to take whatever It needs: fire, food, garments, oil, cooking utensils—all of which they give It gladly . . . as a kind of oblation, I suppose. And afterward, when they're questioned, it's not as if each one had a different story— Oh, no! they all agree: black braided hair, brown eyes, prominent nose, over six feet tall—"

"Have *you* seen It, Rusa?" the king inquired skeptically, as the swallow flew away and the fledglings began to cheep.

"No, but my son—the youngest—has, and the boy's far from ignorant."

"Well, naturally they all agree—what would you expect? They've been telling each other tales about the creature for a thousand years, have paintings of It, statues—"

"Yes, of course—if you'll excuse me, sire—that was my reaction too, at first. However, in none of their paintings, none of their statues or stories has Agdistis ever been represented with an infant in Its arms. That's something new."

Now, for the first time since Rusa raised the subject, Midas leaned forward, evidently interested. "Infant?"

"Yes. That's the other point on which they all agree: wherever It goes, Agdistis takes with It an infant, cradled in a cotton sling—a sort of homemade marsupium—suspended from Its neck."

Once again the king was silent, absorbed in his own thoughts, but whether about the hermaphrodite or the queen, Rusa hadn't the temerity to ask. After a rather lengthy pause, he stood up—at his full height Midas wasn't much taller than the back of the throne, slightly over five feet—and went into the courtyard. Rusa followed until he realized that the king was going nowhere in particular but was merely restless, wandering aimlessly, though more or less in circles, around the sacrificial altar. Observing this, Rusa stepped back out of the sunlight into the shade cast by the east wing of the palace—the apartments occupied by the seventeen princesses and their husbands—and waited patiently.

Midas had a mannerism, when walking, of lifting his feet high off the ground, as if he were tramping through tall grass, and of turning his head jerkily from side to side, as if his eyes were set in his temples and on the constant lookout for an assassin—a mannerism reminiscent of a game bird. His squat build and colorful clothes served to reinforce this impression. He wore the traditional Phrygian cap—a phallus-shaped hood with long pendent earflaps suggestive of wattles—snug-fitting leather trousers spangled with electrum, buskins, a belted chiton and an elaborately embroidered, open, sleeveless coat. Like the feathers of a game bird, the royal finery merged with its surroundings—the powder-blue, bronze-green, and crimson colors of the palace—until the two were almost indistinguishable, each the complement of the other.

From time to time Midas stopped and looked expectantly in the direction of the north wing, which contained his sleeping quarters, as well as those of the queen and the royal concubines, but seeing nothing, resumed meandering around the sacrificial altar. Presently, at a moment when the king's back was turned, Tyana, the queen's handmaid, came out of the palace. As soon as Rusa saw her, he raised his brows inquiringly. Tyana stopped, shook her head in the negative, and then proceeded toward the monarch.

156.

Even before she reached him, the king could tell from Tyana's cautious gait and apprehensive expression that she was the bearer of bad tidings, but Midas waited to speak until the woman had abased herself at his feet. "Well?"

"The queen, my lord" —Tyana tried her best to sound auspicious— "has given birth."

"Another girl?" he said dryly. The handmaid's response—if, indeed, there was one—was inaudible. Tyana remained with her forehead touching the hot flagstones, her scarlet himation covering her head. "Is she still alive?"

The handmaid's expression brightened as she looked up. "Oh yes, my lord, crying heartily."

"Not the child, imbecile! the queen." Tyana quickly lowered her eyes, licked her lips, and nodded imperceptibly. "More's the pity." For a moment Midas stared grimly at the sacrificial altar. That he had never had a son, not even with his concubines, and still, at fifty-six, remained without an heir, rankled sorely. No matter how faithfully he followed the priests' prescriptions for begetting a son—subsisting on a diet that excluded everything but egg yolks boiled in myrrh and honey or consuming huge quantities of ginger, garlic, cinnamon, and sparrow tongues—the queen invariably broke out in spots, suffered nosebleeds, and her nipples turned black: the surest signs of carrying a girl child. But since Midas was neither content to attribute his misfortune to the Fates, nor prepared to blame either the gods or himself (the former being sacrilegious, the latter inconceivable), he held womankind wholly responsible. "All that soft ensnaring flesh, those female-producing loins," he muttered now to himself, as if he were about to make a hecatomb of the entire distaff side of the household, and could already see them with their throats cut, bodies flayed, vitals wrapped in folds of fat broiling on the altar. "Go!" he commanded Tyana, "tell your mistress to keep out of my sight—*all* of them—tell them all to keep to their quarters, if they value their lives!"

Hearing this and seeing the handmaid flee across the courtyard back into the palace, Rusa was in no hurry to rejoin Midas. But the king, for his part, was facing Rusa now and shielding his eyes against the sun, as if he were looking for Rusa, so the chancellor steeled himself and went over to express his regrets. By the time he reached the king, however, Rusa realized that Midas was not, in fact, looking for him but at the gilded lions on the Hall of Honor, shielding his eyes not against the sun but the glare from the gold.

"If only I knew *then*," Midas mused regretfully, "what I know now."

"When, my lord?"

"When it came to ransoming Silenus—I would have asked for *sons.*"

"If you'll forgive my saying so, my lord," Rusa remarked, "there isn't that much difference between the two—gold and sons—both bring heartache."

"There's a great deal of difference" —Midas took his eyes off the lions and scowled at Rusa— "when it comes to primogeniture!"

"Who can say? For all we know, it might be a blessing."

"How so?"

"After all, if you did have sons, the eldest would automatically accede to the throne. Whereas, this way, you have a choice—complete freedom to choose among your sons-in-law, grandsons, even—"

"There isn't one I trust!" Midas turned and walked away toward the orchards.

"In that case," Rusa went on, keeping abreast of the king, "you might consider nephews."

"Such as your youngest," Midas remarked with irony, "the one who saw Agdistis?"

"The boy has many remarkable qualities—" Rusa broke off, seeing the king stop in his tracks, obviously struck by an idea. "Yes, sire?"

"This infant, Rusa?"

"Which infant, sire?"

"The hermaphrodite's—has it a sex?"

"No doubt, but no one's mentioned it—no one, I imagine, chose to get that close."

"Well, have someone find out!"

"The child's sex?"

"Yes. Send someone to Its lair— It's supposed to live in the woods, isn't It, at the source of the Sangarius? Disguise someone as a woodcutter then, and send him there—*alone*, though, so as not to alarm the creature."

"If you'll forgive me, your highness, there isn't a man in the kingdom who would dare go near Agdistis alone."

"What? Not even that son of yours? Surely he's brave enough—if, as you claim, he's qualified to be my successor. Let's see what he's made of, Rusa. Yes, by all means, send your son— No, wait! Better yet" —a cruel self-satisfied smile animated the king's expression— "send the queen!"

As relieved as Rusa was by this sudden reversal, it left him utterly incredulous. "The *queen*, my lord?"

"Yes."

"Alone, my lord?"

"Yes—no! . . . No," Midas drawled, glowing with delight, "not alone. Have her take with her that newborn babe of hers."

"The princess, my lord?"

"Yes."

"And the palace guard—"

"Will escort her to the woods—no farther. She's to go the rest of the way alone."

"And-and, if Agdistis should assault her?"

"So much the better: what more fitting end for a breeder of females?" Pleased with himself, the king turned back now toward the palace and revealed the rest of his plan with mounting excitement. "If, by some stroke of luck, the hermaphrodite's child should prove to be a male, the queen is to exchange it for her own. She will then return to the palace without, needless to say, a word to anyone—unless she wants her tongue pulled out"—Midas looked hard at his chancellor—"the same holds true for you, Rusa—she'll return to the palace and raise the child as my heir." The king paused and stroked his beard pensively. "Really, when you stop to think about it, what could be better than to have as your heir the son of a deity? . . . Who knows, perhaps the gods themselves have had a hand in this, have sent the child to me—that would certainly explain the hermaphrodite's appearances of late. Yes, yes, it all begins to make sense somehow, perfect sense. Go! have a wagon—not the royal one—made ready. Inform the queen of my instructions. She's to set out as soon as she's regained her strength, not later than three days from now. And Rusa," Midas called the chancellor back, "impress on her the fact that, despite her opposition, she's going to bear me a son after all."

Left alone, the king looked up once more at the gilded lions and began to laugh, delighting in his own humor, irony, ingenuity, impending triumph over the queen, but most of all he laughed with joy because he knew himself to be a favorite of the gods.

At dawn, three days later, Queen Tabal, wrapped in a drab himation which covered not only her head, most of her solemn face and a threadbare tunic that reached to the top of her high-laced buskins, but also concealed a crying baby, walked without glancing either to the right or left past the king and assembled foot soldiers into a waiting wagon. The interlaced leather-strap floor yielded under her heavy tread, giving the queen a foretaste of her imminent insecurity and peril, and she was relieved to reach the corner and sit down on a chest stocked with provisions for the journey.

Once settled, she slipped her right hand under the himation, not to comfort the crying child, but to reassure herself that her gold filigree bracelet and diadem were still in her bodice where she had hidden them earlier. As the wagon lurched forward, a drop of water from the cotton awning, which had been wetted down to guard against the summer sun, fell like a tear onto her cheek. Tabal, who was quite prepared to die but not to shed tears, wiped it away brusquely. Presently she caught a whiff of pears, realized that the wagon was skirting the orchards, and wondered if she would ever smell their fragrance again. A little farther along, at the gateway to the palace, she wondered too whether she would ever again hear the consoling sound of the massive folding doors being closed behind her. Not since she had come, as a bride, from Cappadocia thirty years ago had Tabal set foot outside the citadel. But now—what with the awning, the agitated baby and the steep decline of the hillside—she scarcely glimpsed the walls before the wagon reached the highroad and she was obliged to veil her face against the dust.

As far as Amorium, the city south of Pessinus, the trip was altogether tedious, uneventful. But once the wagon left the highroad and set out across the steppe, the combination of extreme heat and dust, constant bumps and jolts made both the queen and princess sick, and Tabal finally ordered the wagon stopped, dismounted, and went the rest of the way on foot.

By the time they reached the edge of the woods it was late afternoon. The captain of the guard advised the queen to postpone her mysterious mission till the following day, but Tabal was eager to get the ordeal over with. After a brief but unrefreshing rest, during which time the soldiers set up camp, she called for a water bag, some bread and cheese, and a lantern. Ready then to venture into the woods, she spoke again to the captain. "You have your orders?"

"Yes, your highness."

"If I'm not back by dawn the day after tomorrow," she quoted Rusa's words nonchalantly, "you're to return to the capital without me." The captain frowned and parted his lips, about to speak. To forestall discussion, the queen requested that the lantern be lighted. Though still daylight, she wanted to be prepared for all eventualities. Tabal looked up to observe the position of the sun. "If I keep the sun in front of me, facing into it, I'll come to the source?"

"Yes, your highness." The lighted lantern was brought back, and the captain handed it to her. "May the Great Mother be with you."

Since Agdistis was the offspring of the Great Mother, Cybele, Tabal could not help but smile at the irony. "Thank you," she said and, turning, walked away in the direction of the declining sun.

Encumbered though she was by her infant and provisions, Tabal was only too glad to leave behind the blazing heat and choking dust of the steppe, to feel the cool air on her cheek, the submissive moss and matted leaves underfoot, to hear the birds singing in the trees, to be alone and proceed at her own pace into the peaceful woods from which she fully expected never to return. And yet she was not afraid. From time to time since that fateful morning when Rusa brought the news, the queen had felt convinced she was being exiled, that all the talk about trading babies with Agdistis was just a pretext to get rid of her. At other times the tale seemed too fantastic, too obsessive to be a fabrication. About the deity Itself, she entertained no doubts: for as long as she could remember, Tabal had believed unquestioningly in the existence of Agdistis. That It lived at the source of the Sangarius, she knew to be a fact. That It was double-sexed, she also knew. That It had somehow borne or acquired a child didn't sound at all unlikely. But that she would be able to wrest the child away from Agdistis—whether by bribery or wile—seemed utterly infeasible. Either It would strike her dead, drive her mad, tear her limb from limb, or turn her into a tree, but she would never see her family again—of that she was absolutely certain, absolutely accepting. After all, she had fulfilled her destiny—whatever Midas thought—had borne and raised seventeen daughters—eighteen, now—

Tabal stopped, put down the lantern, and peeked under the himation. The infant was asleep. . . . How much the poor thing would be spared, how much deprived of . . . . Raising her grave rugged face, the queen looked up into the sunlit leaves, as if for an example of something beautiful the child would never see, but soon realized that she herself had never set foot in these woods, and that more than likely the child—were she to live—would never leave the confines of the citadel—so that was not an issue. What difference could death make to an infant? It would be, for this one, much as it had been for the other two: the stillbirths. As for herself—the queen picked up the lantern and continued on her way—she had seen quite enough of life to be quit of it—if the gods so willed. Her one regret was that she would never again set eyes on Cappadocia. For thirty years she had dreamed of returning one day to her homeland, of seeing once more its lava cones spiring the landscape, of leaving Pessinus forever and going back to the natural rock out of which she had come. O, to see again those towering waves of hollow rock molded by the elements into forms of fabulosity: a whole city in the shape of dromedary humps and mammary glands mounting in swirls and swells and sweeping curves of polished stone, smoother than her baby's cheek—a whole city without a single rough edge, sharp point, straight line or squared-off corner. The cones of Cappadocia had spoiled her for everything to come: for the citadel of Pessinus, the palace, temple, tumulus, terraces, Hall of Honor—for any man-made structure, no matter how sublime. The cones of Cappadocia made all of man's creations unimaginative, inhuman. People had not been meant to live according to the rules of geometry. Imagine having to be born out of a geometric womb, having to feed at a cubic breast! "How would you like *that*?" she said aloud to the sleeping infant. . . . No, if she *had* to die and couldn't do it in Cappadocia, she was glad, at least, to be far away from Pessinus, far from the palace, out of that endless maze of cubicles and rectilinear passageways.

Tabal stopped short, her usually solemn eyes suddenly alert, ears cocked to a faint roar coming from the distance. Quickly she checked the position of the sun—no longer diagonally overhead, but well below the treetops—listened intently, realized that the sound was coming from the west, and concluded she must be approaching the source. The queen heaved a sigh and her heartbeat quickened as she hurried on, prepared to meet her fate.

Farther along, she stopped again to listen, uncertain this time what she was hearing, whether the song of a nightingale or someone playing a flute. But what would a shepherd be doing in the woods? Nor, for that matter, could it be a nightingale: the song was too prolonged, unearthly. It seemed to issue, together with the roar, out of the source itself, and yet to remain detached, independent of it, to rise above it like smoke from a fire, drifting upward into the atmosphere, even as it drew Tabal, as if she were ensorcelled, toward it now, intoxicated not only by the eerie sound, but by the distinct aroma of burning sandalwood, coming from the same direction as the increasingly loud piping and roaring of the source, ringing in her ears and filling her nostrils with its aromatic smoke—no longer a figment of her imagination, but visible in the fading light—a dove-gray smoke, filtering through the very trees through which she herself was advancing now with evident awe, though trying the while to keep her wits about her: holding high the lantern to herald her approach and repeatedly pronouncing in a hushed and reverential tone the name of the god whose summons she knew beyond doubt that she was answering. "Agdistis? . . ."

In the next second she heard the music stop, saw a smoking fire, saw a lean-to, saw a half-dressed Amazon with a crying infant tucked under one arm and a javelin jutting from under the other, leap into her path. Throwing down the water bag, the bread and cheese and lantern, Tabal prostrated herself at the deity's feet and held out the princess, who also had begun to cry, as if to make an offering of the child.

"Who are you?" Agdistis demanded gruffly.

"A mother," Tabal said, her forehead pressed to the ground, her shaky voice projected backward through her bended knees, perspiration saturating her cotton dress, "like yourself."

"What business have you here?"

"I'm lost . . . banished."

"From where?"

"Pessinus."

"Sh-sh, little one, that's enough: there's nothing to fear."

It took Tabal, who was still prostrate, a moment to realize that these soft-spoken words were not addressed to her. Relieved as she was by the god's changed tone, she dared not raise her head or open her eyes until Agdistis remarked, "What about *yours*? Why do you thrust it from you? Comfort it!"

Bringing the princess to her bosom, Tabal sat back on her heels and began to hum a lullaby. Unlike Agdistis, who appeared unable to quiet the infant in Its arms without constantly observing the creature's expression, Tabal was experienced enough to attend to the princess at the same time that she began, before it grew too dark, to satisfy her curiosity about her surroundings. As soon as she had assured herself of the javelin's whereabouts—it was standing now, propped against a nearby tree—she turned her attention to the god. Compared with Its majestic height and powerful build, Agdistis' delicately braided and beribboned hair—there were six plaits in all—looked incongruous. Tabal could not, as yet, see the baby's face, but its naked body was well proportioned, quite large, in fact, for its age, which she guessed to be about seven months. Their living area was nothing more than a lair, a shallow pit carpeted with oddments—some beautifully embroidered, others merely rags—canopied by what must once have been some commoner's himation. Strewn, as if by a landslide, outside the lean-to was an assortment of cooking, storage, and serving vessels so numerous and varied, Tabal had never seen its like, not even in the royal kitchen. This domestic debris was grouped, more or less, around a makeshift hearth, straddled by a tripod that held a steaming cauldron whose contents were indiscernible because of the sandalwood's predominant aroma. "May I ask what you're cooking?"

Agdistis eyed her with suspicion. "Lamb."

"And for the baby?"

"Lamb," It repeated impatiently.

"You mean to say it has its teeth already?"

"No, but *I* have." Self-evident as this statement was to Agdistis, It could see that Tabal was puzzled. "I chew first, then feed the child."

". . . Oh, I see. There are, you know," she ventured politely, "certain dishes it could eat on its own. I'd be happy to prepare one now, if you'd like. I have some cheese right here, all I need's some greens— Please don't look so suspicious. I'll taste the food myself, when it's ready, to prove it isn't harmful. Shall I?"

Agdistis weighed the worrisome proposal in silence. After what seemed a full minute, It finally nodded, but cautiously.

"Good." As soon as she was on her feet, Tabal said, more to win Its trust than for the sake of practicality, "Will you hold my baby too, while I get started?"

Agdistis put Its hand up, keeping her at arm's length. "How will we tell them apart?"

Until this moment the queen had completely forgotten the purpose of her mission. Reminded now, her heart began to pound, and she swallowed hard. "Is yours a boy or girl?"

"I don't know."

Taking this mysterious reply to mean that Agdistis was still uncertain whether or not the child would turn out, like Itself, to be a hermaphrodite, Tabal smiled inwardly, enjoying the possibility of Midas' being foiled by the gods. "May I look at it?" To reassure Agdistis, she said again, "You hold mine"; whereupon—the offer being accepted with a half-hearted shrug—they exchanged infants.

The moment Tabal beheld the child's face her mouth fell open. Never in all her years in Pessinus—in the course of which she had had dealings with more than a hundred fifty babies, related in one way or another to the royal household, plus her own twenty— never had she seen a baby as beautiful as this. Its hair was aubergine purple, curly and soft as a Persian lamb's; and its huge black eyes, over which the merest suggestion of eyebrows spread like the wings of a swift, were already as shrewd and expressive as any Tabal had ever looked into. At the moment, they were regarding her somewhat saucily with a combination of curiosity, dry amusement, and absolute self-confidence, as if to say, Well, what do you think? to which Tabal replied aloud, "Beautiful."

Pleased by the sound of this new voice, the softness and smell of this new body, the infant began to grasp and pat Tabal's broad nose, prod her cheeks, and probe her mouth with intense concentration.

Tabal had long since noticed the baby's penis, but hesitated now to mention it to Agdistis as the most obvious way of differentiating between the children. She had, in fact, half a mind to follow through her husband's plan, not in order to satisfy Midas or to save herself, but simply because she was too smitten to give the baby back. She had never felt this way before—possessive, yes, but never covetous; covetous, moreover, of someone else's child, the child of a god, no less. Such a desire was worse than a crime, it was an overstepping of the bounds, a sacrilege for which she would surely be destroyed! Come to your senses, she cautioned herself. "We can easily tell them apart" —she turned the infant toward the god— "by this."

Agdistis' eyes shifted from the princess to Its own child and back again several times with increasing confusion, as if, till then, It hadn't recognized the difference.

Tabal's attention, meanwhile, was still riveted on the bewitching boy who by now had squirmed around to face her once more. "What do you call it?"

"Little one."

"Its name, I mean."

"It hasn't any."

"You must call it Attis, then."

"Attis?"

"For 'beautiful boy.' " The suggestion being met by silence, Tabal glanced up. Agdistis looked bewildered. Interpreting Its expression to relate to the child's possible androgyny, she added lightly, "Until, that is, there's some proof to the contrary."

Instead of dispelling the god's perplexity, her remark seemed to make it worse. For some reason—either because It didn't understand her humor or was preoccupied with Its own thoughts or couldn't see something to Its satisfaction in the dusk—Agdistis suddenly went and picked up the lantern, came back to where Tabal was standing, and held the light first over one child, then the other. Still not satisfied It transferred the princess to Tabal's free arm in order to examine both infants more readily. Seeing the lantern flicker and hearing a prolonged sough, Tabal imagined for a moment that the wind had risen, but soon realized it was Agdistis, breathing heavily. Its eyes were so intense now, It looked half crazed as It began to finger the children's genitals; and though It

165.

did so gently, Tabal was, nonetheless, frightened—frightened not only by the look in Its eye, but by her own uncertainty about what It might do next.

For the longest time Agdistis continued to study and compare the infants, as if It were only now discovering—consciously, palpably—the biological distinction between male and female. But gradually the focus of comparison shifted from the boy and girl to the boy and Itself or, more precisely, to a comparison of their penises. This shift became clear to Tabal the moment Agdistis began to feel Its groin—through the sheepskin cloak at first, then by reaching under it—at the same time that Its eyes ceased to fluctuate, remaining fixed on the boy alone, Its expression totally bemused, as if It were trying hard to correlate the organ in Its hand with the one It had Its eye on, trying to comprehend the mysterious elements of form and change and growth, trying, in short, to figure out how in the world an infant ever got from *that* to *this*. Then all at once, for no apparent reason, Its expression changed— Its eyelids closed, brows knit, lips twisted, fingers clenched—and It appeared to be in pain, *was* in pain, but whether over something It was feeling now or merely remembering, Tabal couldn't tell; and though she wanted very much to comfort It, she didn't quite know how, didn't know what to do or say. As it turned out, there was no need to do anything. Whatever had come over the god, shortly passed away. Agdistis opened Its eyes, gazed in wonder at the boy, put down the lantern, and stretched out Its arms, clearly requesting Tabal to give the baby back. When she did, Agdistis hugged it to Its bosom and said in an impassioned whisper, "Attis!" After a moment It held the child out admiringly at arm's length, and, as Its lips began to tremble and Its eyes to fill with tears of joy, It said again, "Attis!" then raised the child high overhead and looking up—the child, in a tremor of excitement, looking down and shrieking with delight—said once more, this time in a tone of adoration, "Attis!"

Not wishing to interrupt the god's rapture, yet wanting to get started on the meal, Tabal waited for an appropriate moment to entrust the princess to Its care.

When the moment came, Agdistis surprised her by saying, "What do you call *yours*?"

The princess, on being separated from her mother, had begun to cry, and for that reason Tabal decided there and then to call her Ia. The appellation pleased Agdistis, and the god repeated it several times, though adding each time in counterpoint the name Attis.

Tabal had planned to prepare a kind of cheese-and-spinach

166.

pudding, but—there being no spinach on hand—made do with beet greens. As she worked she imparted to the god the recipe not only for the dish in progress, but for countless others, as well as for certain household remedies such as a tonic made with cumin seeds—interspersing her discourse with a good deal of free advice on weaning, teething, toilet training, and any other bits of domestic wisdom that came to mind.

When the pudding was ready, Agdistis couldn't stomach it and turned, instead, to the lamb, but Attis gobbled it up. After Tabal had finished feeding him, the child chanced upon the gold bracelet concealed in her bodice, and she parted with it willingly. Fascinated by the play of the firelight on the filigree, Attis began to talk in earnest to the bracelet, put it into his mouth, and drub Tabal's bosom and nose with it. Agdistis was no less fascinated than the child by this new toy, but Attis wouldn't part with it. To placate the god and avert a dispute, Tabal promptly produced the diadem. Agdistis smiled broadly, took the ornament and slipped it around Its right breast. Large as it was, the breast wasn't quite large enough to hold the diadem in place, and it kept falling off, much to Agdistis' frustration. Again and again It tried in vain to put it on. Finally, Tabal, whose awe of the god had successfully checked her laughter, demonstrated how the crown was meant to be worn: with its three gold ribbons to the back of the head. But Agdistis wasn't satisfied till It figured out a way of securing the diadem by wrapping the pliable gold ribbons around Its breast. Then, content at last, the god yawned mightily, carried Attis into the lair, stretched out on the mats, and went to sleep, leaving Tabal and Ia to fend for themselves.

Exhausted as she was, Tabal had great difficulty falling asleep, not because she was unused to sleeping on the ground, but because she couldn't stop mulling over and marveling at the day's events; and also because she realized suddenly that she was going to survive those events (at least for the moment), that in the morning she would have to leave this wonderland and return to Pessinus where she would either be put to death by Midas or be obliged to resume her dull routine—neither of which prospects heartened her now that she had encountered the deity and the holy child.

By the light of day Attis was even more beautiful, if possible, than he had seemed the night before. The gleam in his otherwise pitch-black eyes was so alluring, Tabal had, on looking into them, literally to gasp for air and turn away to overcome a touch of vertigo. Once again she was tempted to carry out her husband's plan—but how, now that the children were clearly differentiated,

and she had squandered her jewelry, and Attis was safely seques-
tered in a cotton sling suspended from Agdistis' neck? When the
time came for Agdistis to escort her out of the woods, she pointed
at the sling and remarked, "Isn't it too hot for that?"

"Not for me. I'm used—"

"For Attis, I mean."

"Perhaps you're right."

"I'll carry both," Tabal volunteered, as Agdistis removed the infant and disposed of the sling, and she saw for the first time since
last night the gold diadem girding the god's right breast.

"Why, when I'm so much stronger?" Agdistis protested, tucking
Attis under one arm and Ia under the other, and setting out in the
direction of the rising sun.

Despite the fact that Agdistis was carrying both babies, Tabal
couldn't keep abreast of It, and she was winded by the time she
caught sight of the wagon through the trees and heard indistinctly
the soldiers' voices coming from the distance. "We'd better part
here," she suggested.

"Thank you," Agdistis said, "for naming the child."

Once again Tabal prostrated herself before the deity. "Thank *you*
for permitting us to spend the night." When she was back on her
feet, Tabal was suddenly overcome by an impulse she couldn't
explain, couldn't control. Against her will and better judgment,
against all common sense and piety, she nonetheless found herself
reaching out quite consciously and taking not the princess but Attis
from Agdistis. Folly though it was, she simply couldn't help herself. Besides, it wasn't in any way her own fault, but the fault of
the gods for creating a creature as irresistible as Attis; and though
she dreaded the consequences, she turned around now, her heart in
her mouth, and walked slowly toward the wagon. In the next second, however, she was scared almost out of her wits by Agdistis,
who laid a heavy hand on her shoulder. Too frightened even to
look back, she waited in terror till the god came around in front of
her and she could see It holding Ia in one hand and pointing with
the other at the child's vulva. Though she tried to laugh the matter
off, Tabal felt herself flushing, in a sweat. "Oh! I-I didn't— I—
mistake—please—no harm—" But Agdistis was so relieved to
have caught the mistake in time, It grinned from ear to ear; whereupon Tabal apologized again, lowered her head in shame, and
slouched away, just as she had come, carrying the princess.

Alerted by the sentinels, Midas and Rusa were waiting at the
palace gates when the wagon returned. Tabal could not help but

observe with amusement the king's expectant expression. Scarcely had she dismounted, than the infant was snatched from her arms and examined with regard to its sex. As soon as Midas realized that she had brought back the princess, he became livid with rage, and would have hurled the child to the ground or crushed it to death, had not the queen intervened. "The *other*, the child of the god," she explained forcefully, "is also a hermaphrodite!"

Midas looked amazed. "You saw Agdistis?"

"I did indeed," she continued with uncommon boldness, attributable only to her encounter with the god. "And you would do well, hereafter, to accept your fate with a little more humility." So saying, Tabal recovered Ia, walked proudly down the ramp, across the great courtyard, and into the palace.

VI

A sudden breeze stirred the sheer curtains veiling Aphrodite's couch. The goddess, who was lying on her back, her left hand holding her groin as if to stem the outflow of some internal force, her right hand covering her eyes, not casually but purposely to occlude her vision—the goddess, feeling the draft on her cheek and sensing the movement of the curtains, turned her head, but did not uncover her eyes. "Is that you?"

"Yes," said a naked boy, as he alighted on the marble floor and drew in a pair of pearly wings which came to rest flat and sleek against his youthful back, the wing-bends invisible below his delicately sloping shoulders. In his cupped palms he held a small amount of something wrapped in cheesecloth—something whose sharp aroma Aphrodite sensed, in much the same way that she had sensed the boy's arrival, without opening her eyes.

"You've brought the camphor?"

"Yes." The boy kept the cheesecloth at arm's length to prevent tears from filling his amber eyes.

"Where did you find it?"

"In the East."

"Good! Quickly now, steep it in water," she prescribed with urgency.

The boy, his heels never touching the marble floor, moved to the washstand, dropped the camphor into a gold goblet, filled the goblet from a gold pitcher, and proceeded to blend the contents with his nimble fingers.

"Quickly, Eros," Aphrodite called to him, "quickly!"

When the potion was ready, Eros carried it over to the couch, parted the curtains, lifted the goddess' head with one hand (Aphrodite's own hand still covered her eyes), while with the other he brought the goblet to her pale lips.

"Disgusting!" she remarked on swallowing the dosage, and, thereupon, sank back down among the pillows and waited with her hand still over her eyes for the medicine to take effect. Presently she began to perspire, moderately at first, then profusely, as if she were feverish and the fever had begun to break. To add to this impression, the goddess murmured half-deliriously a name or word of which all but the vowel sound *a* was indistinct.

By the time she stopped perspiring, the pillows and linen were soaked, and her ordinarily lustrous fluffy hair was a mass of tiny spit curls and serpentine strings. Uncovering her eyes at last, she smoothed back the hair from her temples and smiled at Eros to signify that the ordeal was over, that once again she was at peace with herself. "Not since I first laid eyes on Adonis," she remarked, "have I suffered a seizure like that."

"But why, if the boy delights you so, did you kill your desire, Mistress? Why not have satisfied it?"

Aphrodite heaved a sigh. "Because, alas, I myself have earmarked him for others."

Eros' eyes brightened at this, and he raised and lowered his wings just once, very rapidly, involuntarily, as if in anticipation of flight. In the early morning light his iridescent feathers glowed parti-colored: pink and pearl, azure and apple green. Instead of his usual soft round self, he suddenly looked angular: his straight nose sharp, the outline of his parted lips as pronounced as a drawn bow, nipples erect, the tongue of his headband standing upright at the center of his scalp like a little vestigial horn. "What others?"

"Patience, my pet." The goddess swung her shapely legs off the couch, slipped her feet into a pair of sandals, and waited while Eros laced them up. That done, she went to the dressing table to arrange her hair. "Where is your switch?" she asked, glancing at the boy's reflection in the mirror.

"Outside, on the bench."

"Go and get it."

A moment later Eros returned carrying a young weeping willow branchlet, out of which many lesser branchlets sprouted like cords from a cat-o'-nine-tails. A thrill surged through Aphrodite as she looked into the mirror and saw the boy behind her back test the switch by lashing the air savagely three or four times—an exercise that produced a nasty hissing sound, and made Eros bare his bright teeth and contort his beautiful features with cruelty.

As if she herself had been stung by the switch, the goddess sprang to her feet and whispered with emotion, "Go now, Eros, go to Agdistis—dazzle It, daunt It, drive It to distraction with desire for the boy! Let It learn today—*my* day, the first of spring—exactly who Aphrodite is and what tribute she demands—even from the gods. Let It lose all sense of Itself today, all sense of the world— the source, the steppe, the stars—of *everything* but Attis. Let Its being depend from this day forth entirely on Attis, without whose charms and favors let Agdistis find Itself committed evermore to nonentity. Go now, Eros, go!"

The boy was only too eager to execute her orders. Like a peregrine swooping down on its prey, he descended all the way from Olympus to the source of the Sangarius without a moment's deviation—either to wheel or glide or ride the wind—but worked his wings tirelessly till he spotted the lean-to. Even then, Eros didn't alight to catch his breath and creep up on his quarry, but dived instead directly at the sleeping Agdistis who, ever since Attis had come to pubescence, had left the lair entirely to the boy and bedded on the ground just outside the lean-to.

Even before It opened Its eyes, Agdistis was aware of an unusual light, so intense and bright it clearly penetrated Its eyelids. For a moment It kept them tightly shut in hopes that the light would disappear and let It go back to sleep, but the light remained intense. When at last It opened Its eyes, the light was so blinding Agdistis put a hand up to protect Its sight. Once It realized that the rays could not possibly be coming from the sun, which had scarcely risen, It was at a loss to understand the glare. To further complicate the enigma, the light was easily as hot as the sun at its zenith—the hermaphrodite's brow was already beaded with sweat—and seemed, moreover, to be changing constantly from rose to blue to green.

In an effort to make some sense of what was happening, Agdistis sat up and rubbed Its eyes. Attis was still asleep. The boy had kicked off his cloak and was lying naked on his back, head turned away from Agdistis, cheek resting on his right shoulder, right hand compressing his thick black curls, legs spread wide, the right one bent at the knee and leaning against the side of the lair, the left outstretched, left hand cupping his erect penis, the scrotum drawn tight, testicles upended and perfectly defined.

If Agdistis had ever seen Attis or, for that matter, anyone but Itself with an erection, It had not been particularly conscious of the

fact. Over the years It had even lost interest in Its own erections—
if, indeed, It continued to have any, other than in dreams. Though
It had come in time to accept Its emasculation, It had failed, because of Its concern first with Nana, then with the infant Attis, to
pay much attention to Its waning virility. Now, however, seeing
the sleeping youth, Agdistis was reminded of that afternoon of
butchery, reminded less of the blood and pain and shock, than of
the loss It had suffered and the enduring scar, which It proceeded
now to examine with a mounting sense of lack.

In the brief interim since It had sat up, the mysterious light had
not only shifted, but also changed color again. No longer blue, it
had become completely nacreous and was focused now on the lair,
flooding through the lean-to, bathing Attis in a luminescence which
accentuated irresistibly the cotton-wool softness of the down covering his pelvis, chest and limbs—a luminescence which, far from
washing out his honey-colored flesh, made it seem so succulent, the
saliva flooded Agdistis' mouth. Not since It had first found Attis
fourteen years ago, had Agdistis had such a powerful urge to eat
the boy—or, if not to eat him, at least to lick his body, bite his
flesh. Then suddenly, as It struggled to resist this impulse, lest It
actually devour the boy and lose him forever, something even more
phenomenal than the issuance of the light occurred. Agdistis felt a
strange but extremely pleasurable sensation, as if someone had
begun to stroke It with a feather—not just in one place at one time
with one feather, but everywhere at once with a multitude of feathers, tickling and titillating It till what had been a purely oral appetite spread to the rest of Its body—to Its buttocks, breasts, hands,
and loins—dispersing pleasurably the thrust of Its desire, while
tempering, to Its great relief, the imminent threat to Attis.

So long as the feathers continued to caress It, Agdistis was perfectly content to remain in repose, ogling the boy at a distance, utterly enraptured by his beauty. But presently, as It went on leering, the feathers turned to tongues of fire, licking and burning
Agdistis, bringing It back down to the ground where, in a terrible
sweat and short of breath, It began to roll in the dust, slapping Itself and kicking Its legs, trying in vain to extinguish the flames, till
It was forced to struggle to Its feet again, stumble through the underbrush, and plunge into the pond.

Once the water reached Its chin, the fire went out; and once the
fire was out, Agdistis' thoughts turned again to Attis. In Its mind's
eye It saw the sleeping youth and yearned to see him bodily. Assuming Itself safe once more, Its ordeal over, Agdistis came out of
the water. But the instant It set foot on shore, Its shoulder blades

began to sting, not as if It were still on fire, but as if someone were whipping It now—whipping It in no ordinary fashion: one stroke at a time and then the next with pauses in between to raise the lash, but whipping It relentlessly, murderously, wielding half a dozen whips at once, so that Agdistis hadn't hands enough to protect Itself and had to run away, driven in the direction of the amphitheater. In the next second, however, Its assailant overtook It and lashed It in the face, lashed It on the breasts and penis, lashed It till Agdistis turned and ran the other way—the whiplash stinging Its buttocks then, stinging Its thighs, driving It in no time through the trees and back to the lair where, the next thing It knew, Agdistis found Itself crouching over Attis.

Once again It was dazzled by the luminous light: blue and green and rose; once again It felt the feathers, flames and whiplash, no longer in succession but simultaneously, exciting and tormenting It till Agdistis thought It would faint from the pleasure and the pain; once again It saw the boy's tempting body, saw his penis standing firm above the bulging testes; once again Agdistis was reminded of Its own deficiency and, wanting now not only to regain what It had lost, but also to take into Itself Attis in the flesh, satisfied Its craving.

Attis responded drowsily at first, though not unwillingly. But by and by, as Agdistis lavished Its love on him, the boy grew more and more impassioned—arched his spine, locked the hermaphrodite between his thighs, kneaded Its flesh, and commenced to moan, as he tossed his head from side to side till the passion took possession of him, and Attis lost his reason, lost control, lost everything heretofore familiar to him, *became* what he was feeling, became the frenzy and the straining and the ravishment from which he gained release at last, not by death, as he expected, but by a paroxysm that shook his frame from head to toe, drained him altogether of himself, and left him exclaiming ardently, as if to denominate that missing self's replacement, "Agdistis! Agdistis!"

Agdistis took the last unswallowed drops of sperm and rubbed them like a balm into Its breasts.

Opening his eyes, Attis gazed with adoration at his guardian who had somehow managed in a trice to transform completely the world and everything in it, including Itself—Agdistis looked distinctly different now: softer, more vulnerable, as well as more august—and all at once it dawned on Attis that anyone capable of performing such a feat could not possibly be mortal. "Oh," he said in a hushed tone appropriate to this revelation, "you're a god!"

"Yes, my love"—Agdistis wiped the perspiration from the boy's brow—"and you're my chosen consort. That makes you immortal too."

"Me?" For a moment Attis' ebony eyes shone with a celestial light that did, indeed, make him seem divine. But in the following instant his whole expression changed, and he looked gravely troubled. "No, surely not. Surely what just happened now could never happen twice. Surely, if I'm not already dead, I won't live out the year."

"Don't say such things."

"I have a premonition."

"What foolishness! Don't talk like that. 'Already dead!' You'll *never* die. You're much too beautiful. You'll stay this way forever—forever young, forever beautiful, forever with Agdistis—the two of us as one . . . forever. I'll never let you die, I promise you. I couldn't-couldn't live without you. For you to die, I too would have to die, and that, you understand, can never happen. So, you see. . . . 'Already dead,' indeed! Look here." Agdistis drew Its forefinger down the length of the boy's abdomen from the navel to the groin, inducing a little spasm. "See that? See how the hairs stand on end? Dead, you say? And here" —It traced the outline of Attis' nipple— "see the goose bumps? Already dead? Listen to your heartbeat! Feel your pulse! Look at the perspiration—it's pouring out like the sap poured out before. As for *that*," It added with a chuckle, "not only can it happen twice, but a hundred thousand times—forever: like the two of us: eternal." Struck by an idea, Agdistis exclaimed, "Wait! Stay right there—you'll see." Hurrying away, Agdistis fetched the aulos, came back, sat down cross-legged at the edge of the lair, and began to serenade Attis.

The melody, whose method seemed based entirely on the building up and relaxing of terrific tensions, consisted of three strong beats, sustained for the duration of a full breath and interspersed at regular intervals by a series of free-ranging modulations, so charged with emotion the effect was that of a protracted cry. At its completion, the passage was repeated note for note, except that the opening beat was sounded one higher on the scale, with the result that the melody grew increasingly shrill, urgent, and insistent, the cry increasingly inordinate with each successive cycle. Sitting cross-legged, Its eye trained on the boy's loins, lips pressed to the primitive pipe, producing strange impassioned sounds, Agdistis looked amazingly like a snake charmer. In keeping with this impression, as Agdistis went on piping, Attis' penis began to stir, the shaft to wax and wobble, inclining upward gradually, even as the glans started to reveal itself, rosy in the filtered sunlight, responding with ever-growing vigor to the music's spell, rising with the rising notes, swelling with the swelling cry till, at last, it stood erect, perfectly stiff and proud, whereat Agdistis flung aside the instrument and fell upon the boy a second time.

After It had worked the sperm into Its breasts once more, Agdistis remarked ironically, "Never happen twice?"

Attis smiled a smile of utter joy that showed his teeth, dazzling white, and brought the nimbus back into his pitch-black eyes—two pinpoints now of penetrating light which pricked Agdistis to the heart and made It long to give the boy some lasting emblem of Its love.

"Wait!" It suddenly exclaimed again and went, just as It had gone before, over to the kitchen area, got down on Its hands and knees, swept away a pile of potsherds, and began to dig up the ground.

"What are you doing, Agdistis?"

"Don't look! Lie down! Cover your eyes!"

Attis obeyed reluctantly. "When can I look?"

"When you're told."

Before long Agdistis dug up what appeared to be nothing more than two crude chunks of clay, one about the size of Its fist, the other slightly larger. "Don't peek!"

"I'm not."

Satisfied that the boy was telling the truth, Agdistis stole down to the pond and dipped the chunks into the water, swishing them back and forth to loosen the clay. Presently, as the silt began to wash away and the water to clarify, the hermaphrodite's hands seemed to turn to gold; and by and by It drew from the pond Queen Tabal's diadem and bracelet, glistening in the sunlight. Hurrying back to the lair, Agdistis knelt down facing Its beloved, put aside the diadem and held out the bracelet. "Now!"

Attis sat up. Though visibly excited, his eyes flashing as brightly as the still-dripping ornament, he obviously had no idea what the object was.

"For you, my darling," Agdistis explained, "to consecrate our love." As It slipped the bracelet around the boy's wrist, Agdistis added in a whisper, "Forever," and then, bending down, kissed his penis.

In expression of his gratitude Attis embraced Agdistis fervently. But even so, that didn't seem enough, the moment remained incomplete, unilateral; whereupon, noticing the diadem, Attis picked it up instinctively and placed it on Agdistis' head, repeating the whispered vow, "Forever." Then, as the two embraced again, lovingly, lingeringly, Attis murmured, "Can it happen three times?" and Agdistis proved it could.

After the seventieth time or so, the two lost count. By then, however, the whole of Pessinus was keeping track of their love-making, which neither Attis nor Agdistis did anything to conceal. The spectacle of the two going at it like livestock in an open field, down on all fours in an olive grove, head to toe in a bean patch, sporting underwater in the Sangarius, lubricating each other with oil in the market (the emphasis of Agdistis' pilfering shifted now from necessities to luxuries: silks and scents and body oil)—in short, the spectacle of their coupling in almost every conceivable posture and place became a totally familiar sight. Their liaison captured the imagination of the populace to the point of mania. In imitation of Attis every man and boy in Pessinus donned a Phrygian cap, and every woman not only fashioned herself some kind of crown or garland modeled on Agdistis', but also bared her breasts. Whereas in former years examples of spring sickness, though numerous, were relatively mild, now the condition gripped the population like a plague. Honeycombs went uncollected, haymaking and harvesting fell behind, sickles left out overnight began to rust, potters' wheels stood idle, looms accumulated dust. Men developed incurable cases of priapism against which they strove in vain with man and beast to find relief; and women, though officially forbidden to leave their huts, risked having their eyes put out to catch a glimpse of the god and Its paramour, after which they came back home to exchange wanton tales, however true, such as seeing the two playing at quoits, Agdistis using Its diadem to ring the boy's upright member.

The authorities, who fully understood the extent of Agdistis' hold on the popular imagination, were at a loss to curb the craze. Neither injunctions nor force was effectual. As a last resort, King Midas dispatched his chancellor to the oracle at Ephesus, but the divination with which Rusa returned— "The son must die, and the daughter too," —baffled everyone, especially Midas, who still remained without an heir and feared more than ever for the future of his kingdom.

"Go now, Eros," Aphrodite sang out in a voice as vibrant as a lute, "go to Apollo—"

"Apollo, Mistress?"

"Yes, my pet, Apollo—don't look so incredulous—Apollo who, years ago, persuaded me against my better judgment to punish Agdistis for lack of respect, while he himself remains more contemptuous of Aphrodite than anyone in all creation"—her anger made the goddess hiss—"except, of course, for that lynx, his sister. Certainly Apollo!"

"But you haven't sent me to Apollo, Mistress, since—I-I can't remember. Was it Hyacinthus?"

"All the more reason to go now, before you too are taken in by that endless string of epithets: Apollo the 'deliverer,' the 'reasoner,' the 'dispassionate,' the 'levelheaded,' the 'law-giver,' the 'ever-distant,' the 'pure'—what rot! The self-deceived would be more like it. Haven't you ever noticed his lips" —she gave her own lower lip a tug, revealing the raspberry tissue, dewy and delectable— "how fleshy they are? Almost as fleshy as the cheeks of your behind, my pet. Brutish, too, brutish and venereal like the lips of a satyr—a satyr who espouses moderation—ha! Have you ever heard of such a thing? A satyr who insists on keeping his distance, repudiating his appetites, favoring his intellect at the expense of his emotions—who thinks he knows himself and enjoins his followers to do the same—to know their limitations, the limitations of their nature, when, in fact, he himself doesn't begin to know the nature even of his lower lip— That's it, of course!" The goddess smacked herself resoundingly on the haunch. "You'll shoot him *there*."

"In the rump, Mistress?"

"No, you fool, the lip, the lower lip. Go now, quickly, fetch your bow."

"The switch as well?"

"No, you'll never get that close. A single dart should do the trick: awaken the desire."

Eros stopped in his tracks. "But for whom, Mistress? You haven't said."

"Haven't I?" Aphrodite smiled darkly. "How negligent of me. Why, Attis, of course, Attis the irresistible. I had almost forgotten that other earthlings still exist." For a moment the goddess lapsed into a reverie from which she promptly freed herself with a jerk of the head. "Go now, Eros, go to Apollo. Aim the shaft with accuracy, deadly accuracy, deep into the most tender flesh. I want to see his moderation utterly destroyed, you understand? I want to see Apollo fall in love *im*moderately."

"Yes-yes! you will!" Unable to contain his excitement, Eros fluttered his wings. "He's just outside in his usual spot of late: at the far end of the colonnade. Listen." From the distance came the faint but soothing strains of a lyre. "Hear him playing?"

"Yes." Aphrodite made a face. "Ugly instrument," she remarked as she ushered Eros out the door. "Quickly now, before he gets away."

Forsaking his usual vigor, Apollo was standing still, leaning languidly against a fluted column at the northeast corner of the council porch—standing, moreover, as he had stood for an hour or so every day since the start of spring, gently plucking his lyre while he gazed down from Olympus at the earth below, keeping a sharp eye on Attis.

He had first taken notice of the youth months ago when Attis failed to cut his hair and dedicate the shorn locks to Apollo, as was the custom for boys at puberty. But the god had overlooked the slight, partly because he didn't expect the protégé of Agdistis to know any better, and partly because of the boy's matchless beauty. To Apollo's eye Attis was more beautiful by far than Cyparissus had been, more beautiful even than Hyacinthus who, heretofore, had set the standard for youthful beauty. Sometimes, after studying with care Attis' profile, his annuent muscles, the double wrinkle which appeared above his armpit when he raised his arm, the dimples in his buttocks, the birthmark on his thigh, Apollo would rebuke himself for doting on the boy's individual charms instead of prizing Attis as the prototype of all pubescent boys. At such times, of which the present moment was a good example, Apollo was grateful not only for the distance which separated him from Attis, but also for his lyre which soothed his nerves, restored his sense of harmony.

Today Apollo had been watching Attis and Agdistis hunt a warthog, a stocky yet terribly fleet and ferocious boar with magnificent tusks, that had led the two a merry chase and was still very much alive—more so, in fact, than Attis, who had long since dropped out of the hunt, leaving Agdistis to pursue the beast alone. Attis, meanwhile, had taken shade under a solitary tamarisk at the edge of a grassy plateau. He had scarcely had the energy, it seemed, to drop his knife, unbelt his chiton, and remove his sweat-stained cap, before collapsing, winded and exhausted, to the ground. Apollo could tell how hot it was, not just for Attis but in general, from the conduct of a nearby flock of sheep, most of which had also settled on the ground and were breathing heavily. Even the flies were sluggish today. For a while Attis lay on his back, looking up dreamily at the drooping tamarisk leaves, but soon dozed off, whereupon Apollo began—as if some rule of decency had hitherto prevented him—to ogle the boy in earnest. The fact that Attis' sleeved chiton and knee-high buskins concealed all but his head and hands, in no way deterred the god, who was perfectly content to dwell on the boy's beautiful face, particularly on the fleshy cheeks and slightly parted lips.

In his imagination Apollo had just insinuated himself into Attis' open mouth, when suddenly he was distracted by a shadow cast on the column to his left, the last in the row. Glancing up, he spotted in midair Eros armed and in the very act of drawing back his bowstring, the arrow aimed point-blank at Apollo. Without delay the god ducked into the colonnade, putting the column he had been leaning against between himself and Eros, whose malignant expression left no doubt in Apollo's mind that the boy meant business. Like every other living creature except his sister and Athena, Apollo was utterly vulnerable to Eros' arrows, utterly defenseless. Even the bow with which he had killed the Python and was armed this minute, posed no threat to the imp who, like himself, was immortal. Only the columns of the colonnade, which were set too close to accommodate Eros' wingspread and still leave him room to maneuver, could possibly protect Apollo now. Aware of that, as well as of the fact that Eros would surely try to take him by surprise again, the god stood fast, facing east—the one direction open to attack.

The attempted assault left Apollo feeling not only indignant, but puzzled. He simply couldn't figure out what he had done to antagonize Aphrodite. Had he crossed her inadvertently? Sided with Hephaestus in their latest dispute? Was she taking out on him a grudge she bore against his sister? . . . As the god pondered this question, Eros reappeared. The imp had flown clear around or over the council roof, and came in now, as expected, from the southeast, wielding his bow as before. Once again Apollo was quick to put the column between them—moving, this time, westward—just quick enough, as it turned out, to escape the imp's insidious arrow, which barely missed his ear and chinked the marble column. The next attack issued from the west, and the one thereafter from the north, at which point the contestants, having come full circle, started all over: Apollo growing increasingly irate, Eros increasingly vicious.

By the third time around, Apollo, who was back in his original position, facing northeast, lost patience and cried out, though his assailant was nowhere to be seen, "What is it, boy? What do you want of me? Go about your business!"

"You *are* my business," came the reply from above, where Eros was evidently perched on the roof just overhead.

"Why?" Apollo demanded in outrage, "why *me?*"

"Why not? . . . after such prolonged neglect. . . . There are those who would deem it an honor."

"A virgin, perhaps, who's never felt your sting."

"Is that what you're afraid of, Phoebus, a little sting?'"

179.

"I'm not afraid—" Apollo hesitated. In his mind's eye he saw the Python he had slain in infancy swelling up out of the miasma to overpower him, impair his vision, blot out his discernment, obliterate the very order of the universe. The image was accompanied by breathlessness and a feeling of distress in his intestines. Apart from "feelings" in general, what Apollo mistrusted more than anything was the *imaginary:* that which couldn't be perceived or known, but merely felt or fancied.

" 'Not afraid,' you were saying," Eros persisted.

"Of anything."

"Then why do you shun me?"

"Because I like to be clearheaded, and for that, one must maintain his distance." To dispel the image of the Python and restore his full sense of reality, Apollo rubbed his eyes and took a hard look at the earth again. To his surprise and delight, there was Attis, still asleep. During his flight from Eros, Apollo had forgotten about the boy, but now, seeing him once more, he stopped a moment to stare. But in that moment, as the god reached out in sympathy to brush away an insect that had settled on Attis' lower lip, several things happened in rapid succession: Apollo, blinded by a brilliant light, almost lost his balance; felt something sting his own lower lip; exclaimed in pain; heard, as if in echo, Eros laugh triumphantly; saw the imp perform a dizzying double loop, feathers flashing before his eyes; did indeed then lose his footing; lurched forward, grasped at the ledge of the porch, gripped thin air, and fell headlong from Olympus.

Feeling something brush his lips, Attis awoke, startled to see a beautiful shepherd, armed with a bow and carrying a lyre, bending over him.

"Don't be alarmed," Apollo said softly. "It was just a ladybug. . . ." As if to prove the credibility of his statement, the god touched the exact spot where the bug had been with the tip of his forefinger.

"Why is your hand so cold?" Attis inquired.

"I've come from the mountains—high high up—in search of my flock."

"Oh, so they're yours— I wondered."

"And your breath" —Apollo could feel its warmth now not only on his fingertip, but coursing through his hand and arm into the rest of his body— "why is it so hot?"

"I was hunting," Attis answered summarily, his attention obviously elsewhere. "Your hair—I've never seen a shepherd—anyone—with golden hair . . . and curls like yours: all in a perfect row like that, so orderly, and bound in the back."

"I've never seen a boy with hair like yours."

"But everyone has hair like mine: the color of an eggplant."

Removing his hand from Attis' lip, Apollo ran his fingers through the boy's hair with evident pleasure. "I wasn't speaking of the color, I meant the locks."

"What about them?"

"They're unusually long for a boy your age. How come you didn't dedicate them to Apollo?"

Attis shrugged. "Should I have?"

"They're his by right."

"How so?"

"In return for the other hair he's given you."

"What other hair?"

"Here." Apollo laid his hand gently but firmly on the boy's groin. "Is it also the color of an eggplant?"

"Lighter." As Attis raised his arm, the god feared for a moment that the boy was about to push his hand away, instead of which Attis placed his own hand squarely on top of Apollo's without a trace of modesty. "Your hand is warmer now."

"Where did you get that bracelet?" Apollo surprised himself by his jealous tone.

"From my lover."

"You must have many."

"No, only one."

At this point the god and the boy exchanged a long soulful look in silence. "Two . . . now," Apollo said at last, his voice husky with emotion, mouth agape. Then, seeing his lust reflected in Attis' eyes, and feeling the boy's penis begin to stiffen under his hand, and the hand itself being squeezed by the boy to encourage him, Apollo, breathing heavily, pressed his open mouth to Attis' and brought his full weight down on top of the boy who groaned with pleasure.

To Attis, who heretofore had been familiar with only Agdistis, the beautiful shepherd seemed more like a force of nature than a human being. With Agdistis there was never a doubt in Attis' mind what his guardian wanted—Agdistis always came straight to the point—first to possess, then to please the boy. But with the shepherd it was different. Besides wanting to possess Attis, the shepherd seemed to have some other, more urgent need, altogether unrelated to Attis, a need to release something inside himself. It was this extra need that made him seem now so much like a natural force—a thunderstorm or earthquake compelled, no matter what the consequences, to run its course, discharge its cosmic energy.

At first Attis felt a trifle stunned, a trifle awed to find himself in the grip of this preterhuman force so powerful and self-assured as to seem virtually holy. And yet it didn't scare him off or rouse him to resist, nor did it leave him passive. On the contrary, the feverish activity of the shepherd's hands and haunches, teeth and tongue drove the boy quite wild. He had never been kissed like this before, never been entered by anyone's tongue; had never had his earlobes nibbled, canals explored, neck and nipples bitten, buttocks pinched; had never been scratched the length of his spine, licked from head to toe, held in the vicelike grip of a pair of thighs, handled as if he were a tot: turned upside down, folded over, rolled into a ball, raised like a sacrifice on an altar of knees; he had never been mounted from the rear, penetrated to the core, known the meaning of carnal intimacy; had never heard anyone, man or beast, grunt the way the shepherd did when, in the final throes of convulsion, the earth itself began to quake, the tamarisk to quiver, the leaves to fall, and all at once, as the heavens resounded with a riotous cry, Attis felt his insides infused, flooded.

When, at last, Attis, who was lying prone, bearing with pleasure the shepherd's weight, regained his breath, he murmured, "You're a god." For some reason, which mystified and troubled the boy, these words caused the shepherd to recoil.

"What makes you think so?"

"Please" —Attis ignored the question— "don't pull away from me."

"I won't."

"Never?" Attis pursued the point. "Will you— I don't even know your name."

"Phoebus."

"Will you stay with me forever, Phoebus?"

"If only I could!"

"Can't you?" The shepherd didn't answer. "Must you go back to the mountains?" The shepherd remained silent. "Can't you take me with you?" Still, the shepherd didn't speak, but thereupon something happened that was even more mystifying than before: Attis felt the shepherd's chest begin to tremble, felt a tear fall on the nape of his neck. Reaching up, he touched the shepherd's tear-stained cheek. "What is it, Phoebus?"

"O, Father," Apollo uttered plaintively between sobs, "let me! . . . let me stay . . . let there be an end to distance . . . let Delphi lose its deity—I have a mortal need!"

"For what? I don't understand. Who is Delphi? Where is your father?"

"It doesn't matter. Just stay like this, close—I need to feel your

182.

closeness." Attis obliged by raising his rump. "Yes! That's it. Closer still . . . conjoined . . . forever."

"I thought you had to go away," Attis reminded him.

"No! Never! I'll never let you go. I'll take you with me everywhere."

"Will you? Really?"

"Yes! You'll be my own Ganymede."

"Your what?"

"Poor *ugly* Ganymede. O!" Apollo exclaimed impulsively, "let me see your face again." Disengaging himself from Attis, Apollo turned the youth over tenderly.

For a full minute the two gazed into each other's eyes enthralled. Then Attis, smiling, reached up and fingered the shepherd's hair. "I've mussed your curls—they're no longer perfect."

"I'm glad." Apollo smiled back. "And yours—may I cut them now, now that you're no longer a boy?"

"If you like."

"Have you a knife?"

"Yes" —Attis gestured toward his clothes— "over there. Be careful, though, it's very sharp."

Straddling the youth, Apollo took a lock of Attis' hair in his right hand, the knife in his left. But no sooner did he start to cut, than a javelin came hissing through the air and stabbed the ground just inches from his knee. Turning, the god saw Agdistis, a hundred yards or so beyond the dormant sheep, charging at him, Its head down and howling, across the open plain. As Apollo and Attis scrambled to their feet, so too did the sheep, which began to bleat and bound away in panic. At the same time Attis ducked behind the tamarisk, imploring Phoebus to do likewise, but Apollo stood his ground. He could see the hermaphrodite now brandishing overhead one of the warthog's gory tusks, could see Its own huge canines bared and hear It bellowing, "Death! death! death!" the distance between them diminishing by the second, as Agdistis bore down on him steadily, and Attis began to scream, "Look out!" and Apollo answered, "Good-by, my love, I'll sing of you forever," and the hermaphrodite hurled the tusk with a virulent cry at the naked shepherd who transformed himself so rapidly Agdistis didn't even see the hoopoe fly up into the tamarisk.

"Where is he?" Agdistis demanded in fury, dragging the boy out from behind the tree and shaking him violently. "Where is he?"

Attis was too perplexed and terrified to speak. He also had not seen the metamorphosis and was dumbfounded by the shepherd's

183.

disappearance. Nor had he ever seen his guardian in such a state: flushed and glowering, Its breast heaving, veins distended, teeth bared, froth on Its chin.

The boy's silence drove Agdistis to exasperation. Though there was no one in sight for miles and no place to hide, It began to run every which way in search of the shepherd, but finding only the javelin, It seized the shaft and started stabbing the ground obsessively and shouting in a shrill falsetto all sorts of obscenities. After a while, Its jealousy and rage unabated, Agdistis turned to the shepherd's cast-off garments, snatched them up and tore them to shreds, using the shreds in turn to thrash Attis who, still naked, had only his arms to protect himself. "Never! never! never! no one! ever! understand? mine! you're mine! mine! this! and this! and this" —Agdistis lashed the boy across the face, across the groin and buttocks— "they're mine! mine alone! say it: mine!"

"Yours, yours," Attis surrendered, falling to his knees.

So prodigious was Its fury Agdistis might have gone on flogging the boy indefinitely, had It not been startled by a hoopoe which all at once uttered a rasping squawk, swooped down out of the tree, interposed itself—pecking savagely, its wings wildly aflutter—between Attis and Agdistis, gently brushed the boy's cheek with its wing tip and then soared away, straight up toward the sun, leaving Attis stroking the spot the bird had touched and staring after it bemused; leaving Agdistis altogether quelled not only by the hoopoe, but by Its sudden dreadful suspicion that the boy's seducer may have been a god.

"Go now, Eros, go now empty-handed—"

"Empty-handed!"

"You heard me. I don't want any impishness: no switch this time, no arrows, nothing but your feathers, understand?" Eros nodded. "No need to look so sullen—you'll just restrain yourself for once. Have I your word?" Eros remained silent, noncommittal. To gain the boy's consent the goddess slowly wrapped her arms around his neck, extended her right leg, shifting her weight to her left, dipped her body to his height and, leaning back, created a partial lap of her loins into which she drew the unresisting Eros. "Please. I'll make it up to you, I promise." The boy looked at his mistress lovingly, his amber eyes totally submissive, ready to receive her orders. "Good," she murmured without moving, still holding him close. "Go now, Eros, go to Ia, caress her with your scapulars . . . but lightly, gently, barely brushing her skin, stroking her neck, toying with her nipples" —even as the goddess dem-

184.

onstrated her instructions on the boy's body, she herself was experiencing their voluptuous effect— "exciting and delighting her till her maiden lips turn red, her breath comes hot in heaving sighs, her eyes go out of focus, roll back in her head, and Ia faints with longing for the boy."

"What boy, Mistress?"

"Why—" The name stuck in Aphrodite's throat.

"What is it, Mistress?" Eros disengaged himself from her embrace. "Why are you crying?"

"You'll understand soon enough."

"For Attis?"

"Yes, of course, for Attis! Go now!" Throwing up her hands as if to defend herself from both herself and Eros, Aphrodite turned her back on the boy. "Quickly! before I find a way to stop you."

As Eros darted through the door, he heard his mistress pound her fists against the wall and cry out, "Why? O why must beauty always be mortal?"

Like everyone else in Pessinus Ia was consumed with curiosity to catch a glimpse of Attis and the deity. When, however, she asked her mother's permission to leave the citadel, on the pretext of having to replace a broken embroidery needle, Queen Tabal refused. Since she could not then turn to her father, who had decreed years ago that he, King Midas, would not so much as look at his youngest "until she was ready to bear an heir," the princess went instead to her mother's handmaid. Tyana was reluctant at first to cross the queen, but her own curiosity finally got the best of her, and the following dawn she and Ia, disguised as commoners and carrying their lunch, slipped out the secret sally port in the southeast corner of the cyclopean wall and descended toward the city.

Excited as Ia was by the prospect of seeing the workers' district, in which she had never set foot, the reality proved a disappointment. By sunrise the day was already hot—unusually so for the end of September—and there wasn't a single shade tree or arcade to be found in all of Pessinus. The air seemed made of dust and flies. The alleys that had always looked so quaint from the citadel were, in fact, oppressively narrow, tortuous, filthy, foul-smelling and, worst of all, deserted—without any of the bustle and excitement that Ia had anticipated. (Since the start of the Attis-Agdistis mania, all unnecessary pedestrian traffic had been outlawed, but, luckily for Ia and Tyana, the one time they encountered the king's foot patrol, the captain recognized them both.) The men were either in the fields or workshops or out at the salt and clay pits, while the women remained indoors, spinning and weaving or working in their wretched back yards, not visible from the streets. Even the children were nowhere to be seen, and when from time to time someone did appear in a doorway, his expression was invariably hostile. Except for the occasional hammering of a blacksmith or armorer, the silence was ominous, the mood menacing, the sun merciless.

Then all at once, toward noon, the streets near the perfumery became so crowded Ia and Tyana had difficulty getting through. Despite the ban on public assembly, there were several hundred people, including children, in the throng, all dressed in imitation of Attis and the deity. The one exception was the uniformed members of the foot patrol, who were also there, but, oddly enough, making no effort whatever to disperse the crowd. Like everyone else the soldiers were transfixed, standing in silence and waiting with rapt expressions for something to happen—though for what, Ia, to her dismay, could not see. Just as she was about to ask Tyana to pick her up, the crowd as one, including Tyana, fell to the ground and covered its head—the women using their himations, the men placing their hands on top of their Phrygian caps—and when the dust began to settle, Ia saw the majestic figure of Agdistis, moving slowly toward her, the mass of Its body blocking from view the young god to Its rear. At the same time she could feel Tyana tugging at her skirt, trying to make her prostrate herself, but Ia was too astonished by Agdistis' appearance to move.

The deity's cloak-covered diadem and full-length skirt, bared breasts, heavy braids, bold nose, enormous hands—in one of which It held like a straw a six-foot scepter or javelin—made Agdistis seem twice as powerful and two heads taller than anyone Ia had ever seen. This impression was reinforced by the comparatively average height of Its consort, whose beribboned cap was visible now over Agdistis' shoulder. As the two came closer, Ia strained to catch a glimpse of the young god's face, and when, at last, she did, her enthrallment was complete. For an instant her heart stopped beating, and then it beat so violently she thought she would topple over. To her surprise, however, she remained upright, staring stupidly, mouth agape—though neither drawing nor exhaling breath—her throat closed tight. She was not even conscious of Agdistis when, presently, the deity walked right by. Her eyes were fixed on Attis, who had doubtless noticed her, but showed no sign of interest until he reached a point a yard or so away, and all at once his eyes met hers, and he too came to a standstill, staring dumbly. As they gazed into each other's eyes, Ia felt her body hair stand on end and the blood rush to her cheeks, heard herself heave a sigh, sensed for the first time since that morning the heady smell of sandalwood, rose water, myrrh, and musk in the air, became uncomfortably aware of the noonday sun, producing a haze of heat, an almost blinding glare against which Attis, still staring, stood in partial darkness, his outline sharply etched in light, as if aflame, his face aglow, eyes ablaze, emitting beams more brilliant than the sun's, his features swimming now before her eyes, her eyes rolling back in their sockets, her body all at once weightless, falling, sprawling senseless at his feet.

When Ia came to, Attis was kneeling at her side, holding her head between his hands. Once again she stared into his pitch-black eyes, though questioningly now, almost at a loss for words. "Will I . . . will we? . . ."

Attis understood. "Tomorrow at noon," he whispered, "in the woods north of the city."

Ia confirmed the rendezvous by lowering her eyelids—she hadn't the strength for more—but by the time she raised them again, Attis was gone, hurrying to catch up with Agdistis.

On their way back to the citadel Tyana kept begging the princess to tell her what Attis had said, but Ia ignored the question—if, indeed, she heard it—so completely lost was she in reverie. The moment, however, they reached the palace, Ia dispatched the handmaid to request an audience for her with her father.

"Don't be silly, child," Tyana objected. "You know the condition on which that depends."

"But I'm ready now," Ia stated firmly.

The handmaid was at once dumbfounded and intrigued. "To bear an heir?"

"Yes."

"Is *that* what he told you—the young god—was that his annunciation: a miraculous—"

"Please" —Ia took Tyana by the shoulders, turned her around, and headed her toward the Hall of Honor— "do as I say."

"It's a miracle, a miracle," the handmaid repeated over and again, shaking her head and holding her cheek, as she hurried away.

From time to time in the course of her fourteen years Ia had seen her father seated on his throne, seen him presiding over a sacrifice or in the Hall of Honor after a banquet when the women were permitted to assemble in the gallery, but she had always seen him from a distance, never, as far as she could remember, close enough to exchange a single word. So that now, shortly after he had

granted her request, she found herself abased at the feet of a verita-
ble stranger.

"Rags? Are those rags you're wearing?" Midas complained almost unintelligibly, his speech impaired by numerous missing
teeth. "Is that the way your mother dresses you—worse than a
slave? . . . Stand up, child. Let me see you. . . . Turn . . .
turn. . . . 'Ready to bear me an heir?' Why, you're not even ready
to release the blood! You're wasting my time. . . . Don't lower
your head like that. Look at me! Hasn't your mother taught you to
speak?"

At last Ia dared to look the old man in the eye. Half blind,
hollow-cheeked, and wizened though he was, he seemed in no
way feeble. If anything, the wasting away of his flesh had left him
looking tough and spare. He sat perfectly erect, head held high and
tilted back, as if to peer out from under his cataracts. "I-I've met
the man who will marry me, sire."

"Closer, come closer, child." When Ia had done as she was told,
Midas, clearly pleased by what he saw, his expression noticeably
softer, reached out and traced a bony finger along the line of her
eyebrow. "You pluck them?" Ia shook her head. "They grow that
way?" Ia nodded. "Beautiful," he remarked, but whether about her
soulful eyes or arching brows, Ia was uncertain. "What is his
name?"

"Attis, sire."

"Attis!" The old man burst out laughing. "I believe you're not
alone in that. Isn't that the wish of every woman in the kingdom—
to marry Attis?" Midas turned to his chancellor. "Tell her, Rusa."

"It would certainly seem so, sire."

Turning back to his daughter, the king went on. "Have you ever
seen him, child?" Ia nodded. "You have? Where?" Ia was reluctant
to answer. "Here in the palace, perhaps?" Midas laughed at his
own joke, but in the next second he stopped short, turned again to
Rusa, and said soberly, "How old is the boy?"

"About your daughter's age, they say, sire."

Suddenly, without another word the king stood up and wandered alone into the courtyard.

"He's thinking," Rusa explained to the princess. "Don't worry,
he'll come back."

Midas was indeed thinking, thinking about the many advantages
to be gained from such a match. In the first place it would achieve
at a stroke what neither law nor force had managed to achieve in
months—namely, to put an end to the dangerous alliance between
Attis and Agdistis—if not to the whole Agdistis cult! Secondly, it

would bring this celebrated youth, who represented for the populace downright anarchy, out of the wilds, into society, into the palace itself, where Midas could exploit his presence to regain control over the kingdom. Furthermore, if the boy was in truth only fourteen, there would still be time to instruct and train him for leadership. Forgetting for the moment any future offspring, the boy himself might be turned right now into the very heir Midas had sought so sorely all these years. Oh, yes! Not only was the match a good one, it had, no doubt, been thought up by the gods themselves in answer to his prayers. "Yes, yes," he said, coming back to the throne, "the idea pleases me. We must arrange a meeting, Rusa—though," Midas hesitated, "just how we'll get around Agdistis—"

"No need!" Ia blurted out before she could stop herself.

"What's that, child?"

"N-Nothing, sire."

"Nothing? Come, come. A moment ago, 'no need,' now, 'nothing'? A strong wind requires time to shift. What is it, child? Tell your father. I'll not be cross, I promise you. Has the meeting already been arranged?" Ia looked down at the ground. "Is that it?" Midas chucked her under the chin. "Have I guessed it? Speak!"

"Yes, sire."

"So much the better! When is it to be?"

"At noon tomorrow, sire."

"Where?"

"The north woods, sire."

"Excellent!"

"You're not displeased? You'll let me go?" Ia asked in the same breath.

"Let you? I *want* you to go—you go with my blessings, child. More than that, I want you—want you to be generous, you understand? . . . liberal, yes, liberal with the boy—though not completely, not to the point— Tell me, child," Midas interrupted himself, "have you ever entertained a man?" Ia shook her head. "In that case you had better go and find Tyana now and have her tell you what will be expected. After that, she's to bathe and then anoint you with some lovely scented oil—not your mother's," he added quickly, "leave your mother out of this—let Tyana borrow someone else's—Kussara's! Kussara's oil is much the best—and have her comb your hair and dress you as befits the daughter of King Midas. Go now. Run along. I'll attend to the rest."

"The rest?" Ia repeated warily, interrupting her obeisance.

"The preparations, child. The dowry, the date—"

"You won't hurt him, will you, sire?"

"Hurt him, child? Hurt my future son? Certainly not! What foolishness. Besides, who is there to hurt him? You'll go alone—be sure to tell Tyana that: there's to be no chaperon—just you, you and Attis. . . . Hurry now. Tomorrow will be here long before you're ready."

By the time Ia entered the woods the following day, she felt totally unnerved. However lovely to look at, the dress she was wearing—a long white embroidered gown, girdled just below the breasts, with long sleeves and a matching Phrygian cap, which completely constricted her upswept hair—proved utterly impractical. The descent from the citadel was far too steep, the road too dusty, the sun too hot, the woods too thick for such an elegant tight-fitting gown. Ia had never ventured anywhere alone, and for that reason, perhaps, had had the constant feeling along the way of being followed, but as often as she looked back, saw no one. Until yesterday she had never spoken to a man and, now that Tyana had instructed her in the ways of courtship, never wanted to again. Nor had Ia ever thought to question her own body until yesterday, when she stepped into the marble bath and Tyana proceeded to give her an anatomy lesson which lasted half the afternoon and left her painfully self-conscious and confused about every aspect of her body, including the armpits. Like her dress, her body seemed now, as she tripped over a root and snagged her sleeve on a briar, altogether alien and inappropriate, and she wished she had another.

He had said the woods, but not *where* in the woods. He had said noon, but how could two people possibly tell when the sun was at its meridian unless they were standing in the same spot? Should she stay where she was or start searching for him? Did she really want to find him, now that she understood just how much more than face and eyes was involved in conjugal love? Was his face as beautiful as she remembered? What, in fact, did she remember about it? Not even the color of his eyes. And what would she say when she finally encountered him? What would *he* say?

"Your perfume—"

Startled, Ia flinched and let out a cry.

Attis tried to reassure her. "Don't be frightened. I'm sorry I'm late. It took so long to give my guardian the slip. At first I thought you hadn't come, I couldn't find you anywhere; then suddenly I smelled your perfume and followed its scent and saw you through the trees—your dress! I-I've never seen a dress like that" —he fingered his chiton self-consciously— "so different from yesterday. Where did you get it? . . . Who are you? . . . What's your name? . . . Won't you look at me? . . ."

Ia had, in fact, already looked—not closely enough to observe

190.

the color of his eyes, but quite enough to see again his astounding beauty—and she dared not look back for fear of swooning as she had the day before. Yet even with her eyelids lowered, she was perfectly aware now of what the boy was doing: spreading his cloak under a nearby tree, taking off his cap and belt and chiton.

"Aren't you hot? Why don't you take off your dress? Come, sit over here." Attis made room for her on the cloak. "How do you like my body?" he asked with pride, as he pulled off his trousers and stood up naked. "Don't you want to look at it?" No sooner had Ia nodded, than she covered her eyes with both hands. The contradiction made Attis laugh. "Let me see yours." Accommodating as she wished to be, Ia had difficulty undoing her girdle and turned to the young god for help. Attis obliged, however clumsily, and between them they got her undressed.

Now it was Attis' turn to fall silent, surprised by the difference between their genitals. Crouching down, he proceeded to take a closer look. After a moment he reached out and caressed her vulva, as if to verify by touch what sight had already revealed to him: that Ia had no penis. Eager then to share this discovery, he drew Ia down to her knees and placed her hand on his penis—his own hand continuing to explore her vulva—as they gazed with adoration into each other's eyes (black! his eyes were black, the lashes longer than her own), and brought their lips together, and savored each other's mouths until they found themselves stretched out in a transport on the cloak, their bodies side by side at first, mouths still kissing, hands still fondling each other's parts; but presently, as his passion mounted, Attis rolled on top of Ia and, wanting the contact of their loins to be complete, removed her mediating hand, and hugged her so tight she moaned. "What is it?" he whispered. "Am I hurting you?"

Ia couldn't speak, could scarcely breathe, could only open her half-dazed eyes and produce a wistful little smile to communicate her rapture. Reassured, Attis resumed kissing her, and though she moaned again, this time her contentment was unmistakable. But all at once, as she took his ardent tongue deep into her mouth, Attis pulled back with a start, cried out apprehensively, "Agdistis?" and reared up cursing, kicking, straining, struggling in vain to free himself from the huge hunting net in which he was already hopelessly enmeshed and being rapidly subdued by four or five booted members of the household guard, who almost trampled Ia as they converged in a rush on the writhing body and secured the corners of the net and tumbled Attis over like a sack of meal, kicking him gratuitously, while other guards stood around laughing and jeering and making obscene jokes about their hot-blooded quarry.

191.

Too frightened to intervene, too outraged to cry, too humiliated to speak, Ia wrapped the cotton cloak around her naked body and stood up unsteadily. Forsaking her embroidered dress, which seemed all of a sudden a hateful accessory to the crime, she gathered up Attis' clothes as if they were his mortal remains, and, sobbing now, trailed after the guards as they dragged the net out of the woods.

Not until Attis was brought into the presence of the king, who instantly ordered his release and even apologized for the scratches and bruises the boy had received, did Ia understand that her father meant him no harm. On the contrary, Midas was quick to call him "son," and though he offered Attis no choice in the matter, sanctioned the marriage with obvious delight and promised his daughter a huge dowry. Attis, for his part, was so surprised to find himself inside the royal palace, surrounded by such extraordinary wealth and wonders, he was perfectly agreeable to everything, especially to the suggestion that he exchange his shepherd's rags, still clutched in Ia's hands, for the garments of a prince.

Well before the audience was over and the nuptials set, word of Attis' arrival had spread through the palace. From every quarter members of the household, both family and staff, soldiers, slaves, and concubines were slipping into the courtyard to catch a glimpse of the celebrated youth. The queen, still unaware of her daughter's involvement, was curious too—more curious, if possible, than the rest, whose curiosity was merely idle, whereas Tabal was eager now to see whether or not Attis bore any resemblance to the boy she had named as an infant. By the time she reached the courtyard, however, the crowd was already two or three deep, crammed together in more or less the same small area, keeping back close to the palace walls, so as not to intrude on the interview and incur the king's wrath. But even after her eyes had adjusted to the sunlight, the queen had difficulty seeing the throne and decided to risk her husband's disapproval to get a better view.

Tabal's surprise, as she stepped out into the open and saw Attis' naked back, was nothing compared with her astonishment at realizing that the young girl standing next to him was her daughter. What on earth was Ia doing there—and in the presence of a naked boy? Why was she wearing a shepherd's cloak? Why the household guard? Why the priests? What was Midas holding, handing the boy? . . . The glare from the gilded lions and gold-plated portals blinded the queen, and she shaded her eyes, as she moved closer to hear what was being said.

"—consult the birds. Unless the omens are adverse, let the marriage take place on the fourth of the month, six days hence—"

Even as she heard these words, another flash of gold distracted her, whereat the queen caught sight of something which, in combination with the talk of marriage, made her blood run cold—the boy was wearing her filigree bracelet! So he *was* the god's son after all. Terrified, Tabal cast her eyes over the crowd and up at the rooftops in search of Agdistis who, she had no doubt, was already among them, preparing their destruction. If the marriage went forward, they would surely die, one and all. It must be stopped! Yet, if she interceded now, she would have to explain just how she came to know that the boy was Agdistis' son. And if she didn't? . . . "Wait!" The queen rushed toward the throne.

"What is that woman doing here?" Midas protested.

"The child must not marry him!" Tabal exhorted her husband as she interposed herself between Attis and Ia.

"Who gave you leave—"

"She'll not survive—"

Midas motioned brusquely to the captain of the guard. "Take that woman away from here!"

"—she'll be destroyed—"

"Take her away!"

"—all of us—"

"Away, I said!"

As the guards took hold of her, the queen cried out, "He is the son of Agdistis!"

"He is the son of Midas now!" the king retorted, "the son you failed to bear!"

"Your son will be your death!"

"Muzzle her! she's raving."

"The death of your daughter, the death—"

"Away with her!" Midas commanded. "All of them! Clear the courtyard!"

When, at last, the queen had been hustled out of sight and the courtyard cleared, Midas, obviously troubled by his wife's forebodings, turned to Rusa. "Go! have the citadel closed, the sentinels increased—let no one in or out until the marriage has been consummated."

VII

To the bride, her wedding day, however busy and demanding, seemed endless. After a full week of preparations, Ia had been awakened before dawn, taken from her mother's chamber (in which she had spent the night for the first time since she was seven), put in Tyana's charge and conveyed by cart to the Sangarius. There, the princess, obeying the handmaid's instructions, disrobed, said a prayer to the river god, squatted in the ice-cold water, facing the current, and waited stoically while Tyana produced a pomegranate, cut it in two and, taking pains not to spill the precious contents, carried the fruit out to Ia whose forehead she proceeded to stain—even as the river cleansed the child's loins—with the blood-red juice. That done, the handmaid separated the countless crimson seeds from the pulp and fed them to Ia a bunch at a time, intoning over every mouthful the solemn injunction, "Multiply." Not until the last seed had been consumed and the rind buried in the ground, did the bride, purified, return to the palace.

Later in the morning she had gone to the courtyard with the rest of the women to watch her father officiate at the sacrifice of fifty heifers—more than enough to feed the large number of wedding guests invited to both the midday and evening meals. By the time the women took their place at the far side of the blazing altar, the goldsmith was already hard at work gilding the horns of the herd whose incessant lowing, usually so soothing to Ia, troubled her profoundly. To her father's left stood seven of her brothers-in-law, as well as Attis and Rusa, lined up in the order in which they would participate in the ceremony. All of them were facing the altar, their backs to the women, so that Ia could see none of the ritual articles they were holding, except for the huge double-edged ax, resting on the shoulder of the third in line. As clearly as she understood the meaning of the sacrifice—it was, above all, an offering to the gods, and only secondarily something to be eaten—Ia dreaded the actual slaughter. At the same time she wished it were over, the animals silent. Instead, the lowing grew louder, the gilding seemed to take forever. As the smith worked on, Ia could not help but think of the beautifully wrought gold—the necklace, bracelet, fibulae, given her last night by her mother—with which she herself was bedecked this minute, waiting for the sacrifice.

When, at last, the herd was ready, her father washed his hands, sprinkled the fire with barley seeds, said a prayer to Aphrodite, and then stepped back while the first heifer, excreting and crying in terror, was pulled by the horns to the altar, its forelock cut and cast into the flames; whereupon, the great ax was raised and brought down on its neck, and the animal, emitting a ghastly bellow (drowned out almost instantly by the even louder wailing of the women), dropped to its knees, its hind legs still erect, though tottering, and Rusa cut its throat, and Attis, holding out an empty

194.

basin, did his best to catch the spurting blood which, nonetheless, spattered his face and hands and clothes, as the animal finally collapsed, and Ia, wailing like the rest of the women, but, unlike them, shedding actual tears, rubbed at her forehead in distraction, trying to wipe away the pomegranate juice.

Even before the second heifer was brought to the altar, the household carvers fell to work on the first: flaying the carcass, ripping out the entrails, cutting up the meat, some of which was wrapped in fat, blessed with wine and roasted on the spot, while other, less-choice parts were whisked away to be cooked in cauldrons. Fifty times the ax was wielded, fifty times the heifers bellowed, fifty times the women wailed and beat their breasts; and when, at last, the sacrifice was done, the flagstones were black with blood, the air reeked of blood, the bridegroom was drenched in blood; there was blood on the king, blood on the chancellor, blood on all the brothers-in-law, and each and every celebrant had swallowed some drops of the sacramental blood.

After the ceremony the women retired, as was the custom at mealtime, to their quarters, while the king and other men of rank crowded into the Hall of Honor which, though large, could accommodate only sixty guests, leaving the rest outside to eat in the courtyard. Ia had no appetite. Instead of eating, she spent the time in solitude thinking about the coming night when, at sunset, she would be conducted in a torchlight procession to the east wing of the palace where Attis had his bedchamber. Try as she did to envision the bridegroom as he had looked last week in the woods, she could only see him blood-drenched, crouching at the altar, could only see herself squatting in the river, waiting to be fed the multitude of bleeding seeds inside the cleft pomegranate. Thus far, the day's events, disturbing though they were, had been easier to live through than to assimilate. She could not sort them out, could not unify the seeds, ablutions, blood, gold, fire, sacrifice, entrails, food. And as for the night? . . . In anticipation of its mysteries Ia inserted her hand, which had suddenly turned cold, between her legs and went on waiting.

When the men had finished eating, the women joined them in the Hall of Honor, a large rectangular room, sixty feet long and half as wide, framed on three sides by a narrow overhead gallery. The low roof was supported by six wooden uprights which created a central open area, two stories high, at whose midpoint stood a huge stone hearth without a chimney. There were no doors, other than the entrance, or windows in the hall—what light there was came from the fire on the hearth and a rather small lantern on the roof through which the smoke escaped as best it could—so that by the time the women entered, the crowded hall was not only airless, dim, and smelly, but filled with smoke and fumes.

Except for the queen, who took her place downstairs on a raised divan to the left of the king's high-backed wooden armchair, all the women filed upstairs with their needlework and distaffs. Ia had to vie with several of her sisters for the best spot from which to observe the bridegroom, who was sitting opposite her father in one of the six places of honor (designated by the six wooden posts)—the other four being occupied by the chancellor, the high priest, the chief of staff, and the palace bard. As for the rest of the men, the great majority were crammed into the area under the gallery—some, like her brothers-in-law, stretched out on comfortable couches, some perched on wooden stools and benches, some sprawled on nothing more than skins, scattered over the mosaic floor.

Ia couldn't concentrate on her needlework (few of the women could); she kept pricking herself and finally had to stop. Downstairs, the little lacquered dining tables in front of each guest were being cleared and a new batch of wine prepared for the already boisterous crowd. As the stewards poured the undiluted wine into a giant mixing crater, Ia was reminded of the sacrificial blood, and, glancing then at the bridegroom's blood-stained chiton, thought again of the night to come and her transfer to the nuptial chamber. At the same time, the sisters flanking her were chattering about Attis, speculating on his physique, temperament, sexual prowess, offering the bride the benefit of their conjugal experience.

"But whatever you do," said the oldest, the wife of the man who had wielded the ax, "don't let him enter you right away. He'll want to, of course—he's young, ardent, inexperienced—but don't let him. Keep him out. Make him rouse you first."

"Aren't you getting ahead of yourself?" the second sister remarked with irony. "She's still a virgin. There's only one thing on her mind just now—isn't there, Ia?—whether or not it's going to hurt."

"Well, naturally it hurts—every child knows that."

"Really?" The second sister evinced surprise. "You don't mean to say that Lugga hurt you? How odd."

"Odd? What's odd about it? Of course it hurts. It's meant to hurt. How could it not hurt?"

"Well, all I can tell you is that Pala didn't hurt me."

"Nonsense! It's so long ago, you've forgotten."

"Long ago! Look who's talking! Believe me, Ia, it doesn't hurt—not if the man knows what he's doing."

"Are you implying—"

"Take a tip from me" —the second sister ignored the interruption— "once you're on your back, just slip a cushion under your rump—"

"A cushion!" the ax-wielder's wife scoffed. "No wonder it didn't hurt—if you had to use a cushion—he had nothing to hurt you *with*. Who knows? perhaps you too are still a virgin. Ha-ha-ha! Cushion indeed. Pay no attention to her, Ia. Listen to me. Forget the cushion. You'll have no need for a cushion—not with a boy like that! All you need—once he gets on top of you—is to raise your legs, right up over your shoulders—you understand?—till your ankles touch your ears. You won't need a cushion then, I promise you."

"Later on," the second sister drawled in reply, "when the contests begin, we'll see whose husband has what to hurt who with."

Ia had lost track of time. She had forgotten the athletic games, forgotten that this was only the midday meal—the celebration had scarcely begun. The new batch of wine had yet to be drunk, the bard to sing, the acrobats to perform, the men to compete in the courtyard at throwing the discus and javelin, wrestling and running, and then to display for hours on end their dancing virtuosity, after which, in the late afternoon, she would have to abide another whole feast with other rounds of drinking and other bardic songs before it came time to be conducted to the nuptial chamber. Contrary to her sister's assumption, the question uppermost in Ia's mind was not whether it would hurt, but whether or not she would bleed and, if she bled, as the heifers had, whether the blood would signify death or regeneration.

When the wine cups had been refilled, Rusa quieted the crowd, whereupon the king rose to toast the bridegroom. For a while he stood in silence, looking not at the boy, but in the general direction of his wife, as if he had forgotten his reason for getting up. But presently he turned toward Attis and raised his brows, and though there was no sign of recognition in his almost opaque eyes, his face became quite animated, his voice vigorous and strident, as he began to speak. "At last we have a son—the gods be praised! At last the son is wrested from the mother, from her murky mysteries. No more moon worship, milk tyranny, night emissions— Beware!" the old man interrupted himself to address the groom directly, "beware the unclean cleft! the source of all disease: cataracts, canker, gravel, pox—polluting and undermining the male. At last the mother-time is done, the son assumes his proper place beside the father. Look! there he sits: sturdy, tough, erect, ready to compete in the games, ready to show his strength and skill, ready to implant his seed in the bride. Let the blood flow, the seed take root, the son regenerate himself. Praise the gods! The state is restored, the future assured." To solemnize this blessing, Midas drained his cup, waited while the rest of the men followed suit, and then threw back his head and barked at the gallery, "Rejoice! Rejoice, you women! Give thanks to the son: custodian of the seed, creator of new life. The son has come, the son is here. Cover your heads, you women! Abase yourselves before the son, your savior. Through him alone shall you attain significance."

The women, cramped behind the wooden railing like livestock in a pen, kneeled as best they could and murmured their thanks. Only the queen remained silent, motionless, recumbent, hands pressed flat against her flanks as if she had just slapped them there in defiance of her husband. Had she borne and raised eighteen girls for *this:* to mark the end of motherhood? Did Midas really think it possible to separate the two—put an end to mother-time without an end to man? Perhaps he did. Perhaps he wasn't lying through his teeth, but simply ignorant, arrogant. Then let him speak for himself, speak as a man of men, not of women, and, above all, not of mothers and sons. Clearly, mothers and sons, like mothers and daughters, were inseparable. The daughter became the mother, the mother begot the son, the son consorted with the daughter—it was as simple as that, the life process. Though not, perhaps, for men. Perhaps men, saddled as they were with so much self-conceit, so many self-delusions about their own significance, the significance of all their earthly doings, were too preoccupied with what they called the state, affairs of state—as if the two were inimical: women and the state, as if men had first set up the state solely to neutralize women's "murky mysteries"—perhaps men were too busy to remember, did forget their mothers, did in truth believe that they were self-contained. Tabal had no way of knowing. But as for herself, she had never forgotten her mother, and never would, never could. Whether or not her mother was still alive, living in Cappadocia, she had no idea; all she knew for certain was that her mother lived on in her. She could *feel* her mother's presence now, not in her imagination or in memory or even as a specter, flittering nearby, but in her body, in her inmost being her mother abode. At this very moment, her entire attitude was unmistakably her mother's. The likeness had nothing whatever to do with physical resemblance, but with temperament, mood, beliefs, emotion, with the very marrow of her creaking bones (the expression itself, "creaking bones," was a favorite of her mother's)—even in her diction, inflection, she was her mother's double. Her mother had molded her out of herself as decisively as the earth had molded the cones of Cappadocia—so decisively, in fact, you couldn't tell just where the one began and the other left off, couldn't know exactly what your situation was: whether your dwelling place was in or on the earth, whether you had come from Cappadocia or your mother, whether Cappadocia was your mother or your mother was the earth . . . . And men, the fools, imagined themselves self-determined, self-contained. Oh, no! Her mother was there with her, present in the Hall of Honor, no less than she, Tabal, was there with Ia, Agdistis with Attis . . . . Glancing up, Tabal surveyed the gallery, on the lookout for Agdistis. Most of the women's heads, though no longer bowed, were obscured by the smoke and shadows. Tabal could not descry the god. And yet she had a feeling, a foreboding—more than a foreboding, she knew beyond doubt that Agdistis was there, if not in the flesh, in Attis.

Just now, Attis, like all the other men, was showing signs of drunkenness, motioning his foot at the cupbearer to refill his cup, which he was holding upside down over his head and to which he kept referring as his "blood vessel." Tabal could see her filigree bracelet, flashing on his wrist—the very bracelet her mother had given her on the eve of her marriage to Midas, and she, in turn, had given Attis fourteen years ago, and which identified him now not as the son of man, as Midas claimed, but of the deity whose godhood utterly refuted every word her husband had just spoken.

No sooner had his cup been refilled, than the bridegroom drained it at a gulp and grinned from ear to ear. Much as he had liked the sacrifice and being custodian of the blood— Why had the king said seed, custodian of the seed, when so obviously the stuff was blood? Attis had, in fact, never seen so much blood at once, and only wished the sacrifice had been a hecatomb, a hundred instead of fifty heifers, and that he had been chosen to wield the ax— much as he had liked the sacrifice, he liked the celebration even more, especially the wine and being the center of attention, seated on a throne; liked the women's vain attempts to preserve their modesty, not to ogle and point at him; liked their mass obeisance; liked the prospect of winning hands down, as he knew he would, the javelin contest and outrunning his opponents by a furlong; liked above all the idea of bringing to an end what the king had called mother-time.

Indebted though he was to his guardian for raising him, Attis was only too eager now to get away from Agdistis. He had had enough of Its possessiveness and jealousy, supervision and surveillance, enough of Its attentions: of being fingered, fondled, pestered—without a moment's peace, a moment's privacy—almost out of existence. He wanted to be free of It, on his own, able to assert himself as he had this past week, not find It coming over him, on top of him first thing every morning, last thing at night, leaving him half dead, sapped of his vitality, his strength. No wonder he had begun of late to feel so weary, sluggish, drained, as if he weren't long for this world—Agdistis was living off of him, feeding on him bodily. It was hard now to believe that the reverse had once been true, that his guardian had once suckled and sustained him, attended to his every need. Agdistis' own need had become so immense, so open-mouthed and unremitting that Attis feared It would not rest until It had taken him over totally, into Itself, swallowed him alive; feared that nothing short of death, his death, could ever satisfy Its need; that the need itself was inexhaustible, everlasting, immortal like Agdistis; feared above all that Its immortality depended in some way, which Attis sensed but couldn't quite define, on his mortality.

Fortunately, these fears had been dispelled by the king's pronouncement on the end of mother-time, which came as a great relief to Attis, a great release from Agdistis. Not only was he feeling carefree now, but positively restless, ready to go outside and do something strenuous: run or dance or fight. He wasn't used to sitting still, especially indoors. Nor was he used to drinking wine. Was it the wine—what the others called Dionysus—that was making him feel so heady, hot, as if he were already in motion, already a man, racing across the steppe, rushing headlong toward his destiny as creator, savior of the state? Had the god of wine come into him, inspired him, set his senses reeling? Yes, surely that was it! Attis could feel the presence of Dionysus now, the holy presence, spreading like a fever through his body, firing his blood, searing his throat, creating an uncontrollable thirst, a craving for more, for absolute communion with the god. "More!" he suddenly cried out, thrusting his empty vessel at the nearest steward and standing up unsteadily. "More blood!" But no sooner was he on his feet, than Attis dropped the cup and fell back into the chair stunned, staring up at the gallery.

The queen was quick to notice the change in his expression, but could not see what, if anything other than the wine, had provoked it, because her couch was situated well under the same gallery on which the bridegroom's eyes were fixed. Ia, on the other hand, saw and recognized at once the towering figure of Agdistis. The god was standing on the same side of the gallery as she, at the far end, just before the turn in the railing. It didn't occur to Ia to question

Its presence. She thought it perfectly natural for the god to attend the wedding of Its offspring. What puzzled her was Attis' expression—why he looked aghast. Was it because of the way Agdistis was dressed: without a chiton, wearing nothing but a shabby cloak? Yet the only other time she had ever seen the god, Its breasts were bared. True, It had on that occasion been wearing a skirt, but that might also be the case today. Ia couldn't make out. Not only was her view obstructed by the crowd, the fumes and shadows, but also by the god Itself who, drawing the cloak closer to Its body, seemed suddenly intent on concealing Its identity or, if not Its identity, the crown on Its head, the aulos in Its hand.

Downstairs, meanwhile, the king had sent Rusa across the room to find out if the blind bard Azzi was ready to recite. Reaching for his cithara, Azzi stood up and began to move with absolute assurance out into the center of the room till he was on a line with the hearth, whereupon, guided by the heat of the smoldering fire, he turned to his left, away from the hearth, heading straight for the rear of the hall, yet clearly conscious of the cupbearer coming diagonally toward him from the right, about to cut across his path—more conscious of the boy, in fact, than the boy was of the bard, so that in the end it was the blind man who stopped and waited for the cupbearer to pass before proceeding to the spot, just under the mid-point of the transverse gallery, where two stewards had, meantime, placed his armchair in full view of all the guests.

The men, however, paid no attention. Though not deliberately disrespectful, they were enjoying themselves far too much to notice the bard. Except for the king and Rusa, Attis alone was aware of Azzi's movements, not because he had dared take his eyes off Agdistis—the boy was still transfixed with dread—but because the moment the bard had begun to move, so too had Agdistis. Stepping back from the railing, It all but disappeared among the women. For a while Attis could see only Its head, as It worked Its way from the side gallery, around the corner post, along the rear wall to the middle of the transverse gallery, at which point It reemerged from the crowd, positioned once again at the front railing, but lurking now behind the center post, directly over Azzi who, having seated himself downstairs, was busy tuning the cithara.

Still the men paid no attention, went on talking, telling stories, laughing, joking, shouting—some were even rolling on the floor, wrestling or fondling each other—until the king himself stood up to silence them. "Enough! Let the bard sing. Sing, Azzi, sing of the siege of Pessinus and the destruction of the Assyrians."

At last the stewards stopped serving and the men quieted down, though not completely. There was still a good deal of noise in the hall—coughing, murmurs, stifled laughter, the sound of stools being shifted, cups clinking—but even so the uproar was over, the bard could begin. Holding the cithara sideways, his right hand on the crossbar, the base cradled in his lap where it fitted so snugly the instrument almost seemed a part of his body, something sprouting from his loins, Azzi poised his left hand over the strings. At the same time, Attis, seeing the look of amassed fury in his guardian's eye and the hideous set of Its jaw (the blanched lips were contorted into a rectangle, the fierce lower teeth bared to the gums) as It peered down at the bard from behind the center post— Attis sensed that something was about to happen, and tensed his feet, causing his heels to rise involuntarily, and clamped his knees together to protect himself from Agdistis who, unobserved by the rest of the guests, reached surreptitiously under Its cloak, pulled out the aulos and brought the mouthpiece to Its lips, just as Azzi's fingertips brushed the strings, so that what the astonished listeners heard was not a soothing chord, but an ear-splitting buzz.

At first no one but Attis and a handful of women realized where the sound was coming from; the rest of the guests were utterly confused, turned their heads this way and that, exchanging puzzled looks. But as the sound continued, the guests grew more uneasy. Some men got up to confer with their neighbors; others wandered in a daze, moving sometimes backward, as if to escape the buzz, sometimes forward, as if to locate it; the king beckoned the chief of staff but the general sat fast, fingering the blade of his sword; the bard, whose hearing was perhaps more acute than the average, clapped both hands over his ears to deaden the pain, while upstairs the women, pressed too close to move freely, began to shrink in a body away from the cloaked piper whose identity still remained a mystery.

As for the sound itself, it was insupportable. Sweeping through the hall like a swarm of wasps, ten thousand strong, aroused to kill, the drone assaulted the assembly not only auditorily, but physically, as if it were, in truth, embodied in a wasp, ten thousand wasps armed with deadly stings. But whereas a wasp will dispatch its victim in short order with a few quick jabs to the nerve centers, Agdistis took Its time, prolonged the torture unmercifully, applying steady pressure, steady venom, inducing steady pain, as It drove the sting bit by bit not into the nerve centers, but deep into the brain stem of each and every guest. If, at any point, It stopped while playing to draw a breath, the pause was imperceptible, the drone persisted, sustained by the immortal lungs, the inexhaustible pneuma. And though the sound seemed, as it went on, to grow

202.

ever louder, more intense and furious, it was in fact absolutely constant, repetitive, monotonous: the same two notes, a strident trill, played at the same tempo, the same volume over and over incessantly until one of the stewards, carried away, seized a ladle and started pounding the metal mixing crater, creating a thunderous percussion in accompaniment to the drone.

In a matter of seconds the entire crowd, prompted by the boy's example and goaded by the god, was on its feet, twitching and shaking uncontrollably, muscles in the grip of some elemental force, impelling all of them to move about willy-nilly like so many globules of grease on a red-hot griddle. Before long, one of the men, the brother-in-law who had wielded the ax, cupped his right palm and began to thump his chest, just below the left shoulder, in time with the steward's pounding. The beat was so infectious that presently, despite the crowd's apparent self-absorption, a second man took it up, and then a third and fourth, till finally all the guests, men and women alike, were beating their breasts—arms swinging in rhythm, hands inflicting hurtful blows—even as their bodies continued to twitch and shake with abandon. The deep, dull, periodic thump, produced by a hundred thirty odd hands striking in unison, was indeed formidable. Unlike the on-going drone, the thumping mounted steadily, growing louder, more impassioned, more insistent with each successive beat. Far from trying to drive the wasps away, drown out the drone, the hands, as one, were petitioning the piper, calling on It to come forth and show Itself, clamoring for It not to stop, not to mitigate their misery, but to intensify it, take them over bodily, expose them to the full extent of Its frightful fury, if not to the fatal sting.

When the crowd had been brought to the desired pitch of emotion, Agdistis broke off unexpectedly, stopped playing altogether, grabbed the center post and, leaping up, stationed Itself on top of the railing—legs astride, head almost touching the roof—in command of the entire hall. For a split second the baffled crowd fell silent, stood stock-still. Then all at once the queen cried out in recognition, "Agdistis!" Instantly the cry was taken up by others. From every corner of the hall, upstairs and down, front and rear, came the call, "Agdistis! O, Agdistis! Look! the god! Behold, the god! Behold, Agdistis!" Straight away the hands began to thump again in unison, but harder than before, the suppliants, unconscious now of their own strength, beating themselves black-and-blue; some sobbing uncontrollably, some panting, groaning, dripping sweat, some calling out in preterhuman voices, some absolutely still, devout in their expression, some entirely antic, jumping up and down—all, in different ways, desirous of the selfsame thing: to be possessed by the god.

In response, Agdistis suddenly cast off Its cloak, extended Its arms to the utmost (one hand still on the center post, the other clasping the aulos), and stood before the multitude stark naked, except for the crown of gold—the living god, a mutilated androgyne: colossal, awesome, omnipotent.

Again there was a brief but deathly hush while the gaping crowd waited spellbound to do the god's bidding. Once satisfied that It had impressed Itself, Its living presence, on the spectators' minds, Agdistis recommenced piping, this time with a vengeance, aiming the instrument straight at Attis, as if It meant to vent on him alone Its wrath, the sting of all ten thousand wasps. But no one was immune, no one was spared. Scarcely had the buzz resumed, than each and every celebrant felt the sudden prick, the pang, the frenzy in his senses. Driven mad by the deafening drone, they proceeded now to snatch up avidly whatever sharp or pointed implements came to hand—knives, needles, skewers, swords—and promptly turned them, in imitation of the mutilated god, against themselves. Women, wailing, dug their spindles deep into their skulls, blood streaming down their cheeks as if they were weeping blood. Others were soon beaded with blood drawn from their flesh with embroidery needles. Still others used their distaffs to scarify their thighs. Ia, unclasping the fibula her mother had given her the night before, stabbed herself so many times her breasts seemed to be lactating blood; Tyana cut one of her breasts clean off; while the queen, having got hold of an iron cleaver, hacked open her abdominal walls, converting her womb into a basin of blood. Those who had no implement rent their clothes, tore out their hair, butted their heads against the wooden beams.

Downstairs, meanwhile, the men, armed with deadlier weapons, were wounding themselves even worse than the women. Many, having gashed their thighs through the sartorius, lay helpless and groaning in puddles of blood. Several, self-eviscerated, remained squatting over the butchery, staring dumbly into space, as if they were defecating their own guts, urinating blood. One man was busy branding his flanks with a pair of coals snatched bare-handed from the hearth. Another, in a transport of piety, flogged himself with a heavy chain until his back resembled a field of mole hills, bleeding. The bard, battering his cithara to bits, used the crossbar to puncture his eardrums from which there streamed two jets of blood; while the chief of staff chopped off his right hand at the wrist and ogled the bloody stump. The great majority, however, whose sorry number included the king and all his sons-in-law, were driven by the drone to emasculate themselves, their severed organs scattered like swill over the furniture and floor, their abundant blood utterly obliterating the delicate mosaic.

Only Attis remained impervious to the god's spell. His familiarity with the aulos made him less susceptible than the rest to its supernatural powers. Instead of drawing him into the vortex, the drone finally drove him away, desperate to escape the palace. To that end, the boy, keeping low and under cover of the west gallery, crept the length of the hall unseen. But at the entrance he suddenly collided with a rabid mob, coming from the courtyard. Lured by the piping, the scores of guests left outside during the meal were jammed now in the shallow vestibule between the portico and hall, straining and fighting to get inside, their progress impeded not only by their own large number, but by the narrowness of the door and those among them who had already fallen underfoot. Turning, Attis tried to brave the mob with his back, but failed. In no time he found himself stalled, stuck fast, entangled inextricably in the mass of struggling bodies. Someone on the floor grabbed him by the wrist and almost pulled him down; someone else, standing right behind him, locked a bony arm around his throat. Trapped now in the crush, Attis couldn't move, couldn't draw his knife, had only one hand free to combat his crazed assailant who clearly meant to strangle him. He could feel the forearm closing on his windpipe, compressing it and causing him to gag, could feel his head being yanked back by the hair, his neck about to snap, as he strove in vain to break the strangle hold.

Then all at once the piping ceased again, and with it ceased the tumult: the wailing and groaning inside the hall, as well as the hubbub without. Instantly the arm relaxed, released Attis' windpipe. For a moment both crowds froze as Agdistis, suddenly aware of the boy's disappearance, leaped from the railing to the floor below and charged toward the entryway. Pandemonium ensued. Pushing and screaming, the women tumbled pell-mell down the stairs or, following the god's example, flung themselves off the gallery and stumbled on, undeterred by broken bones; while those among the men still able to move dragged their maimed trunks over the carnage-strewn floor or staggered blindly toward the door in an effort not to escape the god, but to achieve closer communion.

At the same time, the mob at the door fell back, parted to create a path for the oncoming god. But before Agdistis could reach the door, Attis broke away and fled into the courtyard. Crying out, Agdistis went right after him, followed by the shouting mob.

Once again everyone was struggling to get outside. But only those in the lead arrived in time to catch a glimpse of the bridegroom dashing up the ramp, Agdistis at his heels.

Confident though Attis was that he could outrun his guardian, he doubted his endurance—Agdistis would easily outlast him, overtake him in the end—he had no hope whatever of finally escaping. What made him try to run for it was terror, terror not of dying, but of living, a captive, solely in the service of the god. And so he went now like the wind to avoid as long as possible falling back into Agdistis' hands.

Once outside the citadel the boy turned left instinctively, heading westward, away from the palace, Pessinus, civilization; running headlong toward the steppe, the wilderness, the source of the Sangarius. Despite its innumerable associations with Agdistis, the source was, after all, Attis' birthplace, the only place he really knew, really belonged. The idea of returning to it, even, if need be, to die, gave him an incentive, a destination, a sense of going somewhere, toward something, instead of merely running away, running into endless space until he dropped, nowhere.

As he raced ahead, climbing ever higher out of the valley toward the steppe, the autumn air growing cooler, the midday sun hotter by the minute, Attis kept looking back to check on Agdistis. The god was always there, always coming after him, a hundred yards or so behind—the distance never varied. No matter how fast he ran, how hard he exerted himself, Attis couldn't shake It off. Sometimes, after outstripping the screaming swifts streaming by the hundreds overhead, Attis would imagine himself far in the lead, and then look back only to discover the naked god, Its sweating body bright in the sunlight, still no more than a hundred yards behind, still coming after him steadily, tirelessly, taking giant strides, but at a trot to conserve Its strength. Then all at once, as if to eliminate the need of looking back, the drone resumed. Panic-struck, Attis stumbled, fell, scrambled to his feet again, plunged ahead frantically in fear now for his life.

Not until he reached the steppe did the boy slow down, and then only because the vast expanse of barren space dispersed the goading drone, made him feel, however momentarily, less driven. The swifts had disappeared. There were no birds of any sort in sight. The soil, no longer dry and salt-streaked as in summer, was moist and spongy, sheeted in spots with shallow water. For the first time since he had fled the palace, Attis took heart, encouraged now by the fact that Agdistis, who was twice his weight, would surely get bogged down. Accordingly, he mustered all his strength,

206.

began to sprint, trying to ignore his terrible thirst, shortness of breath, sheer exhaustion. As he raced across the tableland toward the far-off mountains, purple under bulging clouds, the drone grew fainter and fainter, the solitude more palpable, the possibility of escape more feasible, and Attis, revivifying steadily, ran faster and faster till finally he couldn't hear the drone at all, nothing but a ringing in his ears brought on by the altitude and his own velocity.

Assuming he was free at last, the boy looked back once more. A hundred yards or so behind, Agdistis was easily holding Its own, following now at a sure-footed sprint, showing no signs of either clumsiness or fatigue: Its chest puffed up, head held high, hair streaming on the wind, aulos still pressed to Its lips. Startled, Attis swallowed hard. The ringing stopped, the drone resumed, evoking yet again the plague of wasps, the plethora of gore. Wherever he looked, Attis saw blood—blood on his chiton, blood on his trousers, blood on his boots, blood in puddles on the ground, the clouds bloodshot, mountains bloodstained, stones of blood like so many dissevered testicles scattered over the endless steppe—and though he was ready to collapse, the maddening drone drove him on, too terrified to stop.

By the time he reached the source Attis could scarcely stand. Doubled over, dripping wet, retching, the boy staggered down to the water's edge, hugging his heaving sides. Though Agdistis had not yet emerged from the woods, both the drone and the god's approaching footsteps, trampling the underbrush, were distinctly audible and growing more intense, more terrifying by the second, driving Attis along the shore to the utmost possible point of retreat: the tip of the spit. The fact that he was utterly exposed out there, defenseless, cornered, left with no means of escape other than the water, made no difference to the boy, who was too overwrought even to quench his thirst. Facing inland, he braced his back against the pomegranate tree and promptly slumped to his haunches. The ground at his feet was studded with numerous spheres of blood-red fruit, bird-pecked and rotting. The roar of the spring, though loud, was not nearly loud enough to drown out the drone which all at once changed from the familiar high-pitched trill into a shattering peal, as Agdistis charged out of the woods and paused momentarily in triumph.

At sight of the naked god, Attis began to twitch in terror and tear at his clothing till he, too, was completely naked. For an instant, as Agdistis advanced on the spit, the boy was reminded of Phoebus, remembered the shepherd's wish to make an offering of his locks to Apollo, and realized now that he himself was bound to make an offering, the only offering that could placate the god. Seizing his knife in one hand, genitals in the other, Attis sheared off at once his testicles and penis, shouted out over the roar of the spring, "To you, Agdistis—yours at last!" and feebly tossed the dissevered members at the feet of the hermaphrodite.

Horror-struck, Agdistis dropped the aulos and backed away, Its mouth agape, eyes bulging, bent arms pressed against Its sides, palms upraised, rejecting with a shudder the gruesome offering. "No!"

For a long time afterward, as Agdistis went on uttering "No!" over and over without stop, and shaking Its head from side to side, and gazing stupefied at the mutilated genitals as if It expected the penis to move by muscular reflex, the boy's blood flowed unabated like the source itself, seeping into the rich black earth, down to the deepest roots of the tree. Just when it was that Attis finally died, Agdistis was too distraught to notice, but the moment was memorialized by a ripe pomegranate which fell with the boy's last breath to the blood-drenched ground, coming to rest in silence among the other pieces of fruit already moldering in the sunlight.

VIII

For three days and three nights Agdistis sat among the rotting pomegranates, sobbing inconsolably over the dead boy whose head was cradled in Its lap. From time to time It sleeked one of Attis' eyebrows, fingered his standing nipples or fondled the vital-looking curls. But mostly It attempted to resuscitate the youth, either by breathing Its own hot breath into the gaping mouth or hugging the boy with fervor to restore his body heat or holding the dissevered members in place for hours on end in hopes of grafting them back onto the trunk and thus enabling Attis to move again. More than anything else, the body's motionlessness grieved Agdistis. "Move! O, move!" It cried out every so often, shaking the boy doggedly. Since It still believed that Attis was immortal like Itself, It had no way of comprehending what had happened, no sense, as yet, of final loss. Nor was there any reason why It should. After three full days the flesh was just as firm and smooth, fresh and bronze as ever—what was missing was the animating force.

Till now, Agdistis had never given a moment's thought to the force that animates, had no idea where it came from, what it was, who created and controlled it, or how it could possibly stop—any more than the flow of the source could stop. And yet it had stopped, quit the body, slipped away unseen, leaving the arms unable to clasp, tongue to speak, eyes to express the heart—and Agdistis strove with all Its might to bring it back. At first It concentrated on the testicles, sure that the force had resided there, but presently, when the grafting failed, Agdistis remembered Its own emasculation and realized Its mistake. Next It focused on the breath and then the blood, draining Its radial artery, as It had Its lungs, into the boy's open mouth, but to no avail. As a last resort It turned to the water: carried both the boy and the dissevered members down to the pond and immersed them in the spring. When that, too, failed, Agdistis was at Its wit's end. For the first time in Its life It had an intimation of something on earth or in the heavens mightier than Itself, and It began to tremble.

Half in dread, half in anticipation, It scanned the woods and then the sky on the lookout for some hidden god on whom to call for help, but there was no one, nothing. Thereupon, It felt—also for the first time in Its life—alone, absolutely solitary. Standing now waist-deep in the middle of the pond, the middle of Its own domain, It nonetheless felt like an outsider, dispossessed of everything—not only of Attis, but also of Itself, the source, the trees, the sky, the shore—as if It had no business being there, were trespassing on earth. And, indeed, It had no wish to be on earth without Its beloved. The lifeless body, floating on the water, made It feel only that much more alone, more bereft, helpless and afraid. "O, give him back!" It implored the unseen nameless power, mightier than Itself. "Please! O, please, make him whole! give him back!" But neither the body nor the members stirred.

Dripping wet and shivering, Agdistis slouched ashore. Instead of returning to the pomegranate tree, It bore the body up to the lair. There, It laid the boy out under the lean-to, dried his limbs lovingly, and covered him with several cotton mantles, leaving exposed only the beautiful head. From another piece of cotton It fashioned for Itself a loin cloth into which It placed with tender care the boy's dissevered members and bound the organs fast to Its own. That done, It crouched beside the shrouded body and, hugging now not the beautiful head but Itself, Its naked shins, resumed for the fourth consecutive night Its pitiful lament.

In the course of the night, however, a heavy drowsiness came over the hermaphrodite, and, struggle though It did to stay awake, Agdistis finally broke Its vigil, succumbed to sleep—almost as if the unseen god, taking pity on It, had intervened divinely: closed Its reddened eyelids, calmed Its anguished heart, covered It, too, with a cotton mantle—whereupon It dreamed a most amazing dream.

Far off through the trees It saw a faint flickering light, coming closer and closer. Presently, a shepherd, dressed in the Phrygian fashion and carrying a lantern, emerged from the woods, walked without a moment's hesitation over to the lean-to and stopped outside. "Forgive me for intruding. I can see you've suffered some misfortune."

Agdistis, who was feeling too doleful either to greet the shepherd or send him on his way, didn't speak, didn't move, merely glanced up blear-eyed.

"May I spend the night?" Receiving no answer, the shepherd ducked under the lean-to and entered the lair at the foot of the shrouded body. Even in the dimness the beauty of the man, whom Agdistis took to be no more than twenty-five, was strikingly apparent—his glittering curls seemed coils of gold, his skin poreless as polished marble. "Perhaps I can help."

Agdistis shook Its head. "He won't move."

Holding out the lantern, the shepherd edged closer till the coppery light illumined Attis' face. As he gazed down at the parted lips and staring eyes, the shepherd's own lips began to quiver, eyes to brim with tears.

"What makes you, a stranger, cry?" The hermaphrodite's tone was at once proprietary and suspicious.

"That anyone so beautiful should die so young."

The statement brought Agdistis to Its feet. "Die? He isn't dead!"

"What then?"

Nonplused, Agdistis showed Its palms, shrugged in anguish.

"His heart has stopped," the shepherd ventured with compassion, "he isn't breathing."

"But he's immortal!"

"Only the gods are immortal."

"I'm immortal."

"You're a god, but he, alas, is not."

"Not? . . . Dead? . . . No!" Utterly bewildered, the hermaphrodite began to rub Its thighs mindlessly, moving Its hands up and down, up and down, and to pace the length of the lair, prowling back and forth, back and forth, repeating with each successive step, each successive downward stroke, "No! . . . no! . . . no! . . ."

The shepherd, meanwhile, having set the lantern on the ground and crouched beside the corpse, reached out to close the eyelids.

With a sudden outcry Agdistis flew at the man, pushed him over

210.

backward and flung Itself on Attis, as if by warding off this har-
binger of death, It could somehow bring the boy back to life. On
Its hands and knees now, It was straddling the body, Its own body
parallel with Attis' but overarching his, their heads face to face.
"O, my beauty, don't be dead, don't ever die . . . please, O
please, come back!" Unable to support the burden of Its grief, the
sobbing hermaphrodite collapsed on top of Attis.

To comfort It, the shepherd laid his hand, whose touch was
strangely cold, on Agdistis' bare shoulder. "Only the Father
can bring him back—"

"The father?"

"He alone."

"There is no father."

"I'm speaking of Zeus, the almighty. . . . Yet even Zeus is
powerless to reverse the Fates."

"Where is he, this almighty?"

"On Olympus."

"Do you know the way?"

"Every inch."

"Will you take me to him?"

"That's why I've come," the shepherd explained matter-of-
factly, stooping to pick up the lantern, as if he were ready even
now to depart.

"Thank you" —Agdistis kissed the shepherd's foot which, like
his hand, was strangely cold— "whoever you are."

"Some call me Phoebus."

Unwilling now to waste another second, Agdistis scrambled to
Its feet. "Let's hurry, Phoebus."

"There's time enough. First, you must anoint yourself—put on
your robe and diadem."

In rapid succession Agdistis washed Its face and hands, slipped a
belted chiton over the loincloth, a russet cloak over the chiton,
braided Its hair, and set the filigree crown firmly on Its head.

When It was ready, Phoebus extinguished the lantern, and all at
once the stars came out a billionfold. Agdistis saw them now as It
never had before, saw each and every star, even those in galaxies,
glowing individually; saw stars in vivid sprinkles, sprays and clusters, swirling, shooting, flying upward fiery like sparks or floating
at a standstill like snowflakes in a vacuum; saw the harvest moon
one second and in the next saw Pegasus and Pisces, Draco and the
Pleiades drift by at such close range the draft from their passage
billowed Its robe, fluttered Its braids as It was borne, breathless
and afraid, among the stars whose incandescence, though dazzling,

neither burned nor blinded, but merely lighted the way through the black immensity to the portal of a marble palace inside which Agdistis found Itself in no time kneeling before a seated figure, cloaked in a gold himation and crowned with a wreath of gold, but otherwise scarcely visible in the steel-blue semidarkness. "Are you— Am I—" the hermaphrodite faltered, keeping Its eyes downcast, not daring yet, despite the darkness, to look on the solemn figure. "Are you? . . ."

"Zeus."

"O Zeus, a shepherd came and told me—"

"No need to explain, I know."

Encouraged to look up by the god's companionable tone, Agdistis was astonished to discover that the almighty had no eyes. Through the empty sockets It could see the harvest moon and stars radiant in the midnight sky beyond the colonnade. The sight unsettled Agdistis. Conscious though It was of the marble floor beneath Its knees, It nonetheless felt more afraid now, lightheaded and displaced, than It had in midair, and hugged the floor to regain Its equilibrium.

"Do not abase yourself."

"O god, almighty god, give me back my beloved!"

"The boy is dead."

"But you're the Father, aren't you, all-powerful?"

"Not to bring him back."

"Not even . . . someday?"

Zeus shook his head. "Never."

"Then let me die!"

"You're immortal."

"Must I live without him then forever?"

"Only the Olympians have time enough for permanent relationships."

"Then make me an Olympian."

"Have you any idea what it is to be up here: remote, detached, an onlooker at life, our only means of participation—*you*? No-no, give thanks for what you have."

"What have I without Attis?"

"There will in time be others—other boys like other seasons: perennially, for your delight on earth."

"I want no others."

"You will in time."

"Never!" Agdistis declared, seizing Its groin, gripping the loincloth as if to safeguard what remained of the boy. "Only Attis!"

"Come now. You mustn't make the same mistake that mortals

make: clinging for dear life to one, when so clearly life is nothing less than *all*—each and every living thing that ever was or will be on the earth—the ever-diminishing, ever-multiplying all . . . of which you yourself are the matrix. What you have your hands on there amounts to nothing, less than nothing. That loincloth cannot take the place of Attis, any more than Attis can take the place of humankind. Till now, you never thought to question that."

"Till now," Agdistis repeated bitterly, "I had no *need*. I trod the earth unattended, unattached, sported on the steppe, reveled in the woods, took my pleasure where I found it: under trees with maidens, shepherds, she-goats; ate whatever came to hand: berries, beets, tiger cubs; quenched my thirst at mountain springs—the rivers of the earth ran through my veins, the winds of heaven through my lungs; I rose with the sun and slept with the moon from which I was inseparable. Of course! there was no question then of holding onto or parting with anything—how could there be?—since everything on earth was mine, already part of me. And so it was, so it remained, until one day something worked a change. Even as I slept, someone came and cut me down, cut me off—from myself, from everything on earth—and when I woke, nothing was the same. A part of me was missing. *This* part!" Agdistis cried out in anger, indicating Its groin. "Just how it was accomplished or by whom, I still don't know. Nor why! That's something you alone must know—you, the Father—something you yourself must have had a hand in. Why? Tell me now!" Agdistis demanded. "Why was this done to me?"

"Because you had no need. And to be without need is to be without god."

"Was there no other way but *this* to bring me to you?"

"None."

"And now that I'm here—before you on my hands and knees—now that you've made me needful—"

"You must go back—back to earth where need belongs. But first," Zeus added quickly, "take off the loincloth." Agdistis hesitated. "Do as I say!" Reluctantly, Agdistis removed the cloth and clutched the precious contents. "Now give it up."

"To you?"

"It's mine already . . . being dead."

"Yours?"

"I would not be Zeus without it."

"But if it's dead—"

"Give it up!"

Agdistis placed the loincloth like an offering on the stool at Zeus' feet and then stepped back. The hall seemed even darker now than it had at first. Agdistis could scarcely make out the seated figure at whom It was staring utterly bemused, could only get Its bearings now by keeping Its eye fixed on the polestar visible beyond the empty sockets. "Is this Olympus or the Underworld?" Agdistis waited in vain for Zeus to reply. "Are you the god of the living or the dead?" Again there was no answer from the eyeless figure. "Have you no *other* organs either? No earthly organs of your own? Is that why you stole mine? Was I, too, almighty once, before you cut me down?" Hard as Agdistis pressed for answers, none was forthcoming. Zeus remained perfectly mute, motionless, mysterious, as the hermaphrodite went on waiting, staring in the same direction as before, but uncertain now whether or not the god was even there, uncertain of Its own whereabouts, uncertain, in fact, of everything but the polestar's light, vivid in the ice-clear void through which It suddenly was falling.

On waking, the first thing Agdistis did was to reach for the loincloth, but it was gone. Perplexing though the disappearance was, Agdistis felt no sense of loss. On the contrary It felt released and oddly strengthened, as if, like a snake, It had merely molted overnight an outworn skin whose casting off made possible continuance. Relieved to find Itself on solid ground again, the dream over, daylight on the horizon, Agdistis set about at last to bury Attis. Instead of digging a fresh grave, It decided to leave the body where it was and plow the earth back into the lair. By the time It had finished, the hermaphrodite was covered with sweat, and though It could feel the approach of winter in the air, Agdistis went down to bathe in the spring.